Connection

by

Katja Desjarlais

The Haunt Vault

This is a work of fiction. Names, characters, places, and incidents are either the product of the author's imagination or are used fictitiously, and any resemblance to actual persons living or dead, business establishments, events, or locales, is entirely coincidental.

Connection

Contact Information: info@thewildrosepress.com

Cover Art by *Diana Carlile*

The Wild Rose Press, Inc.
PO Box 708
Adams Basin, NY 14410-0708
Visit us at www.thewildrosepress.com

Publishing History
First Black Rose Edition, 2018
Print ISBN 978-1-5092-2144-8
Digital ISBN 978-1-5092-2145-5

The Haunt Vault
Published in the United States of America

"Your core has decided it needs her to live and will do anything it can to survive by getting to her." Jagg motioned for Dominic to follow him out of the pristine bathroom. Once in the living area, Dominic dropped onto the sofa, his head lolling back in frustration.

"So you're saying I can either follow this connection to a woman who drives me insane, or I can go insane anyways and die in the process. Fantastic."

"I said your core thinks it is going to die without her. You won't actually die. I didn't. It will merely be… unpleasant for a while."

"How unpleasant?"

Jagger flopped onto the sofa beside Dominic. "Unpleasant enough to have you spend the next few weeks or months in the bloodslave quarters under Boy's supervision."

"And my choices are…?"

"Spend the next few weeks or months in the bloodslave quarters under Boy's supervision. Or Boy puts you down."

Dedication

To Mark. Back to Back.

Chapter One

Dominic hastily snipped the tips off his fangs, cringing at the sound of the metal clippers scraping bone. With his teeth humanized, he retrieved both pieces from the sink and deposited them in the garbage before leaving his bunk to join Rhys in the training room.

Rhys's dark eyes peered up at him from under the skirt of a recent arrival. He scanned his memory for a name. Tessa? Tina? T-Something… All that mattered was that she was an easy transport from a Utah haunt, she was trainable, and she would fetch a good price on the vampire Tender market.

"We've got a local situation that needs cleanup," Rhys barked, angered by either the intrusion into his training methods or by the plain A-type woman spread before him. "Young defector from the Hanson haunt in California managed to hitch a ride into Denver, take a hostage, and has been holed up south of the airport for the past three weeks. Hanson called it in a few hours ago. I'm going to need you to do a meet-up with this asshole kid and bring the woman back here for assessment."

Rhys pulled his phone from his back pocket and fired off a text. "I'm sending you the location now. Punishment for trespassing in our territory has been assured by Hanson, so your only job is to get the female out of the kid's hands and into ours. Got it?"

"Yeah, yeah," he grumbled, checking his messages and calculating how long the drive would be. "I can get on it tomorrow."

Rhys stared him down for a moment, his dark eyes narrowing. "You'll get on it tonight. I want this cleaned up before Kai returns or you're trading places with Boy for a week. Seven nights working Boy's rounds in the bloodslave quarters might give you enough incentive to get your shit together quickly."

Empty threat. Even if he sat around on his ass for the next century, Kaius wouldn't put him on bloodslave duty for a week. There were perks to being the youngest child of the haunt leader, and exclusion from working the bloodslave quarters was definitely a huge benefit.

With a quick nod, he turned his back to Rhys before rolling his eyes. He could be a disrespectful sonofabitch but he was a smart disrespectful sonofabitch. And part of being smart meant knowing who would shrug off an eye roll and who would delight in removing your eyeballs with rusty pliers. Rhys was more 'rusty pliers' than 'shrug it off'. To date, the only thing he had seen Rhys shrug off was his shirt after a rough night.

He pulled the training room door closed to the sound of renewed female whimpers. Hostile demeanor aside, he had to admire the resident trainer and his ability to turn even the most unyielding women into model Tenders. Tessa-Tasha-T-Something would be ready for trade soon.

Walking through the halls of the haunt, he read through the messages lighting up his phone from

Nichol. Maps, suggested routes, known speed traps, and harsh reminders to watch his surroundings were loaded, read, and deleted. The reluctant *de facto* leader of the haunt during Kaius's frequent absences, Nichol's obsession with order and agendas kept the hauntmates on track. He was good at what he did and hated every moment of it.

With Denver claimed by the Kaius haunt, incidents requiring cleaning rarely happened locally. Vampires traveling through the region were usually smart enough to lay low or scared enough to tiptoe gently. Situations in other territories involved some planning and negotiations before he went in, so having his night upended by a last-minute mission was unwelcome.

His own role appeared far more dangerous and prestigious than it was. In an attempt to push him toward more responsibility, Kaius had assigned him to be the collector, the guy that arrived on site to handle the physical mess while the brains behind the operation stayed back, struck the deals, meted the punishments, and enforced the fines. With the Kaius name standing behind him, the risk was minimal and the job itself rarely took up more than a few nights a month.

But it still involved dealing with bullshit he didn't like dealing with, and he rarely stopped himself from making his displeasure with the work known.

Hence Rhys's current displeasure with him.

That, and Rhys had severe asshole tendencies.

And maybe a rage issue thrown in for flavor.

He wondered briefly if anyone would notice if he staked Rhys on his way out tonight.

He needed to feed.

He sauntered up the stairs into the garage that sat

above the bunker the hauntmates called home. His customized black sports car was an insistent mistress, her pearl finish demanding nightly rubdowns and her slick interior begging for a weekly saddle soaping. She was the only female in thirty years to catch his interest for longer than a perfunctory screw and suck, and she had yet to disappoint him on their nightly excursions.

****

The purr of his baby carried him onto the dark highway and into the glowing specter of the city. Satellite radio serenaded him with angsty males wailing about how damaged some woman had left them, and he figured the hum of the open road would be better company for the night.

Although the collection of women for retraining and distribution lacked any serious threat, Kaius's standing orders required him to work alongside one of the older hauntmates. The rare nights of solo work that Nichol granted him during Kai's absences were a welcome break for both him and whichever brother was playing babysitter.

Caught unaware once, amateur vampire hunters had managed to interrupt a pass-off outside a nightclub by embedding eleven silver-tipped bullets in his back. It had been a brief moment of distraction, but a costly one to both his pride and his independence. Nine bullets had lodged in his spine and two in his ass and it had taken his brother Mick forever to remove the shots in between several lame 'pain in the ass' jokes.

Approaching the airport turnoff, he slowed his baby to a crawl and turned off her lights. While most hand-off arrangements were made with attention to secrecy, skulking through secondary roads in search of a paranoid vampire was never truly conspicuous. Neither was a six-one choppy-haired mutt donning chucks, a threadbare ball cap, and enough knives to give a sushi chef an instant orgasm. He pulled off the road into a gravel turnout and got out, popping the back hatch and prepping the customized transport bay for easy access should the woman he was being handed turn out to be less than agreeable.

Fuck it. Let this asshole come to me.

Dominic crossed his arms and leaned against his car, scanning the area for any signs of the vampire he was supposed to meet. Thirty minutes had passed before he caught movement across the eastern field, two silhouettes becoming clearer as they approached.

"You Dominic Kaius?" a male called out, turning to mutter quietly to his companion.

Adjusting his ball cap, he faced the pair. "That depends. You the Hanson kid interrupting my sparring night to fix his screw-up?"

The young male's shoulders hunched a fraction and he bowed his head. "Wyatt Hanson," he stated, yanking the woman at his side to a halt. "You alone?"

Lolling his head back in annoyance, he took a step forward. "Just pass the woman over and let me get the hell on with my night," he ordered. "Your haunt leader can dole out the spankings. I'm just here to save your ass from the noose of a media nightmare in our territory."

He waited for Wyatt to finish whatever internal debate he was having, taking time to assess the woman swaying on her feet beside him. Five-nine. AB. A heavy gray winter coat concealed her body, but the shape of her calves and ankles suggested a willowy form. Bright blonde hair peeked out of a red woolen cap.

A strong candidate for training.

Wyatt looked long and hard at the woman, his eyes flicking between her and the snow-covered field behind him. "If I hand her over to you, there's no way she'll be released to run to the cops, right? I won't be seeing some drawing of me on the news in a week, right?"

"Tell you what, kid," Dominic said, opening the driver side door. "Take her back to your hideout and wait until we come for you. I guarantee there'll be no news reports when we hunt your sorry ass and take you down for trespassing and confining in our territory." When the young vampire bared his fangs at him, he grinned. "Nichol's been itching for a kill lately. So, do you want to bet with us or against us?"

Shifting his weight, the young vampire cowed back and released his grip on the woman. "You'll tell Hanson I didn't do her any harm, right? See for yourself."

The woman hesitated before bolting across the snow, her shoeless feet carrying her away from the vampires with impressive speed.

While tackling her from behind and shoving her into the transport bay would be effective, he preferred having less struggling, less screaming, and less touching. Preferably cooperative enough to ride up front.

A hostile and hysterical screamer made for a long drive home, and Rhys tended to get cranky when his trainees arrived flailing and howling. Cranky Rhys caused eye rolling. Eye rolling caused fights. Fights meant biting. And half of his fangs were secured in his bunker garbage can to ensure he could pass a quick visual should any humans cross his path.

He tossed his hat onto the front seat and leveled Wyatt with a flat glare as he slammed the door shut in annoyance. "You're an idiot."

****

Running in socks in the freezing cold through a deserted field was not how Molly had envisioned things when she'd taken the young guy up on his offer of a dinner date weeks earlier. A quick groping in the car, a bit of making out in the kitchen, then a roll in the sheets. That was the plan.

Dying in the snow under the fangs of a vampire had never crossed her mind.

Though maybe it should have.

She spared a brief glance at a lone billboard lit up in the distance, a warning sign posted along a highway she knew she'd never reach. The Species Purifiers were hell-bent on placing those signs everywhere, warning people about the dangers of associating with vampires.

The message wasn't lost on her now as she ignored the tingling pain building in her feet and doubled her efforts to make it to the road, stumbling when the new vampire overtook her and stopped in her path.

The vampire watched her, his hands open as he straightened up. "I'm sorry," he said quietly, taking a step back when she crouched in preparation of an attack. "Wyatt's put you in a bit of a situation, and I'm going to need you to cooperate."

Torn between keeping her eyes on the new predator and tracking the retreating form of her captor, she widened her stance. "Go fuck yourself."

His brows lifted and he shoved his hands into his

back pockets. "How are you expecting this to play out? The highway's a good four miles off through at least a foot of snow. I can give you a twenty-minute head start, but all that'll do is delay the inevitable. You and I both know I'm faster, I'm stronger, and your feet aren't going to last much longer in this cold." He took another step back. "We can do this the easy way or the hard way."

Turning back in the direction of the highway, she made it a dozen steps before the pain in her feet brought her to her knees. She could hear the vampire approach her from behind, his footsteps crunching across the snow as his legs came into view.

"You tried," he stated, holding his hand out to her. "Up."

She leaned away from him, ignoring his hand and pushing herself to her feet, gritting her teeth against the pain. She met his turquoise eyes and stared him down until he shook his head and turned around, crouching in front of her.

"Hop on," he ordered. "Frostbite is going to settle in if we don't get you out of the snow. If you're behaving, you can ride up front. If not, I'll toss you in the cargo hold. Either way, you're coming with me."

Taking one last look at the billboard in the distance, she dropped her head, took a deep breath, and climbed onto the vampire's back.

Chapter Two

It wasn't until Dominic stood up with long, nimble legs wrapped tight around his waist and delicate wrists crossed over his chest that the faint scent of honeysuckle crept past the AB blood, throwing his concentration. A snarl formed and died instantaneously in his throat, and he hid the momentary tightening of his grip by shifting his cargo slightly and tucking his coat around the damaged feet locked around him. "How long did Wyatt have you?"

Her hands flexed and fisted. "Twenty-three days? Maybe twenty-four?"

Hot breath ghosting past his ear.

He needed to feed.

"I'm going to need some details about your meals and accommodations," he said, releasing the woman's leg long enough to brush his hair out of his eyes. "I'll be compiling a report for his haunt leader and the more detailed I can make it, the more suitable Wyatt's punishment will be." When she didn't answer, he looked back at her over his shoulder, regretting it the moment her scent smacked at him.

Feed.

Locking his eyes on his car, he sped up. "How about we start with a name."

"Molly."

"Good golly, Miss Molly."

She tensed. "Something like that."

The snow under his feet became shallower as they approached the road and he broke into a jog. "I'm Dominic."

"I heard."

He ignored the venom in her voice, his attention drawn by the peculiar flash of guilt that had rippled through him when Molly spoke.

Need. To. Feed.

As he reached the car, his mind fired through his current options, analyzing each scenario's likely outcomes in an instant. His first option was to secure the woman in the holding bay and be pulling away in under a minute to the sounds of screaming. Utilizing his gift of persuasion was option two, but Dominic found it most effective in small doses since maintaining it for a long time was draining and the strong link that would be needed to get Molly to the haunt would be broken when he passed her to Rhys. Which inevitably led to a screaming woman. And a displeased Rhys.

Option three.

He was good at option three. Unlike his hauntmates, he retained most of his human characteristics and habits. He fidgeted. He blinked. He breathed unneeded air steadily without focus. He knew how to be suave and charming, and how to be unassuming and nonthreatening when necessary.

Adjusting his hold on her, he opened the passenger side door and knelt to allow Molly to get down. "Are we doing this the easy way or the hard way?" He stayed crouched and looked up at her, his nose picking up the demanding scent of her blood from her damaged feet. "I really don't want to have to put you in the cargo hold."

Her dark eyes widened and she glanced at the

trunk. “You wouldn’t.”

“If my hand is forced, I will. But I’d rather you comply and sit up front with me.” He reached into the car slowly and popped the glove box open, pulling out a granola bar. “Please?”

Molly eyed him warily, licking her lips. She craned her neck back toward the highway and took a deep breath before inching past him and sitting.

Placing the bar on the dash, he closed her door and took his cell from his back pocket, firing off a text to Rhys as he walked around the front of the car, tracking Molly’s movements to ensure she didn’t attempt an escape.

B there in 30. Asset acquired.

Better be u useless fuckwad.

Well then.

****

“You won’t survive the jump,” Dominic said quietly, his voice yanking Molly from her absent stare out the window. She blinked to refocus her eyes on the road, her hands still gripping the empty wrapper of the granola bar.

He reached across her and opened the glove box. “Have as many as you need.”

Shaking her head, she returned her attention to the nothingness outside.

Thoughtful. Reflective. Cautious. Wise. None of these had ever been used to describe her. Impetuous. Short-sighted. Erratic. Volatile. Those were used most frequently by acquaintances, employers, and scrawled across her school records since kindergarten. It was her inability to look past the current moment and into the repercussions of her decisions that had brought her to this moment, riding in a car in the middle of the night with a vampire, stale granola bars and all.

It was her, in all her flawed glory, that had spotted Wyatt in the pregame crowd in the lounge and singled him out, drawn to the sullen man with the shaved head and tight jeans. She had done her damnedest to entice him, his one-word replies piquing her curiosity until he relented, ushering her to his car under the guise of an impromptu dinner date and what she had hoped would be a short, uncomplicated relationship lasting twenty-four hours or less.

She was good at those types of relationships.

Men who found her flighty, scattered life entertaining and exciting quickly became frustrated with missed dates, forgotten promises, and her revolving door jobs that left her scrambling for rent every month.

Some believed a strong, responsible man could fix her, could force her disorganized mind to adhere to schedules and routines through lists and timers and sticky notes. But inevitably the sticky notes slid down the walls and piled in the corners while timers went off in an empty apartment. Lists were left on grocery store counters or dropped on the bus.

One-night stands were easy for her. No expectation to remember names or numbers. No one judging her for the work shift she would likely sleep through. And Wyatt had fit the bill.

Had she paused for a moment, had she taken a second to really look him over, she would have noticed the strange clip of his eye-teeth and the slight oval shape of his irises.

But she hadn't paused. Hadn't thought. She never

did.

"We're about twenty minutes out," Dominic stated as he flipped through the radio stations, settling on a classic rock one. "This okay?"

She stared absently at the clock. "Does it matter?"

He placed his hand back on the steering wheel, calm and unflustered, his attention riveted on the road. "It shouldn't."

****

Feed.

Fuck.

FEED.

FUCK.

There was a faint scent of honeysuckle pulling at Dominic, driving him into his primal instincts, into that sphere of serpentine impulses that formed the nucleus of his kind. Vampires layered themselves around that essence to adapt, exist, and blend in to ensure the survival of their species.

Laws and guides and punishments revolved around forming defenses against exposing their baser nature, regulating their inner savagery before they annihilated all in their path that didn't feed that id, that generative force that drove their waking moments and formed their essence.

The moment he'd closed his door, Molly's scent had inundated his senses. The purity of the fragrance registered as innate to the woman, not the result of soaps or lotions or other fabricated scents women doused themselves in. It emitted from her skin like a poisonous gas, eating away at his core's layers.

And she was crinkling a goddamn granola wrapper.

He locked his face into a placid, relaxed expression

and focused on the dark expanse of the highway. He pushed past the alluring scent and latched on to the veiled smell of bleach emanating almost imperceptibly from the passenger seat, willing it to help him regain his slipping control, help him restore all the human nuances that made him an ideal candidate for handling the delicate cases Rhys handed him.

His attempts to ignore the plethora of movements and fidgeting that wafted wave after wave of honeysuckle his way was pointless. The woman moved incessantly. Little twitches of her shoulders that caused skin to dance on her clavicle. Bouncing of knees that rippled lean calf muscles. Flexing of long, delicate fingers on soft, pale hands.

FEEDFUCK.

Lowering his head slightly to hide the increased ovaling of his eyes, he allowed himself a moment to revel in his grim fantasies of the jittery blonde channeling all that energy into an enthusiastic blow job while he drove through the night.

The strange wave of guilt that had hit him earlier returned and he clenched his jaw. His fangs were regenerating quicker than usual as his insatiable hunger bubbled to the surface of his consciousness, easing all logic into the back of his mind.

Something wasn't right.

Buzz.

His phone vibrated in his back pocket, pulling him out of his rising bloodlust haze. Rhys was likely becoming impatient. Ignoring the phone, he focused on his task of returning to the haunt with a sedate, compliant, blonde AB. But the longer they spent on the highway, the more frequent her movements. And the more frequent her movements, the more her scent engulfed him. Quelling her nerves became his priority.

Vampires had many weapons at their disposal in their biological makeup, but he found his gift for releasing a sedative-like pheromone was most effective in his current job. As the balm filled the vehicle, Molly stilled, lulled by an uncontrolled physical response that would soon penetrate her mental responses. The soft lips no longer pursed and relaxed. The delicate upturned nose no longer wrinkled and wiggled. Onyx eyes stopped flitting from window to window. She became tranquil. Docile.

Wrong. She suddenly appeared wrong.

Buzz.

Buzz.

The vibrations brought Molly back to life. She shifted, drawing her legs up tight to her chest and cupping her toes. "How much farther?"

Honeysuckle.

FeedfuckfeedfuckMOLLYfeedfuck.

He scanned the darkness, his lips drawing into a thin line as he realized he'd overshot the gravel road that led to the haunt.

A mistake he'd never made.

But he was hungry and trapped beside a meal that was off-limits.

Distracted.

He slowed at a crossroad to turn around and released a potent burst of pheromone to buy him the crucial minutes he needed to get his mind under control before he returned home.

Chapter Three

Dual hungers pulled at Dominic's psyche as he drove into the blue-lit garage. His cargo slept fitfully, pummeling his senses and beating wave after wave of her scent into the tight quarters.

Feedfuckfeedfuck.

Opening the passenger door, he lifted Molly unceremoniously and tossed her over his broad shoulder, keeping his eyes focused anywhere but on the legs in his peripheral. He sped down the stairs into the bunker, desperate to deposit the woman, transfer control to Rhys, and take shelter in the sanctity of his room before he lost total control and took a bite. In his current state, he knew she would not survive it.

And feeding off the women he was sent to assist was severely frowned upon.

Opening the training room door, he was met with the unwavering navy eyes of Rhys, who was perched on the edge of a chair with his long, tattooed arms crossed over a black singlet.

"Phone lost, Dom?"

He stayed rooted on the spot. Rhys's elliptical pupils were almost fully extended, indicating he was either insanely horny or irrationally angry. With only the two of them and a sleeping asset in the room, Dominic surmised it was anger. Hoped it was anger.

"Problem, Rhys?"

Rhys rose to his full six-four and flashed a fangy

smile. He stalked toward him, ignoring the woman slung over his shoulder.

"None at all, Dom. None. At. All. I haven't spent the last twenty minutes getting ear-raped by Kai over your whereabouts. Haven't had to pull the guys off their duties to send them chasing a scrambled GPS signal. Haven't been fucking texting you like a scorned fucking girlfriend while Kaius rips my ass open about letting you go off without a goddamn motherfucking babysitter." His lethal navy eyes sparked inches from Dom's. "Now where. The fuck. Is. Your. PHONE?"

He eased his free hand into his back pocket, moving slowly as he confronted the unpredictable predator. With cautious movements, he passed the phone to Rhys, ever conscious of the sleeping woman draped over him. Even with the amplified testosterone possessed by male vampires, he had rarely seen Rhys's control so dubious.

The tattoos were rippling as muscles tensed and arced. Neck tendons were taut, corded along his Adam's apple. Rhys's hand gripped the offered device and the two vampires froze momentarily, assessing each other as though meeting for the first time.

He broke the standoff first, averting his eyes from Rhys's rage and risking a glance at Molly to ensure his mental connection was holding her inert. Flashing his gaze back to Rhys, he caught a flicker of apprehension in his furious brother before the navy eyes reverted to pure fury.

Rhys took a step back, turning the phone over as an eerily calm smile passed his rough features.

"Oh look. Full power. It appears you have a few unopened messages, Mini."

At any other time, calling him 'Mini' started an insult war that could last hours. Tonight, he merely stood his ground and listened silently as Rhys opened text after unread text.

"Let's start from your last text to me, shall we? What was it? Oh yes. B there in 30. Asset acquired. Sent an hour ago. Whatever, we all know you couldn't judge time to save your useless undead life. And I said… ha… I should use 'fuckwad' more often."

Rhys was disturbingly conversational. He tightened his grip slightly on Molly. Rhys's mercurial temper was legendary among his kind, and he was wary about both the cause of the rage and potential fallout. He moved pointedly to a training bedroom, never turning his back on the unpredictable vampire. Rhys watched, unblinking, as he laid the woman on the bed and arranged her long legs on the mattress.

His hand subconsciously smoothed her skirt down before he snatched the offending appendage back. He straightened and assumed the posture of a beta male, indicating he was ready for Rhys to continue. Rhys's gaze held for a moment before he handed the phone back to him.

Kai: Trouble??
Kai: Location. Now.
Rhys: Call me cocksucker
Rhys: Kai freaking where r u
Kai: SNAP OUT OF IT AND CALL ME NOW.
Mick: Dude I can't lock on you where r u?
Nic: I had nothing to do with your GPS GOT IT
Rhys: I'm coming for you mini
Kai: I will be home ASAP. Whatever that was,

call me.

He took an unnecessary breath. Of course Kaius would have felt the surging bloodlust, the rollercoaster of primal needs battling against his rational thoughts. The last time his internal restraint had wavered in public, Jagger had had to pull his pathetic bullet-ridden ass across his lap and deliver his bleeding, snarling little brother to a very displeased Kai. That slip of control had been momentary. Tonight, he would have bombarded Kaius with thirty, maybe forty minutes of pitiful weakness.

Heavy footfalls in the hallway signaled the approach of another hauntmate. A stealth species by nature, the emphatic stomping was a warning that Rhys and Kaius were not the only ones on the warpath for his head. The training room door swung open, revealing an enraged Nichol. His hazel eyes latched onto him as his fist made contact with his jaw.

The hit would likely have killed any mortal on contact, shattering bone and fracturing the skull. His head swung to the right on impact before he resumed his beta male stance of slightly hunched shoulders, hands clasped behind him. Nichol was close to thirteen hundred years older and he knew he was no match for the old vampire, that he deserved Nic's rage.

"One condition, Mini. One condition was all you had when I gave that scrambler to you. TAKE IT OFF FOR WORK!" Nichol roared, his fury matching the rage still emanating off Rhys. "Kaius is out for MY blood now, you halfwit asshat. If I get Boy's jobs assigned to me because you're too stupid to follow one simple direction, YOU will take my place. GOT IT?"

He merely nodded. He didn't trust himself not to

lash out, verbally or physically. The scent of honeysuckle was slowly thickening in the air, spurring his hunger once again as the spacious training room became stifling, suffocating. His precarious hold on Molly's mind was faltering and she stirred. His instincts were urging him to preserve his sanity and maintain his sleeping hold on her while simultaneously imploring him to wake her and drain her to ease the hunger that was impairing his judgement. *Blink. Breathe. Blink.*

Buzz.

All three males turned their scrutiny to his phone.

Kai: Call

"I… I should probably call Kai now. I'll be in the hall. And then be back. Hallway and back. There. Right outside the door." Rhys and Nic continue to level him with their glares, neither breathing, neither moving. "Rhys, you'll have me in sight the whole time, man. Nic… I'm sorry, man. I didn't think. I'll cover whatever you need. Talk to Kai. I'll talk to Kai. This is totally on me."

He backed out of the training room, his attention divided between maintaining Molly's current restful state and stretching his senses in case his other hauntmates were coming after him.

The youngest amongst them, he was well versed in the pecking order and he was both tormented and spoiled by the older vampires. Having two of the oldest in the haunt assessing his undead life's value was causing his usual inborn insolence to take a back seat to self-preservation. The lethal beasts held position as he pulled the training room door closed, freeing his senses from the honeysuckle onslaught.

A split-second hesitation and a fleeting glance at

the woman on the mattress did not go unnoticed.

He pulled up Kaius's number and double-tapped it, ensuring he was visible from the training room and that he, in turn, could monitor his hold on Molly's mind. He could feel himself tiring from the effort of maintaining a connection this long. But to release her now, in a room with two males who were very obviously vampire and very obviously pissed off… there would be screaming. Screaming, maybe some crying, and he couldn't talk to Kaius with that kind of commotion going on.

Kai answered on the first ring. "Dominic."

It wasn't a guess.

It wasn't a greeting.

It was, in its tone and finality, a demand for information.

"Hey, Dad. Sorry I'm late."

A low, menacing growl rumbled through the phone, a warning to him that Kaius's patience had long since dissipated. Kai had been inordinately indulgent of him since the beginning, but unlike the other hauntmates, Kai's obliging of his whims and attitude were never tempered with combativeness or a well-deserved beat down.

He was, for all intents and purposes, a spoiled brat amongst warriors. While he could hold his own against mortals, his relative youth and inexperience left him the weakest in both physical strength and internal control in the haunt. Kaius, ever cognizant of the young vampire's inability to regulate his hunger effectively, maintained an open blood link to him as often as possible.

His lightning-quick mind processed multiple stories he could weave for Kaius, then abandoned them all.

Kai was monitoring him close enough to sense mistruth, despite his physical distance.

"I cleaned up the Hanson debacle and sent Wyatt Hanson on his way home," he stated, vague yet honest. "She's sleeping in the room now."

Silence.

He shifted his feet. Glanced at Molly through the door window.

"And what," Kai rumbled lowly, "was that."

Another demand.

Dom paused. "The mess I cleaned up."

There was no reason to lie. Kaius would have felt the abrupt surge of hunger, flash of lust, and unraveling control. Whether he had regained his full capabilities instantaneously or not was irrelevant. Kai would be categorizing the episodes, comparing them to past ones, and locating the correlation. Kai went silent again. When vampires went silent on the phone, there was no breathing, no sound of clothing rustling, no shifting of the phone. Silent and still. Kaius had perfected silent and still two thousand years earlier. He was the master of silent and still.

"Put Rhys on."

Chapter Four

Dominic paced the length of the training room. His faculties were weakening, drained from maintaining his tenuous mental hold on Molly while Rhys stood outside the door, phone tight to his ear. While his brothers had long lost the human instinct to breathe, he hadn't. He didn't require the oxygen, but his body remembered the action so clearly that in moments like these, moments where honeysuckle was slowly suffocating him, he had to make a conscious effort to turn off his lungs.

Focusing his physical efforts on not breathing and his mental efforts on the woman lying prone on the mattress was chiseling away at his control. He ran his tongue along his fangs. They had regrown quickly tonight. Almost complete, razor sharp.

Hunger.

Feed.

Rhys remained in the hall, staring unblinkingly at him while talking to Kaius in stealth whispers to avoid any superior senses picking up the conversation. Nichol's attention had turned to tweaking the various monitoring systems in the training room, the doctored GPS long forgotten amid wires and cables. Molly stirred. Twitched. Scratched. Sniffled. Pursed. Stretched.

And he caught every movement in his peripheral.

Mindful of Rhys's unwavering attention, he kept his eyes on his boots, the door, Nichol. Anywhere but directly on the woman until Rhys crooked a finger, silently calling him. He passed the phone and strode back into the training room.

Straight toward Molly.

"Dominic."

Breathe.

"Dominic."

Fight.

"*Dominic.*"

He turned his back to the door, the image of Rhys crouching down to inspect the newest arrival no longer in his sniper vision crosshairs. "Yeah. Yeah, Kaius. I'm here."

"Transfer hold over this woman to Rhys immediately," Kai instructed. "I will be indisposed for a few more days, possibly a week before I can return. In the meantime, you will be on house arrest. And by house arrest, I mean any step you take outside your bunk will be accompanied by Mikhail or Rhys."

"You mean outside the bunker."

"I mean inside the bunker. You are on full escort until my return."

He snarled. "Babysat in my own fucking home? Like a fucking inmate?"

"Yes. Nichol will be chaperoning you to your room now. While he does, tell him I said 'no' to the upgraded sound system in the games room. Boy will be standing guard during daylight. You are not to leave your room until Rhys or Mickey joins you at dusk."

Click.

As he reentered the training room, Nic stood and flashed to his side. Rhys's navy eyes flickered up. "Hand her over."

He moved to the bed.

Hesitated.

His pheromone was the only thing that allowed him to hold her mind still. While Rhys could take over, he couldn't grab a mind that wasn't already in stasis, and the chance of Molly waking during the transition was high. The chance of her waking and screaming was high.

When Rhys booted him in the back of the leg, he reluctantly withdrew the slithering hold gripping Molly's mind, his fingers flexing as he felt her regain her footing briefly before Rhys's snakelike tendrils dove in and stilled her. Rolling his shoulders out in relief at the relatively smooth pass-off, he turned toward Nichol.

And then she moved.

The asset stretched, arched. Her skirt slid up, revealing pale thighs.

FEED.

FUCK.

FeedfuckfeedfuckMollyMOLLYMOLLY.

Nichol pulled him out of the room as his fangs completed their regeneration.

****

Dominic sat motionless, his back rounded against the door of his bunk, shoulders hunched, and his arms draped over his knees. One of the haunt's communal Tenders lay weakened on his bed, her pale complexion and shallow breathing a testament to the unrelenting feeding he had unleashed on her. With his physical hunger temporarily sated, he sat awake in the mid-morning hours.

'Dying for the day' was nothing more than a myth

created and perpetuated by vampires themselves to give mortals a sense of power and safety. In truth, it was only the sun's light that impeded vampires from moving amongst the human population during the day. Vampires required rest to regenerate, to refuel, but were not bound to coffins by dawn. Tucked far beneath the earth's surface, he had no fear of the sun yanking him from the thoughts cycling through his head.

And he needed to think, because something was wrong.

His core was agitated and restless, the familiar ennui he knew replaced by a craving he couldn't put his finger on, one that wasn't fulfilled with A-positive blood. It was augmented by the twinge of guilt that rippled through him every time his thoughts flickered to the woman sleeping in Rhys's training rooms. Guilt he neither deserved nor owned.

He'd cleaned up dozens of messes for other vampires and other haunts over the years. The Kaius haunt, named for the sire of the males within its walls, was the only haunt in North America taking in the humans vampires no longer wanted or needed. Less than a century ago, Molly would have been killed without thought by Wyatt, her body abandoned as he moved on to greener pastures, his mistakes a mere blip.

But times had changed. And the Kaius haunt was, as always, a driving force in that change.

Killed and abandoned.

A gruesome vision crossed his mind and he shook the thought from his head violently, rising to his feet and frowning at the bed. Since waking the worn Tender was considered poor form among the hauntmates, he resigned himself to taking his rest on the sofa.

"I'm crashing now. You can stand down, Boy," he called to the silent sentry outside his door, knowing Boy would neither acknowledge him, nor obey.

****

Dom woke at dusk to an empty bunk, the Tender having slipped from his room at some point during the day out of respect for his desire for solitude when he woke. The haunt's Tenders were highly trained, highly skilled, highly intuitive, and highly adaptive to each brother's preferences. He knew he was discussed at length among the women, his refusal to sleep alongside a supple body, the unhealthy lengths he went between feedings, and his voracious appetite afterwards providing enough gossip to keep them entertained during the monotony of many of their evening tasks.

Almost a decade had passed before he was granted use of the Tenders without direct supervision. It had been awkward, his hauntmates standing guard in the same room as he partook in the blood and bodies of various women. But his impulsiveness, refusal to adhere to early signs of hunger, and the unfulfilled frustration he felt after every encounter made him a danger to the pampered Tenders in his early years.

Rhys maintained an indirect supervision of all the haunt's feeding sessions, demanding Tenders advise Boy of their location prior to participating in sessions with any brothers who were overtired, injured, or ravenous. While the need for interference was rare among the others, Boy had often had to intervene in his feedings, pulling him back before the Tender was drained.

Control had never been his strength, as a human or a vampire.

And he just didn't care.

He stripped on his way to the shower, leaving a trail of clothing behind him that would be picked up when the Tenders on room duty came in to clean and change his sheets. The scalding water warmed his cool skin and he relished in the act of washing the previous night's events from his body. His hunger abated for now, his mind felt clearer, more controlled.

His reaction to Molly last night had been nothing more than the result of waiting too long between feedings. Her scent had been nothing more than an unexpected experience from his usual prohibited indulgences of stoned or drunk prostitutes that reeked of booze, chemicals, medications, and the odor of unwashed men. His desire to remain at her side was nothing more than his baser instincts screaming to be satiated by her blood.

Her raspy voice was aggravating.

Her constant fidgeting was annoying.

Her faint scent of bleach was nauseating.

And his traitorous body was reacting to it all. He snarled, realizing his hand had subconsciously moved to grip his thick member and was stroking it roughly, relentlessly. Releasing his hold, he turned off the water and snatched a towel off the rack.

He needed to deal with his tampered GPS. Make things right with Nichol. Maybe see if Jagger was up for a sparring match. Polish his steel toe boots.

Pulling well-worn jeans over his slim hips and a black singlet over his head, he strode barefoot into the bunker hall to greet his nanny. Mickey was leaning against the wall, hands jammed in his pockets and arctic blue eyes hidden behind shaggy blond hair.

The tallest of the hauntmates, Mick hid his impressive six-seven with the slouch of a wary male attempting unsuccessfully to meld with his surroundings. There was a disharmony between his sculpted, lethal form and the compassionate, perceptive crystal of his eyes. Just shy of two and a half centuries old, Mikhail was the second youngest member of their haunt. His keen strategist mind had made him invaluable to their survival, and his empathic abilities had diffused many testosterone-fueled altercations.

Kaius had chosen a good nanny for the evening.

He raised an eyebrow at Mick, a little trick Kai had helped him learn during his first few months. “What’s on the agenda tonight, Guard?”

Mickey grinned. “Don’t know about you, but I’m spending my night following a brain-dead pussy around the compound while he sulks about being in the company of the hottest motherfucker around.”

“You bite your momma with that mouth?”

“Naw. My momma had class, man. Jagg’s mom is the one that likes to fill my mouth.”

“You’re a nasty bastard,” he laughed. When Mick was having a good day, he was a great distraction from anything you wanted to escape. And he was grateful for anything that would keep Molly’s dark, fiery eyes out of his mind.

“How about we head over to see Nichol and then down to the gym?”

“Whatever you want, window-licker.”

He led Mick on a detour to the garage to grab the modified GPS system. He considered opening it up and messing around with the innards to provide a little humor at Nichol’s expense. The guys had been known to purposely break electronics just to witness Nic's exasperation at the 'incomprehensible stupidity required to achieve such a feat'.

Nichol's obsession with order and completion wouldn't allow him to leave a task unfinished, and Nic had yet to meet an electronic he couldn't master. During a particularly quiet month, Rhys had once explained away his trashing of the entire compound surveillance system as Reactionary Boredom Disorder with his destruction acting as both a symptom of his own RBD and an antidote to Nichol's. For leaving the bunker blind to threats, Kaius took Rhys's fangs every night until the system was functional again.

Nichol, the vindictive bastard he was, worked unusually slow during those three weeks.

He decided that after last night's events, it would be safest to return the GPS intact. Perhaps while groveling. With a little mercy begging.

Maybe toss in a scrumptious Tender for luck.

The males made their way to the bunker's office, passing a pair of Tenders on the way. Mick smirked rakishly at the women and held out a hand. The brunette clasped it and was instantly pinned to the wall, her playful shrieks and laughter echoing down the halls as Mickey nipped at her neck and tongued her cleavage. With an atrocious attempt at a Transylvanian accent, he growled into her breasts, "I vant to suck your blood!" Then he pulled away, bending low at the waist. "You know, if you're cool with that, Amy."

The brunette, Amy, ran her fingers through his shaggy mop of hair. "Only if I can untangle this mess for you, too."

"Deal. Dawn?"

“Of course.”

And with a quick kiss on his cheek, the Tenders carried on with their evening and Mick continued into the office door.

He envied the casual way most of the hauntmates interacted with the Tenders. They were companions and friends as much as a meal and a warm body. When Mick was on, the Tenders fell over themselves to be chosen to fuck him, feed him, or watch television with him. When he was in a low, they flocked to him like mother hens, doting and fussing over him until he locked himself away to escape their overwhelming nurturing. In his current high, the Tenders were hyperaware of Mickey’s presence in the compound and were all anxious to spend time with him before he inevitably plummeted.

Rhys’s relationship with every Tender was unique, as he was the one who brought them into their new reality, alleviated their fears, and trained them in blood giving, home care, and sex. He had inadvertently witnessed portions of the training as he brought in the latest rescues or stopped by to receive cleanup instructions. Rhys was meticulous, known amongst vampires nationwide for his beautiful, competent Tenders. His Tenders fetched higher prices than any other, and his women had become symbols of wealth and status for their kind.

He caught up with Mick and Nichol before thoughts of Rhys’s abilities led to thoughts of what Rhys was currently accomplishing with those skills. The males were hunched over a computer screen, quietly discussing the information displayed.

“Nothing for family? Friends? What about a

roommate? Landlord?"

Nichol shook his head. "No familial links found. Boyfriend a nonissue. No sign of anyone who would notice. Little fucker lucked out."

He frowned and looked over Nichol's shoulder. "What's up?"

"That woman you brought in from Wyatt Hanson last night," Nichol mumbled. "I wasn't sure what kind of online cleanup would be required, but I think this may be in the clear. No social media, no credit score, no friends or family. Can't find anything in her name for more than three months at a time. Hanson's youngest must shit horseshoes with that kind of luck."

He backed away from the screen, forcing himself away from learning any more about Molly Wagner and her apparent inability to stay with a cell phone company for longer than a few months. There was no need for him to know she had been employed at dozens of restaurants, bars, and clothing boutiques across the state. No reason to catalogue her sporadic list of previous residences. He had no use for the knowledge that she had no school records past tenth grade.

"I'm thinking this chick's a bit flaky," Mickey laughed as he scanned dozens of outstanding bills from utility companies. "If Rhys can get her on board, Wyatt might be the best fucking thing that ever happened to her."

"Shut it, you inbred trout sniffer," he growled, stepping back as his temper flared needlessly. He tightened his grip on the metal box in his hands. "Hey Nic, I brought the GPS along. Figured you could get it functional again before Kai gets back."

Nichol took the outreached electronic and locked

his amber eyes on him. "Whatever Kaius felt from you last night had him really tense. I'm pissed you didn't take the working locator because it left all of us feeling pretty helpless and it was my fault. You think you're invincible, but there's no regenerating from a pile of sludge on the road."

The office atmosphere began to grow heavy, weighted by the seriousness of Nichol's words. He had taken many reckless chances in the past few decades, testing his skills and strengths, pushing the limits of the power backing him in both haunt name and power. "I'm truly sorry, Nic. I didn't th—"

"Dude," Mick interrupted, "Nic and Kai may have been worried, but I was kind of hoping I'd inherit your bunk. I'm pretty sure it's bigger than mine."

"You're a heartless bastard," he grinned.

"And I don't give a fuck about you, so we're good, right?" Mickey kissed air at him.

"So how many fucks did you start with?" Nichol inquired.

"I dunno. Not many. The Fuck Fairy skimped out on my fucks," Mick replied, pulling his jeans pocket inside out to illustrate his lack of fucks to the others.

"The Fuck Fairy doesn't hand out fucks, you dumbass," Nic argued. "She blesses you with hot women."

"Your Fuck Fairy felt bad for your ugly ass so she kept her fucks and helped you get laid. Some of us don't need help." Mickey stood to his full height, brushing his hands down his iron chest.

"Whatever, man. The Fuck Fairy bestows pussy."

"That's the Pussy Fairy, you illiterate slob. The Fuck Fairy gives you fucks to give and when you run out, she decides if you're worthy of more."

"Wait," he interjected; "There's a Pussy Fairy?"

"Of course there's a Pussy Fairy. She explains how hideous trolls like Nicky-Boy over here get laid. Or at least used to get laid. I banged her a while back."

"You did not bang the Pussy Fairy," Nichol barked back. "She's, like, virginal and shit."

Dom snickered. "Could we stop arguing over mythical fairies and head down to the sparing room now? Nic, want to join?"

Nichol nodded and strode out the door. "You're just pissed because the Fuck Fairy screwed you over and the Pussy Fairy knows you're hopeless."

And with that, they tackled and shoved each other down the hallway toward the bunker's gym.

****

Frigid water pummeled Dominic's broad shoulders, sending icy channels down his spine and chest. While Mick hooted and howled as Nichol rinsed the blood off them, he grit his teeth, focusing on the divots his extended fangs made in his lower lip. Nic was relishing in the act of hosing down the bloody, beaten vampires, oblivious to the knowledge that he would be next.

Although temperature had little effect on their bodies, ice water blasting skin was uncomfortable and irritating nonetheless. They had sparred tirelessly for hours, choosing hand and fang combat over weapons to work their aggression out on each other. The scouring of the blood-splattered stainless steel walls and ceiling had focused their blood lust afterwards and left them more unwound and relaxed. Until the freezing hose-down, at least.

The saturating assault ended and Mick shook his blond hair out like a dog after a bath. “That felt fucking fantastic!” he shouted, voice reverberating off the steel covered concrete walls. “Bend over, Nicky-Boy!”

Mick wrestled the hose away from Nichol, escaping with numerous bleeding fang marks on his arms. Nic stood stoically as he was blasted, flinching only when the hose passed over his dick.

“Watch the haunt’s pride and joy, dipshit,” Nichol grumbled.

He snorted as he pulled on his jeans. “Gotta respect the weapon, Mickey. It could be the secret to stopping Armageddon.”

Mick rolled up the hose, stepping over the large drain in the center of the room. “Yeah, like some teensy tiny little key for saving the world.”

Nichol flipped him off, strolling out of the room. “See you later, jealous bitches. I have useful shit to get done.”

He and Mick finished setting the room to rights, replacing the weapons that had been knocked off the walls during their scuffles and turning the training benches upright again. The barbell Nichol had thrown was embedded in one wall and Dominic knelt to assess the damage. “We’ll just tell Kai it was there when we got here.”

Mickey agreed with a fist bump as they left the sparring room. “You bled like a fucking geyser,” Mick commented. “Probably a good idea to round up a Tender for you. Let’s swing by the training area and see who’s available.”

The two walked down the winding hallways into the rooms that the haunt’s Tenders and trainees called home, their bedroom doors lining the hall that led to a central kitchen and living area. The scent of woman in this area contrasted sharply with the slightly damp, pungent smell in the rest of the underground bunker.

Bouquets of flowers, scenic oil paintings done by artistic Tenders, and soft welcoming colors covered every surface, creating an oasis of daintiness in a primarily masculine enclosure.

He didn't spend much time in the Tenders' quarters. His infrequent feedings meant Kai usually sent one to his room when he felt he was reaching a critical point.

Selecting one from the group always felt awkward since he had done nothing to foster any kind of relationship with them, and he envied Mick's ease and playfulness with the women charged with keeping the hauntmates fed and satiated. He preferred to get his kicks during his rare solo outings, when he could slip from the bed without another word, his cravings satisfied anonymously.

The Tenders held no real draw for him.

But as the males turned into the training wing, he caught a scent and froze, his pupils dilating and fangs extending.

Feed.

Fuck.

Mollymollyfeedmollyfuckmolly.

Chapter Five

Molly could feel a soft presence caressing her mind as she woke, her frenetic thoughts lulled by what she likened to fingers grazing across her consciousness hypnotically. She stretched slowly, arching her back and flexing her toes. Her eyes opened, adjusting to the candles illuminating the room before she began to register the unfamiliar surroundings, scanning the room methodically in search of clues of her whereabouts. Lounge chairs. Settees. Throw pillows as far as the eye could see. All shades of red, black, and silver. Very bordello, she thought as she took in every nuance.

Movement.

Her eyes flitted to a far corner where a shadowed form lounged in what appeared to be a leather recliner and she recoiled, drawing her legs in tight to her body. "Wyatt?"

A deep chuckle reverberated throughout the room.

"Wyatt's probably halfway to Nevada by now, sweetheart."

She squinted in the low light, fragments of the previous evening dancing in a jumbled mess through her head as she began to recall the cold. The snow. The other vampire.

"You aren't Dominic."

"Accurate assessment, angel."

Lowering her feet to the floor, she inched closer to the wall as she assessed the stranger cloaked in the shadow. His jawline was more rigid, more defined than she remembered Dominic's being. Black hair was swept back, not falling loosely over blue eyes. No day-old whiskers. "And you would be…?"

Silence.

He stood and walked slowly toward her, stopping his approach when she drew further from him.

"That's not your natural hair color."

Glancing toward the door, she readied herself and tore across the room.

One moment, the door was in reach. The next, her hand was grasping at taut muscle under soft, ribbed fabric. She snatched her hand away and spun on her heel, frantically searching for another way out.

"Bathroom's that way," the vampire stated calmly, gesturing to her left.

Realization began to settle in.

Wyatt's put you in a bit of a situation, and I'm going to need you to cooperate.

She blinked slowly, processing the elegant decor, the livable layout of the rooms. The kitchen. For a species that didn't need one. "I'm not leaving, am I?"

The vampire remained silent, watching her with his dark unblinking eyes as she shifted feet, flexed fingers, twitched a shoulder, wrinkled her nose.

"Sir?"

"Rhys. Never 'sir'.' Are you always this," he scanned her form, "squirmy?"

****

She sat on the extravagant red and black sofa, her legs bouncing as her fingers stroked the swirled pattern on the armrest piping. Blonde tendrils were escaping her bun en masse now, providing more movement fodder for her jittery, restless body. Her legs crossed and uncrossed, feet flexing and pointing as she pushed her hair behind her ears only to tug it forward again to wrap the pieces around her chipped neon orange fingernails.

With each movement, her mind processed another nugget of information Rhys was disclosing about her current predicament.

For her, there was no more basement. No more Wyatt with his bags of gas station food and skittish mutterings. No more zip-tie restraints and unpredictable tirades punctuated by nights alone in an unknown place.

The extravagant surroundings she now sat in were a different kind of cell.

"Your situation is somewhat unique," Rhys said, stretching his arms across the back of his chair and drawing her eyes to the intricate tattoos looping over his biceps. "Our typical retrievals are women who've been placed with vampires for decades or those too far gone to consider for anything outside of the bloodslave quarters." He drummed his fingers on the cushion.

"Our haunt specializes in rehoming humans that vampires have accumulated but no longer have use for. Those that show an aptitude for Tender training, or who have completed the training previously, are brought to me. Those that aren't fit for training are housed in our bloodslave quarters." He gave her a fangy smile. "Barbaric, sure, but the other option is giving free rein to the less enlightened haunts regarding their human disposals methods. And those are truly questionable."

He glanced toward the exit, cocking his head. "Unfortunately, you fall between those lines. You're obviously unrefined in speech, education, and manners.

No experience in blood management. Training you would be an extremely time-consuming task. But we got to you quick enough to avoid the worst confinement effects and Wyatt left you fairly intact physically and mentally, I assume."

Her lips drew into a thin line and she fixed her eyes on the bowl of fruit sitting on the coffee table between them. "Then let me go home."

Rhys smirked, his fangs visible. "If I wasn't clear enough earlier, let me state it now. You have two choices here. Train under me as a Tender, a vampire courtesan if you will, and I'll find you a suitable placement when you're ready. Or I can walk you down to the bloodslave quarters now and spend the next few hours fumigating the stench of a cheap hair bleach job from my chaise."

"What would the first option mean?" she asked, her stomach clenching at the thought of being one of those bloodslaves she'd heard about from vampire exposés on late night television. "It's, like, housekeeper training?"

The smirk turned into a full grin. "Some of it." Rhys counted off the requirements, tapping one finger at a time on the sofa as he rattled them off. "Preferred blood flavorings and how to refine them. Money management and basic accounting. Ballroom dance, though that's becoming less of a demand in recent requests. Housekeeping, as you mentioned. Any artistic talents you have will be developed. Manners. Elocution. Cooking." He frowned and stared at his thumb. "Oh, right. Fucking."

Her eyes widened as the urge to run rose inside her.

"Once you have a good handle on every aspect of the training, you'll be placed with a vampire requesting a companion with skill sets best matching your strengths." He licked his lips. "Should you disappoint your purchaser, your fate will rest in his hands. He may drain you, discipline you, or send you back to me. And I do not take kindly to returned products."

This wasn't her life.

Neither her mind nor her personality was suited to any aspect of the training outlined. Her moods and mannerisms were as volatile as her decision-making. Her food knowledge expanded little past identifying which french fries came from which fast food joint. Money management had always been not losing her check on the way to the bank. She cleaned her house when a smell required identification. Without the fortitude to stick with any activity, she had no identifiable artistic skill and tabletops were the epitome of her ballroom dance skills.

This wasn't her life. But it would be her damn choice how her life came to an end.

She stood, squaring her shoulder in resolve. "I'll take door number two, sir."

Rhys quirked an eyebrow.

"It's been some time since someone has made that choice. May I ask why?"

****

Dominic opened the training room door, his eyes locked on Rhys as he stalked into the room with Mickey flanking him closely. Rhys addressed them, his attention on the woman sitting on the edge of the sofa. "Good timing, gentlemen. Our newest enchantress was about to explain why she's decided death would be preferable to the eternal company of handsome guys like ourselves."

His jaw flexing, he risked a glance over at Molly. Most Tenders chose life at the onset, their self-preservation surpassing their fear of the unknown. As they grew accustomed to the lifestyle, few had ever expressed regret, and those that had did so mostly in cases where the masters had met untimely deaths, emotionally devastating the Tender. Especially now, with the women Rhys trained being brought in from the mistakes and whims of lesser vampires, he had yet to see one of them choose the bloodslave quarters over the training.

And Molly was, in his estimation, perfect for it.

Though few would admit it within the vampire hierarchy, Tenders were the backbone of their lifestyle. The strength behind the vampire. Those who had tied themselves emotionally to the women were fiercely protective, aggressive to the point of recklessness should she be endangered. There were those cases where Tenders were used, abused, drained, and replaced, but the Kaius haunt had taken steps over the past few decades to deal with those situations.

Rhys looked over at him and lifted a brow. "She's strong enough for the quarters, right? I suppose putting her down is the other option…"

His eyes latched onto the new trainee as her gaze flicked between him and Rhys and she leaned forward a fraction.

She didn't know what she was asking for.

He crossed his arms. "I'll do it."

Molly's jaw dropped. "What? No! Rhys, I never agreed to that!"

"Semantics," Rhys grinned, his silvery fangs elongating. "You chose death, sweetcheeks, and it appears Mini here is more than willing to do the dirty work for me." When she leapt to her feet, he looked up at her. "Don't worry. Dominic's always quick."

Ignoring the slight, he flashed behind Molly and yanked her head back by her bun, careful to scare her without damaging her. His fangs grazed the milky skin of her neck without puncturing, her piercing scream stopping him cold. He glanced over at Mick and Rhys, waiting for the nearly imperceptible nod of confirmation that his tactic was working. "Still want to die, Miss Molly?" he whispered against her flushed neck.

"Door number one," she whimpered. "Please. Door number one."

He released her without another word as his core reared up, demanding he finish what he had started.

****

Molly's hand rose to her throat, her fingers finding the fading reminders of Wyatt's only feeding from her. Dominic stormed from the room, the blond vampire giving her a quick wave as he followed.

Rhys scratched at his arm for a moment and strode over to a set of doors at the back of the training room. "This is where you'll be staying until your training is complete. Or I eat you in frustration. Either way, you should find everything you need here. You can use anything you find in the en suite bathroom. When I return tomorrow evening, I'll have Nichol bring you a computer so you can start selecting clothing and whatever you deem necessary to look beautiful."

Flash of fangy smile.

She followed, shoulders hunched in defeat amid the luxurious surroundings. "Where are you going? You aren't staying?"

Rhys paused and scanned her methodically. "I have a Tender shipping out in the morning and I need to meet with some of the others to discuss what we can do about that bleached nightmare you call a hair color."

He hesitated in distaste. "If I could get headaches, I'd have one from the stench of that peroxide disaster. Some of our resident Tenders will be by shortly with food," he said, his large fingers wrapped around the door knob. "They're good women. You'd be wise to try and befriend them as we will use many of their skills in your training. This door will be locked during the day until I feel you have control over your behavior. Although we'll begin your formal education tomorrow night, you have an assignment to complete today. Make a list of things that make you happy. Anything. I'll be requesting it when I return," Rhys instructed over his shoulder as he exited the room, pulling the door tight behind him.

She sank onto the luxurious sofa, numb.

****

Dominic kept his hands fisted in his pockets as Mickey stood across from him. "What?"

"Nothing," Mick replied, feigning an intense examination of the back of his hands. "It's just that I think I've got a pretty good handle on you, man, but I couldn't tell if you wanted her to live or die."

He ran his tongue over his fang. "Doesn't matter to me. I was only trying to make sure the chick understood where her decision would lead." He looked down the hall as Rhys approached them. "All good?"

"I'll give her a try," Rhys said, smacking Dom's hat off his head as he passed them. "If you see Justine in your travels, let her know I have a bleached blonde that needs rescuing," he called out. "And if you see Dahlia, tell her I have a job for her."

He watched Rhys turn the corner and held his tongue until he was certain the old vampire was out of earshot. "We should go check on her."

"Don't even think about it, Mini," Mickey warned. "Those messed-up vibes you've been giving off since last night aren't fading. I'm not sure going back in there is going to help."

"Five minutes," he bargained. "Give me five minutes in there to prove I'm all good. Then you can report to Kai that there's no reason for you to tie your ass to me, and we both gain our freedom back. Yeah?"

Mick's blue eyes narrowed. "I'll give you two. But I'm going in with you, and I reserve the right to haul your ass out of there if I sense anything I don't like." He gestured toward the Tender quarters. "After you, princess."

He sprinted back to the training room. A formal introduction, a quick hey-sorry-I-offered-to-drain-you, and he could smooth everything over. After all, the woman was going to be in the haunt for a while.

He needed to establish a cordial relationship.

His brief hesitation before he flicked the exterior lock didn't go unnoticed.

"We don't need to be here," Mickey said quietly. "We can hit the sparring room for an hour or two. Or head out for a run."

He shook his head and opened the door.

Goddamn honeysuckle.

Knowing Mick would make good on his threat if he reacted, he strode into the training room, coming face to face with Molly. She eyed him warily, her fingers knotting in the hem of her skirt. He opened his mouth to speak, then snapped his jaw shut.

What the fuck was he going to say?

As the silence stretched out, Mickey finally took over.

"Dominic wants to know what you're hungry for," he stated, glancing over at him and grinning.

Asshole.

She took a step back. "Anything, I guess."

Ignoring Mick's elbow as it dug into his ribs, he shoved his hands into his pockets. "We can order in anything you want," he offered. "Name it. Anything. Whatever you want."

Accommodating. Friendly. Not at all desperate.

Fuck.

The woman's onyx eyes lifted from the floor. "I guess bacon would be nice," she ventured, the glimmer of hope on her face nearly bringing him to his knees.

Clenching his fists in his pockets, he nodded tersely. "We'll put it on the list," he said gruffly, his voice harsher than intended as he fought to appear unaffected by the woman's presence. "You, uh… take care."

If the woman's slight furrowing of her brows hadn't let Dominic know he sounded like a complete idiot, Mick's dead stare would have.

Take care.

He turned away from her and walked out of the room, Mick pausing to lock the door before catching up to him in the hall.

"Not bad, right?" he said, his head clearing the further from Molly he got. "Text Kai and report to

Nichol. No problems. Totally fine."

"That chilled-out slouch may work on Nichol," Mick stated, crossing his arms over his chest, "but there's no fucking way I'm signing off on babysitting duty anytime soon, Mini."

****

Molly turned to inspect the room, free of watchful eyes. Looking past the opulence of the decor, she assessed the layout of the central area. The lavish seating area and bed were the central focus, their soft upholstery and rich colors drawing the eye. In the back right corner was an easel and numerous dainty carousels of paints, brushes, and oils. Blank canvasses of all sizes rested against the wall below a myriad of stunning art pieces hanging above.

Her eyes flicked to the opposite corner where mirrors lined the walls behind a ballet barre. Atop the dark polished hardwood sat an intricate sound system and what appeared to be a wardrobe. Curiosity got the better of her and she wandered over to look inside.

A copious number of scarves, castanets, ribbons, veils, finger cymbals, and fans filled the drawers and adorned the hangers. Her fingers grazed the delicate items and she allowed herself to relish in the beauty of the collection.

Having spent most of her twenty-seven years in that delicate balance between broke and destitute, she had owned few elegant items. The rare times she had indulged her desire for an unnecessary but alluring piece, she had turned around and sold it to cover her rcnt.

Reluctantly pulling away from the treasures, she wandered into her new bedroom. Grays and blacks dominated the decor, with hints of deep rose accenting the room and softening the design.

A small step stool was nestled beside the raised king-sized bed, obviously meant for shorter women who would struggle to climb into the high bed. It served as a glaring reminder that this was not her room, not her home.

The en suite bathroom was as opulent as the other rooms. The soaker tub sat below a black marble multi-jet shower. Chrome fixtures shone against the dark stone, the only other color in the room provided by the plush white bathrobe and towels, and the deep red pillar candles placed around the countertop and tub ledge.

Opening the large mirrored medicine cabinet, she examined the multitudes of oils, body scrubs, shampoos, and lotions. Selecting a collection of jasmine-scented bottles, she turned on the faucets, locked the door, and climbed into the majestic tub.

****

Soft voices lilted from beyond the bathroom door, pulling Molly from her circular thoughts of drowning, escaping, accepting, reveling.

And Dominic.

If she hadn't been locked in a room by vampires who wanted to mold her and sell her off, she would have felt bad for the guy. The way he froze up, the hunching of his shoulders as he spoke, the apologetic glimmer in those oval irises…

She dipped her head back under the hot water and shook the image from her mind.

Fingers and toes pruned, she toweled herself off with the plushest towel she'd ever enjoyed and slipped into the waiting bathrobe. An unusual self-consciousness seeped in regarding her blonde locks, so she wrapped her hair in a towel and hurried out of the bathroom. When the aroma of unprocessed food hit her nose, she gave a little hop of excitement.

It had been weeks since her last fresh meal.

Tearing out of the bedroom, she stopped short as two stunning brunettes turned to smile at her.

"You must be Molly," said the taller woman, her bright brown eyes sparkling with excitement. "Rhys told us you might be hungry."

"But the brute refused to allow us to take you to the kitchen," chimed the shorter woman, playing with her brown pixie cut.

She eyed the women suspiciously, searching for any sign of duress, any proof of abuse.

Her silence didn't faze the cheerful women at all. The taller woman gestured to a spread of breads, fruits, baked dainties, sliced smoked meats, and an array of cheeses. "We weren't sure what you'd be in the mood for. Since most of us are in bed by morning, there wasn't anything in the oven…"

"But there will be at dusk!" the shorter female exclaimed. "Bacon. Lots of bacon! One of the guys put in a special order."

As she moved to the table to sample the warm bread, the taller woman followed and chattered happily.

"My name's Amy. This is Dahlia. We're so excited to have a new face around here! Paten was selected and moved so quickly that we didn't get any goodbyes or have any closure or a party…"

"And we didn't like Paten because she was kind of a bitch," interrupted Dahlia, her fingers poking at her hair until it stood out in wild spikes around her gentle face.

"Be nice!" gasped Amy. "She was an extremely talented Tender. It's no wonder her training time was cut short. And yes, she was a haughty bitch. I lost the time bet by two days."

Curiosity brought her voice out. "Bet?"

Seemingly thrilled with the interaction, Dahlia hopped excitedly over to her side and offered her a muffin. "Oh yes. We bet on how new Tenders will do. You know, who will excel, how long their training will take, whether they're chosen to stay here, whether or not they drive Rhys into the pits of rage…"

"And I bet Paten would excel, please Rhys, and be traded within three months. It was three months, two days," Amy lamented. "Two miserable days. Miserable because she was still here!"

"So," she began, half chewing, "what's the bet on me?"

Amy looked away and giggled. Dahlia stuffed a cheese ball into her mouth before answering, "Well we can't very well tell you, can we? But I'll tell you this… The wager is high on you!"

She frowned and set her muffin down and glanced around. "So, if everyone is sleeping now, why are you two here?"

Amy grinned. "Rhys caught me in the hallway leaving Mick's room after dawn. And Dahlia's being punished."

"Punished?"

"Yup!" Dahlia laughed. "According to Rhys, I'm on disaster duty for the foreseeable future. That's you."

"What did you do?" she asked, curious about what counted as punishable misdemeanors here.

Dahlia stood with a flourish and spun in a circle. "I chopped two feet off my hair! You like?"

"That's not all of it, Dahl," Amy interjected, her voice turned conspiratorial. "Dahlia was supposed to be traded last week to a vampire with a major obsession with long hair. So she cut it off and tied it around Rhys's doorknob so she could stay here with us."

"And Paten went in my place!" Dahlia exclaimed, pleased with the events leading to her punishment. "Amy's just mad I didn't do it earlier so she could win the bet."

"That I am."

She stared at the two women. "So you want to be here," she stated, not asking as much as confirming what the confident, perky women were radiating. They were healthy. Happy. Not chained, drained, pillaged.

Both women became serious, their playful eyes locking on her, smiles softening in sympathy. "From what I heard, you aren't like most of us," Amy began. "Most of us were taken in from other haunts. We know how the system works, what's expected of us. Paten was a retraining from an affluent haunt up north and Dominic selected me and Dahlia from a haunt in the Midwest that was restructuring and downsizing. But you…is it true Wyatt Hanson kidnapped you?"

She recoiled at the mention of his name. "I don't want to talk about it."

"Of course you don't," Amy crooned. "But you'll have to provide the details to the guys eventually so they can write up a damage report." She placed her hand on Dahlia's arm. "We should go. Let you rest up. Rhys says you're to do your homework before he arrives tonight. It was nice to meet you, Molly," she said politely, smiling warmly as she escorted Dahlia toward the door.

Dahlia waved over her shoulder and with a click, the door was locked again. She ran to the door, peering through the window as the women gossiped down the hallway. "Did you see Gabby after she went to Dom's?" Dahlia asked her friend.

"Met her on my way over here. She said he tossed her out as soon as she got there. Apparently, he was a raging mess…"

The voices went too soft for her to hear any more. She went into the bedroom, climbed atop the mattress, and willed the thoughts in her head silent as she fell into an exhausted sleep.

Chapter Six

Molly awoke just after four in the afternoon. She stretched out, slowly untangling herself from the knotted sheet and comforter as she familiarized herself with her recent situation. The women, Amy and Dahlia, had seemed to be more like sorority girls than mindless bloodslaves. They exhibited no fear of the vampires, apparently going so far as to blatantly defy them without the fear of physical punishment.

She had fought Wyatt on the rare occasions he entered the dank cement basement he'd held her in. And she'd gone hungry for days every time.

In comparison, this wasn't terrible.

Yet.

She got up, brushed her teeth and hair, washed her face, and returned to the bed with the intention of finishing her assignment. She sat for over an hour, thinking and writing, shifting and scribbling until the click of the main room lock broke her concentration and she set her pen aside. Rhys stood in her bedroom doorway, his unblinking eyes scanning her form, the room, and then resting on the notepad in her hand. She extended it toward him and he moved with catlike grace to retrieve it.

"Sleep well, dear one?"

"Yes, sir."

"Rhys."

"Yes, Sir Rhys."

Despite not needing to breathe, she thought she caught a hint of an exhale.

Rhys looked over her list as he moved to the couch and patted the seat beside him. "This is it?"

She sat next to him, her knee bouncing nervously and fingers drumming the plush upholstery. "Yes, sir."

"Rhys."

"Yes, Sir Rhys."

"Pretty things. Soft things. Bright things. This is your list of specific things that make you happy."

"You didn't say to be specific. All those things make me happy."

Rhys tore the list off the notepad, folded it, and shoved it in his back pocket. "Your writing is atrocious. Like a twelve-year-old girl with a boy band crush."

"I didn't dot my 'i's with hearts though, did I?"

Silence.

"Sir Rhys?"

Rhys's navy eyes met hers. He was definitely handsome, she mused. A strong, clean-shaven jaw. Chiseled cheekbones. Dark brows above deep blue eyes. Stray strands of slicked-back hair dropping seductively over his forehead.

Lethally pretty. Movie-star handsome.

And not really her cup of tea. She preferred her guys a little scruffier. A little less tailored.

Guys like Dominic.

Without the fangs.

She shook her head to clear her mind and refocus on what was important. Rhys was her captor. Dominic was his accomplice. Bad, bad guys that would drain her without a second thought.

Rhys's hand dropped to her knee forcefully,

stopping her bouncing. “I find myself at a loss. I don’t know where to start with you. You’re a total project.”

She froze. “Are you going to force me to door number two?”

Silence.

“I’m not prepared for the shit-storm that would arrive if I did,” Rhys finally stated, rising. “Let’s start with your hair.”

Flicking his phone out, Rhys sent a text and moments later Dahlia and a blonde woman entered the room with a cart. “What are they going to do?” she asked anxiously, remembering Dahlia slicing her hair off in protest.

“These two beautiful women will be putting your hair to rights. I’ll be back to check the progress in a few hours.”

“But I like…”

“But I don’t. Ladies, make her stunning.”

As Rhys strolled out the door, Dahlia giggled, “He’s such a crank.”

The blonde woman rolled her eyes, “You know damn well he heard that.”

Dahlia winked at her. “Of course he did. He’ll also hear me call him a jerk, brute, and jackass.”

Rhys’s low voice echoed down the hall, “You wound me, angel. You used to call me a god.”

Dahlia blushed.

The blonde grinned.

Molly’s eyes widened at the implication.

“So,” Dahlia recovered, “Gabby and I are going to make you biteably gorgeous.”

****

Dominic stalked out his door, shouldering Boy on

his way out. Boy turned his head and walked away, his babysitting duties done for the evening.

Sleep had eluded him all day as he bounced between rage, guilt, curiosity, and desire. He had fixated on the images of the two healing fang marks on Molly's throat, their lengths indicating Wyatt was a sloppy, careless feeder. Shifted to the determination in her eyes when she'd bolted across the snow in sock feet. Flashed to the wariness of her stance when he'd returned to the training room to trip over his own tongue.

BUZZ.

He glanced at his incoming message.

Kai: Who is with you?

Looking around, he fired back*: No one.*

Mick appeared immediately. His blond hair was brushed back and he appeared happily sated. The brunette from the morning before must have been more fulfilling than the one he vaguely recalled sending away.

"Text Kai back. Tell him I'm here and he can stop SHOCKING MY BLOODY HEAD!" Mick yelled, willing his voice to travel to whatever mysterious place Kaius had disappeared to again.

He grinned and pretended to put his phone in his pocket. Mickey tackled him to the floor and the males wrestled with fraternal aggression over the device. Mick held back his strength at first, allowing him to gain some ground before flipping him to his back and snatching the phone.

"Mick is here and doing a great no… spectacular job of babysitting my sorry punk ass and I will be eternally grateful for his sacrifice for my… sanity? You aren't really nuts. Just kind of, I don't know, off. How about eternally grateful for his sacrifice keeping my dumb ass from being a total fuckup. Send. Done! Wanna go for a run outside tonight?"

He rolled his eyes. "Any chance we should trim the canines before we go?"

"Fuck that. I hate the feeling of regrowth. All tingly and sizzly and shit. We'll stay in the backwoods. Suit up, my man!"

They went topside, scenting the air for unknown odors and scanning the darkness for movement. Assured that all was clear, they took off running through the dense trees. Although Mick's age made him fast, his own hearing and sight were extremely advanced, giving him a slight edge in the forest.

He dodged wayward branches with ease, relishing in the profanity Mickey emitted when one caught him in the face or chest. The vampires covered over a hundred miles in three hours as they wound through the thick woods, their feet crunching on the untouched snow.

Mick's whooping and cursing punctuated the rhythmic pounding of their feet intermittently. He felt his mind reassembling itself, restructuring its order and control.

Molly was here to stay and he needed to deal with the situation. She was pretty. She was want-to-fuck-you-until-dawn pretty, but that was manageable. All Tenders were beautiful. He could handle beauty.

She smelled like honeysuckle. With his thoughts and abilities under control, he could avoid scenting the air when she was around. Or when she had been in a room. Or pretty much stop breathing entirely since that scent would likely permeate the entire goddamn compound once she was no longer a flight risk. But he could do that. It would take effort, but it was doable.

She was aggravating. The constant jiggling, wiggling, shaking, bouncing, twitching was exhausting to process even for a vampire. She had no impulse control. She made stupid decisions. Stupid decisions that got her locked in basements with losers like Wyatt Hanson.

Her impetuousness would feed his own, and he had enough experience as a man to know that without a staying hand, he was destructive to himself and those around him. And as a vampire, his lapses of self-control were both violent and deadly. That made her bad for him, and he was wise enough to know that bad for him wasn't good.

And she was too damn tall.

As the males closed in on the haunt, he felt his resolution strengthen. He could exist in the same space for the duration of Molly's training. Whatever pull she had initially had on him was a freak incident, nothing more than some stupid crush brought about by boredom with his surroundings. His judgement had been impaired by hunger, his control weakened. But now, rejuvenated, she was relegated to the status of every other woman he'd brought back to the haunt for trade.

He and Mickey wandered down the hall, closing in on the Tender wing. Jagg came up behind them, his long gait allowing him to overtake them. "Last one there gets the A-positive," he called before breaking into a full run.

Mick took off, leaving him alone in the hall to assess his readiness.

Calm. Controlled.

Kai would be proud.

Looked like he was getting an A-positive tonight. Oh well. Dahlia was a sweet girl.

He walked into the living area of the Tenders and was greeted with soft smiles, waves, and a smack upside his head from Mick. The males lounged on the couches with Tenders perched at their sides, never breaking conversation.

"Oh it was funny!" Dahlia laughed, claiming a spot beside him. "She ran her hand right through the dye and it went everywhere!"

"I could hear Dahl and Justine screaming from out here, and Gabby went running toward the shower," Amy chimed in with a giggle. "When Rhys said he wanted her back to rights, I don't think he expected to be replacing furniture."

He shifted in his seat, catching on to who the women were discussing.

"That chaise is definitely destroyed. The carpet, too," Dahlia whispered. "Good thing we got most of it off her skin. She was almost leopardized."

Justine, the perky blonde sitting on Jagg's lap, let out a loud laugh. "The first time was funny, but by the fourth, I swear I saw Rhys's neck vein twitching."

While Rhys's temper was epic, he had never lost control with a Tender. It appeared Molly was going to break that record. Soon.

He adjusted his position slightly, leaning forward and allowing his hair to fall into his eyes. He could easily picture uncertainty, anger, and defiance on Molly's face. The slight jutting of her jaw, the pursing of her lips. But fear…

Molly and fear didn't sit well in Dominic's gut.

"Although, it did turn out pretty fantastic," Dahlia smiled. "Justine can match roots better than anyone I've ever met!"

Justine blushed, causing Jagg's nostrils to flare slightly.

Amy grimaced. "Hope we won't have to go back in there tonight to finish clean-up. I don't want to be around Rhys when he's around her any more than absolutely necessary."

Mickey licked Amy's neck, slurping noisily. "I'll tell him you're busy. Far too busy. Work?"

A shy smile. A nod.

Dahlia refocused her attention on Dom, who had remained motionless throughout the conversation. "Will I be cleaning up tonight? Or…"

"Why didn't you finish cleaning up earlier?" he asked, curious only for discussion's sake.

"Rhys called Boy in."

****

Molly shifted her weight, her hands twisting around a blackened bathrobe as Rhys sat silently and stared at the black stains on the red satin chaise. Periodically, his gaze would flick down to the soiled oriental carpet.

The vampire Boy stood unseeing in the corner of the room, blending seamlessly into the shadows.

With labored movements, Rhys held a bag in her direction. "Put these on."

She gripped the bag and scurried into the bedroom, certain she was holding some latex contraption. Or lace lingerie. Maybe leather.

She opened the bag.

Low slung faded jeans and a black shirt with a glittering rainbow appliqué across the chest. Matching bra and panties.

She smiled.

Returning to her bedroom, she felt infinitely better. Less exposed. Standing before an irritated vampire in a stained bath robe was unsettling. Wearing something she would have picked for herself made her feel more in control, more capable of handling whatever was thrown at her. Whatever being the vampiric statue in the corner.

"Justine is highly skilled. Despite the reek of dye in here, you look much more appealing now."

She frowned. "Thanks?"

"Discussing this," Rhys gestured to the damaged furniture, "will have to wait. I have a more pressing issue we need addressed tonight."

Her eyes flickered to the statue in the corner.

"Yes. I think you would be easier to train and possibly happier having a little more freedom of movement within the compound. However, I believe you're also a flight risk. That's where Boy comes in."

Boy stepped out of the darkness. His long blond hair framed his face and his empty blue eyes. Tall, lean, and lithe, he moved with the presence of a stalking lion. Her flight response kicked in and she moved away from the male, putting Rhys's muscled form between them.

"I don't normally bring Boy in this early, but you're… special."

Her tongue had barely breached her lips when Rhys caught it in his fingers.

"Mute Tenders are a commodity among some of the more archaic in our society. Do not give me a reason to rip that tongue out of your head."

Tongue snapped back in her mouth, she nodded in acknowledgment. If she had to choose between hiding behind Rhys and his tongue removal threats or facing off against the silent vampire across from her, she'd take her chances with Rhys.

"If you want freedom, you need to be tracked. To be tracked, you need to be tied. Tonight, you'll be tied to Boy. Tomorrow, the training room will be unlocked and you will have limited free movement. The other Tenders will assist you in knowing where you may and may not go. Agreeable?"

She nodded reluctantly and held out her wrists, prepared to be shackled to the frightening blond vampire.

Rhys chuckled, his low throaty voice reverberating throughout the room. "No, dear one. Tied. Boy will bite you and drink while you bite Boy and drink."

"Fuck that!"

Boy stood unflinching. Rhys grasped her chin and turned her face to his. "Not. A. Choice."

She whimpered. "I can't bite him. It's… the sensation… I'll puke!"

With an audible sigh, Rhys removed a small knife from his boot. "Boy. Arm."

Boy raised an arm, eyes remaining fastened at a point past the walls. With a movement too fast for her to register, Rhys sliced Boy's wrist and brought it to her mouth. She pinched her lips together, fighting the liquid from entering her while Rhys's grip gently forced her jaw open and the blood dripped onto her tongue.

She gagged, pulling desperately, ineffectively, out of Rhys's hold as Boy leaned down and sank his fangs into her neck. Fear and revulsion eliminated any pain she should have felt as the sensation of her blood being pulled out of her body set in. As she kicked, hit, and writhed fruitlessly, she could hear Rhys's exasperated voice.

"This is why I wait. Getting kicked in the fucking balls so you can go hang with the girls? Fucking ridiculous. You aren't dying. Wait. Boy. That's enough."

Boy retreated instantly to the corner, her blood staining his fangs.

She continued clawing and kicking, frantic to escape Rhys's hold. He tightened his arms around her and lowered them to the ground. Her desperation to escape amplified as Rhys attempted to soothe her through his embrace.

The tighter he gripped, the more violent her struggle. As she whimpered incoherently, begging through unrecognizable sounds to be released, Rhys held tight until Dominic's voice broke the unintentional power struggle.

"Molly."

Through tears, she looked up into Dominic's blue eyes.

"Could I help you up?"

Hiccupping nods.

"Okay. Rhys, I'm going to take her arms. You can let go."

Rhys waited until Dom had a grip on her before he unwound his body from hers. "I'll wait in here. Get her settled."

Dominic grunted in acknowledgement and guided her to her bedroom. Keeping one hand firmly around her wrist, he pulled the bedding down before lifting her onto it.

****

Dominic had witnessed varying levels and intensity surrounding Rhys's training methods. Knowing the vampire was skilled beyond reproach had always left him somewhat awed at the transformation Rhys could bring about in the women they brought him.

He had seen former bloodslaves become gentle artists, painting and arranging flowers while discussing Rembrandt and stock prices. He had seen prostitutes perform graceful fan dances, then sit with their masters and examine budgets and meal plans for guests.

He'd witnessed the most foul-mouthed women recite poetry in sweet voices while knitting blankets before they headed into the kitchen to create delectable-smelling French cuisine.

He was no stranger to the blood tie Boy formed with every Tender. He'd even witnessed a few exchanges while conversing about sparring techniques with Nichol and Rhys. The tie served multiple purposes for Rhys and the Tenders. Boy monitored the women's whereabouts, their general emotions, and could identify shifts in their mental state.

Rhys adapted his training techniques to meld with the information the tie with Boy provided. The Tenders were granted more freedom, many leaving the haunt during the day to run errands or attend events. As the women were traded, many of their masters formed stronger ties and overrode the delicate one they had with Boy.

In rare instances, Rhys had intervened after a trade when Boy had noticed patterns of fear, pain, and helplessness.

The tie was necessary.

And as he watched Rhys physically subduing Molly to force the tie with Boy, he discovered he didn't give two shits about necessity. He entered the room, determined to maintain his control as Rhys lowered the frantic woman to the floor.

Rhys had made the call too soon.

Boy's blood tinged her chin pink. The scent of honeysuckle mixed with the permeating scent of terror and crept into his psyche despite his lack of breathing. He faintly registered Boy in the shadowed corner, his tongue slowly caressing the last of Molly's blood off his silvery fangs.

From what he had seen in the past, most Tender trainees welcomed their first blood exchange and completed it with eagerness.

Molly's reaction was uncommon.

Molly's everything had been uncommon so far.

His hands flexed and fisted as the image of Boy's blood on her lips looped in his mind. A low growl began to fill the training quarters, a subconscious territorial warning to the other males in the room. While he didn't recognize it for what it was, Boy and Rhys exchanged a quick, knowing look. He frowned and stared past her, determined to maintain his feigned indifference.

Something was wrong.

He needed out. Now.

Chapter Seven

Molly stayed tight to Dahlia, amazed at the stark contrast the intensely masculine bunker held against the gentle calming rooms of the resident Tenders. The dark charcoal paint and tiled stone floors balanced between enclosing and embracing, the wall sconces of artificial candlelight that lined the halls casting shadows and augmenting every movement.

She was enjoying her first foray into the extensive halls of the underground bunker, Dahlia's lighthearted chatter keeping her from dwelling on the events of the previous evening. Although she knew it was nothing more than an illusion, the freedom she was experiencing was more than she'd had in almost a month, and she was finding it more exhilarating than she cared to admit aloud.

Dahlia paused outside two large glass doors and peered in as she knocked. "Okay," she smiled cheerfully. "We can go in!"

Pushing the heavy door open, Dahl led her into the huge common room where Dominic and the blond vampire sat cross-legged on the floor, engrossed in a racing video game.

Dominic's shoulders tensed suddenly and he dropped his controller, cursing under his breath when the other guy began hollering in victory. "Shut it, Mick. Hey Dahlia."

The blond, Mick, turned toward them, his eyes

widening a fraction. "Oh hey." He rose off the floor and walked over to them, extending his hand to her. "Mikhail. Mickey or Mick if you prefer."

She shook his hand reluctantly, watching Dahlia's reaction to the huge vampire. "Molly."

As Dahlia started pointing out the various entertainment equipment set up in the room, Dominic stood and stalked closer to her, his turquoise eyes almost completely hidden by his hair. "I'm going to need to take some of your time in the next few nights to compile a report about Wyatt," he said quietly before calling out to Dahlia. "Don't touch that! Nichol will freak out."

Dahlia snatched her hand back from the stereo. "Ooooh, right. Molly, honey. Don't adjust any settings in here. Ever." She walked back to her and grabbed her hand. "Let's go check out the sleeping quarters. You guys want to come?"

Dominic took a step toward them before Mick held his hand out to stop him. "You ladies have fun. I'm going to kick this dickwad's ass a few more times."

With a shrug and a smile, Dahlia waved at the vampires and led her down another hall, its lighting dimmer than the rest of the bunker. "We try to keep it pretty quiet when we're in this wing," she said. "That's Mickey's room. Kaius's. Nic–"

A striking man with light brown hair, hazel eyes, and dark freckles across his nose and cheeks was exiting the room as they passed and he turned, his strange eyes meeting hers. Without looking away, he addressed Dahlia. "This is the difficult female?" he inquired, cold eyes never losing focus.

"Sure is!" Dahlia chirped, her perky demeanor a

stark contrast to her own skittishness.

"She smells strange."

"It's the dye. Take a whiff!" Dahlia reached over, pulling her hair tie out and letting the black waves tumble to her waist.

The hazel-eyed male leaned forward, scenting the air. "So it is. Rhys deserves a raise."

"Who do you think you are?" Molly blurted, insulted when he wrinkled his nose.

Her mind took a moment to register her new place against the wall. Feet dangling helplessly, she gripped the vampire's hands around her throat in a feeble attempt to free herself.

"I am not Dominic. I am not Rhys. I have no patience for obstinate little bitches and even less for ones that smell as offensive as you. Next time you enter this hall, do so with a silent tongue and appeasing odor."

And he was gone.

Dahlia flitted over, wrists wringing and worry marring her dainty features. "Oh honey! That's Nichol. He doesn't like anyone. Don't take it personal."

She coughed, pulling oxygen into her burning lungs as quickly as possible while Dahlia helped her up and led her back down the hall. "We should probably get b–"

Two massive bodies launched into the hall and fell to the floor, fists flying and fangs bared. She flattened herself against the wall as Dahlia shrieked and cowered, covering her head with her arms.

Dominic and Mick.

They rolled around on the ground for a few minutes, the snarled cursing coming to an end when

Mickey gained the upper hand and locked Dominic underneath him. He shook his blond hair out of his eyes and looked over at her. "Maybe you should get back the training rooms. Rhys will be by shortly."

Dahlia nodded, grabbing her arm and dragging her away from the scene. "Maybe…let's not mention this to Rhys."

Too stunned to speak, Molly merely nodded and followed Dahl back to the relative safety of the pastel rooms.

****

"He went too fucking far," Dominic growled, snapping at Mick's arm until his brother released him. "Nic's a goddamn asshole."

Mickey stayed seated on his chest. "Yeah, well, that asshole could end you with one finger if he wanted to. You're fucking lucky I took you down. What the hell's up with you?"

What the hell was up with him? Something was fucking wrong, and that something was just triggered by Nichol's threats to the new arrival.

Forcing his muscles to relax, he waited until Mick rose off him and offered him a hand. "Nothing's up."

"Obviously."

With his brother's eyes on him, he skulked to his bunk and flung the door open. "I need a minute."

He could hear Mick slide down the wall to wait for him as he locked himself in his room to decompress.

Mickey had just saved him from a beating he probably wouldn't have survived. Nichol was old, permanently angry, and had more strength in one hand that he and Mick combined. Even Rhys deferred to Nic, and Rhys didn't do that easily.

Whatever weirdness was going on with his core, he needed to gain a grip on it.

Needed to figure out what the hell it wanted.

Because he was damn certain it wasn't Molly.

There was nothing about her that separated her from the other women that had come and gone through the haunt over the three decades he'd been there. She wasn't exceptionally beautiful. Wasn't alluringly well-spoken. And he didn't know enough about her to form any kind of attachment or real desire for her.

"Mick?" he called out, listening as his brother stood. "Can I ask you something?"

"Nine and a half inches."

He rolled his eyes and slammed his fist against the door. "Fuck off and get in here."

Mickey poked his head in and grinned. "Jealous?"

"Help me up," he grumbled, chickening out. "I need an hour or five in the sparring room."

****

Dominic checked himself over in the mirror for the third time, running his hands through his hair to push it out of his eyes. He grabbed his laptop off the table and gave Boy a quick wave. "Rhys will be down in the training room with me," he called out, banging on Mickey's door as he passed. "You've got the night off."

He met up with Rhys at the entrance to the Tender quarters and followed him past the kitchen and into the open living room. "This'll probably take a few hours," he said, opening his computer and starting a new document. "Nic's on my ass to get the report compiled so Hanson can submit proof of punishment."

Rhys unlocked the training room door and called for Molly, rolling his eyes when she replied with a flippant "all right already." "I'm going to remove that tongue one of these nights. Remove it and smack that insolent look off her face."

His irises narrowed with the empty threat toward Molly and he ducked his head to avoid saying or doing anything that would give away his reaction.

It didn't matter that he'd never known Rhys to raise a hand to a Tender. He was pissed.

Molly ran over to the door, skidding to a stop when she saw him. "What's going on?"

He didn't miss the flash of fear in her eyes.

Hunching forward to make himself look as non-threatening as possible, he gave her a tight smile. "Remember that report I need to put together? Procrastination time's up and I need to submit by dawn."

Rhys looked between them for a moment. "I'll be holed up with Nic in the com room for the night. We good?"

He nodded, the realization he was about to be alone with her slowly settling into his head.

Molly flopped down on the other sofa and waved Rhys off. "Yeah, yeah, Warden," she called out. "See you later."

Waiting until Rhys's footsteps disappeared into the main haunt, he angled his computer at Molly and sat back. "It's usually best if you type it out yourself and then I'll go over it and fill in the missing information. Does that work for you?"

She pulled the computer onto her lap and began immediately, a myriad of expressions crossing her face as she worked. After a few minutes, he tugged his cell from his pocket and opened the music app, selecting playlist he'd put together a few weeks back.

Four songs in, Molly looked up from the screen. "One-hit-wonder compilation?"

He slid his phone across the coffee table. "Good call. Almost done?"

"Almost."

He didn't want her to be done. He wanted to stay there as long as he could, watching her type to the beat of the music, her lips moving to the lyrics as the genres flipped between rock, country, hip-hop, and industrial. He was inordinately fascinated with the speed in which she typed with four fingers, with the frequency she shifted in place.

When she finished, she passed the laptop over to him and sat back. "I can't spell."

Scanning it over, he latched on to the most glaring omissions.

"The description of the initial feeding is good, but we need to make note of how many other times there were, how long they lasted, and the length of time between them."

"That was it," she said, drawing her legs up to her chest. "I was exhausted for probably a week after, so maybe he felt bad or something."

Starring the single feed and entering a quick note, he moved on to the other missing piece. "You didn't mention any of the… um… physical interactions."

She frowned and crossed the room to sit beside him. "There. And there. And there."

He reread the hastily typed record and shook his head. "The zip-tie thing is good to include. Shows he had some sense of what he was doing, since most vampires don't run around with a pocket full of them unless they intend to use them. I'm talking about anything… physical."

Molly's proximity was strangely soothing, and he was struggling to stay focused on the task at hand.

She crossed her legs, her knee bumping against him. "I didn't really see him much," she said, looking down at her hands. "After he fed off me on that first night, he kind of avoided coming into the basement unless he had to." Her eyes widened and she looked up at him. "He's not going to get away with it, is he? I mean, kidnapping and starving me has to come with some jail time, right?"

Setting the laptop down, he rested his elbows on his knees and ran his hand through his hair. "Vampire punishments are a little more barbaric than jail time," he opened, speaking slowly as he riffled through the information he could safely provide. "Wyatt's primary charge is trespassing, which actually carries more weight than any of the other charges. Confinement, assault…all those are essentially misdemeanors we'll use to prop up the trespassing claim and provide a time frame for the offense."

"That's bullshit!" Molly exclaimed, grabbing the computer and pointing to the screen. "He tied me to that room for weeks!"

Risking a glance at her, he shrugged apologetically. "It's the way things are here. But the trespassing charge alone warrants the steepest penalties we can request, so Wyatt's going to have a really bad time of it once he gets back to the Hanson haunt."

Molly's lips pursed and she glared angrily at the coffee table for a few minutes, her knee bouncing beside him. "Promise?"

"Guaranteed," he assured her. "Once we receive proof of Wyatt's punishment, I'll show you."

Seemingly appeased, Molly closed the screen of the laptop. "I don't want to think about this anymore," she said, leaning away from him. "Why was he so freaked out by you? You don't seem that scary." She paused, her hand touching her throat. "To other vampires," she amended.

Angling his head away to keep his fangs hidden, he smiled. "I'm backed by the Kaius name. I'm probably less than a decade older than Wyatt, but our haunt is stronger and better connected than the Hanson haunt, despite their greater numbers."

She sat forward. "So where does 'Kaius' come from?"

"The old bastard that created us," he replied. "I'm the youngest. Then Mickey. Jagger. Rhys. Nichol's the oldest."

"Boy?"

He grimaced. "Boy's been around for centuries. No clue who his creator is. Probably some rogue. I think Kai took him in at some point and the bastard never left." His mind flashed to the mute male and his empty eyes. "Stay away from him. Nichol, too. As you saw, he can be kind of a dick."

****

Molly took another bite of her apple and pointed at Dominic with it. "Seriously. Don't look it up. It's just… wrong."

Rhys had come and gone twice in the past few hours, both times to remove the bag of chips she'd grabbed from the kitchen and passing her the bowl of fruit as she and Dominic talked. Once she'd typed out her recollections of Wyatt and the basement, the topics of conversation had flown around from concerts to vampire myths to the memes she'd missed during her confinement.

Dominic passed his phone back to her. "I think the others have seen the Deepfryer videos, but I didn't realize they were online, too."

"Everything's online," she replied, shivering as she recalled the night she witnessed her first and only Deepfryer execution on an ex-boyfriend's big screen TV. It was a video out of Turkey, the most recent country to invest in the shower-like glass enclosure that emitted a solid stream of ultraviolet rays that would ignite a vampire quickly while slowly baking a human. It was gruesome, horrifying, and extremely effective as both a punishment and a deterrent. The glass walls allowed observers an unobstructed view of the appalling experience.

The memory of it was burned into her brain.

The United States was marching toward Deepfryers ardently. Europe was already following in the Middle East's footsteps, turning toward public execution as a punishment. Hell, most of society had witnessed one, thanks to the internet. It was definitely nothing she needed to see again.

Some schools had even discussed showing live video of such events to students, but a handful of level-headed government officials had determined the trauma of witnessing such a violent death would outweigh any incentives to avoid associating with vampires. Unfortunately, between parents and the internet, most school-aged children were well-versed in the consequences of cavorting with the undead.

Abominations.

Atrocities.

Soul-stealing sycophants.

But what had stuck with her long after she'd seen the video wasn't the chanting crowds or the small group of protestors on the fringe. It wasn't the flames or the screams. It was the way the strong, lithe body of the ignited vampire curled around his human companion, shielding the sobbing woman from the punishing rays.

He had twisted around her form, spreading himself open to the light as it torched his sinewy body and marred his handsome face. Most deemed that act, witnessed in Deepfryers across the globe, as the vampire's way of ensuring the human burned as quickly as he did, engulfing the human in flames and selfishly securing the imminent death of their co-accused.

In many countries, those who publicly proclaimed the act as protective were silenced, sentenced to the Deepfryer as sympathizers.

That shut the rest of the sympathizers up. The Deepfryer was indeed an effective deterrent.

Shaking off the morbid thoughts, she selected a B-side song from Dominic's incredible collection of music, smirking when he narrowed his eyes. "Come on," she cooed. "It's on your damn phone. Name it."

"Playtime's over," Rhys yelled into the room as he approached.

Dominic jumped to his feet and grinned down at her. "Looks like we're still tied." He hooked his laptop under his arm and offered his hand to help her up. "If Rhys is cool with it, I'll load up an old MP3 player with everything I have and bring it by tomorrow night."

He elbowed Rhys on his way out of the room.

"Bedtime, angel," Rhys said, gesturing toward the training rooms and following her in. "Tomorrow's going to be a long night."

"Yes, sir," she said, saluting the vampire she was quickly discovering had a loud bark and little bite. She closed her bedroom door, the sounds of Rhys moving around in the training room almost comforting in their normalcy.

She didn't want to be here.

But so far, it wasn't terrible.

****

Dominic rose before dusk and tapped his laptop to life, pleased to see the sizable file transfer had finished. Unplugging the MP3 player, he tossed it onto his bedside table and scrambled to get ready for the night.

He was hungry.

And experience had taught him that hungry and Molly weren't a good combo for him.

He fired off a text to Rhys, requesting that Gabby swing by for a quick bite.

On it.

Within minutes, her soft voice was in the hall and there was a knock on the door. He opened it, stepping aside as she came in with a smile and lifted her hair. "Rhys said you need a quick bite?"

"Yeah," he muttered, a strange tightness building in his throat. "Thanks."

He licked his lips and ducked down to her neck, recoiling as his fangs touched her skin.

What. The hell.

He pushed past the unpleasant sensation as it spread through his limbs, forcing his teeth into Gabby's vein and drawing deep. The blood was sour on his tongue, the few mouthfuls he managed to swallow sitting like stone in his gut. He unhooked his fangs, using his sleeve to wipe the last remnants from her skin. “All good,” he choked out, opening his door and urging her out of the room before he gagged.

Mickey was at his side in a flash, his blue eyes scanning him over. “You okay?”

He sat down on the edge of his bed as the feeling began to wane. “Fine. I don’t know what she’s eating, but it’s fucking foul.” He shook the last of the sensation off and rose to his feet, slipping the MP3 player into his back pocket.

Chapter Eight

Molly pushed her headphones down around her neck and gave Dominic a smile, waving her newly acquired MP3 player his way.

He set the pile of packages and letters on the coffee table and looked over her shoulder at her chosen playlist for the evening. “Seriously? Hair metal?”

She shoved the player into her pocket and tapped at the spreadsheet she was attempting to complete. “I’m trying to amp myself up to get through this,” she grumbled, glancing over at Rhys. “Math really isn’t my thing.”

Her trainer looked up from his phone. “Nothing about you needs amping. Except maybe your focus. Dominic, get the hell outta here.”

“Yeah, yeah,” Dominic muttered, rearranging the stack of mail and lifting one corner to show her the contraband he’d snuck into the training rooms. “Are we still good for me to walk Moll through basic haunt practices tomorrow while you take a sparring session with Nic?”

Rhys’s dark eyes zeroed in on Dominic for a moment. “Helpful little vamp lately, aren’t you? Be here for eleven and stick to the talking points I emailed you last night.”

He turned back to her and pointed at her paperwork. “That would be a lot easier if you opened the textbook."

Using the text as a shield, she inched the smuggled chocolate bars out from under the envelopes and tucked them into the pages of the book. "See you tomorrow, Dom."

The past week had been a strange combination of emotions and events for her. Frustration and anger at being contained against her will was battling with the growing sense of security she was experiencing from having a guaranteed roof over her head and a full fridge she could access whenever she wanted.

Or, at least, whenever Rhys wasn't doing a 'full assessment of strengths and weaknesses'. Accounting was, decidedly, a weakness.

As was dancing, elocution, and budgeting.

She'd excelled in table setting and floral arrangements, though, so the week hadn't been a total bust.

Since her experience with Nichol in the main haunt, she'd remained close to the Tender quarters, venturing out only when accompanied by Rhys or Dominic.

And she infinitely preferred Dominic's company to that of Rhys. Her trainer commented on her every breath, every movement, every word, and every twitch. She spoke too quickly, breathed too shallow, walked too heavy, moved too much. Her hands were never where he wanted them, her posture was never proper, and her language was, in his words, more trucker than Tender.

By contrast, Dominic was a quickly becoming a welcomed diversion from Rhys's incessant corrections and criticisms. Every evening since she'd given him her report on Wyatt Hanson, he'd swung by the training rooms for a few minutes, sometimes longer if Rhys was busy elsewhere.

They'd talked music and movies. He'd listened intently as she described the last festivals she'd attended, and she sat in awe at the bands he'd seen live during his human years.

He'd brought her the MP3 player she was currently attached to, swinging by the next night with a charging cord and headphones. When she'd mentioned how much she missed flipping through music magazines at the gas station, he'd slipped two under the locked training room door while she was being schooled in the correct way to sit.

Last night, he'd walked in on her and Rhys in the midst of a heated argument about her aversion of vegetables. Rhys had stormed through the Tender kitchen, emptying the cupboards of all foods he considered 'junk'.

And nestled in her accounting textbook sat two chocolate bars.

A small voice in the back of her head continued to remind her Dominic wasn't an ally.

He was one of them.

But he was also a distraction from the barrage of fears, anger, and frustrations she was feeling, moving from one prison to another.

And in a strange way, she was looking forward to tomorrow.

****

Dominic crossed his arms and continued his stare-off with Mickey, unwilling to give on his simple request.

"Sorry, man," Mick stated, straightening up to his full height. "Kaius's orders. Where you go, I go. He and I are both getting some heavy vibes off you, and until we know you can deal with them, the best I'll offer for tomorrow is hanging back and shutting up. And no closed doors. I want full visual at all times."

Lolling his head back in annoyance, he grunted his agreement. "I don't even get why you're still anchored to me," he huffed, loading a boxing game into the console. "I'm totally chill. Totally on track."

Mickey snatched up the blue controller and sat on the floor. "Chill? The only time you aren't wound is when you're in the training room with her. Your control is precariously balanced right now. If Kai can feel it from wherever the hell he is, it's a lot more serious than you think. And we've done six runs into town this week. That's five more than I like to do in a month. What the hell are you doing?"

"Kicking your ass is what I'm about to do," he retorted, changing the subject and loading the first match.

Mick's question was legit. He had no idea what was compelling him to clip his fangs every night and drive to the gas station on the outskirts of Denver, spending upwards of an hour selecting magazines and chocolate bars and bottles of orange soda. His bedside table was stuffed with items he'd grabbed on a whim in case Molly mentioned them. Beef jerky. Gum. Crossword books. Anything he saw other people place on the counter to purchase, he added to his own collection.

He knew it was weird. And knowing Mick was witnessing it didn't help his growing concern over the compulsions that were taking root.

He'd experienced crushes in his human years. And this was definitely not a crush.

He rose every evening with an urgency to see her and lay awake long into the early afternoons planning his excuse to do so. He hung around in the Tender quarters after Rhys sent him away from the training rooms, making polite small talk with Dahlia or Gabby while he glanced casually toward the small door window to check on Molly.

Supplying her with those few pitiful tokens from her former life was fast becoming his favorite activity. Every pathetic offering was met with excitement, her delighted acceptance of them temporarily quelling the strange unease building in his core.

Mickey tossed his controller in the air, catching it right before it hit the floor. "And that, Mini, is how you kick ass. Take notes, brother. Take notes and bow to the king."

****

Molly craned her neck to watch Mickey standing outside the common room, his long blond hair falling into his eyes as he hunched over his phone. "Now?"

Dominic glanced behind him and nodded, arching back slightly and lifting his shirt to tug the package of beef jerky he had hidden. He lifted the plastic to his mouth and averted his eyes from her, as though ashamed of the fangs he was using to slice the package open.

"It's not Mickey I'm worried about," he whispered. "He's heard everything and is pretending not to for your sake. But Rhys could probably hear a dime drop on the highway two miles away. If he's in this wing, we're screwed."

She slid the salted meat out eagerly and gnawed a piece off, chewing and chewing until she could finally swallow. "Fangs would probably be good for this kind of thing," she mused. "They seem super useful."

Dominic wrinkled his nose. "I guess. They come with a lot of drawbacks though."

Tucking one leg under her, she leaned closer to Dominic. "Could I see?"

He hesitated before he opened his mouth and drew his lips back enough for her to inspect the glossy whiteness tinged with a hint of silver. His stillness encouraged her exploration as she reached up to touch the razor-sharp peaks. "They're so pretty," she whispered, forgetting momentarily that the fangs belonged to a male, not a caged zoo animal.

Dominic leaned away from her and pushed his hair out of his eyes. "I won't be adding that description to my memoirs."

"Smartass," she grinned. "Okay. I've met Nichol and Boy. You, and Rhys. Who else?" Mickey cleared his throat loudly in the hallway and she waved in his direction. "And Mick, of course."

Dominic flipped Mickey off and stretched his arms across the back of the sofa. "Kaius and Jagger."

Scanning her memory, she nodded slowly. "Kaius is the haunt leader, right?"

"Yup."

"Why?"

He looked back at Mick and received a thumbs-up. "When a vampire moves out and starts creating his own line, he's considered the leader, and all his turnings take his name. So you get Dominic Kaius, Rhys Kaius,

Mikhail Kaius, et cetera."

"So if you leave home, you'll be the head of the Dominic haunt?"

There was an audible snort in the hall and Dom grimaced. "Pretty much."

She bit her lip and pulled another piece of jerky from the bag. "Not nearly as badass sounding as the Kaius haunt."

Mickey chuckled and Dominic rolled his eyes. "And that's why I'm never moving out."

"And who's Jagger?" she asked, getting more comfortable and taking another bite of the heavily spiced meat.

He and Mick exchanged a look and Mickey shook his head. "Jagg's around, but he keeps to himself a lot. You'll meet him eventually, but he doesn't spend much time around the Tender quarters. I'll introduce you one of these nights, okay?"

Satisfied, she set the half-eaten package of jerky down. "Is the lesson over? Because I'm dying to watch TV."

****

Dominic sauntered down the hall, slipping a bag of gummy bears into the band of his cargos and fluffing his shirt out over it. Mickey followed at a distance, his attention on his phone as he muttered under his breath about the recent Supreme Court rulings about vampire-human interactions.

"Rhys okayed an hour in the common room," he called over his shoulder, pushing the door open to the Tender quarters. "We can meet you there if you want."

Mick shook his head and leaned against the wall, his hair falling forward while his thumb flew across the screen. “Didn’t work last night. Or the night before. Or the night before. Kudos for your persistence though, Mini.”

TV time had become a nightly event for him and Molly over the past two weeks.

Provided she finished the tasks Rhys gave her for the evening, she was allowed an hour or two in the common room to watch whatever caught her attention. Sometimes it was a talk show or a comedy special, other nights she kicked back to infomercials. Never the news, and never a movie.

He craved every minute of it.

They would talk on their way to and from the common room then sit quietly on the sofa together, him on one side and her on the other. He would pass her whatever candy he’d smuggled past Rhys, and her eyes would light up as he tore the bag open.

For at least one hour a night, he was calm, relaxed, and content.

The other twenty-three hours were an entirely different story.

“Hey,” Mick muttered. “You eat recently?”

“Unfortunately,” he grunted, the memory of last night’s feeding still haunting him. “Something’s messed up with my taste buds.”

His brother lifted a brow and looked back at his phone.

He scanned the large training room for Molly before sitting on the newly replaced sofa to wait. The scent of honeysuckle was strong, powerful enough that it would linger on his clothes long after he returned to his bunker alone.

Her bedroom door opened and Rhys walked out,

his hands running through his hair in aggravation. "This is fucking impossible," he snarled, yanking the door shut and pacing the room. "Wyatt Hanson picked the most stubborn, air-headed woman in Denver. You submit the damage report yet? Because we're adding this in."

Molly slipped from her room, smirking sheepishly as she walked over to the sofa, giving Rhys wide berth.

"Tell him what you did," Rhys ordered.

She pushed her tongue against the inside of her cheek. "I started a bath and forgot about it."

Rhys crossed his arms. "And?"

"And I used all the clothes in the closet to mop up the mess." She dropped her gaze from the trainer's piercing glare. "And I didn't tell you until you stepped in it."

His eyes dropped to Rhys's bare feet, noticing the wet hem of his cargos slopping against his ankles. "So is TV time off?"

Rhys looked between them, navy irises ovaled in anger. "Go. Molly, wait with Mick in the hall. Dominic, I need a minute."

Scampering across the floor before Rhys changed his mind, Molly was out of the room with impressive speed. He waited until she was out of ear shot and stood. "What's up?"

"Writing's on the wall, Mini," Rhys said, walking over to a large cabinet and removing a stack of plush towels. "I'm doubling down on her training starting tomorrow night. That means no more visits, no more hangouts, no more wasted hours."

His muscles tensed as he listened silently.

Rhys tossed the towels toward Molly's room and

scratched at his tattoos. “Whatever you think this is with you two? It isn’t. Her time here ends with one of two roads: the bloodslave quarters or trade. I get that you might feel bad for her, given the circumstances that brought her here, but she’s not your problem. She’s a few months away from being someone else’s problem permanently.”

****

Molly drew her knees up on the huge sofa and watched as Dominic stared blankly at the infomercial, turning the TV remote over and over in his hand. “You okay?”

He blinked, something she’d noticed neither Rhys nor Mickey did. And it was strangely comforting for her. “Yeah. Sorry.” He gave her a smile that hid his fangs. As he always did. “Want me to change the channel?”

She shook her head and leaned forward to set her empty bag of gummy bears onto the coffee table. “We can head back if you’re not into this tonight,” she suggested, not wanting the evening to end but becoming increasingly aware that Dominic was far more sullen than usual.

“Where would you be tonight if you weren’t here?” he asked, ignoring her offer. “I mean, if there had never been any Wyatt. What would you be doing on a Friday night?”

She pursed her lips and thought hard about it. “Maybe working. Though I was one more screw up away from getting fired when… I don’t know. Out at the bar? Dancing? Maybe on some lame-ass date. Why?”

“No reason,” he muttered, turning the volume up.

They sat in silence for another few minutes before Dominic continued. "Does the vamp thing freak you out? I mean, obviously now since you're caught up in the whole bloodslave/trade shit. But back a few months ago… were you more Species Purifier or…" He trailed off and locked his eyes on the television.

"The Species Purifiers are wingnuts," she replied, scooting a little closer. "I was pretty young when that feeding footage from the state fair hit the news, so I was certain vampires were going to bite me every time I stepped foot outside after dark. Drove my mom crazy." She watched Dom run his tongue over his fang absently. "But by the time I was in my early twenties, I just kind of forgot to be afraid."

He scoffed and side-eyed her. "That worked out well for you."

"You know, there's so much focus on the biting thing on TV. A bit on the bloodslave thing. But this trading thing? I'd never heard of it until, well, you told me." She settled into the sofa. "This is a lot scarier than a bite."

Dominic nodded slowly, his hair dropping into his eyes. "We don't like to advertise it, obviously. A lot of haunts are still old-school in the way they do things. We're trying to get in with the times, but we're caught between modern human society and thousands of years of vampire society." He looked over at her. "I'm sorry you're trapped in it."

She dropped her head onto his shoulder and turned her attention back to the over-excited woman on the screen peddling another magic kitchen gadget.

****

Dominic reached for the remote as smoothly as he

could, desperate to avoid jostling Molly as he reluctantly powered off the satellite box. “Time’s up,” he stated, tentatively resting his cheek on her head and relishing in the warmth that seeped into his body.

“Nah,” Molly replied. “Time’s only up when Rhys comes in here yelling.”

He closed his eyes for a moment.

She’s not your problem.

His eyes snapped open and he arched his neck back to see Mickey’s long legs stretched across the hallway.

Running wasn’t an option. Kaius could track him easily and even if he managed to get Molly out, she’d be hunted, caught, and killed swiftly if she was lucky. Boy’s blood in her system was a homing beacon, and an effective one at that.

“Okay, okay,” she sighed, lifting her head. “I suppose we should go. Thanks for being my chill-out buddy.”

She leaned over, kissed his cheek, and paused.

If he had a beating heart, it would be pounding out of his chest as she brushed her lips against his gently. He remained completely still, the triumphant howling of his core muted by his confusion and uncertainty.

“They’re barely noticeable,” she said softly, pushing herself to her feet, wrapping her hands around his arm, and tugging.

Dominic stood up, almost flush against her. “What?”

“Your fangs. You always hide them, which actually makes them more of a thing than they are. But when you aren’t hiding them, they’re barely noticeable.” Molly rose up on her toes and grazed her lips against his again. “See?”

When she didn't step away, he ran his hand through her hair and kissed her hard enough for her to feel his fangs. "How about now?"

She responded by kissing him deeper, her fingers trailing up his arms and up the back of his neck. He followed her lead, his brain nearly short-circuiting when her tongue danced across his lower lip.

"Whoa!" Mickey's voice cut through the room, his heavy footsteps closing in fast on them. "Oh, no. No way. Come on, Miss Molly. Back to the quarters you go."

She released her hold on him and grinned sheepishly. "I'm going."

He stayed rooted on the spot for a few seconds before following, passing Mick on his way. "You're an asshole," he muttered, too quiet for Molly to hear but more than loud enough for Mickey.

"An asshole that's saving your own right now," Mick hissed, picking up his pace as he escorted Molly back through the halls. "You're lucky I'm not going to report this to Rhys."

Rhys stood at the entrance to the Tender quarters, arms crossed while he scanned the trio over. "In you go," he barked, adding an extra snarl when Molly paused to give Dominic a quick wave and a smile. He waited until she disappeared into the training area. "Does she know?"

He shook his head, not trusting himself to respond.

"Fan-fucking-tastic," Rhys grumbled, turning down the hall. "Now I'll have to do it."

Mickey shoved his hands in his pockets and stared at him. "That was really fucking intense, Mini. Nearly knocked me face-down." He shook his head. "Fuck,

Mini. This is bad."

Rolling out the tension in his shoulders, he stormed toward his bunk. "It's fine."

****

"Go fuck yourself!"

It had become Molly's mantra over the past week. Nonplussed, Rhys handed her another plate and reclined in the luxurious black velvet sofa that had replaced the casualty of her hair color restoration.

"Heel. Toe. Smaller steps. And stop looking down, for fuck's sake." Rhys's judgmental eyes appraised her hunched form as she struggled to walk the length of the training room in four-inch stilettos.

"I walk just fine in wedg–"

"Wedges are nothing more than glorified Frankenstein boots. Straight back, eyes forward."

"I did this well enough yesterday. Can't we just move on?" she whined, her toes aching from the pointed shoes.

"Until you can switch heel heights with ease while carrying a dish on a flat palm… stop wrapping your damn thumb around the edge…we'll practice every night. You lack grace. I can hear you clomping through the halls all day like a rabid elephant on speed."

"Maybe you should be spending more time sleeping during the day and less time being an ass about how I walk. You'd probably be a hell of a lot more pleasant."

Rhys smiled, fangs elongating and shimmering in the light. "There. Pleasant. Now fucking walk."

She rolled her eyes and resumed teetering across the floor, inching her thumb over the plate's rim as stealthily as possible. Two days into the practice, Rhys had given in and brought a shovel into the training room to remove the larger shards of broken glass.

The plate quality had also taken a drop, with the intricately embossed dishes from the beginning replaced with heavy, cumbersome bulk plates from a box store. When Rhys had walked in on the third day to find all the heels carefully smashed off the red soles, he had disappeared until the following evening, returning with cheap brands that blistered her feet and were half a size too small.

Rhys, she determined, was a vindictive prick.

Focused on Rhys's assholeness, she lost the heel-toe rhythm and stumbled. Though his natural speed could easily save the plate from its inevitable demise, Rhys had watched every single one fall to the floor and shatter. By day four, he appeared to become more resolved with every twinkling shard of glass. His jaw would twitch slightly, hardening for a moment before he would stand, replace the dish, and resume observing her attempts at elegance.

Not every moment of the training had involved walking. Though he insisted the heels of varying heights remain on her feet, she was being schooled in accounting, basic cooking skills, and delicate hand gestures.

History had been abandoned by day five when "Just like that movie!" had been interjected one too many times for Rhys's liking.

"How someone has scatterbrained as you managed to sit through any movie is a mystery," he'd commented that night, almost baffled by her ability to not only sit through a film, but to remember enough to match it to a history lesson.

She didn't have the heart to tell him she never lasted more than half an hour before reading the full synopsis online.

Tonight's training was going no differently than the previous ones had. Rhys pushed. She pulled. Rhys demanded. She refused. Even when she acquiesced, Rhys's eyes remained guarded, prepared for a verbal or physical onslaught. All lightweight items of value had been removed to preserve them from her frustrated aggression.

"Go soak your feet."

Rhys brought out his phone and sent off a text. As she limped to the bathroom, she heard Boy entering the training room to sweep up the remnants of the evening's failures. Boy had continued to remain as quiet as he had the night of the blood exchange. He entered rooms in a ghost-like silence and disappeared from them the same way.

It was easy to forget his presence as he blended mutely into the corners of rooms. Though she had been tense the first two nights he had joined her and Rhys, she quickly became accustomed to his fleeting, unseeing presence in her tiny world.

The one saving grace she had was music. While she couldn't play a single instrument, Rhys had been mildly impressed with the rampant knowledge she displayed about every song that would filter through the Tender training room from the radio in the kitchen. Concentration had been frequently interrupted by her turning to her trainer and mentioning some random fact about a bassist or a piece of history regarding a lyric.

The night before, Rhys had walked into her room holding a small stereo and plugged it in. Flipping from station to station, he had allowed a few bars of music to play before turning to her and demanding she name the song and the artist.

Two hours later, Rhys's music test had become a game she refused to lose.

"I should just send Dominic in here," he had muttered when he finally gave up and stormed from the training rooms. "He wastes his life on this crap, too. He could put you in your place."

As she sank into the tub, she wondered briefly where Dominic was. Ignoring the stinging of her blistered feet when the water hit them, she allowed herself a moment to be disappointed that he hadn't shown up again that evening, that he was still MIA from the training quarters.

She'd asked about him the first few nights, but Rhys's noncommittal replies every time finally sank in.

Her situation had changed. Again.

Her only companionship outside of Rhys came from the Tenders on the sporadic occasions she saw them. They were always polite, quick with smiles and offers of assistance, but they were busy, flitting in and out of the quarters under Rhys's detailed instructions.

For the first time since her arrival, loneliness was sinking in.

****

Dominic had had an extremely successful and productive week. He had run more, sparred more, and fed more in the past seven days than he had for the past six months combined.

"I'm far too pretty to work this hard," Mickey complained as the males meticulously scrubbed the rims of Dom's car. Again. "Too much fucking dirt under my nails."

He grinned. "Suck it up, princess. It's this or another run in the woods."

Mick tossed his sponge into the bucket. "Screw this. Let's check what came in on the post office run."

They descended the stairs leading into the bunker and rounded the corner in time to see Nichol storm into the office. His rhythmic footsteps faltered briefly as the lingering scent of honeysuckle caught him off guard.

He had avoided all interaction with the new trainee for a week now. At least, all physical interaction. Reality aside, he'd been less successful ridding the jittery woman from his daydreams. A short buzz in his head from Kaius refocused his attention on Mickey's ramblings about proper air guitar technique.

"... and if you keep making up finger placement, you're gonna screw yourself over when you actually get the guitar in hand. Because you're, I don't know, practicing it wrong."

They reached the bunker's common room and attacked the stack of letters and packages.

With vampire prejudice rising across North America, prepaid post office boxes were the securest way to ensure mail arrived unopened, if at all. The haunt maintained three, each in a different county, each paid for annually with cash and registered under its own alias to identify what type of delivery each box was used for. Tenders emptied the boxes once a week, leaving the collection of packages for the hauntmates to distribute as needed.

"I don't see anything from the Cam Pewter box," he frowned. "Nic will be pissed the GPS parts aren't here yet."

"Thcrew him," Mick grinned, slicing open a large box with his fang. "We'll just… fucking tape glue thtuck on my tooth… give him a pair of these to cheer him up."

Mick pulled a pair of red panties out of the box and slingshot them at his face.

"The hell!" he laughed. "Whose package is that?"

Mick dropped the bra he was sizing on himself and checked the label. "Mr. L. Othario. Probably an order for Miss Mol…"

Mick froze, mid-word.

Silence.

He grabbed the bra from Mick's hand and tossed the lingerie back into the box. "We should drop all these off before the meeting."

Mick rose from the floor slowly, cautiously. "You know, I can bring these down to the training center while you let Nichol know his new toys didn't come in."

With a huff, he stacked the mail under his arm. "It's fine. I need to update Rhys on the Hanson punishment before our meet-up later. Two birds, one stone and all that."

Mickey followed him warily. He knew the past week had been intense for Mick as he shadowed his volatile little brother around, and he was grateful Mick's mood was in a high zone. Despite his feeble attempts to dampen his emotions, he knew echoes of his intense reactions continued to ricochet through Mickey's mind, the hunger, desire, and rage providing a constant pulsing base.

Pushing his physical limitations had done little to curb his growing craving for the new Tender trainee, and he had overheard Mickey mention to Nichol that he was having difficulty distinguishing his own emotions from Dominic's. The hauntmates, under Kaius's direct instruction, had done what they could to keep him occupied and sated, but Mickey was uniquely privy to how frequently his mind conjured thoughts of the stunning woman.

Stunning and irritating.

Rhys, ever meticulous and diligent in his training of the women, had hardly been seen since he'd refocused his training efforts with Molly. The resident Tenders had run errands in town, bringing back boxes of plates and bags of shoes under Rhys's clipped demands on his walk from the communication room to the training room.

Snarled mutterings of "hot mess," "rabid elephant on speed," and "tonight she dies" were repeated like a twisted mantra, as though solidifying Rhys's resolve to turn Molly into a quality Tender before he killed her in exasperation.

Gossip amongst the bunker's women revolved around Molly's sparking temper, her blurted commentaries, and her bullheaded refusal to view Rhys as anything more than a verbal sparring partner.

While watching Rhys's control tested to the brink was humorous for him and the rest of the males, Molly's presence was becoming dangerous for his own control. No amount of blood had fully reigned in his primal beast, and every attempt he'd made had resulted in a wave of nausea he'd not felt since he was human and hung over.

Although volatile since he was turned, he knew Mick could feel the renewed inner battle for control he was experiencing every waking minute. He'd been an unwilling turning to begin with, at the twilight between life and death when Kaius arrived on the scene of the car accident and yanked him into his new reality.

His date for the evening hadn't survived long enough to be brought over.

Not that Kaius would have taken on the burden of a female vampire anyway. Rumor was they were ten times more powerful, dangerously unrestrained, and prone to mass annihilations when the mood struck them.

He'd never met one. And he wasn't anxious to change that.

Since his turning, he'd existed under the obligation to survive. He trained, fought, fed, and fucked under a sense of duty or need, but relished none of it. He hadn't asked for it, hadn't ever wanted to live longer than he had to. Moving from one drunken weekend to another was replaced by moving from one sparring partner to the next with no end in sight.

As the youngest member, the rest of the hauntmates save Boy indulged him, with Kaius closely monitoring his moods to ensure he didn't walk into the sun out of pure apathy. Mick's empathic abilities helped Kai when distance limited the eldest vampire's connection and had been invaluable in keeping him alive during the first mercurial decade.

Over the past thirty years, he had accepted that he wasn't allowed to die. Kaius and the brothers coddled him, hoping someday the camaraderie of the haunt would create a fire inside him to thrive. Pushing him into the role of a fixer was the most recent effort to bring him into the fold, to provide him with a sense of purpose.

Or, as Rhys eloquently put it, to pull his head out of his selfish ass and contribute something to the haunt other than smartass comments.

As the males neared the Tender kitchen, Dahlia's sweet voice was speaking solemnly.

"You need to figure out something you can do. Paint?"

Silence.

He and Mickey froze, eavesdropping on Dahlia and her companion.

"What about dance?"

Silence.

"Can you sing?"

"Like a crow with a chest wound."

Molly.

Dahlia sighed. "You need to think of something you can do to fetch a good price. If not… well…skilled Tenders usually go to better vampires…" Her voice drifted off, the clear warning left unsaid.

The reverberating crash of metal on metal was the only warning the stealthy males had before a flurry of black hair came storming out of the kitchen, onyx eyes blazing then zeroing in with deadly accuracy as they found him.

"You."

He remained motionless, not breathing, not blinking.

"I'm going to end up getting chewed by some fanged psycho because of you," Molly hissed, rising onto her toes to level her gaze with her prey, finger digging deep in his chest. "Why didn't you let me run? Let me out? I hope you burn in fucking hell. I hope you end up in a Deepfryer so I can watch as y…"

Neither Molly nor Dahlia's human senses would have registered the speed in which Rhys shot out of the training room. His tattooed arms wrapped around Molly as he sped back through the door, his stunned cargo over his shoulder.

Mickey's cautious gaze locked on him, assessing him for a reaction. Dahlia stood still, mouth agape, before bowing her head in deference to the vampires and backing slowly from the room.

He stood frozen, a slight twitch in his jaw the only movement as screams of rage laced with sobbed apologies echoed from the training room. Mick waited, following his lead as long as his emotional turmoil remained manageable.

Minutes passed before he blinked, his turquoise eyes registering the box still tucked under his arm. "We should drop this off and head into the office for the conference."

Purposeful strides toward the hysterical screaming belied the rolling waves of fury, possessiveness, and need washing over his psyche. He opened the door, Mickey hot on his heels, and strode to the bedroom where the scent of honeysuckle and fear was concentrated.

Molly's lithe form was stretched against the side wall, arms held tight above her head by iron manacles Rhys was currently securing to an inconspicuous hook in the ceiling. Her thrashing legs bounced off Rhys's steady figure, causing no more disturbance to the hulking vampire than a fly bouncing off a window. Deaf to the scorching insults peppered with pleas for mercy and promises of obedience, he approached Rhys with the letters and box.

"Mail delivery."

Dominic kept his attention on Rhys's muscled shoulders as they rippled with tension, unwilling to look at Molly while she was shackled. With a final tug to ensure the manacles held, Rhys turned slowly. "Put it out there on the sofa, Mini. I'll be right out."

He backed out of the bedroom, packages in hand and Mickey tight to his side as Rhys turned to Molly with a snarl. "You would be wise, princess, to shut the fuck up right now. I'll be back before dawn."

Slamming the bedroom door, Rhys joined them in the living room, tossing the box to the side and turning his attention to the pile of letters. "Anger projection isn't uncommon with rescues," Rhys stated, brow knotting as he read the contents of the particularly thick envelope. "I'm usually the recipient of it, though."

He shrugged, anchoring his feet to the floor before he broke down the bedroom door and ripped the shackles off the wall. "No problem."

Rhys carefully folded the message, standing to tuck it in his back pocket. "We should head over to the office."

****

As Dom took his seat, he kept his gaze fixated on the papers in front of him. Nichol had set the video conferencing up on a long table to allow all members of the haunt to see their leader during this week's meeting. Kaius had yet to return to the bunker, and all the males were anxious for the opportunity to discuss the myriad of issues that had arisen in the almost two months of his absence.

Mandatory weekly meetings among the hauntmates

ensured each member was kept abreast of all aspects of the operations and undertakings among the brethren. It also provided an opportunity to address personal disagreements and concerns that often arose between the testosterone-fueled predators.

Kaius's calm guidance was frequently sought and when that proved ineffective, his indisputable decrees were quick to end any disharmony that interfered with the males' ability to work cooperatively.

Over the past two weeks, Dominic had begun to despise the assembly. The hesitant glances his way, the fabricated jobs only he was qualified to do that kept him conveniently tethered to the compound, and Rhys's vague reports of his training sessions all tested his patience. Rhys, his usual reporting style as detailed and as crude as he could make it, now only reported that "the acquisition is not advancing as anticipated."

A sharp ring and Nichol began connecting the video call. Kaius's usually stoic face held a hint of a smile as he laid his blue eyes on the assembled males for the first time in nearly two months.

"Evening, boys. I am short on time tonight, so let's go over our reports and delay any gossip until the end. Jagg?"

Jagg, his icy eyes focused on Kai's lips, stopped his steady humming and spoke in his low, rumbling baritone. "Nichol and I have a bead on acquiring a Deepfryer through the European underground. I'm hoping to use it to create some protective wear that can withstand the rays. I've also just received a new shipment of multi-length retractable blades and have been creating a practice regime for us to begin next week."

Kaius spoke slowly, enunciating clearly for Jagg's benefit. "I'll ensure any funds required for the testing are readily available. Email me a list of supplies you may have difficulty locating and I'll do what I can. Nice work. Nichol."

Jagg resumed his hushed humming while he began compiling a sloppily written list of supplies. Nichol moved closer to the screen, his hazel eyes glinting with excitement. "GPS repair is slow going, since parts supplies are ridiculously backed up, but I did manage to tweak the exterior monitoring system to provide a clearer visual during heat view. And I was able to break into the back walls of the Species Purifier website and get a detailed list of all members, along with their residences and workplaces. With this little baby."

Nichol paused to hold up a tiny metal chip. "We can track each member's online presence and monitor the group's plans."

A slow round of impressed applause from the brothers preceded Kaius's vote of approval. Kai's eyes sought out Boy against the back corner. "Boy. You are well?"

Boy's empty blue eyes flicked to the screen and an infinitesimal nod affirmed his status before he resumed his detached staring at the ceiling.

Kai turned his attention to Mick. "Report."

Mick stood, his imposing size filling the video feed. "I miss you, daddy."

The strained atmosphere of the room dissolved briefly while the males barked with laughter.

Kai raised one eyebrow, his mouth turned up in amusement. "And?"

Mick grinned and sat down. "And my networks are

reading a lot more anti-vamp chatter across North America as a whole. My eyes in the Senate report that legislation will be presented for debate regarding a registration system. The proponents are looking at ways to permanently mark us for quick identification. While we can do little to stop this from passing, I have my guys pushing to legislate fines over detention as the punishment for breaking the law. Most vamps can afford any fine levied, but detention hasn't had a good history amongst our kind lately…"

Mick trailed off and let the idea take root.

Kaius gave a solemn nod. "Email me daily updates. Start preparing contingency plans for us and others to deal with the possibility of a registration system. I would also like you to begin preparing various scenarios should the decision to detain arise. I will forward you case studies from Dubai."

"Yes sir," Mick answered, his eyes glazing over as his mind likely began flashing through any way to gain a strategic advantage.

Kai turned his attention to Rhys, and Dominic held an unneeded breath. "Report."

Rhys stared at the papers in his hands, his neck taut with tension. He rose slowly and moved pointedly away from Dominic's reach. He tracked his brother, anxiety rising as Mick inched subtly closer.

"Our donor requirements for A-positive have finally slowed, but B-negative is running low. We lost three out of the pool last week due to self-harm. I need Dominic to meet a contact in Amarillo next week to replenish our pool. He has a collection of eighteen of various types he's aiming to unload, and that should meet our current orders. The number of injured vampires seeking orders has leveled temporarily, but if the legislation Mick mentioned passes, I anticipate a surge in orders. I suggest we double our collections and increase our storage capabilities to stave off any backlog we may experience."

Kai nodded. "Make it happen. Boy. Ensure there is sufficient room for the donor influx next week and increase the sustenance distribution down there."

Boy, glazed eyes unseeing, merely blinked in acknowledgement.

The rustling paper in Rhys's hand drew attention back to him, reminding Dominic that Rhys had yet to address the tumultuous issue of the confined trainee. He stilled in anticipation. Mickey placed a staying hand on his shoulder, prepared for whatever reaction occurred with Rhys's report.

"The acquisition is not…" Rhys paused, focused on Kaius's steel-blue stare, and continued. "The trainee Molly fits most of the requirements laid out in a request I received this evening. If I can get her on board within the next week or two, I'll be accepting a lowball offer of twenty thousand dollars for her. If not…" He rolled his shoulders out. "She isn't a strong candidate for the bloodslave quarters, so if the sale doesn't pan out, I recommend she be put down as humanely as possible."

****

In the millisecond it took for Dominic's control to snap, Rhys watched as Mickey threw him to the floor, barely restraining the snarling male until Jagger jumped in to assist. The low growl of possessiveness rumbled through the room from the prone vampire, punctuated by snapping fangs and hissed curses as Dom sliced into Mickey's forearms.

Kaius's attention remained locked on Rhys, both males focused on ignoring the growling beast being dragged from the room. "You feel she will be receptive."

"If she's not receptive, I have to put her down," he reiterated, hoping against hope Dominic didn't hear his words. "She doesn't have the physical strength to survive the bloodslave quarters for long."

A savage howl rang through the hall. Nichol quietly rose and closed the office door. Boy maintained his silent vigil in the corner. He looked away from the penetrating stare on the screen.

"I leave it to your impeccable judgement," Kai stated, his cool voice hiding the strain Dominic's emotions were likely placing on his mind.

With a nod of farewell, Kaius disappeared from the screen, leaving him, Nichol, and Boy to process the night's events against the dull roar of a possessive growl. After a few minutes, Boy slipped from the room.

"This is all kinds of fucked up."

He looked over at Nichol. "Yeah, man. It's…I have a job to do."

Nichol hummed in agreement. "Isn't he a little young for this?" he mused as he deconstructed the video conferencing system. "I mean, that was some serious primal shit going on. I've heard that sound from vamps over the years, but they were usually centuries, not decades, old."

He turned the letter over in his hands. "Don't know. Maybe Jagg can help. If we remove the girl…fuck. I don't know. Out of sight, out of mind? Does it work that way?"

"Hope so. If I ever make that sound, I'm walking

myself straight into the Deepfryer. If I'm too gone to do it myself, your useless ass needs to push me in."

He chuckled. "Yeah, I'll make sure you're dead within the hour. Promise."

The males worked in contemplative silence, setting the office back to rights. As he moved to leave, Nichol grabbed his arm. "Dom's our brother, always will be, but we all know he isn't all there. That bit…woman…would break him, drive him back into the sun and you know it as well as I do. You can feel her destructive force when she passes by. Sell her, kill her, whatever. But get. Her. Gone."

Chapter Nine

Molly's senses pinpointed the stream of light coming from under the bedroom door and the hushed whispers of her fellow Tenders. Her shoulders screamed for relief from the manacles she had been placed in hours earlier. Her throat, raw from screaming, cried for salvation in the form of ice water.

None came.

Straining to hear what the women on the other side of the door were saying, she groaned in frustration. "Please," she called out, her normally husky voice graveled from abuse. "Dahlia? Amy? Please help me!"

The whispers stopped. The sound of retreating footsteps let her know exactly where she stood among the sisterhood of Tenders in the compound. Angry tears dropped down her cheeks.

Fuck Dominic. Fuck Rhys. Fuck Wyatt Hanson and his stupid fangs and zip-ties. Fuck Amy and Dahlia and Gabby. Fuck the vampire Boy with his hollow, evil eyes. Fuck walking in high heels. Fuck memorizing history and practicing recipes that always turned out slightly off. Fuck eloquent speech and stupid paint that dripped down the canvas.

Fuck it all, she was going to be killed tonight and she was fucking ready.

The time passed tortuously slow as she waited for Rhys to come back and drain her dry.

She hadn't intended to lash out at Dominic. Hadn't

intended to wish the Deepfryer on him.

He hadn't been the one who placed her here.

But he was a convenient target for the rage and fear she was feeling, a convenient target whose dejected turquoise eyes were flickering through her mind.

She dropped her head forward.

Truth be told, the three weeks had been exhausting, but safe. There was a constant supply of delicious food, a warm shower, and companionship. She hadn't had the stress of keeping a roof over her head or the embarrassment of being fired for incompetence.

Though she supposed it was that very incompetence that was going to kill her tonight.

At least embarrassment wouldn't be a part of it.

Small victories.

The bedroom door opened slowly, light assaulting her sensitive eyes. She tracked Rhys as he approached her, studying her in that cold, calculating way he had the night they met. A minute passed. Two. Ten before Rhys finally spoke.

"You have two options," he began, fingers gripping what appeared to be a letter.

"What's door number one?" she whispered, replaying her first night with the vampire.

"I drain you. Five minutes and all this," he waved an arm across the room, "is over."

Fighting tears, she averted her eyes. "And door number two?"

Rhys held up the letter. "We clean you up and move into the final training stage tomorrow night." He paused a moment to allow her time to digest the idea. "Should you choose door number two, you will spend the next week confined to this room. The Tenders have been instructed to avoid all interaction with you. You will be fed according to your behavior and effort, subject to my discretion. We will spend most of the next 168 hours preparing you for your new master. His expectations for a Tender are… negligible to say the least. In return for your service, you will be housed, clothed, and fed. He already has competent staff handling the daily operations of his haunt and he is a male of simple entertainment tastes. This is, for you, the best you can hope for. You have until dusk tomorrow to decide."

"But I want…"

The words died on her lips as Rhys's penetrating gaze narrowed, a low chuckle rumbling from him as his silvery fangs appeared to elongate in the dim light. "What you want, sweetheart, is no longer my concern. Choose life or choose death. I will deliver. Right now, however, I'm going to go against my intuition and unshackle you. With the first insolent bullshit spewed from your mouth, you will lose your choice in this matter."

Her arms dropped to her sides in agony, the pain bringing her to her knees as she gasped through the muscle spasms. Using the toe of his boot, Rhys tilted her head to look at him. "Whether you choose door one or door two tomorrow, make sure you look your best. I don't train mongrels and I tend to get violent when my meals are unappealing."

****

Dominic hovered in the red haze of his mind, relishing in the numbness and surreal experience of an aware dream state. He could sense stilted movement around him, could feel his own body being adjusted and jostled, could taste a bland metallic liquid dripping in rivulets down his throat.

Voices surrounded him in static, staccato blips. He was blissfully unaffected by the activity around him, reminiscent of the stupor of his human drinking nights. Vampires didn't get drunk on alcohol, didn't have a twilight of awareness to revel in. They were dead or alert. This delusional bubble he found himself in was pure euphoria and he clung to it as one might an umbrella in a hurricane.

Enchanted serenity.

An electric jolt tore through his mind, ripping him from the sea of peace.

With the second shock, he landed reluctantly into hyper-awareness. Movements, sounds, taste, odors. All assaulted his senses as his efficient brain scrambled to categorize his situation.

He was in his bunker. In the shower room in his bunker. On the floor of the shower in his bunker. A-positive blood in his mouth. A-negative residual taste coating his molars. Another unidentifiable taste, almost spicy in flavor, coated his tongue. Dahlia and Gabby. Faint humming. Jagger. Arm restraining him from behind. Hand gripping his jaw, forcing it to remain open. Mickey.

"Dom."

Another shot in the brain. Kaius.

"Dom."

He struggled to unbind himself from Mickey's sturdy grasp. "The fuck!" he growled, "Let me up." His speech felt strange, sounded sloppy.

Mick's hold loosened on his jaw but remained locked around his chest. "No can do. Kaius's orders."

He scanned the room, assessing the destruction surrounding him. Gabby's blonde hair was visible through the doorway, her immobile figure stretched out while Boy stood guard monitoring her faint heartbeat.

Dahlia hunched in the corner holding a towel to her leg, a scarlet stain growing against the white fibers. Her stuttering heart rate told him she was better off than Gabby, but not by much. Streams of blood gathered in the grout lines of the tiled floor.

Splattered droplets reached the shower ceiling. Jagger knelt silently at his feet, a clean laceration healing along his forearm.

"Dom."

Mick's voice snapped his attention back.

"Okay, Mini. Jagg's gonna text Kaius, let him know you're awake. Jagg? Tell Kai he can cut the pulses. Dom, we're just gonna sit like this for a little while until we get a few things under control. Understand?"

He attempted to lunge forward out of Mickey's constricting hold. Two long vices locked around him and he turned his head instinctively to bite at the offending limbs just as Jagger cinched his legs.

"What the fuck happened to my fangs?" he snarled, enraged at his captors and his confusion.

"Look around you, Mini," Mick growled, his voice low and patience obviously wearing. "What the fuck do you think we did with them?"

His eyes locked on a pile of torn flesh and blood in the opposite corner of the shower. Two glimmering pink-tinged peaks amongst the chunks of muscle and skin. He stilled as his mind processed what atrocities his baser nature had committed in that room. As

Gabby's heartbeat regulated, Boy gently picked up Dahlia from the tile floor, left the room, and pulled the door tight behind him.

He slumped against his brother, empty of both fight and flight.

"What's happening to me, Mick?" he murmured. "What's wrong with me?"

****

Mickey leaned back against the cold tile of the shower, accepting the weight of his younger brother physically and mentally. He tightened his arms in reassurance as his eyes closed. The past six hours had been nothing less than hell as he and Jagg fought to restrain Dom and bring him back out of his core impulses.

The vampire core had connected so vehemently and unexpectedly to Molly that neither the hauntmates nor Kaius knew what to do. He had struggled to keep from falling into the primal ferocity Dominic was projecting and had nearly been lost himself shortly before Kaius had begun sending jolts to Dom. Those shocks provided enough reprieve for him to pull himself above water before he drowned alongside his broken kin.

The blood of the Tenders, a catch-all for vampire injuries, had only served to further infuriate Dominic. Gabby had been thrown from the room, the crisp snapping of her bones ending before he or Jagger could react. A drop of Dahlia's blood on his tongue and the livid vampire had torn a hole from her thigh, snapping for more as Jagg ripped Dominic's fangs from his gums.

He had felt the moment Dominic's inner vampire

had decided it wanted Molly weeks earlier. He and Jagg had been running coolers of blood to a few of the local injured vampires when a jolt of possession rocked his mind in a blinding flash. Having never experienced the moment of connection himself, he shook off the shock and continued to unload the cumbersome coolers. It wasn't until the call came in from Rhys regarding Dom's unknown whereabouts that he was able to pinpoint who the emotion belonged to.

And it wasn't until he heard the soft, rumbling growl of possession radiating throughout the bunker halls the next night that he realized exactly what Dom's emotional jolt had been.

A territorial marking.

A warning.

Dominic, since the night of his turning, had fought to separate his human and vampire instincts. Fought to crush the vampire until it surged forth in a haze of blood and violence. By refusing to merge his dual natures, Dom had left himself unable to identify his impulses for what they were. And right now, he was treating his unexpected connection to the new trainee as he did his baser hunger. As a physiological need he could ignore, starve, until the inevitable detonation.

Hours into the howls and incoherent screams, Jagg had taken matters into his own hands, slicing his arm open and dropping his own blood into Dominic's snarling mouth. He could feel Jagg's resolution as his predatory side roared in protest against the bloodletting.

An unconnected male spilling his blood for any reason beyond siring went against all the core instincts of their kind. Between the strength of Jagg's four-hundred-year-old blood, Kaius' jarring pulses, and

Mickey absorbing a portion of his rage, Dom had slowly pulled out of the abyss.

He met Jagger's crystal eyes, the sacrifice of three pints evident in the male's posture. "Is this how it... Did you... Is this what happens? Is this what you were like? I don't remember it being so strong on my end."

Jagg focused studiously on his lips. "The intensity, yes. There was a lot of distance between you and I at the time, so you were spared the worst of it. It took me many months to regulate the connection enough to be more than a lovesick fool. But I was three centuries old with far more control than Dominic has. Or will likely ever have. And not once did anyone threaten to kill or screw my Seline. That would have ended far more unpleasantly than this has."

"Worse than two injured Tenders and six hundred years' total of strength huddled on a shower floor?"

"I drained a man for licking his lips in her presence."

"Oh. This connection thing is some serious shit."

"Very."

He looked down at Dominic, who had slipped into his day rest. "What do we do now?"

Jagg stood slowly. "On some level, he is successfully fighting the connection. They aren't tied. Once the female is gone, it's likely he'll settle. I need to feed and rest. I'll send Boy to stand guard. Keep your phone ready in case he wakes."

He watched Jagg retreat from the room. Calling out loud enough to provide a reverberation for Jagger's damaged ears, he ventured to ask the reserved vampire a question he'd been wondering since Jagg returned to the haunt decades years earlier. "Why'd you come back?”

Jagg stilled. “After Seline’s death, I returned to the only place that would accept me, broken as I was.”

****

Molly paced the bedroom floor, her hands twisting at the long ringlets of her hair. Donning the only dress in her closet, she stopped frequently to adjust the laced bodice of the black frock. Her bare feet padded across the room as her mind flipped between door one and door two. She had concluded she was not deliberating between life and death, but rather a quick demise or a slow one.

Knowing she would not decide on an answer prior to Rhys’s arrival, she had spent her evening soaking in lilac bathwater and curling her long hair into ringlets that were quickly losing their bounce. She had plucked, preened, and scrubbed religiously for hours, preferring to focus on avoiding iron burns instead of on her impending fate. Her stomach was empty, making its displeasure known loudly despite the copious amounts of water she drank to stave off the hunger.

Rhys arrived at dusk, entering the bedroom as calm and collected as usual. She stood still before his appraising gaze, obeying the twirl of his finger and turning in a slow circle to display the gothic gauzy ensemble. Content with her scent and appearance, Rhys presented her with a granola bar.

While years of poor financial circumstances had left her hungry for far longer in the past, her time in the vampire compound had spoiled her stomach with a constant supply of delicious food. She moved to take the bar as Rhys removed it just out of her grasp.

“Manners.”

She bit the snark out of her lip. “Please.”

“Please, what?”

Recognizing he was testing, baiting her, she held her tongue. “Please, Rhys, may I have the bar?”

“Master.”

She stared at Rhys, her brain screaming insults while simultaneously recognizing that were she truly craving an immediate death, it would be her mouth throwing the words, not her mind. “Please, Master, may I have the bar?”

Rhys’s dark eyes narrowed, assessing her intent as he handed her the food. As her lips closed around the ration, Rhys came out of his daze. “Eat it facing the corner. On your knees.”

Her mind screeched in protest, every fiber of her being urging her to fight back. Every fiber except the self-preservation one that overshadowed all else and she moved her feet swiftly into the corner. She knelt silently, her stomach grateful for the sustenance even if her frail pride was currently doing nothing to cushion her aching knees.

An hour passed. Fearful of retribution by fang, she remained in the corner, fingers twisting and wrapping the delicate skirt fabric as Rhys appeared determined to test how compliant she could be under distress.

An imposing overlord in her peripheral.

****

Rhys’s flexible mind ran through countless scenarios, numerous ways he could prepare Molly for her future. Each one ended with her incapable of the obedience her new master would require, resulting in death if she was lucky. Never one to cater to the sadistic impulses in which many of his kind relished, he was at a loss.

Despite her numerous flaws, he had found himself both frustrated and entertained by the woman. She was quick-witted, quick-tempered, and found everything fascinating until it no longer was. Molly had interest in everything and skill in nothing. And at two weeks into their ten hour a night training, she had not once looked at him with anything but humor, determination, or anger.

And that hung around his neck like a noose.

At some point in the near future, he had to bed this woman for her own safety. A woman with zero desire for him. A woman his hauntmate was inexplicably connected to. And he had the obligation to train her before she learned the hard way how different sex with a vampire could be from screwing human men.

While the vampire appetite for blood and sex was high, the act itself was dangerous for human partners. The speed and force of the coupling meant tensing at the wrong time often resulted in strained muscles or broken bones. In a frenzy, it was common for males to shatter the woman's pelvis. Sex in a state of anger was sometimes deadly, and he had a few of his highly trained tenders ended years into their service because they momentarily forgot the rules.

Molly was unlikely to survive the month.

"Stand and face me."

She rose, smoothing her skirt and straightening her back.

"Tonight, we review the rules."

"Okay…"

"Yes, Master," he corrected in a hiss.

"Yes, Master."

Molly's forced compliance did nothing to assuage the whispering guilt he felt for his role in her situation. Though he had to acknowledge that Molly did indeed have more self-preservation than he had anticipated. It would serve her well since any Master with such ambiguous requirements was not looking for a companion.

In any other circumstance, with any other Tender with six to eight months of training, he would have laughed the vampire's request off. But Molly had to go. And his job was to ensure she went with as much preparation as he could provide.

"Tonight, I will teach you the one rule you must perfect. We'll practice its application across a variety of scenarios. At the end of the night, I will allow questions." He lowered his head before reestablishing eye contact with Molly, ignoring her twitching fingers and subtle weight shifting. "This will keep you fed. Safe. Alive. Understand?"

"Yes, Master."

He crooked a finger, beckoning Molly to follow him into the living quarters and motioned for her to sit on the new black sofa as he crouched low at her feet. "I live to obey, serve, and please my Master. Say it."

"I live to serve…"

"Obey."

"I live to obey and serve…"

"Obey, serve, and please."

"Ob…"

"I live to obey, serve, and please my Master."

"Oh for…"

Before her exasperated rant could take root, Molly was on her back on the sofa, and he hovered over her as his fingers clenched her throat. "I. Live. To. Obey. Serve. And please. My Master."

"I live to obey, serve, and please my Master! I live to obey, serve, and please my Master!"

He released his hold, pulling Molly back up and resuming his position on the floor. "You will repeat that one hundred times while I explain what exactly the rule encompasses. Start."

Molly breathed deep, her voice shaky with anxiety, and began to chant the rule as he continued to glare at her.

"The only appropriate response to your Master's requests is 'Yes, Master.' 'No' is no longer in your vocabulary. Nothing distracts you from fulfilling his every request, spoken or unspoken. You will learn to read him, anticipate his needs and wants, and respond without prompting. You will never speak out of turn. Never raise your voice to him. Your entire existence revolves around his whims. Seventy to go."

Molly continued her chant, hopefully absorbing all he was saying.

"Anything you need, be it food, clothing, or attention, you will rely on your Master to provide. Do not, under any circumstances, attempt to fulfill your needs yourself. Express gratitude for everything you are given, regardless of significance, or you will find yourself going without entirely. Keep your eyes averted, looking directly at your Master only when you receive instruction. Forty left.

"Do not argue. Do not disagree. If a task appears impossible, figure out a way to complete it. If a request is unappealing, swallow that tongue of yours and do it anyways. And Molly… stop chanting… look at me…

Molly. Do not ever fight back. Ever. You will be dead before your body hits the floor. You will never win, never gain the upper hand. You will never be stronger, quicker, or more skilled. The first time your insolent mouth overrides your intelligence will likely be the last time either are used. Am I clear?"

Molly nodded, tears rolling down her cheeks.

"Twenty-two to go. Resume. None of the humans in your Master's retinue are your friends. As a Tender, you are above them in the hierarchy, and there may be those that will go out of their way to eliminate you. Never speak ill of your Master to others because he will find out. He will find out and he will punish you."

"Pu…"

Face down on the floor and sprawled beneath a massive body, Molly struggled for a moment before she stilled in submission and awaited instruction. He maintained his hold on her as he lowered his fangs to her ear. "You were not given permission to speak."

He rose, leaving Molly on the floor to debate her next move.

"You may stand," he commanded. "List your errors."

With a steadying breath, Molly kept her onyx eyes locked on the floor. "I spoke without permission. And I fought back when you punished me."

"And?"

Molly's brows furrowed. "I don't know."

"Were you given permission to look at me?"

"No."

"No, what?"

"No, Master. I did not have permission to look at you. I'm sorry."

He moved closer, placed his hands on her shoulders, and bent down to level their vision. “And now I’m going to let you in on a secret that may save your ass. Vampires are predators, hunters. The chase excites us, weakness disgusts us. However, our desire to both dominate and indulge our Tenders on a whim may be the key to your survival should you forget your place or… pull a Molly. The moment you recognize you have fucked up, stand tall, expose your neck, and offer your wrists. This will appeal to your Master on multiple levels. The human morals of his day will acknowledge the show of responsibility for your error. As a Master, he will accept the open position as trust in his methods. His vampire urges will be appeased with the inner strength such a pose requires and will be accepting of his willing source of sustenance. And Molly? Do not mistake deference for weakness. Play. The. Game. Do you understand?”

“Yes, Master.”

He walked over to Molly’s beloved radio and turned it on to a retro music station. “Now, sweetheart, you and I are going to do a little role playing.”

****

Dominic flashed into consciousness. He could feel the vice grip of Mickey’s arms still secured across his chest. He ran his tongue over the razor edges of his emerging fangs, their rejuvenation sped up by the four-century-old blood coursing through his veins. Scenting the air, he noted the pungent odor of bleach overpowering the fading smell of Tender blood.

He scanned the pristine floor and walls of the bathroom, every splatter of flesh and blood from the previous night erased from sight. Not a speck remained.

Boy's exceptional senses would have ensured nothing was missed, no evidence of his uncontrolled fury lingered.

Testing Mickey's grip, he eased forward to assess how cognizant his sleeping hauntmate was. As the biceps rippled, he relaxed back against his brother.

"How long does Kai want you to play Big Spoon?"

Mick snorted, his eyes still closed. "You don't like cuddling me, Mini? Aren't I pretty enough? Nic says I'm plenty purdy. Says I have purdy lips."

He grinned, picturing his snarky brother describing anything as 'purdy.' "I don't like being this close to your junk. Who knows where your dirty ass has been. I probably have crabs now, you raging manwhore."

Mickey's barking laugh echoed in the tiled shower. "Vamp crabs. That's a scary fucking thought, man. Could you imagine it? Little red bastards with fangs and inflated egos? Screw that idea. Fucking without consequence was probably my favorite thing during my first few decades… Anyways… Jagg and Boy should return soon. Until then, you're my bitch."

He turned his head to glance at Mick. "What's going to happen to me?"

Adjusting his position, Mick loosened his hold slightly. "Honestly? I dunno, man. My best guess is Jagg and Kai are going to be calling the shots for the next little while."

"What are you…" He paused, unsure if he wanted to hear the answer, "What are you, I don't know, picking up from me?"

Mick's hesitation hung in the air.

"Mick."

With an uncharacteristic sigh, Mickey adjusted his

grip again and closed his eyes. "You're killing me, Mini."

"Mick."

"I wish I was fucking kidding, Dom. Yeah, you're in control right now. But underneath it, it's like your core is melding with that rage you've carried since the night Kai brought you over. You've always been kind of… fragmented. You gave off three separate vibes. Anger has always been strongest, but your… youness I guess… that part that feels everything else has been nearly as strong. Your core used to kind of pulse. Like a heartbeat. It was strange. I can pick up changes in everyone's baser instincts, but yours was this steady beat of emptiness. And now? Now that emptiness is filling with your rage and I've been fighting off that beast since you snapped last night. So yeah, Mini. You're killing me."

He stayed motionless as the weight of Mickey's words hung in the air.

"Mini?" Mick muttered quietly.

"Why can't I feel any of that? Is it because I'm going fucking nuts? Am I, like, delusional or something? Psycho?"

"Ahhhh Mini," Mickey chuckled, "you're no more insane than you ever were. Now instead of being a fuckup mess, you're a fuckup mess in looooooooove."

"Go fuck yourself."

"See? You two even sound alike. Seriously, though, I know absolutely nothing about this connection shit. My job right now is to keep you from offing yourself or anyone else, and part of that is internalizing as much of your rage as I can without falling into it myself."

He side-eyed Mick. "You can do that?"

"Damn right."

"That's some intense shit."

"It's been an intense few hours."

The males fell into a contemplative silence. He could feel waves of fury and possessiveness lapping at his psyche, only to have a them pull back before they breeched the shore. Focusing on the steady rhythm, he recognized the moment Mickey took on each wave. Before they would crest, an unseen vacuum would pull the driving force backwards, leaving little more than a gentle ripple of rage.

"You're doing it right now, aren't you?"

"Yup."

"Is this why you're so moody?"

"Fuck off, Mini."

"Let me up and I will."

A low rumbling laughter shook Mick's chest. "No chance in hell."

The soft humming in the hall alerted the males to Jagg's arrival. He could feel Mick's grip loosen, his confidence in the four-hundred-year-old vampire allowing Mick to relax his intense vigil over the unstable hauntmate. Jagg entered the bathroom, scrutinizing Dominic. Apparently satisfied with what he found, he turned his attention to Mick. "Status?"

"Tired and hungry. Could use a shower. An hour with a Ten… maybe fifteen minutes with a Tender. Who am I kidding. Ten minutes."

He grinned despite the situation.

Jagg's stoic face and icy eyes remained impassive. "Go. Boy and I will take it from here. Report back when you're ready."

Mickey stood slowly, disengaging from him. "I can… ease up?"

Jagg nodded and he could feel the waves of anger increase in magnitude as Mickey began walking out of the room. Mick glanced back. "I'll find you in a bit, Mini."

The door of the bunker closed as Mickey left and Boy arrived. The presence of Boy increased his apprehension. Boy, with his hollow blue eyes, silently held mouth, and vacant expressions, was unreadable for all the brethren.

Rising to his feet slowly, he attempted to demonstrate to both Jagg and Boy that he was, in fact, lucid and in control as he hooked his thumbs into his blood-spattered pockets and stared his elder hauntmates down.

"Boy," he began slowly, "are Gabby and Dahlia… okay?"

Boy's blank expression held, save for the slight nod of his head.

The males stood in the silence as he fought to maintain his precarious control in Mickey's absence.

"That's not anger you are experiencing," Jagger stated.

His eyes narrowed at Jagg, but he remained mute.

"It's desperation."

Silence.

"It's truly a messed-up setup, this connection thing. Your vampire core thinks it's dying of starvation, dehydration, freezing to death… however you want to think of it. And it's pissed. For some godforsaken reason, your core has decided that the Tender-in-training you brought in…"

"Molly," he muttered absently.

"Molly. Your core has decided it needs her to live and will do anything it can to survive by getting to her." Jagg motioned for him to follow him out of the pristine bathroom. Once in the living area, Dominic dropped onto the sofa, his head lolling back in frustration.

"So, you're saying I can either follow this fucking connection to a woman who's leaving in days, or I can go insane anyways and die in the process. Fantastic."

"I said your core thinks it's going to die without her. You won't actually die. I didn't. It will merely be… unpleasant for a while."

"How unpleasant?"

Jagger flopped onto the sofa beside him. "Unpleasant enough to have you spend the next few weeks or months in the bloodslave quarters under Boy's supervision."

"And my choices are…?"

"Spend the next few weeks or months in the bloodslave quarters under Boy's supervision. Or Boy puts you down."

Chapter Ten

The pulsating baritone growl emanating through the walls of the haunt had become little more than white noise to the occupants since it began the week prior. It had erupted shortly before dawn the first night, a relentless warning call to the hauntmates that refused to ease even when the sun had engulfed the sky.

The brothers were initially on edge, restless from the constant assault on their sensitive hearing. They closed doors, ran water, and blasted music through the haunt until eventually most were able to tune out the snarling attack.

Mickey had lasted less than four hours into the second night before Nichol was given a phone order from Kaius to arrange a temporary move for the empathic vampire from their haunt to another three states away.

Rhys stared at the training room door.

In one night, he would be handing over his newest Tender to her new Master and the hell of the past month would be over.

Theoretically.

Realistically, no one knew how long Dominic would remain the feral, snarling animal he'd become so suddenly. Anchored to the wall, Dominic had begun a territorial growling vigil. Despite Jagg's assurances that removing Molly and her scent would speed up Dom's recovery, he had his reservations.

He had gone to see Dominic twice, but the moment Molly's residual scent hit Dom, the snarling amplified and he had exited the room quickly to avoid getting caught by the snapping fangs.

One more night of training.

Once Molly's self-preservation had kicked in, her ability to be a subservient, compliant Tender had impressed him. She continued to lack grace, eloquent speech, and appealing mannerism, but she held her tongue and was quick to navigate the various scenarios he had presented.

While he would not call her a success, he had mentally upped her survival time to three months if she took to tonight's lessons as well as the previous nights.

He had sat in his bunker all day contemplating tonight's lessons and he came to two conclusions. One, he did not want to fuck Molly. Never one to hold on to his human morals, he was uncomfortable with the sudden attack of wrongness that sleeping with his hauntmate's connection conjured. The brothers had shared Tenders without hesitation or jealousy for decades, some for centuries. And yet the thought of bedding Molly was disconcerting, almost guilt-inducing.

His second conclusion was that Molly's survival depended on being schooled, and he was not the only male in the compound capable of providing her with a crash course.

As he entered the Tender training room, he hid his amusement behind an unaffected facade. When dawn had arrived, his final instruction to Molly was to prepare herself as she felt most comfortable for this evening's tutelage. He reasoned that she would be more pliable if she wasn't maneuvering in stilettos and fidgeting with satin.

Naturally, this was one instruction Molly obeyed easily.

And she was a disaster. Raven hair brushed straight and parted unevenly. Pink lipstick, too bright for her pale complexion, required reapplying. Charcoal eyes rimmed with too much onyx eyeliner and mascara dangerously close to clumping.

Faded denim with tears that looked suspiciously fresh. A white shirt with a rainbow splattered across her breasts held an almost imperceptible hole where Molly's thumb dug and twisted the thin fabric.

Bare feet with rainbow nail polish.

He briefly contemplated cutting the losses her sale would earn and simply drain her immediately.

"It's still going."

His unblinking eyes held Molly's anxious, flitting gaze. "It is."

"Will it stop after I leave tomorrow?"

"We believe it will."

While the incessant growling had been wearisome for the enhanced hearing of the males, the Tenders had reacted strangely, pacing anxiously and exhibiting signs of distress despite their average senses. While Molly had remained focused, subservient, and silent during the past week, she had developed a slight rhythmic rock shortly after Dominic had been secured in the bloodslave compound.

He gave Molly his nightly signal to spin slowly for his appraisal. "You worry for him."

Silence.

"You have my permission to speak freely."

Silence.

"Kitten. Tonight, we'll lift the Master-Tender protocols. This will be… intense enough as it is. You need to ask, answer, and comment freely to get three months of information into that stubborn rock you call a head."

A grin. The visible drop of her shoulders brought back the same feeling of wrongness he experienced every time he thought of screwing her. Shaking it off instantly, he crossed the room and spread himself across the black sofa, securing his hands behind his head and slowly toeing off his boots.

"I have grand plans for us tonight, sweet cheeks," he announced, "and I hope you'll be on board with everything I want to do."

Molly rolled her eyes.

Rolled. Her. Eyes.

"Whenever a man claims to have grand plans, I usually end up bored and thinking about what kind of french fries I prefer. I ain't holding my breath."

"What kind do you prefer?"

"Burnt on the bottom, soft on the top."

"That's not a kind."

"It's my kind."

Her playful banter was offset by the hesitant steps she took toward him. "So how do… what's the plan? Or do we, I don't know, just… start?"

"We aren't going to start anything. Grand plans, and all. You, my dear, are going to accompany me on a little tour of our facility."

He strode toward the door, his sock feet silent on the hardwood. He noted Molly's initial reluctance before her curiosity overcame her uncertainty and she padded quickly behind him.

The duo walked in silence through the corridors, the muted snarl rolling through the halls.

"Why is he doing that?" Molly finally asked.

"You, honey."

"Me, what?"

"That sound, angel, is the sound of a connected vampire being held from his target. And you are the lucky bullseye." He slowed his pace. "Think of it as imprinting. Like baby geese do. I saw a video online about that once. Very apt."

Molly halted, hands on her hips and black eyes narrowing. "I barely know him. Hell, I haven't even seen him in over, like, two weeks!!"

He turned, placing firming hands on her shoulders. "I'm not going to push you into this. Given your unique circumstances and our shortened time frame, I'm only going to provide the opportunity. If it happens, it happens, if not, I have some videos we can review and discuss. Though they aren't as effective."

"Videos," Molly bit, her eyes flashing as her temper rose, "for what… Oh."

"Yes. Oh."

"But he's… that sound… he's an animal," she stuttered. "He'll kill me!"

"I theorize he won't."

"You theorize he won't. THEORIZE? Are you fucking insane? Listen to that!"

"Yes, I theorize," he chuckled. "No, I am not insane. Yes, I can hear that. Much better than you can, for that matter. And I'll be there to ensure your safety."

Molly shook herself loose from his grasp. "That's creepy. You want me to… and you're going to just hang out and watch?"

"I believe this is the best solution for all involved."

"You're fucked in the head."

"I'm logical."

"I'm not doing this."

"I won't make you," he said, stopping to lean against the wall. "You also have the option of Jagg or Mick, but they have some weird kinks even I don't like to think about."

"Why not you?"

"You want to fuck me?"

"No."

"Then…"

He let the options hang in the air.

Molly's eyes locked on the ceiling as her fingers twisted and twirled her shirt, the once tiny hole growing larger as she subconsciously tugged at the fragile threads. "He stopped coming by just like that. What if he doesn't want to? Or he's too messed up?"

"I have a theory."

"Your theories suck."

"As do I, darling."

****

Even barefoot, Molly was aware of the seemingly deafening clomp of her feet beside the graceful, striding male at her side. As the pair descended the long, sloping halls into the basement of the compound, she could feel the resolve she had clung to for the past week wavering.

Sex was sex was sex, she chanted. Done this hundreds of times before. Dozens of men. One more to add to the meaningless notches of forgotten names and faded faces.

She had been prepared for tonight. Although she hadn't been thrilled by the idea of sleeping with Rhys, with his flashing eyes and sarcastic retorts, her inquisitiveness was elated at the thought of knowing exactly what sex with a vampire entailed.

Before internet searches had become monitored by the government, she had read story after story of women recounting their affairs with vampires. The biting, speed, intensity, encores… it had appeared to be the work of fiction writers.

Tonight, she had the opportunity to experience it.

And then she would be gone from the training center and into the home of a strange Master with an unknown temperament.

With that thought, Rhys brought her to a stop before a looming steel door. The baritone rumble was impossible to ignore as it washed rhythmically over her.

"Ready, princess?"

She nodded at her trainer while he pulled a key from his pocket and popped the lock. Rhys moved in front of her, blocking her view of what lay inside the dim room.

"Dominic. Dom. Mini. I need you to look at me and I need you to stay right where you are." He spoke as if calming a wild dog. A caged animal.

She stepped back as the growl amplified and the clanging of metal chains reverberated in the dank hall.

"I see Boy gave you a good hose down… yes, I know you can smell her on me," Rhys said, speaking slowly and calmly. "I want to show you someone, but it's real important you don't eat her. Grab my hand, kiddo."

Run.

She reached toward Rhys, allowing him to pull her gently into the faint torchlight of the cell.

As her eyes adjusted to the darkness of the room, she could make out a hulking figure straining forward, his wrists anchored to the ceiling and his ankles shackled to the floor. Short chains kept the snarling beast from reaching the door. Wet, black strands of hair moved across his forehead, with quick flashes of tormented turquoise eyes visible as he thrashed against his restraints. She squinted and stepped minutely closer.

"Dominic?"

Stillness.

Silence.

"Dom?

His eyes flicked up, locking on her ebony ones.

Recognition.

"I'm just going to… uh… sit over here. This wet cement is freezing my feet. Course, now my ass is going to freeze. Whatever though. I have enough padding on that," She grinned nervously, backing against a side wall and sliding down.

The growling resumed as Dominic's eyes traveled to her bare feet. "Rhys," his rough voice called hoarsely, "a few blankets for the asset?"

A tattooed arm appeared in the door, gave a thumbs-up, and disappeared.

"Why are you calling me that?"

He blinked and looked at the wall behind her. "Reminding myself of what your function is."

"It's rude."

A hint of silver fangs flashed in the dark cell. Dominic's eyes refocused on her sockless feet and her subtle rocking motion as the rumbling snarl continued faintly in the small cell.

She tilted her head, assessing the male who had driven her into this strange predicament. "Why do you make that sound?"

"Dunno."

"Can you stop when you want?"

"No. Is it… bothering you?" Dominic's raw voice cracked, hinting at the physical impact the past week had had on him.

"It doesn't stop when you talk. That's kind of cool."

Dom scoffed. "Cool. Yeah."

Stillness.

"It doesn't bother me," she began slowly. "It's actually kind of, I don't know, focusing? Like right now. If I wasn't so fucking cold, I could probably just go to sleep in a snap."

At the mention of her discomfort, the low roar amplified. "Rhys is on his way."

She nodded in acknowledgement, impressed when Rhys appeared in the doorway instantaneously with several thick comforters thrown over his broad shoulders.

"Sorry it took so long, kids. If anyone asks, I have no idea where everyone's bedding went. And for the record, we need more spare blankets in this dive."

Scrambling to her feet, she smiled at Rhys as he made his way to her, tracking Dominic's bared fangs. Unblinking eyes glared as she and Rhys arranged the blankets into a bright nest. When Rhys's hand innocuously brushed against her thigh, Dominic let loose a territorial snarl against the incessant roar.

She started, gripping Rhys's arm as she moved to

place him between herself and the chained beast.

Rhys, in turn, raised his hands in deference to Dominic's sudden burst of possession. "Mini. Enough. You're being an ass and scaring the lady."

Blink.

Dominic refocused on her, his growl softening slowly. He cleared his tired throat, "She's not a lady."

Rhys grinned, "We all know that, Mini, but we don't say it with her standing right here."

She released Rhys's arm, pushing it forward in the process. "You can both go fuck yourselves."

"See, Dom? One does not have to verbalize Molly is unladylike. Her vocabulary advertises it for her."

Dom slunk back against the wall, his shackles clanging as they slackened.

"All right, kids. I'm going to loosen these chains a bit before I go," Rhys stated, taking his position beside Dominic and cranking the pulleys. "Molly try not to be excessively annoying. Mini, don't drain her. It's tempting, I know. But if you do, I'm out twenty grand. That give you enough range? I'll be in the hall listening to my music and playing Solitaire."

And he was gone.

She glanced at the empty doorway. "That's just creepy."

Dom cocked his head.

"He's like, right there. Listening. All creepy-like."

"What is he listening for?"

She hunkered into the nest of blankets, freeing her arms. "For us to... you know. *Eeeeek eeeeek wonka wonka bom chicka wow.*"

Dominic stared as she used her hands to crudely demonstrate her point. As realization overtook his confused expression, she looked away. "He wants us to…you know…fuck. This is so awkward. You don't have to, or anything. We could, I don't know, just hang out. Like before. Or I could go. I should probably go. Rhys said I could probably figure it out from some videos he has…"

Enraged snarl.

"She's not going anywhere, Mini. Calm the fuck down," Rhys called into the cell.

She huffed. "I thought you were listening to music."

"I'm a vampire, sweetheart. I can hear a pigeon shit on a limo twenty-miles away."

"So fucking creepy," she muttered as Dom's flashing gaze fixated on her and she looked down at her hands working the hole in her shirt. Her nerves relaxed slightly against the gentle growl and her lulling rock resumed. "You should say something. I mean, I'm totally fine with it if you're up for it. Up for it," she repeated, grinning at her own crude joke.

Dom remained motionless.

"How is someone with your horrendous humor not still a virgin?" Rhys called out.

"Fucking. Creepy!" she yelled back.

"He likes you," Dom commented quietly, his raw voice scratching.

"Do not!" Rhys retorted from the hall.

"Ignore him," she demanded. "Tell me what you want to do."

Dominic crouched on the floor, keeping his distance and looking as nonthreatening as he could be in his current situation. "I don't," he began slowly, "I don't want you…"

"Go fuck yourself!"

With a strangely human sigh, Dominic continued. "Don't want you to sleep with me for some course requirement. It's not right. And I'm not… right… right now, and I know where you're going tomorrow. I get where Rhys is coming from, but I could end up more insane than I am now. Or I could lose control and hurt you. Or kill you."

"Do you really think you'll hurt me?"

Dominic's eyes glazed over. "I don't think so. I don't want to. But who knows. Whatever this… this connection thing is, I don't know what to expect."

She narrowed her eyes as Dominic's shoulders slumped in defeat momentarily before returning to their broad, strong position. "Well, you're kind of a selfish prick, you know that?"

Dark eyebrows shot up in surprise laced with a hint of amusement. "Am I now?"

Wrapping a thick quilt around herself, she stood up and tip-toed tentatively within reach of his loosened chains and sank to her knees. "Yes, you are. I've been ripped from my life, crappy as it was, to become some glorified bloodslave so that no news outlets pick up on the messed-up crap some of your species does. But *now* your morals are stopping you from helping me learn what I need to stay alive in the situation *your kind* chose for me?"

Silence.

"Add to that the fact you abandoned our TV time, and I figure you owe me."

"I owe you."

"Yes."

Dominic sat back off his haunches and draped his

long, bare arms over his knees. Her eyes traveled over his thick forearms, up his flexed biceps, and across the wide, sloping plane of his shoulders. "You're doing this under duress," he grumbled.

"I'm doing this because I might want to get laid once more before I'm drained for disobedience. Or swearing. Or breaking some antique vase. Or whatever else sets you guys off. And if we don't, and it's just too weird, I want one more night to prove I know more about the punk movement than you."

Dom met her eyes. "And what if I hurt you?"

"Rhys is right outside the door being creepy. He'll stop you."

Silence.

With a sigh of resignation, Dominic's head dropped to his chest. "Bring the rest of the blankets over here. It's cold, I'm wet, and I have no body heat to warm you up."

****

Dominic watched silently as Molly dragged her nest of quilts over to him and haphazardly arranged them before him. He could feel his vampire core warring with the remaining morals of his humanity.

The scent of honeysuckle that had driven him mad weeks earlier was now soothing and familiar, with her mere proximity providing a mental clarity he hadn't had in days. With Rhys out of the room, he could now recognize that his lingering scent on Molly was casual without a hint of carnality.

Visions of Rhys bedding Molly had tortured his thoughts for much of the past week, and the relief of knowing it hadn't occurred unknotted something deep inside him. He eyed her with a faint amusement as she inadvertently locked her legs in the pile of blankets and fell forward onto her knees. "Elegant."

She rolled her eyes and got comfortable. "Always." Molly crossed her legs and tilted her head. "So, do you prefer vinyl or disc?"

"Vinyl," he replied instantly. "I miss wasting an entire Saturday flipping through boxes of records in sketchy stores. Probably more than I miss pizza."

"I could probably kick your ass at a rock-off," Molly stated confidently.

"I'd give you a run for your money," he answered in challenge, temporarily distracted from the chains securing him to the damp wall.

She looked up at him and pursed her lips. "So, what happened to you? How did you become a vampire?"

His eyes darkened and he could hear Rhys moving closer to the doorway. "I was driving too fast on an old road in winter, hit a pothole and spun out. I panicked and hit the brakes, which flipped the car. Kaius happened to be in the area and brought me over, but it was too late for the girl I was driving home. I basically murdered her because I was a bad driver."

Molly stood up and cupped his face with her hands. "Poor road maintenance killed her. I thought you were a great driver when you brought me here."

"I drive a lot now." He tugged at his chains. "Or, at least, I did."

The taste of raspberry lip gloss and the scent of honeysuckle overcame him as her soft lips brushed against his.

He could feel the tentativeness of her kiss, her uncertainty of his reaction. As his brain caught up with what was happening, he felt her move away. Desperate for more, he grabbed the base of her neck and pulled her back, his clanking restraints echoing in the cement cell. His lips captured hers gently, his knees almost giving out as her soft tongue, usually so quick with retorts, slid sensually into his mouth.

Molly's tongue flicked over one fang, then the other. As a low purring growl erupted from his throat, she caressed each fang slowly, testing his self-control while he lowered them to the cold floor.

Mollymollymollyfuckmolly.

He'd had been hard since his connected-addled mind had first recognized her presence in his cell. Her scent, her proximity, her complete imperfection had kept him aching despite the fog of hunger and possessiveness. As she crawled up and settled on his lap now, he realized that he was dangerously close to erupting like a teenage boy in a back seat make-out session.

Fuck.

He grabbed her hips, stilling the barely perceptible rocking of her ass against his straining member. Incapable of breaking away from her luscious lips, he lowered her slowly onto the nest of blankets and settled over her, subtly testing the slack in his restraints. As his free hand captured the hem of her shirt, she broke her lips from his.

"It's ripped."

He blinked. "Ripped?"

"My shirt. I tore a hole in it."

He looked down. Linking his fingers in the offending tear, he ripped her shirt up the middle. "I did, too."

As the fabric fell open, he had to pause. Full, round breasts encased in a plain white satin bra. *Fuck.* He lowered his head, sliced the bra open with his right fang, and sat back up to admire the pert rosy nipples against the alabaster white of her skin. As he marveled at the total perfection of her breasts, she squirmed, her arms raising to cover herself. A snarl of warning detonated from him, freezing her in her place.

He took a deep, unneeded breath. "I'm sorry. I just really, really want to… just… don't try and hide your body from me. It's like taking water away from a dying man."

She rolled her eyes.

"I wish I was exaggerating," he murmured, lowering his head to flick his tongue against one tight bud. "But for vampires, modesty during sex is viewed as a tease and can bring out our predatory side at a very inopportune moment." He turned his attention to the other breast, tracing the fullness slowly, memorizing its contour. Her breathing had become shallower as her blood raced from arousal to the surface of her skin.

He traced his tongue from her sternum to her carotid artery before scraping the soft skin lightly with his fangs. "This is, for obvious reasons, the most common site for feeding. Close to the heart, easiest to monitor, easiest to access." He paused and reached up to brush his thumb across the smooth skin of her cheek. "Yes?"

She licked her lips and nodded. "You'll stop if I freak out?"

"Immediately."

He struck swiftly, pulling the nourishing AB into his mouth. Molly tensed as he broke the skin, but stilled instantly, one shapely leg bending up to caress his hip as he fed. Detaching his fangs from her neck, he licked her wounds tenderly to allow the coagulant in his saliva to halt the bleeding. "Well?"

Molly raised one eyebrow. "Let's just say my mind was not blown."

With a barking laugh, he rose on his arms and looked down at her. "You also aren't dead, so at least we're on the right track."

His lips traveled from hers, down the perfect slope of her breasts, tracing the waist of her jeans. His fingers deftly popped the button and tugged the zipper down. As Molly raised her hips to allow him to pull the clothing off, he was hit with an overwhelming scent of honeysuckle. Using the clamor of his restraints to center his lust, he pulled the jeans off and tossed them aside.

His own damp jeans were no help in controlling his pulsing erection. Only the obnoxious rattle of his chains kept him grounded as he took in the sight of the raven-haired goddess displayed before him in nothing but white panties adorned with…

"Does that say… Tuesday?"

"Yes."

"It's Sunday, isn't it?"

Positioning himself between her thighs, Dominic hooked a fang in the Tuesday-not-Sunday panties, caught Molly's eye, and waggled his dark eyebrows before pulling them slowly down.

"Don't rip them. They're a set."

"How many do you have left?"

"Tuesday and Friday. I think Saturday is under my bed, though."

Using his finger to pull the garment off her legs, Dom held the garment up for approval. Molly's pleased smile unknotted another rope in his stomach, her simple pleasure at having unripped Tuesday panties perfectly at odds with the sensual swell of her hips and deftness of her fingers as they traced intricate patterns across his shoulders. He reverently lowered his head into his own personal heaven and hell, running his tongue between her wet folds.

He was rewarded with a gasp.

Another slow lick savoring the taste of honeysuckle.

A low, throaty moan.

He focused his energy on the small nub, each flick of his tongue receiving praise.

A twitch of her hips.

A hand gripping his hair.

Nails in his shoulder.

Heels digging into his back.

Gasps, panting, whimpers.

He relished in every movement, every sound, cataloguing each moment while he stored them in his memory. As he slid one finger into Molly's taut body, her back arched and she began mumbling incoherently. Adding a second finger, he worked her slowly, before building up speed. As his tongue and fingers surpassed human speed, Molly's body began tightening around him.

He was torn between tasting her as she came or indulging in her femoral artery. As he debated internally, Molly's incoherence became a string of panted pleas to the gods interjected with cursing combinations he wasn't sure he'd ever heard. The intensity of Molly's approaching orgasm was pushing his own control dangerously close to the edge.

As her body began convulsing on his hand, he turned and bit into her thigh, his own orgasm threatening to overtake him as her blood hit his tongue and her body clenched around him. He allowed himself to relax into the moment briefly as Molly arched and moaned. As the tight grasping turned to soft flutters, he sealed the punctures and slowed his movements in her sensitive body.

He kissed his way up her glistening body, ignoring the twitch of his dick as it realized how close to the promised land it was. Molly's eyes opened, blinking and glazed. He gently ran his hand along her skin as he stared at her intently, awaiting her assessment.

Nothing.

One minute.

Two.

Four minutes.

Suddenly Molly shook her head quickly. Ebony eyes locked on aquamarine. She grinned, the slight crookedness of her eyeteeth mimicking tiny fangs themselves. "Mind half blown."

He rolled his eyes. "I call bullshit."

With a laugh, Molly's soft hands reached for his jeans. He held an unneeded breath as her fingers fumbled with the closure. After a few moments of struggling, his patience snapped and he jumped to his feet, metal clashing around him. He deftly unfastened the damp fabric before an aggravating realization entered his mind.

"I can't pull these off over the chains."

Molly sat up, brows furrowed. "Just push 'em

down as far as they'll go."

"I'm not doing this with my jeans around my ankles."

"Rip them off?"

He looked down. Briefly acknowledging that he could, in fact, be pantsless and at the mercy of his brethren for the foreseeable future, he determined it was a trade-off he was willing to make. As he tore the jeans up one side and down the other, he could hear Rhys chuckling quietly outside the cell.

Fuck Rhys.

"I would definitely ride that pony."

He met Molly's eyes, her appreciation for his assets emanating in her tone, her bitten lip, and in the blatant perusal of his form. She brought her hand up, crooked a finger, and gave a twirling motion.

"You're kidding."

"Turn around for me, pretty boy. I want to see all the goods."

With a short head shake, he turned around, then back again, ever conscious of the heavy restraints around his ankles.

"Now do a push-up."

"I'm not doing a push-up."

"Then get over here," Molly ordered, her knees falling open as she reclined into the nest of blankets.

"Yes. Ma'am."

"You know," he mumbled gruffly as he lowered himself on top of her, "you shouldn't be giving orders. You're the lesser species, and commands will not be tolerated by your..." His voice broke off, unable to verbalize the dark cloud hanging over their union. "They just won't be tolerated. Remember that."

Molly nodded solemnly, her playful mood dissipating. He watched her long, delicate fingers reach between them and grip him firmly. Teeth clenched, he couldn't tear his eyes away from her hand as it guided him into the folds of her wet heat. He took in a deep, unnecessary breath and pushed into Molly slowly, allowing her tight body to acclimate to his size.

Her female heat, so much more pronounced in his vampiric state, clenched around him, drawing him in further until he was fully sheathed in paradise. He could feel his core surging forth, desperate to connect, to take her hard and fast. With great control, he moved slowly, exposing his length to the chill of the cell before encasing himself again in the heat between Molly's thighs.

He felt her soft hands working through his tangled hair, trailing across his shoulder blades as contented sighs and gasps lessened the harshness of clanking metal. Faint voices in the hall entered his consciousness briefly before he was pulled back into the sanctity of Molly's body.

Her legs rose, wrapping around his slim hips.

"Do not restrain our kind," he muttered, continuing his rhythmic thrusting, "It's an act of aggression."

"But you…"

He paused briefly before slamming his hips into her at a bruising, punishing speed. "I. Am. Not. Your Master," he bit out, his frustration over their predicament reverberating in the cell.

As Molly went rigid, he halted and cupped her chin, guilt ricocheting through his head. "And never tense up. Don't fight against any position change. Expect to be put in any position your new M… expect to be tossed around like a doll. Stay limp, stay pliable." His voice cracked at the implications. "Please."

He was torn.

Torn between the welcoming heat of her body and the sobering bleakness of his cell.

Torn between his primal desire to savagely take all she could give and his male desire to satisfy his female.

Torn between losing himself in the imperfection of this moment and grounding himself in the knowledge she would be gone by next sunset.

Gone.

He rocked inside her slowly, the quiet clanking of his chains keeping his focus on the present, on the woman underneath him. As Molly's breathing grew quicker and shallower, he increased his speed and opened his eyes to watch while his connected female came undone.

Her hand fisted in his hair and pulled his lips to hers. As her body clenched around him and Molly's tongue ran across one fang, he released with a snarl. All thoughts left his head, the tension and frustration of the past month a distant echo as he came down from his high.

Molly's hands tangled in his hair, brushing the damp strands from his forehead as he slowly returned to his senses.

"We should play Twenty Questions," Molly suddenly said, pushing up on her elbows.

He blinked, his mind not fully firing as he slowly rolled off her and on to the blanket nest. Every muscle in his body was unwound, a complete relaxation unlike anything he'd experienced in either his human or post-life. Molly was busy cocooning herself in the nest, with only her onyx eyes peering out of the jumble of fabric.

Seconds, minutes, hours. He had no idea how long he and Molly lay curled up in the cell as Twenty Questions became Forty Questions before morphing into a long discussion about the advances in junk food options over the past three decades.

The longer he and Molly whispered in the stark room, the calmer he became. The pull of the connection no longer snapped against his mind, no longer intertwined with his every thought.

He was sated.

Complete.

Gone.

Without warning, his vampire core finally acknowledged Molly would be taken from him.

Hundreds of miles away, Mickey felt the break.

Chapter Eleven

In bringing Molly to Dominic, Rhys's agile mind had run through every scenario, assessed every obstacle, and created contingency plans for every possible outcome. Boy had been aware of the plan, though he had never been assured if Boy's silence meant he supported the idea. Between the two of them, with the strength and speed of age on their side, he was utterly confident in the situation.

What he hadn't accounted for was the connection.

The initial reintroduction of the pair had achieved more than he had anticipated. His brother had fought past his feral core quicker than expected once he removed himself, and his scent, from the cell.

That should have alerted him of what was to come.

The initial texts had come in quickly.

Group Kai: Location of Dominic stat

Group Boy: Secured

Group Kai: As of?

Group Boy: Now

Group Kai: Status

Group Boy: Resting

Group Kai: Mick?

Group Mick: Barely notice him. Background hum

Boy's and Mick's responses to Kaius bought him time, but he knew it wouldn't be long before the hauntmates were sent to check that Dominic was indeed secured. And he was. He was secured and having the strangest sex conversations he had the displeasure of hearing.

He had been the one secretly trashing the tacky Days of the Week underwear for two weeks. Worse than wedge heels, and a good reminder why he needed to double-check all purchase requests his Tenders made through the system.

Despite his distance from the haunt, Kaius was strongly linked to all he sired. Dominic's sudden change from savage to amorous could be explained through the rare dreams vampires had, but it wouldn't last long.

And Dom was lasting longer than Rhys figured he would.

One by one, the hauntmates had wandered through the bloodslave quarters and into the hallway where he stood guard. Boy had arrived first, his vacant eyes fixed on the open cell.

"All good, Boy. Thanks for covering with Kai. I'll call if I need you."

Boy moved to peek in on the couple.

"She's fine. You know it. Don't go in there. Your scent could set him off."

He turned and resumed his bloodslave duties, silent and stoic as always.

Nichol was the second visitor that night.

"Explain," Nichol demanded in his harsh baritone.

"Training," he responded, not bothering to look up from his Solitaire game.

"Explain."

Rising to his feet, he emitted a long, drawn-out sigh. "One night. The kid gets one night with his woman, she gets the basics, I don't have to fuck her and her constant insane commentary. Win, win, win."

Nichol cocked his head, then shook it in disgust. "Waste of time, what he's doing. In, out, walk the fuck away. Something's wrong with that kid."

He smirked at Nichol's characteristic display of contempt for females. "Leave Mini alone. Can I trust this won't be getting back to Kaius any time soon?"

With a short nod, Nichol had sauntered out of the hall and he had continued his futile attempt to block the sounds coming from the musty cell. As he completed what felt like his thousandth Solitaire game, a quiet humming indicated Jagg's arrival.

"Dangerous game you're playing."

He looked up, ensuring Jagg had a good view of his mouth. "Just cards, man. No one dies in a solo game."

Jagg's icy eyes had moved toward the open door of the cell. "We agreed to remove the girl."

"And I will. The trade happens tomorrow an hour after sunset. Cash in hand, pain in the ass gone, Dominic recovers and we return to normal. Badda bing, badda boom."

"Mini is aware of this?" Jagg questioned.

"He knows the purpose of the Tender training program. So yeah, he knows."

"This will make it worse."

"I tossed the kid a bone. One night. You can rat me out to Kai tomorrow."

Jagg narrowed his eyes. "You should've asked me about this."

He had risen to his full height, forcing Jagg to look up at him. "I don't question you about your training methods in the weapons room; don't fucking question me on mine."

As Jagg stormed off, Rhys focused his attention on the sounds echoing in the cell. Gasps. Whimpers. Skin on skin. Chains grating and striking against cement. Tuning it out, he had flopped back onto the hard floor and flicked through his music playlist until a pause in the din grabbed his attention.

He had spent centuries training Tenders throughout Europe and North America. He'd bedded thousands of women in his long life. Sex was no more intimate than a passing nod on a subway, no more exhilarating than a quick run in the woods. Women came, usually hard, and went.

Both his nature and his career kept him incapable of forming attachments to the multitudes of women he encountered and knowing the Tenders he trained would be warming the beds of other vampires never entered his consciousness past their training.

But as indifferent as he was toward his bedmates, he couldn't help but feel a bit for his youngest brother as Dominic fought through the knowledge his connected would belong to another vampire within hours. Hearing his hauntmate's voice crack nearly pushed him to cancel Molly's assignment.

Nearly.

Many discussions among the hauntmates had occurred regarding Molly, Dominic, and the connection. The consensus was that Molly had to go. Jagg assured the brothers that Dominic would survive the separation after an undetermined amount of "recovery" time. Nichol assessed that Molly, with her flightiness and ineptitudes, would be hazardous to

Dom's mental health in the long run. Mickey had called in to discuss his concerns that Molly may be bringing Dominic too close to primality than a vampire Dom's age could handle.

Kaius and Boy had remained mute on the subject, in both presence and voice.

He was stretching his long legs across the hall and contemplating how quickly he could grab a chair from the Tender bunker when he picked up a new scent in the musty air. He knew this scent. One of Dominic's specialties was a calmative pheromone, and that pheromone was quickly becoming stifling in the enclosed space.

Calmative pheromone.

"BOY!" he hollered as he shot into the cell to find an unconscious Molly, a diminishing heartbeat, and a feral vampire frantically dripping his own blood down the throat of the ashen woman. As he dove toward Molly, an enraged snarl erupted from Dom and he knocked Rhys into the wall, pulling the dying woman back into his arms.

Boy appeared in the doorway, his usually vacant eyes momentarily confused before he launched at the pulleys controlling Dominic's restraints. As the chains tightened, Rhys advanced on his snapping, growling hauntmate.

"Drop her," he commanded. "Drop her now on the blankets before Boy tightens those chains more and you smash her head on the floor."

Boy hesitated, assessing Dominic's intent.

Dominic tightened his grip, the creak of ribs crackling in the chamber.

With a quick glance at Boy, he lunged for Molly as

Boy yanked the restraints flush with the wall. Dom howled, his savage eyes locking on Molly, now unmoving over his shoulder. A flicker of regret before the unrelenting territorial snarl began again.

Boy had appraised the manacles and followed him quickly through the ascending hallways into the Tender compound.

****

"What the *fuck* just happened in there?" Rhys thundered, setting Molly roughly on her bed. "How did you not feel what the *fuck was going on there*?"

Boy's leveled gaze merely infuriated him further.

"Just… *fuck* … just do your thing. Fix her. Whatever it takes. Make yourself fucking useful," he hissed as he stormed out in search of Jagg.

Jagg.

Fucking Jagg.

He tracked Jagg down immediately after leaving Molly in Boy's hands. He found his closest friend scowling at his phone and texting angrily, a staccato hum in the air. He glanced up. "Kai is on his way. You should get out now."

Rhys leveled his gaze. "Tell me what happened down there."

"You were there."

"What. Happened."

Jagg hunched forward, resting his elbows on his knees. "What Mini knew in his mind didn't translate to the core. Remember Mickey's warning? That Dom is running on three separate waves, and they aren't talking to each other? My guess is once the core figured out what was going on, it went on the defensive."

"He was like that when we got there and it eased

when I left the room. What made him snap?"

"You tell me."

Fuck. When Dom went from trainer to lover.

He ran his hand through his hair. "How did Boy not notice Molly was in trouble?"

"That freaky pheromone is my guess. Molly wouldn't have known she was in danger, and he wouldn't sense any changes. Same reason you didn't notice right away. That shit works on us to a lesser extent, but probably just enough to distract you," Jagg mused. "If you take off now, I won't tell Kai I saw you. Maybe give it a few weeks."

He crossed the room and flopped onto a chair. "I don't run."

"Because you're a masochist."

"I thought I had it all worked out."

"The connection is unpredictable. Apparently, Dom's is slow to think and fast to react. Sneaky shit, though, using that scent."

"I should have foreseen this. My scent on her, her scent on me… it set him off every time. That kid has a freakish sense of smell," he commented, noting his bootless feet. "See? Can't run anyways. No shoes."

Jagg grinned. "You have maybe two hours before Kaius arrives. What are you going to tell him?"

"Maybe he won't notice his youngest is frothing at the mouth. I'll say Boy did it."

Jagg laughed, his quiet baritone echoing in the sparse room. "Seriously, Rhys. When Dominic went full-on primal, Mickey called Kai. If he felt that in Washington, you can bet Kai is going to have questions."

"Fuck," he grumbled for what felt like the

hundredth time. “Think I can plead good faith? I didn’t know he’d go all Super-Vamp on me. Jagg, it was nuts. Kid threw me like a pillow. Boy was straining to work the pulleys. Why didn’t you warn me connected assholes were so strong?”

“I did. I told you that you were playing a dangerous game.”

“Maybe ‘Hey, Dickwad. Be prepared for Dom to toss you like a fucking golf ball’ would have been more helpful.”

“I still warned you.”

The duo sat in silence for a few minutes before Rhys’s phone buzzed.

Boy: Tender stable

Rhys: How

Boy: Tender stable

“Molly kept calling me creepy for hanging outside the cell. I should let her spend some time with Boy. That bastard is weird as they come,” he commented. “Him watching over Mini is like crazy leading the crazy.”

Jagg grinned. “She all good?”

“Apparently stable. Hopefully well enough to go tomorrow. I need this hell behind me. Far, far behind me.”

****

Rhys despised imprisonment. The lack of luxuries and unappealing scents that accompanied every cell he’d been in never ceased to raise his ire. Being chained in his own haunt, steps away from affluence, only heightened his displeasure.

He was two months into the punishment Kaius had commanded for him, and he was desperate for a hot shower, a soft bed, and a wet woman. His cellmate had been a horrendous conversationalist, muttering only one word throughout the entire sixty-one days they had been bunk buddies. The warden was even more useless for intellectual discussion, silently arriving weekly to supply cold bagged blood and hose the prisoners down.

He had spent a large amount of his almost eight hundred years chained in dungeons. Cells. Vaults. Despite the terminology, they all had the same things in common. They were cold, hard, damp, reeked of mildew, and every noise reverberated off the walls and wreaked havoc on his exceptional hearing. The continual jolts from silence to clanking metal wore on his temper more than the actual imprisonment.

He knew he damn well deserved it.

He adjusted his position on the chilled floor and eyed his anchored cellmate. While the muscles of vampires were not permanently affected by immobility, weeks or months of the same position was uncomfortable at best. Dominic's lucidity had been returning at an alarmingly slow rate, and the warden felt it was in everyone's best interests to keep Mini as stagnant as possible until he recovered.

Recovered.

He snorted. His freedom was tied to the mental state of a rabid animal. Had Jagg elaborated a little more on the connection, neither he nor Dom would be here.

Thinking back, he realized that hell was infinitely preferable to his current perpetual state of dampness. Dominic stirred again, his head lifting, long matted hair obscuring his eyes as he searched the dim room.

"Molly?"

He sighed, leaning his head back. “Still just me, Mini.”

Turquoise eyes sharpened briefly, the glimmer of Dominic emerging before the oval pupils dilated and closed again.

At least the snarling had ceased a week ago.

Small victories.

****

Kaius sat stoically as Nichol flashed image after image of the growing Species Purifier followers. What had begun as a grassroots movement months before had taken hold and swelled, boasting a membership of thousands and growing incrementally daily. Not even a mind as dexterous as his could keep track of the increasing number of names and faces marching in streets around the continent.

The weekly reviews of anti-vampire rhetoric had become so lengthy, he had been forced to request that Nichol and Mick summarize the most aggressive and worrisome statements in nightly emails to himself and the remaining hauntmates.

The remaining hauntmates.

With Mick working three states away, Rhys imprisoned, and Dom…he glanced around the table. Nichol’s presentation was as concise and stringent as always, his only sign of strain being the subtle grinding of his fangs in the sullen atmosphere. Jagg perched on a stool across the table, his back hunched as he flipped a small blade through his fingers.

His incessant humming gave a hint of life to the quiet room, but the repeated minor melody did little more than provide a soundtrack to the unspoken frustration resonating from Jagg’s pale eyes. Through the monitor, he could see the toll that separation from the haunt was having on Mick. While his hosts were affluent and welcoming, Mick's mind had steadily drifted into a darkness that settled deep in his blue eyes.

Despite his limited time home in the haunt, even Kaius was becoming irritated with their situation on all fronts. Only Boy appeared unaffected by the weights pushing on the haunt.

He glanced back at the screen where Mick sat expectantly.

"My apologies. Please repeat."

Mick leaned forward, enunciating clearly for Jagg. "I said maybe it's time to regroup."

Jagg's humming ceased and the room fell completely silent as all eyes looked to him.

"You feel you're ready to return," he stated.

"I think… we think… things are getting bad out there and we need all of us there. All."

His unblinking eyes scanned the room slowly. "You've discussed this."

Slow nods.

"You."

Mick nodded in confirmation.

"Rhys."

Another nod.

"Dominic."

Mick's eyes flicked to Jagg. "Yeah, him too."

He contemplated the request. "No. You may return, Mick, but under close monitoring and with the understanding that any reversion will see you sent back to Washington immediately. Rhys will continue his punishment, and Dom hasn't shown enough lucidity to be released."

"Fucking bullshit!" Mick snarled. "We have Tender requests piling up by the fucking boat load, violence against vamps is hitting European levels, the bloodslave pool is shrinking, and we're sitting around night after night monitoring internet chatter instead of actually doing anything!"

The conference table was halfway to the floor before the hauntmates registered Kaius's movements. "Mind your tone, Mikhail," he hissed, his elongated fangs shimmering against the light of the computer screen. "I am well aware of what we are coming up against. More so than you do. More than any of you. I have seen this play out across millennia, child, and I promise you I am *well fucking aware* of our challenges!"

"We need to resume trade," Mick pushed back.

"Too dangerous."

"Then we need to make a move on the Senate."

"Too much risk."

"Then let's plan a relocation north."

"What we face is global."

"Then tell us what the fuck we should be doing," Mick snapped. "Other than playing on our goddamn computers night after night."

"I have to go online and order another table," Nichol mumbled, ignoring Mick and Kai in favor of returning his control room to rights.

"We are gaining intel. Knowledge is power," he retorted, "and we have unlimited access to knowledge in this day and age."

"Without action, knowledge is as useful as a fairy tale."

He and Mick locked stares, ovaled blue eyes

flashing with resentment and exasperation. Mickey leaned back from the camera, his arms crossing defiantly on his broad chest. "You used to be a leader, dad. We were the most advanced haunt in the Western world. We were fucking *legends*. Now we're sitting here holding our dicks while the world burns us out of existence."

****

The scent of mildew grew stronger the deeper into the bloodslave quarters Kaius went. His eyes flickered down the hall, noting the multitude of empty cells lining the deepest area of the compound.

Fucking legends.

The Tender training had been one of his greatest achievements, next to bringing over an unrivaled brethren of superior males. For centuries, he and the haunt funded their existence through the refining of women, schooled to meet individual requirements and desires, and sold for astronomic prices. He had initiated the shift to rescue as well, recognizing that the archaic ways of most established haunts were becoming an increased security risk.

It had also been him who had read the winds well in advance of the revealing of vampires to humanity, and the haunt had been ready with hundreds of bloodslaves during the few years of hunting in the open. While vampires had been dealt a brief reprieve from hiding in the darkness, the younger ones required far more nourishment than civilized society was willing to accept.

And it hadn't been long before all missing humans were attributed to the fanged ones. Bloodslaves were a form of damage control. An expensive, coveted form of damage control.

The idea had come to him while watching a pizza delivery commercial.

It had been him who insisted their haunt begin stockpiling blood as the novelty of vampirism wore down around the world. The compound's tremendous freezer system once held thousands of pints ready for delivery to those too injured to hunt their own. A little less than half full now.

Again, a late-night advertisement had inspired him. Neatly packed airless bags of sweaters and blankets. The order appealed to him.

He dug into his pocket to retrieve the key to the cell two of his stock had called home for the past two months. Dominic, his shackles holding his arms and legs flush with the damp cement wall, was in a restless sleep. Day and night had long ceased to run Dom's internal cycle, and he was almost grateful for the numerous nights he was granted a suspension from Dominic's id-driven emotions.

Rhys, on the other hand, was sprawled across the frigid floor with his long, tattooed arms behind his head as he grinned at him.

"Welcome back to our humble abode," Rhys drawled in an atrocious southern accent.

He sat, resting his head against the wall and closing his eyes. "Boy is keeping you fed?"

"Yeah."

"How is Dominic feeding now?"

Rhys arched to glance over at his suspended brother. "Better. He doesn't fight it anymore. Boy still has to open the bags, though, since Mini refuses to bite in. But he allows Boy to pour it down his throat, so that's an improvement."

He nodded slowly, contemplating. "How has he been handling his fangs?"

"Boy stopped pulling them a few weeks ago. No problems since. But Dom has been secured pretty tightly, too."

"So no more incidents?"

"Well, he can't reach his arms, so yeah, no more incidents. The mumbling hasn't stopped, though."

He frowned. By the end of Dominic's first month in the cell, he had begun muttering incoherently during his periods of rest. The frequency had increased as the territorial snarl dissipated, with "Molly" and "chains" the only discernible words.

He had hoped whatever link Dominic had formed during his core's failed attempt to turn Molly would fade, perhaps be taken over by the Tender's new master. He glanced over at his youngest.

Perhaps the female should have been put down after all.

"Do you think Dominic could handle being less restrained?"

Rhys paused. "If I say yes and he gnaws his arm half off again, do I add time to my sentence?"

"No," he chuckled softly. "I won't be extending your time here if Mini decides to make a meal out of himself. I feel he has enough control over his core now to avoid another extreme incident."

"The core is fucking insane, Kai."

"Yes, it can be. Have you noticed any improvements to Dominic's lucid moments? Is their frequency increasing? Duration? I am not always fully tuned to him."

Rhys rose to his feet, looming over his creator as he stretched his long arms out before crossing them over his chest.

He was beginning to despise that pose.

"What's this about, Kai?"

He remained seated on the cement. Amongst others of his kind, such a display of passive aggression would require a response from the old vampire. A forceful, bloody response. But amongst his own hauntmates, he met the display with an eye roll.

"Sit your ass down. I've had enough of back-talking children tonight."

Rhys cocked a brow and sat, his curiosity piqued.

"It has been suggested," he looked pointedly at Rhys, "that the unfolding global situation requires more action than I have currently authorized, and that our haunt needs to regain an active leadership role in the vampire community."

"So, someone thinks we need to stop jerking off and start militarizing."

He dropped his head onto his knee. "What is it with the masturbation references tonight?"

"Apparently, I'm not the only horny one."

"Dick issues aside, our blood reserves are hitting critical levels, we are three members down, and we are, at most, weeks away from the implementation of a tattooing law across North America."

"What's the big deal? The marks would be gone within days."

He looked meaningfully at Rhys's tattooed arms. "The government is aware of the use of mercury for permanence."

"And how the fuck would they know that?"

"We have some theories," Kaius stated, running his long fingers through his hair in frustration. "Nichol has been able to gain sporadic access to the White House servers and was able to intercept an email between a Senator Green and someone using the initials K.D. The email Nic found was traced to Pennsylvania, but the path became untraceable from there."

"What did the email contain?"

With a frustrated growl, he jumped to his feet and began pacing the enclosed space. "It would appear K.D. is our elusive Deepfryer manufacturer. The good Senator was looking for a good price for a bulk purchase."

Rhys stared blankly at him as the weight of the information registered and fused within Rhys's exceptional memory.

"K.D."

"Yes."

"Fuck."

Chapter Twelve

The faint scent of organic decay and earthy musk registered in her blurred mind long before Molly opened her eyes.

Rain again.

In that precious moment before movement rattled her collar, she could almost pretend she was home.

Dingy apartment home.

Acquaintance's couch home.

Tender compound home.

Dominic's cell home.

The musky odor brought her mind gently to that night in the cell. Her last night of imprisoned freedom, where she could move unfettered by links.

Dominic liked red, but rarely wore it because he felt it was too vampy.

He respected the Beatles but felt Elvis's influence on modern music was greater.

He had never eaten sushi.

And, as Dom and she had feared, he had snapped.

She had awoken the next night, bound tightly in the back seat of a minivan while a radio preacher extolled the virtues of humanity in its fight against the Beasts of Darkness.

And it was the turquoise eyes of one of those beasts that now kept her anchored to her ever-shortening survival rope.

She wanted to know more about him, wanted to

know if the inexplicable draw she felt toward Dominic was real or if she was romanticizing him more and more with every passing night in her new inhospitable surroundings.

As the dampness sent a shiver across her arms, her collar clanged softly and pulled her from those intense eyes, dropping her soundly into her reality.

Ensuring she had not tangled herself in her leash while she slept, she eased out of bed and carefully unkinked the links that had ensnarled themselves. The few precious inches the untwisted links provided may have little bearing on her movements now, but experience had taught her to secure the largest range of motion possible. Stepping gingerly toward the bathroom, she dragged her restraints across the ceiling track and ran an unbearably hot bath.

Dove preferred her pale skin to hold a pink tinge of health, and hot water was the quickest, most effective way to please her Master. It also gave her a few minutes of peace as her senses were drowned by the running water, the weightlessness of her limbs calming her while her hair swirled against her ears. The lapping of the minuscule waves shielded her briefly from the perpetual clinking of her leash throughout her waking hours.

Rhys, she thought in the solitude of the water's white noise, would be pleased with her ability to stand immobile for hours on command. Perhaps, if she saw him again, she would recommend Dove's patented Tender training system for those women prone to continual movement. Or disobedience. Or the very human twitching of muscles under strain.

It was almost Pavlovian in nature. Clink. Thwack.

Clank. Thwack.

"Master expects you downstairs in twenty minutes."

She rose reluctantly from her watery solitude. "Thank you, Diane. I'll be down in fifteen."

Dove, she had learned painfully, subscribed to the belief that five minutes early was on time and on time was late. And each minute of Dove's time that was wasted was worth five lashes on the backside followed by an hour of sitting motionless on the floor.

After her fourth reminder, she had figured out the unspoken rule.

Learning to dress around her collar had taken some practice, but she had quickly become an expert at shimming clothing up over her hips, then contorting her arms and shoulders to squeeze through the more open necklines of her approved wardrobe. The complementary kitten heels slipped on easily while she ran a brush through her damp locks.

Complementary kitten heels.

With the hours upon hours Rhys had spent training her to walk in high heels, he had spent no time teaching her how to assemble outfits. Upon discovering this deficiency in her training, Dove had taken it upon himself to teach her the precise combinations he preferred. It was simple. Dove would place several dresses and shoes before her, and then tighten her leash until she made successful matches. With correct pairings came full lungs. It was an effective method.

Reviewing the intricate path of tracks along the ceiling helped her center herself mentally. The precise measurements, the visual rigidity of the steel course against the glaring white paint of the ceiling provided a focal point for her mind.

Room by room, she memorized, studied, and practiced moving through the metal maze.

Imprinting paths in her mind.

Training her movements until they became instinctual.

A final glance in the mirror, a touch of lip gloss, and she was prepared physically to start her evening. With a practiced flick of her chain, she turned and moved hastily across her room and through the hall to the great room where Dove paced leisurely. Her presence was acknowledged by nothing more than a raised hand.

Stop.

Motionless.

Dove ended his phone call and assessed her appearance.

"Diane."

Diane appeared quickly, the rattle of her restraints echoing in the large room. "Master?"

"Its hair. I feel it could do with a cut. But its femininity is already so precarious…"

Diane backtracked her movements, then followed Molly's course to assess her more closely. "I could perhaps take a little off the bottom, then add curling to its morning regime. It may help soften that drowned rat look it seems so fond of."

Dove joined Diane, his cold hands running through Molly's hair. "Let's begin that tomorrow. Turn."

She turned hesitantly, battling her survival instincts to face away from danger.

"You've done well with its clothing, Diane. I'm pleased with the latest outfits. From the neck down, it's a perfect picture of delicacy."

Dove ran his icy hands across the cinched waist and fitted bodice of her teal dress before flicking the full skirt out for his appraisal. "And it's finally an acceptable size. Well done, Diane."

She was hungry.

Diane curtsied, pleasure at being complimented for her skills evident only in the slight upturn of her sour lips as her hard, gray eyes remained emotionless. "May I go, Master?"

With a short nod from Dove, the retreating clank of chains disappeared into the kitchen.

Dove moved silently to the ornate French doors and peered across the dark gardens. "I am expecting guests tomorrow evening. Formal wear is required. Am I to assume we will not see a repeat of last time?"

She nodded. "You will not see a repeat of last time, Master."

Last time. Two months seemed like two decades ago. She had pushed last time back in her mind, far behind the realm of consciousness. The only tangible reminder was a series of fading scars across her back.

"When my guests are pleased," Dove spoke quietly, the threat in his deep voice palpable, "I am pleased. And this meeting is… critical… to me." He turned, locking his gray eyes on her pale neck.

Molly tilted her head slightly and drew a preparatory breath before Dove's fangs sunk in.

No flinch.

No recoil.

Rhys would be proud.

The strain of her leash kept her head tilted back, her airway constricted against the unyielding steel.

A single track from the kitchen's labyrinth led to a garage she had never seen. She mentally traced a path from the locked garage door to her room before starting back at the door and reviewing less direct options.

Options were good.

A practiced relaxation.

Purely pliable.

With a quiet exhale, she began reviewing the placement of the dozens of metal stoppers scattered throughout the intricate track system. Maneuvering down the fourth instead of the fifth track in a room meant the difference between an uninhibited exit out the other side or a sudden stoppage and backtracking.

Dining room. Track two. No. Track three. Yes. Four. Five. No. Six loops back.

One no. Two no. Three yes.

Four no. Five no. Six back.

Turn. Approach from the other door.

A slight tightening of her leash. Sharp clinking morphing into a muffled clang.

The kitchen track system was the most difficult to navigate. The combination of intersecting pathways and stoppages was difficult to memorize and was further compounded by her limited unaccompanied time in the room.

Hence her current "acceptable size."

Some rooms were easier to master. Bathrooms, for instance, had three tracks leading to either the toilet, sink, or shower. Hallways had two paths with exits to each adjoining room. By following traffic rules and staying to her right, she had quickly mastered the basic navigation of the halls.

The system logistics were impeccable in their

design. The monitored mobility provided just enough physical freedom to complete tasks while the intricate pattern ensured all tethered to the system were constantly reminded of their confinement.

No track led to the basement. Though many ended at its door.

She maintained a perfect immobility of body while her mind ran the tracks from room to room until the pulling sensation was augmented by the cooling trail of dripping blood.

Her ears focused on Dove's retreating footsteps. She was dismissed.

Mentally reentering her surroundings, she moved quickly to the kitchen to receive her meal and instructions from Diane. The thin, angular woman with her piercing, weaseled eyes was waiting, scissors in hand.

"Sit."

She guided her chain along the appropriate track and sat quietly in the chair. Veined hands passed a brush violently through her black hair, pausing periodically to spray ice water on the locks.

A practiced snipping of scissors.

Aggressive brushing.

The gathering of supplies as Diane moved along her rat maze toward the fridge to assemble a cold, unappetizing meal.

She wanted bacon. Gummy bears.

"You'll wash your hair at night from now on. I'll be bringing a variety of curling irons before morning."

She nodded her understanding as she chewed the cold, gristly pork chops.

"I will also be bringing a variety of dresses to try

for tomorrow evening."

Another nod. The rice wasn't fully cooked.

"Master wants the rules reviewed this evening."

The milk was on the verge of spoiling.

"You will stay on your knees beside Master Dove's chair unless instructed otherwise."

Hard rice embedded in a back lower molar.

"You are not permitted to speak to anyone other than Master Dove and may answer only through him."

Annoyance of the hard rice eclipsed by a string of pork wedged between upper molars.

"All instructions will be carried out without hesitation or question. All. Instructions."

Better to remain thirsty than risk more of that milk.

"Be rested. Master Dove will be displeased if you are inattentive or do something ridiculous like faint."

Swiss cheese is so bland.

"You are to return to your room after your meal and wait for me. Master has instructed you to make an itemized list of mistakes you made last time. I will be by shortly to review it."

That was a lot of cheese.

She traced through the kitchen, washing her dish carefully before returning it to the cupboard. The shrewish Diane maintained her pinched scowl as Molly passed her and escaped to the solitude of her sparse room to complete her homework.

Last time.

It was a relatively simple task, numbering her errors.

1. I spoke without permission.

There were three unfamiliar vampires sitting on the sofa across from Dove when she entered the room for her evening perusal. In just under two weeks, she had learned many lessons in Dove's house. However, she had never been tutored in his expectations around company. Unsure of her place, she approached Dove warily, the distrust in her unexpected circumstances evident in her downturned gaze.

"Gentlemen, my Tender, Molly."

She should have moved quickly to her position kneeling beside her Master. She should have ignored the males across the room. She should have been smart, going with her trained protocol instead of being proactive in her learning.

"Good evening, gentlemen," she said, bobbing her head in a half-curtsey.

Her knees hit the floor before her mind registered the movement, the skin of her cheek stinging above a deep pulsing pain.

"Your displeasing face," Dove whispered in her ear, "remains intact only because I wish it so. Assume. Your. Position."

She rose, her dignity as fractured as her cheekbone felt. She moved cautiously to her place, kneeling quietly and steeling her eyes on the floor. She could feel the split skin of her cheek emitting a small stream of blood down her face. She let it roll, tiny drips hitting her folded hands before continuing their course across the contours of her wrists.

She dared not wipe it away.

2. I looked Master Dove in the eye.

She had spent the next few hours sitting motionless, dissociating herself from the pain of her cheek and knees by reviewing the tracks of the library over and over, forcing herself to imagine escaping from various spots of the cluttered room. The library was a particularly difficult room, as many pathways were interrupted by heavy pieces of furniture, and those pieces were periodically moved into new locations.

"…enjoyable taste, but it is a product of the Kaius Khthonios Haunt, so it is to be expected."

A low chuckle emitted from one of the guests.

Her ears targeted the sound, pinpointing the stalky auburn-haired vampire.

"Rhys Kaius definitely curates a quality Tender. I've considered purchasing one for myself. May I… sample his wares?"

"Certainly."

She had known three things the moment her eyes flicked frantically to Dove. First, she had fucked up. Second, she would be punished. Third, he had been watching her, anticipating her error.

The slimy vampire had enjoyed her wrist while Dove's belt found its way across the soles of her feet.

3. I displayed defiance.

Defiance. Rhys had warned her nightly that it was her defiance that would get her killed.

Sharp tongue.

Impetuous stomp.

Crossed arms.

No, no, no.

As the nasty, stout vampire finished his feed, his towering companions moved in close, their identical strides matching their interchangeable appearances. "May we?" they inquired, twin baritone voices echoing eerily in the room.

She stilled as her Master assessed her.

"Alas, gentlemen, I cannot risk my nightly

indulgence becoming too weak. You may, however, test its other attributes."

"No!"

4. I ran from my Master.

She leaped to her bloodied feet, the terror of the twins overcoming the agony of her torn soles. Then she ran.

Dove stood stoically.

The intersecting pathways made her attempt to flee jolting, scattered. The leash scraped across her neck when she overshot one track, then burned its way across her airway as it tightened, loosened, rotated.

Dove watched her movements intently.

She burst through the great room doors, tearing down the hallway toward her room when she heard her Master's voice. "I'll give you each an artery. And it lives, or I take her price from your bones."

Yes, completing the list was simple. Compartmentalizing the night, however, was less so. She placed her completed list on her bedside table and awaited Diane's unpleasantness.

Chapter Thirteen

The delicate crimson fabric draped gently over every curve, with the elaborate beading of the strapless bodice offset by the simplicity of the chiffon skirt that twirled and flipped with every movement. Long black ringlets fell loosely to her waist, framing Molly's pale skin and accenting her dark eyes. Diane had arrived early in the evening to direct the preparation, and even she had difficulty finding fault with the picture before her.

She was reviewing the path lines in the great room.

Diane was tense, her movements less graceful than usual and her thin lips sealed tightly to her yellowing teeth. She ambled around the bedroom, almost as though she feared leaving the small space.

The *buzz* of Diane's cell phone interrupted the solemn silence.

"Master is ready for you."

With the practiced flick of her wrist, she aligned her leash and strode swiftly down the hall into the great room. Upon entering, she was surprised to see she and Dove were alone, his expected company having not arrived yet.

Her lightning assessment of the situation allowed her to relax infinitesimally at the knowledge she was well schooled in the requirements Dove had in private. With a slow turn, she allowed Dove to peruse her attire, his lack of demeaning commentary a testament to the effort she had put into her appearance for the evening.

Dove gestured for her to assume her position, kneeling silently beside his chair. Taking care to avoid splitting or wrinkling the delicate fabric of her skirt, she knelt gingerly and limited her twitching movements to subtle pressure of each finger against her thighs.

"I expect your behavior to be as appealing as your appearance this evening," Dove murmured, evidently distracted by his anticipation of his guests.

She nodded, reminding herself no question was asked. Yes, asshole, I know what you expect.

As the minutes ticked by, she entertained herself by reviewing the kitchen tracks, then jumped to the multitude of pathways that led to the basement door. Right, right, five steps forward, left. Two steps, right.

Diane appeared at the great room's entrance. "Your guests have arrived, Master. Shall I see them in?"

"Yes. Direct them here."

She remained still, quietly hoping she and her crimson dress would fade into the mahogany of the floor. As footsteps approached, Dove rose to greet his company.

"Senator Green. Pleasure to meet face to face."

****

"It's still grainy as shit," Rhys grumbled, leaning forward for a better view of the screen.

"Shut. The fuck. Up."

"Maybe if I adjust the frequency…"

"Touch it and I'll rip your fucking hand off."

Nichol was in a sour mood, his latest gadget producing a less-than-stellar picture of the events unfolding. Rhys, his senses slightly reduced by the complete gluttony of blood and women over the past few nights, squinted at the monitor. "Fine. But I can't make out the house number."

Mick leaned in, his impeccable eyesight straining to read the address. "Four? Eight? Whatever. Louis will let us know when we touch base."

Nichol continued to fidget, disconnecting and reconnecting wires, adjusting dials, smacking the side of the monitor. "Fucking undetectable? More like fucking useless. Do we at least have sound now?"

Mickey nodded. "Yeah. I'll feel better when the picture is clearer, though."

With a frustrated growl, Nic resumed fiddling with the multitude of dials.

Rhys was almost regretting the last Tender he'd been with. He was definitely too full and too relaxed to be monitoring an infiltration. It had been hard enough keeping his wits about him during the negotiation of Gabby's sale, and he was pretty sure he'd lost money on the deal.

But after Dominic's uncontrolled feeding off her months prior, Gabby was anxious to get away.

And he couldn't deny her.

He glanced over at Kaius and was met with a knowing grin. Kai patted his stomach with a chuckle before returning his focus to the screen. He adjusted his position, taking care not to disturb the hunched vampire at his feet. Dominic had been fed and showered before being tethered to him. He hadn't spoken.

Mick let out a loud cheer. "You did it, you ginger-haired bastard! 448. We'll get the street name when we debrief. Nice work."

With a kick at Mickey's chair, Nichol joined the others, his eyes bouncing between the monitor, the speakers, and the screen. "Better hold. I paid a shit-ton for this."

"And you're certain this K.D. won't be able to track it?" Kaius asked, his awe at the advances in technology evident in his voice.

"Positive. You couldn't."

Kai nodded in acknowledgement. "Good point."

Rhys steeled his resolve to focus on the monitor when a shrew-faced woman opened the door. Her squinted eyes and pointed chin filled the screen.

"Fuck!" Mick exclaimed. "Yikes. Jeez. I mean… fucking hell. That's not a face that should open doors quickly."

With a smirk, Nichol turned the sound up. "She sounds like a harpy."

"Anyone recognize any of this? The woman? This house?" Kai asked, leaning forward for a better view. "You're recording this, right?"

"Of course," Nichol snapped. "Not my first rodeo, boss."

The other males, save Dominic, shook their heads.

The picture on the monitor jostled and bounced as the camera's wearer moved down a long hall and was ushered into a grand room where a tall dark-haired male stood.

"Senator Green. Pleasure to meet face to face."

Kaius dropped his head.

Rhys side-eyed his maker.

"You were right," Kai sighed, his hands running through his blond hair. "Kaspars Dovidas, you sneaky prick."

The males turned their attention back to the screen as Senator Green introduced his vampire bodyguard.

"Shaun Moen is accompanying me this evening. To level the physical playing field, of course. I hope you find this precaution acceptable."

Kaspars affixed his gaze on the vampire behind the minuscule camera. The other hauntmates stilled, willing the old vampire to remain oblivious to the technology. "Your age."

The camera jolted as its wearer bent forward, lifting the hem of his cargo pants. A fragment of a ring above his ankle was exposed before Kaspars Dovidas laughed.

"No problem, Senator. Your bodyguard is welcome. Please sit. Diane, a glass of wine for the good Senator."

He looked over at Mickey. "Thought you said he was around your age?"

"He is," Mickey grinned. "Louis's fifth ring never closed. So right now, our Kaspars Dovidas thinks Green brought a fifty-year-old vampire as backup."

Kaius let loose a barking laugh. "And how do you know this guy?"

"I fed off him in the late 1700s."

With a shake of his head, Kai returned his attention to the monitor. "Can you turn the sound up any more, Nic? Or tune out some of the distortion?"

As Nichol adjusted the sound settings, the males listened in while Dovidas and Green discussed their business dealings.

****

"You buy fifty machines outright, and I'll reduce my cost by ten percent. Anything less than fifty is full price."

Louis was positioned behind Green, the

microscopic surveillance camera tightly secured to the roots of his bright red hair. A tall, lanky male, he was prone to slouching and therefore tended to give the impression he was both nonthreatening and oblivious to his surroundings.

He was neither.

Louis Forbes was a rogue in life and a rogue in his post-life. His leathered, gaunt face housed mistrustful eyes that changed from blue to green to gray, as much a chameleon as their owner.

Tribal and religious tattoos from his human days laced down his lean arms and across his hands, which were currently tucked deep inside his jeans pockets. The vampire that had brought him over had sought to create a minion in the streetwise man and had only succeeded in creating his own destruction.

He did not take kindly to laws. Less kindly to those who attempted to force his compliance with them.

As it was two hundred years prior, his loyalty could be bought for a fair price and trumped for a higher price. Mikhail Kaius, however, was the exception. Initial meeting aside, he and Mickey had almost two centuries of history, most of it involving one bailing the other out of trouble without hesitation. So when Mick called, he answered.

The threat of Deepfryers held little weight for him. His nomadic existence meant he could easily slip from society to society, from country to country, with no ties or responsibilities outside of self-preservation. He had agreed to infiltrate Senator Green's security force solely out of allegiance to Mick.

His isolation made him excellent for undercover work. Despite his penchant for brightly dyed hairstyles, he blended easily into his environment, melting in and out of lives without notice. He kept his head facing Kaspars Dovidas as the two men hashed out the details of their unofficial contract.

When talk turned to less important legislature being presented, he took the opportunity to scan the room slowly, allowing the camera to pick up any identifying detail. Paintings. Furnishings.

A Tender.

He tilted his head, hoping the camera was picking up the woman sitting silently in the corner. Her hands flexed and relaxed rhythmically while her dark eyes flicked from side to side, up and down in no discernible pattern.

While not a purchaser of Tenders himself, he was aware that the pale, slightly malnourished woman kneeling at Dovidas's side was atypical. Her flitting eyes were hard, calculating. The set of her determined jaw was not the relaxed expression of a Tender being treated properly.

He had an inherent mistrust of women.

And an inherent sense of propriety regarding them.

Memorizing her features, he decided he would give Mickey and his haunt a heads-up and leave her situation in their hands. After all, any Tender in this territory was likely the product of Rhys, and every vampire knew Rhys's product.

As he assessed the woman, his eyes were drawn to the iron choker around her neck, its bulky links out of place against the delicate femininity of the Tender's dress. He followed the choker's path, noting with interest the attached chain which led to a metal track above her.

Keeping his movements inconspicuous, he slowly followed the metal tracks as far throughout the room as he could without noticeably turning his head. He traced the paths repeatedly, angling his head slightly differently with each pass to ensure the males watching his transmission saw what he saw.

Kaspars Dovidas was as much of an asshole in Memphis as he was in London.

And Moscow.

And pretty much everywhere he had been rumored to be during the past 450 years.

His business finalized, Senator Green had reclined back on the leather sofa and turned his attention from Kaspars to the woman beside him. "This here," he began, inclining his fair head toward the Tender, "she's one of those, what do you call them? Bloodslaves?"

"Not quite," Dovidas responded, his gray eyes darting up to meet Louis's. "More of a companion. What you call your 'girlfriend.'"

Liam Green laughed heartily. "Girlfriend. Our girlfriends don't take kindly to leashes, Sir. Am I right to assume she's one of those women who get off on the freakiness of you guys?"

"Perhaps."

"Huh," Green stood, moving slowly toward the hostile Tender. "Mind if I have a look?"

Kaspars watched unblinking as the senator crouched before the woman and reached one hand toward her chin. As the good senator's hand brushed against the pale skin, Dovidas snatched it away, the crisp sound of cracking knuckles breaking the silence of the room.

"Look does not mean touch, Green." His voice

acid, Kaspars maintained his grip on the elderly man's hand.

"My apologies," Green stammered before regaining his composure. "I wrongfully assumed you might…share…in the spirit of our newfound partnership. After all, I will be writing you a rather sizable check in the near future. Perhaps you'd entertain the idea? I've heard interesting things about these women."

"Jesus, no."

While Senator Green hadn't heard the whispered curse, Louis and Kaspars heard the woman's words clearly. His face impassive, he continued to observe the events before him. Interference would blow his cover, and a Tender was not worth forfeiting a mission. Kaspars glanced down at his female, a vindictive smirk playing across his chiseled face. "An alternative to a handshake?" he asked.

Senator Green smiled broadly. "Why, yes. I know you vamps aren't fond of touching. This would make an acceptable substitution."

Dovidas nodded his acquiescence. "On my terms, of course."

"Of course."

He turned his attention back to the solemn female, hoping the camera was picking everything up. He could smell her AB-positive blood as her teeth dug deep into her own tongue.

Chapter Fourteen

Dominic lay curled at Rhys's feet, long forgotten early in the surveillance. As the males made notes and pitched thoughts about the events unfolding on the screen, the immobile male had become one with the floor. His lack of participation in the charged discussions made him a fixture of the room, forgotten even by Rhys.

With his fullness still balancing along the rail of discomfort, he leaned forward in his chair, trying to reposition himself more comfortably as Molly's voice came through the speaker system.

"Jesus, no."

While the males had immediately identified Molly once Louis' camera had turned to her, none had reacted outwardly. An unspoken agreement of silence had filled the room as the vampires monitored the recent developments.

Molly did not receive the silence memo.

Upon hearing her voice, the curled gargoyle at his feet shot up, the dark head connecting with his jaw, sending shards of his right fang to the floor.

After two months of lifelessness, Dominic's eyes were alert, fixated on the hostile face of his connected.

Dom's reanimation set all males in the room on alert. After the initial shock, Kai moved quickly within reach of Dominic, prepared to restrain him. Nichol was poised to pull the plug on the monitor, with Mickey shooting across the room to block the exit.

Dominic had merely stared, his eyes narrowing as they took in Molly's circumstances.

Rhys could feel his tongue slicing and healing, slicing and healing as he ran it along his shattered right fang. He leaned forward, attempting unsuccessfully to relocate his jaw, and locked on to Nichol with an unspoken question.

Nichol was quick to move, muting the sound and turning off the monitor before scribbling a quick note and passing it to Rhys.

Still recording. All good.

He quietly slid the message to Kaius. With a nod of acknowledgement, Kai turned his attention from Dominic to Rhys. "Need help?"

Rolling his eyes, he leaned closer to Kai and prepared himself for the shot of pain as Kai snapped his jaw back into place with ease.

****

Dominic couldn't pinpoint which came first, his physical reanimation or his mental one. It didn't matter, though. He was cognizant, in control, and feeling more vampiric than ever. His senses were on alert, cataloguing every piece of information he could glean from the brief time he witnessed Molly on the monitor and assessing every nuance of his hauntmates as he pieced together what was unfolding.

He knew that room.

He'd seen that vampire.

He turned slowly away from the empty screen and rose to his feet, the clanking of metal bringing his attention downwards. Cocking his head, he noticed the manacle and chain connecting him to Rhys. Aware that all eyes were on him, he slowly scanned the males one by one.

“Where’s Jagg?”

Kai answered warily. “Memphis. Acting as middle man between us and Louis.”

“And Louis is…?”

“Our undercover guy. Friend of Mick.”

He nodded. “Anyone going to review the past…”

“Little over two months.”

“… little over two months with me?”

Silence.

“Alright. Anyone want to explain to me what the fuck is going on right now?”

While his tone was agitated, he felt completely stoic, focused. Perhaps for the first time in his existence, he felt regulated. Ordered. Thoroughly controlled.

Mickey and Kaius appeared to be picking up the same auras, as both males relaxed slightly into their chairs.

“We’re doing recon on some shady shit between a Senator and one of our own,” Mick began. “Louis, that’s the guy on the inside, is posing as a bodyguard for one Mr. Senator Liam Green. Two weeks ago, Nichol picked up enough chatter to link a vamp with the initials K.D. to Senator Green. K.D., commonly known as Kaspars Dovidas, is negotiating a sale of fifty Deepfryers with Green. Green, in turn, is pushing bills through to make Deepfryers legal. Dovidas stands to make millions off the initial sale, and currently holds, get this, the only patent on a North American Deepfryer. Tonight was the first time we were able to get a positive ID on Dovidas, though…”

"I suspected K.D. was Kaspars when Kaius first brought it to my attention. Obviously, Kaspars is the Master Molly was sold to. But it was only confirmed tonight," Rhys stated, no remorse in his tone.

He blinked. *Complete control.* "What did you know ab… no… what *do* we know about this Kaspars Dovidas now?"

Kaius leaned forward, large hands running through his blond hair. "More than we have time to discuss tonight and more than you're ready to know. Louis should be touching base with Jagg right about now. The night is running out and I want no discussion while we are not all at our peak. Once Jagg calls for a debriefing, you're all expected to feed and rest. Tomorrow night will require everyone in prime mental condition. Am I clear?"

With muttered acceptance, the males resumed a muted vigil around the conference table.

Recognizing the authority in Kaius's tone, he backed down. Despite the questions he had regarding the events of the past two months, he could sense that logically this was not the time to delve into it.

Logical.

Focused.

If he had to label how he felt, the only term he could apply was 'Kaius-y'.

Fifteen minutes of silence passed before Kaius's phone came to life with a text message. After a quick exchange, he tossed it on the table for the hauntmates. When Rhys refused to stand, he craned his neck to see over Mick's shoulder.

Jagg: Eagle has landed. Now?

Kai: Conference call 8pm tomorrow. Yes?

Jagg: Yes
Kai: Have all you need for 2nite?
Jagg: Yes. Don't text speak.
Kai: :)

Kaius looked around the room. "I think we'll call it a night. Rhys, Dom, you two will remain tethered for now despite recent developments. Boy will be on hand should you need him. And Dominic? We're on this."

He nodded and glanced over at Rhys. "Sorry."

"No worries, Mini. Mobility will be significantly easier now that you aren't a drooling lump."

He followed Rhys's cue, his chain keeping his stride long to match that of the elder male.

Rhys maintained two bunkers in the haunt. As they passed the hall to the Tender training area, he knew Rhys had decided to spend the day in his quarters where the rest of the hauntmates resided.

"We're stuck in these clothes until tomorrow. You going to be ok?" Rhys called over his shoulder as he opened his door.

"All good."

Rhys led them over to his bed. "Well, I guess we won't be maintaining status quo."

He raised a brow. "Status quo?"

"Yeah," Rhys said with a grin. "You've been curling up on the floor beside the bed for the past two weeks. Kind of like my own little puppy. My Domidog."

"I fucking hate you."

"And you probably should," Rhys stated. "Boy is delivering a couple bags for you. I'm still good. Once you're fed, you take the wall side, I'll take the door side."

He frowned. “Why do you get the door side?”

“Because I’m physically dominant and it’s my job to keep your fragile little ass safe.”

“I really fucking hate you.”

“As you should.”

Boy arrived with a brief knock before he entered, deposited the bagged blood, and exited without a sound. The tethered pair moved in sync to fetch the bags before retiring to the sofa.

“Mini, once we know more about our plan tomorrow, I’ll fill you in on what’s gone on since you’ve been… incapacitated. How are you holding up?”

He scented the blood bag and assessed himself. *Controlled. Focused.* “To be honest, I think I feel like you always do.”

“Annoyed? Horny? Disgusted with existence in general?”

He grinned. “Like a vampire.”

One eyebrow cocked. “Seriously?”

“Yeah.”

The males sat in silence as he choked down his meal, then moved in coordination to the large bed. Rhys regarded the situation. “If we get on from the end, then there won’t be any awkward crawling over each other thing.”

“Aren’t you supposed to be all open and not weird about this shit?” he muttered.

“Aren’t you supposed to shut up?”

With a snort, he hopped onto the mattress, dragging Rhys’s leg with him. Gathering his footing, Rhys followed and lay back, placing his tattooed arms behind his head.

"Get some rest, Mini. Tomorrow is going to be pretty intense."

"Sounds good."

"And if anything, and I mean anything, feels off, wake me. I'd rather that than waking up to you chewing on my arm."

"Okay, captain."

"Good to have you back, Mini. Like Kai said, we're on this."

****

Dominic saw it all when he fell asleep, snippets of scenes pulled from deep in his subconscious. Each image held a clarity that dreams didn't usually possess, a haze of emotion tinging the visions as they flashed across his mind. Even now, lying motionless on the bed, he could recall every image perfectly, could feel everything as intensely as he had at rest.

The room.

The vampire.

The thick collar clasped tightly around Molly's neck.

The fear.

The pain.

He stared at the ceiling, willing his body to remain completely immobile to avoid alerting Rhys as his fully awake mind continued to drag up image after image of his connected female.

Chapter Fifteen

Kaius had spent the entire day prioritizing his knowledge and theories regarding Kaspars Dovidas, the Deepfryers, Senator Green, and the extent of his own role in the unfolding events. Political reform was occurring far quicker than he had anticipated as citizens flocked to the anti-vampire movement en masse.

The few grassroots movements lobbying for equality found themselves the targets of the Species Purifiers, the most vocal and influential of the anti-vampire movement. Shouted down at public forums, exposed online, and attacked both physically and verbally on the streets, vampire supporters had gone quiet, their opinions largely held close to the chest.

He couldn't blame them.

He had determined days ago that attempting to thwart changes in laws would be a poor choice of action. There was neither the time nor the support to halt the pending bills and placing his haunt members into the public realm would be akin to waving a red cape at millions of bulls.

Survival of the hauntmates was first and foremost.

Nights earlier, he had broached the idea of moving, relocating to a more remote location in a less hostile country. The motion was met with snarling profanity and quickly dismissed as a course of action.

This left him with the unenviable position of leading his haunt, and in turn the hundreds of haunts scattered throughout North America that looked to him for guidance, in guerrilla warfare. The past two weeks had been spent researching the key players in government and their links to various civilian and vampire enterprises.

The discovery of Senator Green and his link to Kaspars Dovidas was a lucky one. Locating and disabling Deepfryers had risen to the top of the list of targets, and Nichol was fast-tracking his acquisition of one for investigative purposes.

Perhaps Dovidas had a spare he was willing to part with.

He was far more familiar with the sadistic vampire than he could let on to the others. They had shared a complicated history over the centuries, and his own personal battles placed him in a precarious position when dealing with him.

Kaspars had been present at several mass slaughters in his 450 years, whispering in the ears of the politically corrupt or mentally unsound. He thrived on chaos, enjoyed the screams of dying men far more than most other vampires did, and he had made his fortune negotiating black market weapons deals over the past four centuries.

Dovidas was a master at game-playing, the king of chess. He was known for his ability to set up his pieces perfectly, escaping unscathed when the proverbial shit hit the fan.

He would have to tread carefully in this game and keep his presence under the radar.

Molly would be, once again, a complicating factor in tonight's decisions. Dominic's sudden awakening was both a relief and a source of frustration. Had Dom remained oblivious to the world around him, the possibility of Molly becoming a casualty would be a regrettable, but unimportant, detail.

It was widely accepted amongst the North American haunts that while civilian deaths were always to be kept to a minimum in any raid, human members of a vampire's retinue were exempted from this due to their ties and often extensive knowledge. With Dominic cognizant, any plan would require extracting Molly safely.

And that was definitely complicated.

Dom's burst back into reality was so sudden that neither he nor Mickey had sensed any change prior to Rhys's jaw being sent halfway across the room. The males had since been monitoring the youngest brother, anxiously awaiting a reversion. Historically, Mini was easily detectable.

His borderline control and fluctuating anger was often at the forefront of Kaius's mind, refusing to sink into the consistent hum of existence where his brothers resided. Now, Dominic blended in so perfectly with the others that he was left unsettled in anticipation.

With an acknowledgement of his eight p.m. deadline, he laced his combat boots and strode down the hall to Rhys's bunker. Boy was standing guard, motionless and mute. With a nod of dismissal, Boy disappeared down the hall toward the bloodslave quarters to continue his work stocking the freezers.

He knocked, knowing Rhys and Dom were already up and expecting him.

"Come on in," Rhys called. "Your brat is driving me insane."

With a chuckle, he entered the room. Rhys and

Dominic were lounging on the sofa, arms crossed and their tethered legs stretched in front of them. "Would you gentlemen care for a few minutes apart?"

Chained legs extended in his direction and he moved forward, pulling a key from his back pocket and unshackling the males.

Rhys bolted for the shower, steam quickly pouring from under the door.

He turned to Dom. "You are well."

Dom nodded. "Yeah. How long will I be tied to Rhys?"

He contemplated the thought. The rationale for tethering had been two-fold. It served as a safety containment measure for Dominic while doubling as a continuation of Rhys's punishment. However, with Dom's apparent returning to a more controlled, vampiric version of his former self, he was prepared to release the males if tonight's discussions went smoothly.

"I'll re-evaluate the situation before dawn. Tonight, we will be reviewing our options regarding Dovidas. And his retinue."

"And you're going to see if I go nuts when Molly gets mentioned."

"Something like that."

"Fair enough," Dominic replied, brushing one of his shaggy dark strands from his eyes.

The shower room door was flung open, steam billowing into the hall. "Your turn," Rhys muttered as he crossed the room to his closet.

"Put some fucking pants on!" Dom barked as he bolted to the shower.

"Precisely what I'm over here doing."

He stared at the ceiling, having witnessed Rhys's immodesty far more than he cared to over the centuries.

****

Shortly before eight p.m., the conference table was buzzing. Kaius monitored the electric charge of excitement bouncing through the room, ensuring it stayed within manageable levels for Mickey. The hauntmates were eager for action, restlessly awaiting the video call from Jagg and Louis. Their chain reattached, Rhys and Dom sat side by side as Mick gave Dominic a quick rundown of his relationship with Louis.

"So I'm standing there, press ticket in this stupid hat and these brown pants that are three inches too fucking short, and who do I see looking all suave in a black security suit? Fucking Louis. I managed to get a photo of my loss while that smarmy fuckup stood a foot away from her."

"So how much did you lose on the bet?" Dom asked. Kaius grinned at the visual of Mickey playing dress up to see who could get the closest to Marilyn Monroe. It wasn't often he was privy to the antics of his spirited second-youngest.

"One grand and my dignity," Mick replied, a hand running through his hair.

"That's harsh."

"I hate brown pants."

The ringing of the computer screen put an end to Mickey's tales of some of the shenanigans he and Louis had pulled off over the years. With the click of a mouse, Jagg's icy eyes came through the monitor. The hauntmates angled their bodies toward the screen to facilitate smooth communication with the quiet male.

"Jagg. Good to see you. Is Louis with you?" he began.

Jagg nodded, the screen bouncing as he adjusted the distance between himself and the camera. Louis, his fire engine mop of hair spiked tall, appeared beside Jagger. "Hey."

He flicked his wrist, indicating to Jagg he was going to speak. "Louis Forbes. You already know Mickey. Beside him is Nichol, Rhys, Dominic, and I'm Kaius."

Louis's eyes studied each male as the introductions were made. "Nice to finally match faces to names. Your haunt is well known, even amongst those of us who prefer a less structured existence."

"Nichol and I reviewed the footage early into the morning," he stated, anxious to plan a course of action. "You did well. We've established the key players, the locations, and a general layout of Kaspars Dovidas's main rooms. Is there anything the camera did not pick up that you noticed?"

Louis leaned back, tattooed hands disappearing behind his head. "Nothing regarding Green or Dovidas. However, and this is probably in the realm of the infamous Rhys, the Tender I caught on film is malnourished. Dovidas has her leashed to an intricate track system that runs throughout the house. She showed signs of physical abuse, and as you saw, Dovidas seems to pimp her veins out as punishment."

A quick burst of fury emitted from Dominic before his focus resumed and Kai could sense the calculated control take over.

Rhys leaned forward, meeting Jagg's eyes briefly before addressing Louis. "The Tender, Molly, will be a consideration in any plan of action we make. We have the added complication of her being connected to one of our hauntmates."

Louis's brows raised. "Connected? How did she end up with Dovidas?"

Sparing a glance at his youngest, he leaned forward to respond. "Long story short, the connection caught us all by surprise and we decided separation would be best for all involved."

Louis tossed his head back, a roaring laugh erupting before he composed himself. "And your haunt is considered to house the greatest minds in the Americas. So, who's the lucky guy? Mick? You holding out on me?"

"Not likely, man," Mick snorted. "The young one, Dominic. Over there."

Louis leaned into the camera, his angular features filling the screen. "How old are you, kid?"

"In my third decade."

With a low whistle, Louis resumed his position. "Well then. I can see how that would be a bit of a surprise. How are you holding up?"

"Fine," Dom responded to the unknown vampire with a frown.

Louis turned his attention back to Rhys. "How long have they been separated?"

"Over two months."

"Ah. So he's coming out of the looney phase early. I take it none of you are connected, then?"

The hauntmates shook their heads as Jagg spoke up, "I was once. Briefly."

"Separation does nothing to eliminate the connection. Except make it tougher on the male during the crazy phase," Louis stated.

Kaius mentally filed the information away for later assessment.

"But since that's over, kid, you'll be fine as long as the Tender gets returned to you. Preferably alive."

"How do you know so much about this shit?" Mick interjected. "You've never been the victim of connection."

"I'm a fantastic observer."

He flicked his wrist again for Jagg. "So with this added situation with the Tender, we will need to proceed with much more stealth than initially intended. Our goals are threefold. One, get the woman out alive. Two, locate wherever Dovidas is storing those Deepfryers. Three, Kaspars's head on a spike."

"And our good Senator?" Louis inquired.

"Without Kaspars, we believe he has no vampire network and we will resume monitoring him. Eliminating Dovidas will send a message to any other potential procurer of Deepfryers that we will not sit by and allow such traitorous actions."

Louis's gray eyes narrowed before he responded. "If you need me, I'm in. I could use a break from being an apathetical bastard."

He bowed his head. "Your offer is both appreciated and accepted. We'll need you in a far bigger role than you likely expect. What are your strengths? I assure you, any information you share will not leave the confines of this room."

"And am I to assume there will be reciprocation of info?" Louis inquired.

The male's sense of survival gave him more confidence in the young vampire's skills.

"Yes. In fact, we will expose our strengths first. I trust Mickey's skill in character judgement, which places you higher than most on our roster," he responded. "Is everyone in agreement?"

A round of nods.

"Nichol is our tech guy whose primary strength lies in language acquisition. He is fluent in all commonly spoken tongues, with a particular finesse for regional dialects. Mick, as you are likely aware, is strongly empathic with an added proficiency in strategy. And unlike others with strong empathic skills, Mick has managed to maintain his own sanity and identity…"

"Which means I'm only slightly freaky, but you already knew that," Mick interjected.

"Rhys, while being our Tender trainer and primary means of financial stability, is also gifted with agility and strength…"

"Which ties into the whole Tender training, obviously," Louis chuckled.

Rhys grinned with satisfaction.

He leveled Rhys with a look, refusing to show amusement when his tattooed child kissed air in his direction. "Dom, despite his age, has heightened senses. He is also a Soother, albeit an untrained one."

Louis whistled again, impressed. "Been a long time since I met one of those."

"Jagg is our weapons specialist due to his skill and his speed. He's our ghost when needed. I have strength and the ability to maintain a link between myself and my brethren across vast distances."

"You, Kaius, are legendary for your strength. I wasn't aware of the link, though. Can you feel Jagg right now?" Louis asked, his curiosity about the old vampire apparent in his expression.

"I can. He's currently uncomfortable with your proximity."

Louis shuffled over a bit before turning to Jagg. "Should've said something, man. Didn't mean to crowd you."

"Louis will snuggle the fuck outta you if you let him," Mickey laughed as Louis flipped him the middle finger.

"All right," Louis started, "Since our sharing circle is almost complete, tell me about the big guy in the back of the room. Then I'll spill."

He looked over at Boy. "He's not involved in this operation and will be exiting the room." Boy moved to the door.

"Not so fast," Louis growled. "Is he of the Kaius blood?"

He met Louis's eyes. "No. However, he has been a part of this haunt for many centuries. I assure you, on my word, he's trustworthy. Boy runs our bloodslaves, fills orders, and pulls security duty within the compound as needed. His involvement in haunt actions doesn't often extend past those requirements."

Louis took in the information silently and sat back as he weighed the reputation of Kaius Khthonios against the unknown male. "Fair enough. Once he vacates, I'll provide my abilities."

Boy left the room, leaving the hauntmates in a stalemate with Louis until the suspicious vampire felt he wouldn't be overheard.

"I managed to end my sire during my fifth decade. My age rings stopped forming from that day on. I'm over two hundred, but inspection places me under sixty.

I specialize in short term hypnosis which usually gets me where I need to be when I need to be there. I also discovered I have the ability to blend in easily. Despite the hair, I'm readily overlooked and quickly forgotten. Much like I'm assuming Ghost-man beside me is."

Jagg turned his attention from Louis to the camera. "I observed Louis at work. His hypnosis skills are well developed. Entrance into Senator Green's security force would have been impossible in such short time without it."

"Is your hypnosis skill effective on vampires?" Kaius asked, part of him hoping it was, the other wary of the implications of such a talent.

"No," Louis answered back. "I haven't had enough long-term interactions with our kind to practice and develop the ability. However, I think I could hone that craft as well, as I've improved my capabilities significantly since I hit the end of my second century."

He hummed his response noncommittally, unwilling to offer any assistance of such an aptitude that could, at some point in the future, be used against his haunt. "Now that we're all familiar with each other's abilities, let's move on. Louis, we usually spend our first planning stage tossing out ideas before reviewing, eliminating, and tweaking. Is this acceptable?"

"Anything to watch your haunt at work, Kaius."

The ideas came fast as the males suggested various methods of attack, ambush locations, intelligence required, and potential allies for both themselves and Dovidas.

"There's a chance whoever Nichol's European Deepfryer contact is has connections to Kaspars."

"The Zorias haunt in Washington where I stayed last month would stand with us. Supply any backup needed."

"I can access city records and get a blueprint of the Dovidas house, but any renovations made may not be included."

"Do we have time to scout his schedule? Maybe grab him that way instead of mounting an ambush on his turf?"

"Any way to communicate to Molly what's being planned? Maybe she can assist from the inside."

****

I'm going fucking insane.

Dominic subtly dropped his hands under the table and dug his fingers into his kneecaps.

Mick was talking.

Mick. Focus on Mick. Focus. On. Mick.

The mantra did little to stop the scenes unfolding in the recesses of his mind.

I'm going fucking insane.

The sounds rolled through his head in waves, as though he was immersed in a pool and straining to listen through the lapping water. He could pinpoint Molly's voice with ease, but her form remained just outside his view, just outside his grasp. She was responding to a male, her answers clipped as his baritone rumbled in his head without clarity.

"Yes, Master."

His fingers tightened on his knees, threatening to draw blood.

He spared Kaius a quick glance, grateful the old vampire was fully immersed in breaking up a heated argument between Rhys and Mick.

The male voice continued to trickle wordlessly into his mind, the tone growing sharper. He shifted in his seat, bending down to feign the tying of his boot laces as he closed his eyes and fought in vain to bring the scene into the forefront.

A flash of a blue skirt against a mirrored floor.

Impeccably polished men's shoes moving closer.

"My apologies, Master. Please."

He straightened in his seat, violently shoving the daydream back as he refocused his attention to the task at hand.

****

As dawn approached, a tentative plan was reached and Dominic felt a renewed sense of readiness. The hauntmates disconnected communication with Louis and Jagg and went their separate ways to rest for the following night. When he and Rhys moved in unison, Kaius halted their exit.

"I'll untether you now. However, for the foreseeable future, you're roommates. Boy will spend his day at your door, Rhys, should there be any change in Dom's status."

"Thank fuck," Rhys sighed. "I wasn't in the mood for another night of Twitchy McKicksALot."

"Whatever," he snarked back as Kai unshackled his leg. "You're the one rolling and moaning half the night. Like sleeping beside a nightmarish toddler."

Kaius stepped back from the bickering twosome. "Off you go, kids. Seven o'clock start tomorrow."

Rhys was still kicking the chain off his ankle when he shoved him over and bolted to the bunker.

Chapter Sixteen

Molly couldn't stop yawning. The weekly grocery delivery was running late, and she was expected to help receive, process, and store the items before she could go to bed. It had been a long week, with Dove's temper shorter than usual and his nourishment demands higher than the typical two or three mouthfuls. But on the up side, he was so focused on preparing his Deepfryer order that her time around him had dwindled down to little more than a quick snack on his way by.

Diane sat opposite her in the receiving room, her pinched features further scrunched in concentration over a crossword puzzle she was never able to complete. The buzz of the gate was met with a glare. "Get that."

The video monitor was mounted beside the security panel, and it always took her a few moments to remember the order of the buttons. As the delivery man's face appeared on screen, she buzzed him in and moved to the door to await his arrival. Reconfirming him through the peek hole as she was trained, she opened the door and accepted the first of many loads of groceries and household disposables.

As the last of the grocery bags was transferred to her, she felt the hand of the man latch to hers as a paper was shoved quickly into her palm. The man left swiftly, leaving her to secure the door behind him while discreetly pushing the note into her cleavage.

While Diane confirmed each purchased item, Molly put them away hurriedly. She knew the paper was not the receipt, as Diane was currently comparing the receipt with her notes and the groceries. Possibly a flyer, though it felt too small to be that. Whatever it was, the note was her first interaction with the outside world in almost five months, and she was relishing in the possibilities.

With a huff, Diane finished her calculations. "Four things missing. Incompetent jackasses. I guess I'll give them a call. You might as well go to bed. Take your iron and C vitamins with you. Master says you taste bland lately. Double the dose."

She curtsied, anxious to leave the presence of the vile housemate and escape to the sanctity of her bedroom. She moved with ease through the halls and into her room, closing her door before scurrying to the bathroom where she could examine the note with enough warning to hide it should the first door be thrown open.

Diane was not one to knock, and locks were not allowed.

Pulling the crinkled note from her bosom, she unfolded it gingerly for fear of ripping its contents. A masculine scrawl, tall and thin with a strong right slant filled the paper.

Good Golly Miss Molly
The Boys are B…

With a disappointed sigh, she refolded the note. *A song list.* Unsure of what she expected it to be and unhappy with everything it wasn't, she crawled under her blankets, flicked her light off, and fell into an exhausted sleep.

****

Molly sat upright with a start.

A song list.

Good Golly Miss Molly.

Her hand grasped frantically for her lamp as she hung over the edge of her bed, feeling between her mattress and box spring for the small note she had hidden. With the paper in hand and the dim light illuminating her small room, she opened the folds hurriedly.

Good Golly Miss Molly
The Boys are Back in Town
The Pina Colada Song
All Apologies
The Delivery Man

This was something. She placed the note on her knees, her fingers running along each handwritten line.

Good Golly Miss Molly

Easy. Dominic had made that reference the night she met him, which made him the most likely author of the message. She ignored the quick pang his name caused, focusing instead on the hints contained in his letter.

The Boys are Back in Town

Boys. Dominic, Rhys, maybe Mick with the haunted eyes. The miserable freckled male. Perhaps Boy? Regardless, she was certain the clue referred to more than Dominic, and the surge of hope that The Boys might get her away from Dove had her bouncing.

The Pina Colada Song

She paused and re-read it a few times, a smile on her lips when she remembered the correct name of the song. Escape. Hell. Yes.

All Apologies

Face value. Get me out and all's forgiven, she thought, tears burning her eyes at the idea someone missed her, someone was thinking about her, and someone not only knew where she was but also wanted her back. Even if that someone couldn't properly name bass guitarists and had treated her wrist like his personal fountain.

The Delivery Man

The missing items.

The delivery man with the incomplete order would be returning and she needed to have her message ready.

****

"You can't seriously tell me you all thought this would just go away on its own. I mean holy fuck. Dominic, if you don't sit down, there's a good chance I'm going to remove your kneecaps."

Louis watched with amusement as Dominic glanced his way before taking up residence in front of the door. Over twenty-four hours had gone by since Nichol had intercepted a phone call from Dovidas' maid regarding her incomplete grocery delivery.

Mick had taken the call, his Southern accent lacking but his manners impeccable. Miss Diane had been assured the items would be delivered the following morning, complete with a gift card to make up for the inconvenience.

And he had made sure Delivery Man Thomas made good on Mick's word.

The males were holed up in his shack, a light-tight shanty off the main roads on the Arkansas-Tennessee border. Delivery Man Thomas had been Louis' brainchild for instigating communication with Molly without arousing suspicion. Using his hypnosis skill, he could simultaneously skim a few groceries off the pile while instructing the man to deliver the message to Molly discreetly.

The note itself was all Dominic. Though Rhys was dubious.

"There is no way Molly will figure that shit out. Anything longer than five words and she'll probably be off counting tiles in a kitchen or something. No offense, Dom, but your little girlfriend is flighty as hell."

"She'll get it," Dom insisted. "You know she knows music. And it's better than some of that cryptic weird shit Nichol was trying to come up with."

"What if she fucks up?" Rhys demanded, arms crossed.

"What's there to fuck up?" Dom replied. "I'm telling her we're here and we're getting her out. Unfuckupable."

Dominic had won the battle, but Louis suspected had she not been Dom's connected, Rhys would have taken a more dominant stance. As it was, he was impressed with Dom's ability to maintain a cool head while discussing scenarios that didn't always end with the Tender Molly coming out alive.

He had witnessed many connections from afar, often lingering in an area longer than intended solely because of his fascination with the mysterious process. He'd observed the most reserved males frothing at the mouth when their connections left their home to run a quick errand and had watched as feral beasts lurking in the shadows became stable haunt leaders to make their women happy. He had seen connections broken through death, and others that were well into their fifth century.

He wanted none of it. Ever.

Dominic had obviously come through his initial induction into connection with relatively little damage. He chalked it up to his strong blood. For such a young vampire to go through the first connection phase without his female present, he had expected far more mental instability. However, up until an hour ago, Dom had been the definition of vampiric control. Calm.

Even now, with his pacing and the unnecessary breathing of the freshly turned, the male was handling the uncertainty surrounding his connected female's safety with more sophistication than he had seen some vampires have during the most ordinary of couple separations.

He was impressed.

The exceptional hearing of the males picked up Delivery Man Thomas's van long before the decrepit vehicle peaked over the hill. In his impatience, Dominic opened the door a fraction, cursing and snarling as the sun's rays blistered his exposed hand and forearm. Only the advanced eyesight of a vampire would register who slammed the door as Rhys launched himself across the room.

"Frying us all is probably even less helpful than your fucking pacing has been, Mini."

Dom grunted, cradling his blackened arm as the odor of burnt flesh filled the room. "Jeez fuck," he panted, "I kind of lost it for a moment. Sorry. Any air freshener around here, Louis?"

"No. Stop breathing like the rest of us and it won't bug you."

The van came to a stop, its grating motor finally

ceasing. Delivery Man Thomas's footsteps approached the door, halting as he knocked. "One. Two. Three. Four. Five…"

"What's he doing?" Rhys asked him.

"Little instruction I always add to humans coming by here during daylight. Knock and give me ten. It prevents, oh I don't know, accidental sun exposure."

Dominic rolled his eyes and moved far from the door's path as Delivery Man Thomas came in and stood in the open doorway.

"Close the door."

Slam.

"Lock it."

Click.

"Report."

Aside from his complete compliance, the only physical sign that Delivery Man Thomas was under his hypnosis was the slightly mistimed blinking of his brown eyes. "Miss Diane received the items. And the gift card. The younger woman gave me this."

The quick extension of Delivery Man Thomas's arm and open palm as he spoke was likely the only reason both remained attached to their owner, as Dominic snatched the crumpled paper.

"You've done well," he told Delivery Man Thomas. "Keep your new phone with you at all times and I'll be in touch shortly."

He slipped three hundred-dollar bills into the man's hand before dismissing him for the evening. He turned to the cocked eyebrow of Rhys. "Pavlovian. He will associate my calls with money, making his response time quicker should the hypnosis not take root."

"Smart."

"I know."

"Mini. Care to share your love letter with the class?" Rhys called to his hauntmate.

Dominic stood leaning against the wall, his thin lips pursed.

"Dom," Rhys barked. "Read it."

Shaking his head quickly to rid himself of his trance, Dom read the note. "Spiderwebs. Hungry Like the Wolf. Sixteen Candles. I Think We're Alone Now. Kryptonite."

Silence.

"And?" Rhys finally spoke.

Dominic looked up. "And what? That's it."

With a slow nod, Rhys turned to him. "I fucking knew we should have had a Plan B."

He chuckled, peeking out the covered window as the sun sunk below the horizon. "She's good. Jagg should be up in a few minutes."

Rhys ran a hand through his hair. "Alright. Mini, start talking. What's Molly saying?"

****

Dominic focused his attention on what was in the message, and not on what was missing. "The entire thing has been scratched onto a receipt. It's a little hard to make out since there are pen marks beside most of the items, but I'm pretty sure I've got it. Spiderwebs must refer to the track system Louis described. Molly's letting us know she's trapped, not free to move around. Agree?" Ignoring the tightness in his throat he got every time his mind brought up the image of his leashed connection, he turned to Louis for confirmation.

"I'd say so. The system was pretty detailed. From what I saw, many of the tracks had stoppers on them for no reason. Maybe mind games," Louis stated, his brow furrowing. "A human brain would have difficulty maneuvering in there."

"I figured as much. Hungry Like the Wolf… letting me, us, know she's not being fed properly? She looked so fucking thin in that video…" Again he ignored the knot in his gut caused by remembering the protruding collarbones and hollowed cheeks. He glanced at Mick, who responded with a thumbs up. The male had been silent most of the day, his main job to monitor Dominic's moods.

"That's something we need to be aware of," Louis interjected. "Malnourished humans are physically weaker, slower, and their minds are often unfocused. Any plan of action needs to account for that."

Rhys nodded in agreement. "And I can vouch that a hungry Molly is less agreeable than usual. Though that may work in our favor."

Louis snickered as he acknowledged Jagger's waking. "She's probably monitored tightly by the other servant on the premises. That woman looked like a crossbred weasel."

"Molly responded?" Jagg asked, taking a seat on the thread-bare sofa.

"Yeah," Rhys replied, ensuring he had moved into Jagg's line of sight. "We're just in the middle of reviewing her message. She's trapped, hungry, and cranky."

Jagg nodded and turned his attention to Dominic. Once he met Jagger's eyes, he continued. "Sixteen Candles."

"The fuck does that mean?" Rhys demanded.

With a scowl, he focused on the words. *Nothing.*

He took a breath in concentration, regretting it immediately when the odor of his burnt arm filled his senses. “No idea. What about I Think We’re Alone Now? She’s by herself right now?”

“Doubt it,” Louis commented. “Delivery Man Thomas said Diane signed off on the delivery after Molly took in the groceries.”

“Good point,” he replied. “The last one is Kryptonite. I think… Molly may be saying she’s losing her mind? Maybe telling me… fuck if I know.”

He flashed back to his limited interactions with Molly. Flighty, yes. Prone to outbursts? Definitely. But with everything thrown at her in the short time since he’d brought her into her new existence, Molly had never appeared breakable. Picturing her hungry, tethered to a leash in a damp basement, slowly losing her mind… he could feel his anger rising.

“Nope.”

All eyes turned to Louis.

“That woman was definitely not broken when I saw her. She was hard. Calculating. I’m not sure how much you witnessed as the night drew to a close, but there was no pure submission or pliability in her eyes. My assessment? She was plotting an escape long before I got there. Her movements through that maze were deliberate. Even her miscalculations, her progression down a track with a stopper, was purposeful. She was giving a show of uncertainty to Kaspars. Dominic, that woman is definitely *not* going crazy.”

What he witnessed as the night drew to a close. Dominic had been so focused on what was happening to her, he didn’t read Molly’s subtleties on the grainy footage. He met Louis’s eyes, the relief he was feeling at the older vampire's assessment evident. "So if she's handling everything mentally, what does *Kryptonite* refer to?"

Stumped, the males sat in contemplative silence, save for the soft humming from Jagger which came to a sudden stop. "Can I see the note?"

He passed the crumpled paper over.

"There's a question mark. Here. It's faint, but it's there. She's asking about his weakness. What's Dovidas's weakness?"

"Fire."

"Sunlight."

"Beheading."

"Correction," Jagg interrupted, "Is there anything Molly can do, in her current situation, to weaken Dovidas?"

The males fell silent once again. Louis moved to sit beside Jagg, rereading the message. "Vitamin K."

"What about it?" Dominic asked curiously.

"There was a vampire in France a few years back that studied our aversion to vegans. Standard thinking had revolved around the lack of iron in the vegan diet that didn't appeal to us. It was a small study, interrupted by the anti-vampire measures put in place, but he had determined it wasn't the lack of iron. It was the high levels of Vitamin K."

"Get Nichol on speaker. Kaius, too, if we can," Jagg said softly. "I have a vague memory of this study. Probably saw mention of it somewhere and deemed it unimportant."

Rhys propped the laptop onto the cluttered kitchen table and called the haunt.

"What?"

"Hey Nicky," Rhys greeted, ignoring Nichol's lack of phone manners. "Kai there?"

"Yes. What?"

Jagg leaned into the camera's line of sight. "What do you know about Vitamin K?"

Nichol paused. "It's necessary for clotting. Makes us sick as all hell. Why?"

Rhys tilted onto the screen. "Molly responded."

Chapter Seventeen

Dominic stared at the covered window, clenching and unclenching his fists rhythmically to keep himself grounded. Dawn had come and gone, his brothers resting in the corners of the small shack as he forced his emotions to remain flat until Mick finally fell into a deep sleep.

He leaned back in his chair slowly, lurching forward when his skin made contact with the wooden slats.

Mick stirred, snarling for a moment before he resettled.

He tentatively inched a hand across his spine, reassuring himself the flesh was still undamaged. The pain from the imagined lacerations continued to radiate through his body as he attempted to shift positions.

The strikes had begun shortly before dawn.

The first nearly brought him to his knees as he riffled through the fridge hunting for a palatable blood type to soothe the peculiar emptiness in his gut.

By the fourth hit, he had hidden himself in the bathroom, running the shower to hide his involuntary grunts as the assault continued. He had gripped the sink counter, staring into the mirror as an imaginary switch flayed his spine, yet left no welt.

The attack had ended as suddenly as it had begun, leaving him unmarked.

He was going insane.

****

Molly lay naked and motionless on her stomach. The lash marks crossing her back had healed to a slow leak during the day, and the tightening of the inflamed skin was an almost welcomed distraction from the burning pain. Even with the blurred red numbers on her clock blending and morphing from exhaustion, her internal clock let her know sunset was moments away. With a deep breath, she pushed herself onto her hands and knees and gingerly crawled off her bed.

As she stood in the shower, facing the stream of hot water, she prepared herself to wash the blood from her back and out of her hair. She turned.

Sixty.

Counting down would give her an end time, a moment to look forward to.

Fifty-nine.

The water pierced her gashes as she scrubbed shampoo into her hair, arching her back to keep the suds from touching her sensitive skin.

Forty-two.

The hunger cramps had hit so hard. The ease on her failing system was almost worth the lashes.

Twenty-eight.

Seven strikes for seven granola bars.

Seventeen.

Four days had passed since she had placed a crumpled receipt in the delivery man's callused hand.

Five.

Tomorrow was grocery delivery day.

Four.

Tonight was another meeting with Senator Green.

Three.

At least she had a satisfied stomach.

Two.

Someone knew where she was.

One.

She could hold on.

She toweled off slowly and walked over to her closet to assess what she could wear that wouldn't result in her fainting from agony while still appeasing Dove. She pulled a black sequined mermaid dress off the rack. Plunging back. Perfect.

The spaghetti straps of the gown slipped up her arms, the open back framing her lash marks. Looking longingly at the ballet flats in the closet, she turned her attention to the narrow wedges Dove had sent along with the dress.

Glorified Frankenstein boots.

Sitting cautiously on the bed, she awaited Diane's summons. When it came, Diane's pinched face sneering at her stiffened movements, she followed the woman to the great room for Dove's assessment. His eyes narrowed.

"Diane. Its hair is wet."

Fuck.

Diane followed Molly's track to examine the state of her hair. "I can pull it into a bun. It will look intentional."

"Do it. Senator Green is expected in ten minutes."

Diane disappeared briefly, returning with a hairbrush and pins. Her hair was pulled tight, wrapped, and fastened without care for the small metal sticks scratching across her scalp.

"Master?" Diane questioned, gesturing to the new style.

"Yes. Much better, Diane. Go wait for their arrival."

As Diane exited the room, Dove motioned for her to take her place beside his chair. She knelt slowly.

"Turn."

Her eyes flicked toward Dove's feet.

"Face the wall. Senator Green could use a reminder of what happens to those who play games."

She obeyed. The door of the great room opened and she could hear three sets of footsteps cross the hardwood floor.

"I see you've kept your bodyguard close," Dove spoke, his disdain for the vampire guard evident.

"I hope you do not mind," Senator Green's cocky voice replied. "Equal footing."

"Of course. Welcome, Shaun Moen. Come. Sit."

"Actually," Senator Green interrupted, "my guard has recommended a quick tour of your home to ensure there are no unexpected guests to our little meeting. Have you any objections?"

Dove chuckled. It was dark with a hint of indulgence. "I will take you myself."

****

Kaspars Dovidas was a collector of art. Paintings and sculptures lined the hallways and were displayed throughout the sprawling house.

It was a great benefit to Louis's current assignment.

Placing the image of the Tender Molly's back to the side of his mind for later, he used the statues and canvases as an excuse for his swiveling head and roaming eyes while the group moved in sync throughout the rooms.

"Pardon, sir, but is this Egyptian?"

Dovidas paused in front of a cracked urn, its colors faded from centuries of exposure to the elements. "It is. I picked that up last century. One of my favorites."

He hummed in appreciation, tilting his head to the side to angle the minuscule camera along the hall's track system. As the Senator's bodyguard, Louis was afforded the option of falling behind the other men as they discussed minor legislative propositions being put forth in the upcoming weeks.

He scanned the ceilings, noted doors as Dovidas opened them for inspection. As they hit a room at the end of a lengthy hall, Dovidas cracked the door a fraction.

"This is where the woman stays during the day."

Remaining as disinterested as he was in the other rooms, he stuck his head into the tiny bedroom, the scent of blood hitting his senses. Damp splatters on the bedding. The lashing had been recent.

"You don't worry she will leave during the day?" Louis inquired, ensuring he sounded curious enough to ask, not curious enough to care.

"She cannot leave. As I'm sure you've noticed, both the woman and Diane are limited in their movements. Neither have access to outside without my presence. For their safety, of course," Kaspars added for Green's benefit.

Green nodded in understanding. "Some women need a tighter leash than others," he agreed.

As the men continued their tour down the hall toward the dining area, Louis decided to delve a little deeper. "I've never had one myself. A Tender. Always worried one would end me during the day. I applaud your bravery, sir."

Dovidas side-eyed him for a moment. "Never? Likely a wise choice. They can be more trouble than they're worth most days. Never go to rest with one, never give them access to your resting place, and never underestimate the worth of a perimeter collar."

Perimeter collar.

He fell back from the group again as they approached a completely mirrored dining room. Senator Green could not hide his admiration.

"Stunning room, Dovidas. How do you keep the mirrors on the floor from cracking?"

"Special order."

"Of course."

As the men backed out of the room, he made sure he scanned the maze crossing the ceiling before rejoining the others.

"The kitchen is the final room. I trust it has met your privacy expectations so far, Moen?" Dovidas formally addressed him.

"Yes, sir. A quick look in the kitchen and you gentlemen can get to your discussion."

The swinging door leading to the kitchen fluttered to a close behind the males. He walked swiftly around the room. "These doors lead to…"

"The garage."

He tested the far one in confirmation. "And this one?"

Dovidas hesitated.

Bingo.

"Cupboard."

He nodded, silently acknowledging Dovidas' hesitation to disclose his resting place in front of a human. "Shall we?"

****

"There," Dominic barked, pointing at the screen. "Right fucking there. Pause it, Rhys."

Rhys swore under his breath, rewinding the recording of Louis's feed too far and waiting for his cue to pause the recording.

"That's his resting place. Look at the track lines. They end at that door. Fucking fuck. How do we still not have sound?" he snarled. Mick placed a hand on his back, a gentle reminder to keep his rising anger in check.

Rhys dove back to examine the wires tangled below the table. "Someone get Nichol back on the phone. I have no goddamn idea what to do down here."

Mick handed his phone to Rhys. "It's on speaker," he said as the phone's ring filled the room.

"What."

"Nic," Rhys growled. "Still no sound on my end. What the ever-living fuck do I do? Are you getting anything?"

"We have video, but the sound is acting up here, too. Must be an issue on Louis's end. I'll keep playing around, but for now we'll need Jagg to read lips."

Rhys smacked at Jagg's leg. "Hey. Can you make out what they're saying?"

Jagg nodded. "Only when they're facing Louis. Not helpful when he trails behind them like this."

He turned back to the screen to see the males returning to the great room. Molly's back remained to Louis, covered in welts. Mick squeezed his shoulder. "Need a break?"

He didn't need a fucking break. He needed

answers.

"I'm good," he lied distractedly, reaching behind himself to run his fingers along the imagined lashes that continued to throb into the evening hours. "I'm pissed, but I'm in control. Right?"

"So far, so good, Mini."

"I should be pissed, though, right?"

"I am," Rhys interjected. "That's my product he's scratched up."

He booted Rhys under the table.

"What?" Rhys complained, "I put a lot of work into that Tender. Her resale value is dropping. Fast."

Another kick.

Rhys poked his head up. "Kidding, Mini. I'll trade her for a week with your car."

He leaned further forward, grateful for the ease in which Rhys had been keeping his anger and frustration levels from soaring too high. Despite the tenseness of the situation, Rhys's commentary had kept his rage in check, replacing it with annoyance. And maybe a hint of humor.

Anything to keep him from dwelling on Molly's welts. Or the fact their pattern replicated the imagined ones he'd experienced the morning before.

Kaius's voice came over the phone. "We need translation."

He caught Jagg's attention and pointed to the screen.

"I can't get anything. Louis isn't staying on Dovidas long enough to catch a coherent sentence," Jagger said softly, an apologetic glance toward him.

"Dominic," Kaius called out, "what do you see?"

Dom breathed out. "Aside from Molly's ribs? And

those whip marks?"

"Aside from those, Mini."

"Nothing. I can't see her face, either."

"When you notice anything, I want you to call it out. Any of you. Louis seems to be showing us things he feels are important, and the more we notice now, the less time we waste hunting on the replays."

The camera bounced.

"… agreed on a finder's fee. I did not give any indication you and I were partners."

"You catching the audio, Kai?" Rhys yelled, jumping out from under the table and watching an aggravated Dovidas hunched forward in his chair.

"Yes. Shush."

"Partners is a strong word," Senator Green stated. "I'm merely suggesting a more equitable cut of the profits. After all, I need your product, but you need my connections."

"I need no connections from you," Dovidas responded flippantly.

"Yes, you do. Not a lot of humans willing to do business with a vampire. Even a vampire-killing vampire. I can be the human front for your sales. For a forty percent cut."

Mick tapped him on the leg and pointed to the screen. Louis had repositioned himself, angling the camera toward Molly. Her profile was clearly visible on the monitor.

"If Louis can see her face, can she see him at that angle?" Dominic called toward the phone.

"Yes," Nichol responded. "If she's smart enough to look his way."

The males half listened to the argument building

between Dovidas and Green, most of their attention on Molly's eyes as they collectively willed her to look at Louis.

Nothing.

A soft hum came through the speakers. Dominic glanced at Jagg, who remained unaware of the quiet melody.

"Are we boring you, Moen?" Dovidas's voice was clipped.

"Apologies, sir," Louis responded, his head bowing quickly and jostling the camera. "I'm being paid to not listen to your conversations. Humming helps me tune it out."

"It's highly distracting."

"Again, I apologize. I will cease."

Dovidas nodded curtly and opened his mouth to speak.

"Though I'm surprised an art lover such as yourself is not more in tune with music. There are so many interpretations, so many messages in it…"

"Your hum is off-key and offensive," Dovidas barked, his eyes narrowing in annoyance.

"Apologies, sir."

"There!" he bellowed. "She caught it. Fuck, that Louis is a genius! See? Shoulders dropped. Her back isn't as rigid. Holy hell, she fucking caught it!" He breathed, relieved Molly knew they had an ally on Dovidas's turf. "Did you see that, Mick? Sh… what the fuck just happened?"

****

As the conversation between Dovidas and Green deteriorated, Louis moved his attention from the astute Molly to the increasingly aggressive vampire beside her. It was unlikely Green would have survived had Louis been any younger, for the speed required to intercept the attacking male had pushed his skills to their limits. Fang to fang, he held his ground between the snarling vampire and the cowering Senator.

"Your age, Shaun Moen," Dovidas hissed through his elongated teeth.

"Just over five decades, sir," he calmly responded as he assessed his distance from the windows.

"You are no half centenarian," Kaspars growled, his hand grasping his neck. "You move with the speed of three centuries."

"You've seen my age for yourself, sir. Speed is my skill."

Dovidas stared unblinking. "Move."

"I can't do that. My job is to protect Senator Green, and I keep my word when there is a payment attached."

"Mercenary," Dovidas spat.

"Entrepreneur."

Dovidas laughed low, releasing his throat. "Is there truly a difference? Green. Stop whimpering and take your seat like a man. My apologies for allowing my temper to get in the way of our negotiations. As you can see from my… girlfriend… over there, I am quick to anger, but quick to forgive. Woman! Turn. Would you prefer her to be facing you, Senator? You have been quite distracted by her tonight." Dovidas leaned in low. "Is it the curve of her spine that draws your eye? Or the curve of my whip?"

Senator Liam Green sat motionless, his eyes darting between the Tender Molly and the great room doors as he fought to regain his composure. "I feel we have discussed all we can this evening. I should take my leave."

Louis turned his head enough to allow the camera to pick up Molly, whose face was finally visible, while he himself maintained a tight observation of the volatile male before him.

"There is nothing left but the paperwork, Green," Kaspars said, motioning toward the doors. "The deal will be seventy-thirty above expenses, with the elimination of the finder's fee. Have your lawyers draw up the contract. Keep it short. Anything slipped in and there will be nothing the conciliatory Shaun Moen can do to save your flabby neck."

The good Senator hesitated.

He contemplated eating the man himself.

"That is acceptable," Green finally drawled, his concession words a failed attempt to save face. "You will receive paperwork by Thursday."

****

Dominic rolled his shoulders, forcing the tension to release even a fraction.

"Too fucking close," Rhys muttered.

Mick sat back in his rickety chair, grinning. "It's always too fucking close with Louis. But he's never been caught in a gig yet."

"Yet being the operative word, Mickwad," Rhys snarked back.

"Mickwad?"

"Dickwad, Mick-style."

Mickey snorted with laughter before placing a reassuring hand on his back. He relaxed into the physical connection, relieved that Mickey was draining some of the pressure in his head.

"How are you holding up, Mini?"

His shoulder blades twitched as Mick applied more pressure. “Fine. Furious. I’m fine but I’m furious, if that makes sense. You’re doing that thing, aren’t you?”

“Yup,” Mick replied, cocking a brow at Rhys’s curse-laden commentary as he tried to negotiate the saving of Louis’s camera footage. “You’re pretty revved, but you’re still in control. I’m just helping keep you there. Tonight has been a lot to take in for you.”

“I’m gonna fucking de-ball him. Remove his fingers one by one. And his tongue. Think we can work that into the plan?” he grunted.

“We’ll try.”

The males occupied themselves restlessly as they awaited Louis’s arrival. The cold bagged blood from the fridge satisfied their hunger but did nothing to satisfy their tongues.

Rhys licked a cold drop from his fang. “How does he stomach this cold shit?”

“He doesn’t. Have you see him feed once since we arrived?” Mick asked. “That’s right. Not once. Louis is a pure old school hunter.”

“Risky down here,” Rhys mused. “This area is the cradle of vampire hate. Fucker must have a death wish.”

“Never understood that,” he murmured more to himself than the others as his eyes remained locked on the door. “All the voodoo, Wiccan, pin doll business and the moment the unexplainable is actually waving at them, they lose their minds.”

“Like you wouldn’t scream like a little girl if a ghost appeared right now behind you and licked your ear,” Rhys retorted.

“Why the fuck would it lick his ear?” Mick

wondered aloud. "Kind of a weird jump from yelling 'Boo' to licking someone's ear."

"Who the hell gets scared from a little 'boo'?" Rhys defended. "But ear licking? The whole wet willy thing? That's freaky enough on its own."

The front door swung open.

"I'm with Rhys," Louis injected. "Just thinking about it makes me queasy."

Mick vacated his seat, spinning it toward Louis in a smooth, practiced motion. "I'll pull Kai and Nic up on the monitor if you give me a minute. They probably have some questions about tonight."

Louis straddled the clunky wooden chair with a nod and turned his attention to Dominic. Mickey moved closer and leaned close to whisper in his ear. "Your control is still holding," he reassured him. "Just a precaution. Any unleashing on Louis and you'll be signing your own death warrant."

"Dominic." Louis' boots appeared in his peripheral.

He looked up from his hands.

"Before we all get into the details of tonight, I need to clear up something."

Silence.

"Dovidas went for Green. His intention was clear. Molly wasn't in danger at the moment. Even if she had been, I would have had to hold back or risk this entire mission. I'm assuming a Rhys-trained Tender isn't cheap. Dovidas does not strike me as a guy who throws away money, and that's what killing your connected would be. Small silver lining, yes, but it weighed in on my decision to stay the course tonight and protect Green. However, as this mission develops, you need to know where the line is. And as a group," Louis paused to look around, "we need to decide where the woman fits along the priority line."

He remained silent. Mickey stayed behind him, providing a steadying hand on his hunched shoulder. He could feel Mick pulling some of his anger away, allowing his mind to mull over the truths behind Louis's explanation without influence. A few moments went by as the laptop came to life with Kai and Nichol on the other screen.

"Louis. You did well this evening," Kaius stated.

"Thank you. I was just explaining some things to Dominic regarding his connection and my actions tonight," Louis responded, his eyes staying locked on the young vampire before him.

"And I was suggesting that we define the woman's priority in this mission immediately to avoid any second-guessing on my part. Or errors. I may be strong for my age, but Dovidas is still considerably older and hesitation in my responses could be disastrous."

Kai peered through the screen at him. "Mick?"

"He's fine."

"Dominic?"

He looked at Kai, gave a small smile, then turned his attention to Louis. "I get it. I do. It kills me, but I get where we are in all this right now. If you'd gone toward Molly when Dovidas lunged, it would be game over. But Kai?" He refocused on the monitor. "Louis is right. We need to figure out what and how we're doing this. Fast. She didn't look… well."

Chapter Eighteen

Louis was quickly acclimating to the various quirks of Mickey's hauntmates. Rhys's foul language, his penchant for poking the bear, was both refreshing and exasperating after a tense night. His reputation preceded the cocky elder male, and he had to admit he was a little star struck to be working so closely with a vampire known not only for his Tenders, but for his survival in some of the world's worst dungeons.

Rhys was definitely an old badass.

Jagger's incessant humming had become little more than white noise to him during his first mission for the Kaius haunt. Mick had warned him that the icy-eyed male had limited hearing, but the extent had been significantly more pronounced in person than he had anticipated. Having never interacted with a vampire with such a critical sense impairment, he had been awkward in his initial dealings with Jagg.

Cringing internally every time he thought back to the first few days he and Jagg worked together, he had made sure to take his cues from the others now, signaling Jagg before he spoke to ensure the perceptive male missed nothing.

And he really didn't need to yell.

Dominic had risen higher in his estimations tonight. While he knew Mickey had likely intercepted some of the storm raging inside the young male, Dominic had maintained a logical mind in the face of his connected woman's assault.

He wasn't so sure he would have been as rational.

The one vampire he was grateful to have limited contact with was the aggressive Nichol.

Even through the speaker, the male gave an air of gruff impatience, his disdain leaking through whenever he spoke of the Tender Molly. Although he was an obvious asset with his technological abilities, the little interaction he had with Nichol regarding the microscopic camera hadn't ended quick enough.

Nichol was, in his irrelevant opinion, an ass.

He glanced over at Mick as the males arranged themselves in front of the laptop camera. Mickey's empathic abilities were known to him but observing them in action had been a new experience. Over the decades, he had become accustomed to Mick's mercurial moods.

He had long suspected his own flat and unaffected emotions were a balm to the constantly bombarded vampire, and he had periodically extended his time with Mickey in the hopes of relieving a little of the negativity Mick devoured in his normal existence.

Not one to have bursts of emotion, he was fascinated with the way Mick's proximity diffused Dominic and he suspected Nic's combative snarl was tamped down despite the distance between Mick and Nichol. Observing the physical change in Mickey as he pulled from Rhys's joking banter and balanced it with Dom's anger gave him a new respect for his friend.

And then there was Kaius Khthonios.

Kaius Khthonios, with his impeccably curated haunt.

Kaius Khthonios, with his authoritative baritone

voice.

Kaius Khthonios with his long, stoic silences.

Kaius Khthonios, with his straw blond hair and unblinking blue eyes currently fixated on him.

"Prior to opening discussions this evening, Louis, I want to thank you for your vital assistance in gaining intel on Dovidas," Kaius began. "However, you will need to make a decision now before we can establish our final strategy."

He frowned. "Go on."

"I can't have our haunt's scent detectable anywhere near an attack on Dovidas. This includes any extraction efforts for the Tender in his possession." Kaius moved his penetrating gaze briefly to Dom. "Meaning any boots on the ground, should you agree, would be yours and yours alone."

He sat back in the worn chair, crossing his arms as Mick spoke up. "Hold up. Kaspars is over twice his age. It's a suicide mission."

"A suicide mission we will manipulate in Louis's favor."

"And how do we knock over two centuries off Dovidas?" Mick demanded, his concern for his friend's wellbeing evident.

He leaned into the monitor. "Tell me why."

Kaius's unblinking eyes stared hard at him. "Dovidas is familiar with my scent and by extension, would be able to recognize my bloodline. He and I have had… mutual associations… in the past and should the involvement of my haunt in Dovidas's demise be detected by those acquaintances, it would bring down a shitstorm that would decimate not only us, but all who support us."

"And you won't say who these 'mutual associations' are?"

"I cannot."

"But they're strong enough to take you down?"

"They are."

"And they are on Dovidas's side?"

"Yes."

He mulled over the implications of what Kaius had laid out. Any group strong enough to take down the Kaius haunt was not a group he wanted to fuck with. Walking away with his head intact was likely the smartest choice, as his involvement would make his scent a target alongside the others.

"What's your plan if I walk?"

"The peddling of Deepfryers needs to be halted," Kaius stated slowly. "Should you choose to end your involvement, we'll settle for stalling the sales through the use of human law enforcement."

He chuckled. "Your Plan B is calling the cops?"

"An anonymous tip regarding human enslavement."

"So, the woman would be released and Dovidas would be, what, held in a cell for a few days?" he posited.

"In the best outcome, yes."

"And the worst?"

"Dovidas annihilates the officers and the Tender, news of the bloodbath goes international, and we are inadvertently the cause of the immediate legalization of vampire hunting in the Western world."

****

Molly watched silently as a perplexed Diane compared her order receipt against the multitude of excess items on the table. With the other groceries accounted for and put away, there remained eight bags worth of broccoli, cauliflower, and spinach.

"Perhaps we received someone else's order as well," Diane mused. "We don't have enough room to store all this."

She poked at the offending vegetables and wrinkled her nose. *Yuck.*

Diane's eagle eyes missed nothing.

Fuck.

Diane's thin lips smirked and pushed the collection in her direction. "Or maybe you should bring it to your room. Package it up. You'll be eating nothing else until this is gone."

She stood slowly to retrieve bags to repack the repulsive food. Her lash marks tightened and stung with every movement, reopening and knitting together as she went about her confined life. She was exhausted, hungry, sore, and discouraged. In the three days since she had figured out the lithe, guarded vampire with the fire-engine hair was allied with Dominic, she had eagerly anticipated today's delivery.

When the groceries arrived, and the delivery man had come and gone without a word or a quick pass of a note, all the brutality of her week had taken up residence at the forefront of her mind. She was barely holding her composure in front of Diane, and the fear of breaking down around the vindictive shrew did little more than add to the pressure building in her head.

Dove had become significantly more agitated and impatient since his attempted attack on Senator Green, but he had also been leaving the house every night until daybreak. As her role for Dove disintegrated into a quick feed prior to his exit, Diane had taken full advantage of his absence. With a disciplinary wooden spoon in hand, Diane had stood over her as she completed a 'spring clean' of the house.

The metal track and leash system did not allow for the range of motion required and the past three nights had become little more than a game of scrubbing as quick as she could and pulling back for air before she fainted.

It had taken some practice.

She dragged herself and the bags to her room, collapsing onto her bed. Reaching into one of the bags, she pulled a head of cauliflower out. Hunger trumped disgust, and she devoured the entire thing before her taste buds could protest. Knowing Diane would hold tight to her threat of no other food until the greens were eaten, she decided the quicker she ate, the sooner she would have kitchen access again. Yanking a bunch of spinach out, she absently chewed the leaves and allowed herself to wallow in self-pity.

****

Nichol's arrival in Memphis had been eagerly anticipated by the hauntmates. With a plan and all its contingencies firmly in place, Kaius had disappeared once again to wherever it was the ancient, secretive vampire went. Rhys stood over Nic, fascinated by Nichol's ability to recreate the haunt command station in Louis's dilapidated shack.

It had taken the surly male two full nights to drive over a thousand miles and judging from Nichol's grubby appearance when he arrived as dawn crept over the horizon, he had not spent his day in a hotel. Nic had cut his arrival so close that Louis had called Delivery

Man Thomas and razzle-dazzled him into coming by early to collect his additional groceries and unload Nichol's plethora of electronic components into the tiny house.

It did not escape his notice that Louis then tipped Delivery Man Thomas exceptionally well.

With the rest of the males resting against the back walls for the day, he had agreed to assist Nichol to ensure everything was ready to go by the time the other rose. While more of a lover and a fighter than an intellect, he found himself losing time as he connected wires and typed commands.

"I'm going to put your ass out of a job," he declared smugly, his assigned duty of speaker wiring complete.

"Good. Then I can take over your lazy-ass job of eating and fucking."

He grinned at his hauntmate. "Normally I wouldn't argue with that assessment, but considering the last woman I trained was Molly, I think you owe me an apology."

Nichol snorted. "I met her once. I should have drained her. Would have saved all of us a lot of trouble."

"Yeah," he mused as he assessed his work, "But then Mini would be mopey and we'd all be sitting around the haunt jerking off and scanning real estate in Alaska."

"Mini's always mopey."

"Ah, that's where you're wrong, Nicky. He *was* mopey. Now he's turning into Mini-Kai. Mini-Kai with a vengeance issue. Seriously, you won't recognize him," he commented. "Wait. You met Molly? When?"

Nichol spit a wire connector into his hand and continued his job. "When Dom first brought her in. Reeked of chemicals. Sharp tongue on that one."

He chuckled. "I don't think I've ever been told to go fuck myself as often as I was in those weeks. I'm amazed she's still alive. I suspected she'd last a month. Two, tops. But Molly's survival instinct has a shit-ton more control than her conscious brain does."

Nichol's attention moved to the computer monitor. "So, what was with the human and the foul-smelling bags?"

"Nasty, wasn't it?" he grimaced. "It was the only way we could figure to get Vitamin K into Molly without arousing suspicion."

"And you think the woman is smart enough to know they're for her."

"Not exactly."

Nichol paused. "Not exactly?"

"Yeah."

"Quit being fucking cryptic."

"Fine," he huffed. "During her stay in the Tender compound, Molly didn't touch a single vegetable. In fact, she expressed outright disgust and revulsion every time she saw spinach, cauliflower, or broccoli. We theorize that the maid runs a tight ship. She was quick to catch the missing items from the first delivery we altered and knew down to the penny how much was owed. It would make sense that Molly is kept up on delivery days to put the groceries away. There was enough spinach and cauliflower added that she would definitely make that face she makes. The scrunched nose one."

He stopped for a moment, demonstrating for

Nichol. "We're working under the assumption that the maid is in charge of Molly's meals since it would be a task below Dovidas. With the malnutrition we've seen, Dom surmised the maid is a vindictive, evil bitch, and if Molly pulls a Molly and expresses her dislike for the veggies we sent, she will be punished by being forced to eat the shit. Make sense?"

Nichol stared blankly at he, his eyes glazed.

"Nicky?"

Nichol turned his gaze slowly in his direction. "I really don't fucking care. I tried to. Just now. But I don't. Why the fuck am I here?"

"We need to get a bug into that house and an undetectable phone into Molly's hand. Last thing we need is that girl getting it in her head to mount an attack on her own," he mumbled.

Nichol turned to one of the large duffle bags he'd brought with him. "Bugs I can do. An undetectable two-way communication device may be more difficult. Does she have a land line phone she can access?"

"Louis reported her room as bare. No electronics. We're under the assumption Dovidas or his maid check her room thoroughly, so whatever we do has to be concealed. We haven't been able to risk any communication with her since Dovidas called out Louis."

"It would be easier to omit the woman from the mission."

"You tell Mini that."

Nic grunted. "Get some rest. I'll have something prepared by nightfall."

****

Delivery Man Thomas left the small shanty for the

second time in eighteen hours, new instructions in his brain and another small fortune in his pocket. Louis secured the door and turned to the others. “He’s hit his limit. He’s of no more use to us, or I run the risk of frying his mind. He bring everything you needed, Nichol?”

The snarky vampire nodded tightly before resuming his intricate wiring in the small canister.

Louis squatted beside Dominic. “Hungry?”

“I should probably feed.”

“Care to join me on a hunt? Nothing to do here until Nichol works his magic, so we might as well make the most of the evening,” Louis offered.

He glanced over at Mick, who grinned. “Go for it, Mini. Watch the master at work.”

With a momentary hesitation, he stood. “I’m in.”

The males strode out of the house and began the long walk into the city.

“Where are we heading?” he asked. “Do you have preferred hunting grounds or something?”

“We’re going to Graceland,” Louis replied casually. “You think you know the way?”

He stopped cold, his feet rooted to the earth. “We can’t.”

“We are.”

“I can’t.”

“You are.”

He took a deep, unneeded breath. “Why?”

Louis grinned at him and kept walking. “You saw the map. Just a few blocks from there. You and I are going to do a little intelligence gathering ourselves. I know the layout of the house, I know the placement of the windows, and once we get there, I’ll show you how we get inside."

"And what are we doing once we get inside?"

"You're getting a message to the Tender, I'll be slashing phone wires and power lines," Louis exclaimed, his normally reserved tone tinted with excitement. "Delivery Man Thomas is out and we need a way to get the communicator to Molly. I'm merely providing a reason for repairmen to arrive on site tomorrow."

"Kai mentioned my scent, his scent… we can't be found there."

"A quick dip in the Mississippi will solve that temporarily."

He eyed the elder vampire. "You'll take the heat when, not if, when Kai finds out?"

Louis's barking laugh echoed in the dark valley. "Nope." A long, lanky arm reached forward. "Into the river with you."

****

Louis rarely felt any emotion. He felt hunger. Curiosity. Sometimes lust. But watching Dom crawl out of the odorous river, his dark hair covering his eyes as his silvered fangs flashed in the harbor lights, caused a quick burst of levity from him. The snarled mutterings of the soaked vampire also pleased him. Greatly. "You'll forgive me when you see her," he chuckled.

"I reek."

"Don't breathe."

"Molly has to. Fuck. What the fuck do humans do to that river?"

His grin was met with a splattering of water droplets as Dom shook his hair.

The males sprinted through the city, staying tight in

the shadows of the back alleys as they made their way toward Kaspars Dovidas's house. He kept a watchful eye on his companion, ensuring that the young vampire maintained his cool head as they moved closer to the gates of the property. He was never one for the detailed plans the Kaius Haunt toiled over. He preferred to arrive on site and make his decisions from there.

And this was an easy gig.

With his scent already familiar, even if Dovidas denied the males access to his house, he was confident he could make his way around the property undetected to slice the electrical and phone lines leading to the estate. However, gaining entrance would provide Dominic with the opportunity to leave a message for his connected. Maybe see for himself that she was alive and would stay that way.

He liked Dom.

The dank water clung to his hair, clothes, and skin. Dominic was not only undetectable by scent, his appearance was altered enough that as long as he kept his head down, he would be unrecognizable should Dovidas see him anywhere else in the future. He turned to Dominic, giving him a final piece of advice. "Keep your head down, show your rings, and be fucking submissive. Your age means Dovidas will expect you to be skittish around him, so you'll get away with avoiding eye contact. Show no recognition if your connected is around. And don't. Fucking. Talk. Got it?"

Dominic glared at him with narrowed eyes. "Got it."

They approached the gate and he pressed the buzzer, ensuring he was partially hiding his companion from the video monitor. A sharp female voice it through the quiet night. "State your business."

He leaned into the small microphone. "Shaun Moen to see Mr. Dovidas."

The speaker clicked to silence as the males waited. It sparked to life a few minutes later. "Name your partner."

"James Banks. In his third decade."

Silence.

"You may enter."

He strode confidently up the pathway to the front door, with Dominic trudging behind. He knew the young male held onto his unnecessary breathing from his human years, and it was humorous for him to hear a quick breath followed by a soft curse every time the river water odor hit Dom.

Kaspars Dovidas stood in the open door frame, his arms crossed casually across his chest. "Shaun Moen. What brings you here without the illustrious Senator Green?"

"My partner and I would like to discuss a proposal with you."

Dovidas's gray eyes flicked past him. "James Banks. Your proof?"

Dominic, head down, pulled his damp pant leg up, revealing his three narrow rings above his ankle. To the human eye, they would appear to be one thin line. However, the enhanced vision of vampires allowed them to differentiate between the fine slate lines and the infinitesimal strips of unmarked skin between them. Kaspars nodded his approval as Dom straightened himself.

"And what is this proposal?"

He glanced toward the gates. "I would prefer a

more secure location than the front porch. Eavesdroppers and all."

Dovidas hesitated. He assessed both males, his hard eyes searching for any sign of danger. After a moment, he nodded briskly and stepped aside, allowing the duo to enter the house. Kaspars scented the males as they passed him, his nose wrinkling slightly as he took in the smell of the river water.

He braced himself for questioning and was relieved when Dovidas merely rolled his eyes. Young vampires without the guidance of their creators were known for developing strange habits in their early decades, if they survived that long. Secluded resting places in inhospitable places was one such quirk.

Dovidas did not hide his contempt as "James Banks" removed his slopping boots and padded across the foyer, leaving wet footprints in his wake.

He awaited instruction from Kaspars, which arrived as a gesture, before proceeding to the great room. Dom followed, the slurping sounds of his soaked socks echoing in the silent hall. Dovidas brought up the end of the group, and he knew they were being examined closely by skeptical eyes. As they entered the large room, he turned to Dom. "No sitting. This place is nice, and you reek like the hull of a fishing boat."

Turquoise eyes narrowed his way.

But the kid obeyed.

Kaspars, apparently pleased with his control over the young vampire, motioned toward the sofa. "Sit, Moen. I am interested in hearing what you have to say. Diane? Send in the Tender."

He maintained eye contact with Dovidas, using his peripheral to gauge Dominic's reaction.

Perfect stillness.

"Well," he began, "My associate and I are here to offer you temporary perimeter protection in the evenings. At a reasonable cost, of course."

Dovidas grinned, the silver flecks of his fangs glinting in the light. "Two children offering me protection? Interesting. And why, may I ask, do you believe I would need it?"

He leaned onto his forearms. "Not for you, sir. For your house and its contents. It did not escape my notice the last time I was here that you and Senator Green had reached an agreement regarding the Fryers. Negotiating the sales and acquisitions of such an undertaking will take you from the area frequently, am I correct?"

Dovidas paused before humming in agreement.

"You have a perfect setup to keep your humans safe in the house. However, your exterior security is lacking. Vast grounds. Two weak and secured humans. Gates that are easily compromised. Reinforcing your perimeter with security measures would take time and would require numerous humans in and around your house. For a fee, my associate and I could be your guard dogs during those times you are absent."

Kaspars relaxed into his chair as the Tender entered the room. Her eyes fixated on the ground, he was certain she was unaware of her proximity to Dominic as she crossed the floor and knelt beside her captor. Dovidas glanced at the woman. "You assume I care enough about the safety of the humans to invest money into their security."

He raised a brow. "You care enough about your own resting place, located in this house. And you care about your own survival. Humans are easily compromised. There are those among us with the ability to hypnotize humans. A six-foot gate and wooden door are hardly deterrents to a vampire with a grudge."

"You know something."

"I know nothing. However, I know peddling Deepfryers will not sit well with many and I intend to be on the winning side should it come to a war."

"You believe my side to be the winning side."

"Your reputation precedes you."

Dovidas smiled, a feral glint in his gray eyes. "Would you provide your service for no fee, since you feel strongly about aligning with me?"

"A cheap mercenary is a weak mercenary," he countered.

"Are you good at what you do?"

"I saved Senator Green from yourself, sir."

Kaspars laughed deep and low. "You did. Let's tour the grounds and you can attempt to impress me with your suggestions."

He glanced at Dominic. "Would you like James to join us?"

"I assume he will have nothing to contribute?"

"You assume correctly," he responded. "His skills revolve around his senses. Though they are still in the developmental stage."

Dovidas tuned to Dom to address him. "I'll send Diane in with a warmed A-positive. The Tender is not to be touched. Am I clear?"

Dominic nodded, his dark hair obscuring his eyes.

He sauntered beside Kaspars. "No worries. He's young, but quite controlled. And I'm sure his stench will keep your Tender far away from the pathetic beast."

****

Dominic breathed in. *Out. In. Out.*

The overpowering odor of the river water penetrated his sensitive nostrils, lingered on his tongue, and focused his mind.

MollyMollyMollyMollyMolly.

In. Out.

The delicate scent of honeysuckle wove through the reek of decay and gasoline. Louis's low voice was nothing but white noise against the controlled breathing of Dominic's concentration. Seven yards. He was seven yards away from Molly. His eyes downcast, he had yet to look at her. But her scent wafted through his mind nonetheless.

MollyMollyMollyMollyMolly.

In. Out.

As the older males exited the room, he held steady.

One minute.

Two.

Five.

The shrew-faced Diane entered the room, her leash clanging down the hall in warning. Without a word, she thrust a large wineglass of A-positive blood in his direction before she clattered back down the hall. He stretched out his senses. Louis and Dovidas were outside, their voices muffled, indistinct from one another.

MollyMollyMollyMollyMolly.

In. Out

He raised his eyes from the hardwood, willing his feet to remain anchored to the floor as he took in the presence of his connected for the first time in months.

Her ebony hair sat high on her head in a loose bun, displaying her prominent collarbones and gaunt cheeks.

Molly's gaze remained locked on her knees, the delicate satin of her red dress outlining the boniness of them. His eyes trailed up along her thin thighs, noting the rounded softness had disappeared and now connected to jutting hipbones. The unforgiving fabric of her dress showcased Molly's ribcage and displayed a small bosom below the ornate lace of her neckline.

In. Out.

Assured of their privacy, regardless of how brief, he dared a softly spoken opener. "Good golly, Miss Molly."

Molly's eyes never moved.

Her body, however, took in a deep, shuddered breath.

A whisper.

"You reek, Lord Dominic."

He bit back a grin. Onyx eyes rose to meet his.

MollyMollyMollyMolly.

In. Out.

He stayed his feet. His mind knew there were messages, important things he needed to communicate to the frail woman across the room. His body was tight, every muscle battling between racing to his connected and holding his position for her safety. He focused on the river stench, ignored the honeysuckle, then stretched out his senses to locate Dovidas and his maid before whispering frantically to Molly.

"I'm so sorry," he whispered desperately, "So, so sorry about what I did. Why you're here." His head dropped. "Pretty much everything. All I remember is this overwhelming urge to turn you, to keep you safe and away from whatever bastard wanted to buy you. It was all I could thi…no…" He shook his head, small droplets of foul water splattering on the floor. "No excuse. I'm sorry."

Molly's bony shoulders relaxed slightly. She stared at the ground for a moment before looking up at him. "I would make a terrible vampire anyways," she breathed. "No bacon and all."

He listened as Dovidas and Louis began approaching the house. "When you get back, I'll order up enough bacon for you to eat every single fucking day," he promised. "But right now, we need you to eat the vegetables. They'll weaken Dovidas every time he feeds from you. Louis is our guy on the ground, and he needs you to do this. We have a plan in the works to get you out and deal with the Deepfryer problem. Don't try anything on your own. Nichol is rigging a communication device. Watch for it. And when the shit hits the fan, stay away from windows. There's going to be a lot of fire."

Molly's dark eyes teared. "You aren't saving me now?"

His eyes flew to Molly's restraint, instantly recognizing the strength of the titanium links binding her to her collar.

He could do it.

He could snap the chain, escape out the front door, and disappear.

Fuck the Deepfryers.

Fuck Louis.

Fuck the dozens, maybe hundreds of vampires that would inevitably be torched in the Fryers.

Fuck.

As his heel lifted to propel him forward, he felt a zap tear through his skull.

Kaius.

His ears picked up the footsteps of Dovidas and Louis as they approached the house. Valuable seconds wasted on an impractical fantasy. He stared at Molly, willing her to understand. "I'm sorry," he whispered softly before returning his gaze to the floor as the older males reentered the room.

Chapter Nineteen

Diane was a bitch.

When everything in her day went smoothly, Diane was a bitch.

When something minor went wrong, Diane was a bitch.

When she perceived something was wrong, Diane was a bitch.

And when she was inconvenienced, Diane was a massive bitch.

Upon her discovery earlier that morning that the house phone was dead, Diane had proceeded to take her frustration out on Molly. The cell phone Diane carried was linked solely to Dovidas, useless outside of communication with the Master of the house.

"I can still smell that stink in here!" she would yell every time she entered the great room. "Scrub it again!"

And she would return to her game of deep breath, kneel, scrub, rise, gasp.

When she had watched Dominic shuffle away the night before, she had expected to spend her day torturing herself in bed, tossing and turning to the memories of those turquoise eyes and whispered apology.

No fear of that now.

Dove had fed longer than usual after Dominic and Shaun Moen had left and then he disappeared down the darkened stairwell off the kitchen. Despite her blood loss, she was handed her list of chores to be completed before she would be granted breakfast.

She was tired.

Chores complete, she had fled to the solitude of her room to chew on her fading tub of veggies. The respite had been short lived, however, as Diane had been unable to call in her grocery order.

In Diane's mind, a broken phone line was best dealt with by making Molly scrub the odor of river water out of the house.

Fuck Dominic.

The scent clung to everything.

As she scrubbed, she reviewed what she wished she had communicated to Dominic. In eight nights, Dove was planning to leave for an extended time to do whatever it was jackass vampires did when they disappeared into the dark. Through snippets of phone conversations, she surmised Dove was going as far as Asia, though for what purpose she could not establish.

And she had been too stunned by Dominic's presence to mention it.

Too caught up in the possibility of leaving.

There were faint sounds coming from the basement and growing in intensity over the past week. Initially, she had assumed Dove had taken another woman into the house, but his continued feeding from her had negated that theory. Dove did not want them to see who or what was downstairs, and that made it potentially important.

Too caught up in her fantasies of freedom.

She had been desperate to tell Dominic how hungry she was. How exhausted. How much her bones ached and skin stung. She wanted to know how she could kill her Master, make him pay for the past months of hell. How she could escape the leash and the collar now. Now, not later. But nothing had escaped her lips.

Too caught up in that dark mop of hair obscuring those brilliant eyes.

Deep breath, kneel, scrub, rise, gasp.

The foul stench was embedded in the cleaning rags.

Impossible task.

Deep breath, kneel, scrub, rise, *gasp*.

Gasp.

Gasp.

****

Dominic's eyes shot open, his hands flying to his throat as his body lurched forward on the floor.

"What the fuck!" Mick yelled, appearing at his side in an instant. "Mini. Talk to me, man. What's going on?"

He pulled in lungful after lungful of unneeded air, his frantic panting slowing as he became more alert. He held a hand up to Mick, hoping the male would back off long enough for him to process the nightmare that had woken him.

Mick sat back on his haunches, watching him warily as Nichol joined the pair.

"Explain," Nichol demanded, his brows knotted.

Explain?

What the fuck was he going to say? He shook his head. "Just… needed a minute."

Nichol's hazel eyes looked him over. "You do not need to breathe."

"I'm well fucking aware," he snarked, running a hand through his hair and averting his gaze. "It's fine. I'm completely fucking fine."

“You look like shit,” Rhys stated, plunking down beside Mick and assessing him thoroughly.

He lolled his head back. “Could we just drop it? It’s over.”

Rhys and Nichol looked to Mick, whose jaw was flexing with tension.

“Mini,” Mickey began slowly. “Where did you and Louis disappear to last night?”

****

“How the fuck didn’t you pick up anything?” Rhys barked at Mick as he booted Louis’s bedroom door open. “There’s no way Dom was completely calm in Molly’s presence.”

Dominic remained still on the floor under the intense stare of Nichol.

Louis’s spiky red hair appeared in the doorway, his fangs running long at the unexpected intrusion into his rest. “Dominic and I stopped by Dovidas’ under the guise of me wanting security work. Dovidas wasn’t very open to the idea,” Louis lied smoothly. He looked to him for backup. “What’s going on?”

He opened his mouth to respond, cut off by Mick’s frustrated growl. “Aside from Mini waking up choking for air, we just figured out I felt nothing coming from him during your little trip to Dovidas’s.”

Louis cocked a brow and walked over to him, crouching and looking him over. “Maybe your radar is fucked up.”

“Nope,” Mick muttered. “Rhys is in an increasing state of horniness since his leave from the haunt, Jagg has existed in a boredom realm since he began packing bombs. Nichol is bouncing between excitement and exasperation. I’m guessing that’s because there’s explosives involved but we have to wait to use them. And right now, Dom's working real hard to hide how freaked out he is."

Dominic glanced over at Mickey. "So what did you get from me last night?" he asked, stretching his back out before leaning forward on his knees.

"You were pretty quiet," he replied, shaking his head. "I should have received a spike, but you were muted."

Jagger's humming ceased. "Muted? Mick, do you remember that Subduer we met in France? About a century ago? You were very…thrown by his presence."

Mick nodded slowly. "You were right there, and I couldn't feel a thing. Just your existence. Is it possible Dovidas is a Subduer?"

Curiosity piqued, he sat up a little. "A Subduer?"

"It's a fairly useless skill under most circumstances, but a Subduer can reduce the clarity of empaths and ties. Strong ones can mute bloodmates," Jagg explained. "Merely being in that one's presence had Mickey quite turned around."

Rhys stood against the wall, his arms crossed and navy eyes narrowing. "I guess that would explain why Boy didn't report anything to me. He's always the first to know when my Tenders are in trou… oh, fuck." Rhys stared at him long and hard. "Mini. What exactly have you felt since that night you tried to turn Molly? Is it possible you overrode Boy's tie?"

All eyes fell on him as he processed the idea. "Doesn't fucking matter, if Dovidas is a Subduer. I shouldn't feel anything in that case."

While most of the males grumbled their agreement, Nichol stood, towering over him. "You *shouldn't* feel anything? Shouldn't, or don't, Mini?"

He continued to assess the uneven grains of the wooden floor. Even if his young blood had overridden Boy's tie to Molly, a Subduer would make it a moot point.

He was going nuts, and his brothers were figuring it out.

He'd be put down like a rabid dog.

He was carefully crafting a lie in his mind when a shooting pain across his spine snapped him into focus. He leapt to his feet, away from Mickey's hand as it smacked across his back a second time.

Mick stalked toward him. "Take your shirt off, Dom."

He shook his head.

The other males began to circle him, monitoring his retreat and cutting off his escapes.

"I barely fucking touched you," Mickey growled. "Now take off your goddamn shirt."

He was scanning the room for a way out when he was taken down from behind, Rhys's tattooed arms tearing the shirt open before locking onto him and holding him still. "Nothing," Rhys reported. "Not a fucking mark."

****

Mick was siphoning Dominic's rising feral rage as fast as he safely could when Rhys's hand smacked against Dom's back, sending a burst of pain through Dom and into him. Dominic reared up on Rhys, fangs snapping as a low growl overtook the room. When Rhys moved to strike back, Mick jumped in.

"Hold up!" he barked, the pounding fury and confusion from his hauntmates threatening to overtake him. “Rhys stand down. Mini… I really need you to calm. Everyone needs to calm the fuck down so we can figure this out.”

The ratcheting tension eased slightly, enough for him to center himself as Louis stepped between Rhys and Dominic. He held up his hands to Dom, approaching him slowly. “I want you to turn around, Dominic,” Louis said quietly. “No one’s going to jump you. Just turn around and face Nichol.”

Dominic hesitated before he complied. Louis moved in closer to the young male, murmuring as he did. “You’re going to feel my right hand on your right shoulder blade. Any pain?”

When Dom shook his head, Louis looked to him for confirmation.

“Alright, kid. Now I’m going to move toward your left blade. If it hurts, tell me.”

Louis’s hand inched across Dominic’s back, stopping when the muscles tensed. He changed direction, moving down. The process went on for five minutes as the Kaius males watched Dominic’s reactions. With every ripple of Dom’s muscle, Louis changed course until he stepped away and dropped his hand.

“When did it start?” he asked. When Dominic refused to answer, Louis moved directly into his line of sight and addressed the others over his shoulder. “Going from memory, the pain follows the whip marks his connected female carries.”

“Impossible,” Nichol scoffed. “Even if he did manage to link to the woman, the Subduer would mute the link. And pain transmission is not a symptom of connection.”

Louis cocked a brow. "Symptom? Connection isn't some fatal disease, man."

Dominic's anger drained instantly, replaced by defeat as he dropped his head. "I've heard her," he muttered.

He froze. "Heard who, Mini?"

"Molly." Dominic refused to look up. "Seen her, too. I… I think I'm going insane."

He didn't have to scan the room to know his hauntmates heard the confession. The instant bombardment of bewilderment and resignation told him enough.

Vampires who had lost control of their faculties were a danger, dealt with swiftly and irrevocably.

"Good fucking luck to you," Louis suddenly chuckled, pushing his ire up instantly. The red-haired male turned to the others. "Your little brother has managed to reach a connection level on par with that of a millennium-old vampire. I'd wager his attempt to turn the female is to blame. He may very well have progressed far enough in the process to begin a sire link. Combine the two, and you get… this."

The silence stretched out as the males considered the possibility.

"He's too young," Nichol stated.

Louis met his stare and rolled his eyes, far from Nichol's view. "Yeah, well, they all gotta grow up sometime, Nichol."

Mick turned his attention to Dom as he mulled over the new information.

A spike of terror shot out from Dominic as he looked up. "If I'm not nuts, and I really did experience Molly's whipping, then my nightmare today…"

Chapter Twenty

Louis watched the cantankerous Nichol with a mixture of awe and annoyance. The snarky male had managed to hack into the telephone company's servers to determine when technicians would be dispatched to the Dovidas home and had subsequently added his shack to the repair list ahead of the call. Tomorrow. 10:00 a.m.

The phone beside him buzzed. Again.

It was greatly irresponsible for you to bring a young vampire on a recon mission unapproved by me. Especially when said mission is in direct violation of my instructions to keep all males of my bloodline out of scenting distance.

He read Kaius's text quickly before placing the phone back on the table.

While impressed with Nichol's technological abilities, he had spent the past three days awake with the sullen male, ready at a moment's notice to use his hypnotic skills on the workers that would be intercepted and sent off with enough explosives to level a hockey arena. Having a companion with no sense of humor and a penchant for withering glares at the most innocent of questions had flipped the hostility switch of his trademark unflappable demeanor.

The hours of lecture via text was not helping.

Kaius Khthonios was a master of logical guilt.

Another *buzz*.

Did your creator deprive your brain of oxygen before bringing you over? Which testicle you are least attached to?

Fuck.

It had taken longer than expected for Dovidas's maid to arrange a repair. Dominic had risen every evening anxious for news before busying himself with monotonous tasks around the tiny house. Unbeknownst to the others, he and Dom were expected at Dovidas's for a trial security job when nightfall hit tonight.

Although he was second-guessing following through with the plan as Kaius tore a strip off of him, he was certain that placing himself within Dovidas's immediate circle would be instrumental in the Kaius haunt's plan.

In his mind, his plan made more sense. But Dominic's involvement would not be approved by Kaius regardless of the rationale.

With the realization that Dominic's connection to the Tender was not only unnaturally intense, but also cutting straight through the powers of a Subduer, the mission had taken on a new urgency. The males were watching Dom carefully now, reading Molly's condition through the young vampire for any signs of immediate distress.

Aside from intermittent gasps for air in the early morning hours, Molly appeared safe. Temporarily.

The hauntmates had finally decided against stealth in this mission. Although it was their first foray back into the vampire world of political warfare, the haunt had long since been both admired and feared for their covert operations, the true masterminds revealing themselves long after the mission was successful.

Bombing the Dovidas house into dust was anything but a Kaius Khthonios tactic.

He approved.

In the haunt's plan, his job was to send repairmen onto the grounds for two purposes: to plant explosives around the house's base and to enter the house under the guise of line checking. Once inside, the techs were to locate the Tender's room and plant the lipstick communicator.

He was to prowl the exterior that evening to connect the explosives to a series of wires linked to a detonator Nichol could control from his computer.

From there, Louis would lie in wait until Kaspars left the house, be it that evening or nights later. He would then infiltrate the house and release Molly. Once they were evacuated, the detonator would go off, leveling everything in the radius.

Jagg would wait up the street in Nichol's black SUV and trail Dovidas at a distance.

Rhys would be parked behind him in a rented vehicle, ready to receive the Tender once she was free. In the unlikely event of Dovidas returning to the house, the vitamin K weakened Kaspars would be captured by Louis and brought to the shack for questioning.

However, the haunt theorized Dovidas would likely flee the area and head straight to wherever his Deepfryers were being produced. And Jagg would follow his every move. From there, the hauntmates would be able to set up surveillance and establish a covert operation to capture Dovidas, destroy the Deepfryers, and potentially discover if any other vampires were involved in Kaspar Dovidas's business.

It was the uncertainty of time and strength, the

potential for scent recognition, and Dominic's connection to the woman that caused him to adapt the plan. Should anything go awry, he was determined to ensure he was not seen by Dovidas as the enemy in the heat of the moment as it would only be upon confrontation that he would be able to accurately judge how weakened the vitamin K had made the older male.

Working for Kaspars meant his scent around the house would be expected if the bombs did not fully decimate the building. Since the Kaius haunt plan only became personally involved should Dovidas lead them to the Deepfryers' location, he had to be prepared to play alongside Dovidas should his strength not be adequately diminished for capture.

Dominic would be integral.

With his scent unidentifiable, Dominic was his nomination for rescuing the Tender. He could easily cry turncoat on the young male after he and the woman were off the premises. Dom would never be identified by Kaspars or his associates, and he could blame an error in judgment on his perceived youth. On his own, he could not guarantee that the malnourished woman would escape should Dovidas hightail it back to the house unexpectedly.

And he didn't want her death on his head.

So tonight, his fourth night awake, he and Dom would return to the Dovidas house for a few hours to monitor the location as mercenaries. Dovidas had referred to it as a "trial." He intended to use the time to compile a mental list of the locations he would instruct the repairmen to plant the explosives the following day. With any luck, Dovidas would make his outing a short one and he would have ample time to hunt, feed, and rest before his ten o'clock meeting with the telephone repair techs.

Opening a cold bag of blood, he offered it to Nichol who merely grunted while he snatched it. The sun was slowly disappearing as Dom's eyes snapped open.

"Anything?"

"Tomorrow at ten, Dominic," he said. "We have to leave for our date in fifteen."

Nichol's eyes narrowed. "What date?"

"Dominic needs to feed."

"Last time you took him out, you ended up at Dovidas's."

"And I learned my lesson."

Mickey wandered over, his shirt wrinkled and stretched from over wear. He eyed him, well aware that he rarely learned his lessons regardless of the teacher. Glancing over at Dominic, Mick nodded slowly, reached over to grab a lipstick tube off the work area, and pushed it into Dom's hand. "Fine. Clip your fangs and go. Use a blade for bloodletting, not your teeth. I want you disguised on those streets. And Louis? I'm trusting you with my hauntmate. You get that, right?"

The phone buzzed again.

> *You have the foresight of a goldfish and should make it a personal growth goal to adhere to plans instead going off haphazardly in an unrestrained manner.*

He glanced at Mick. "I get it. We'll be back long before dawn. I swear it."

With his friend's blessing, he waited as Dominic's fang tips were snipped and they disappeared into the night.

****

Nichol watched the door close before turning to Mickey. “You know they are blatantly disobeying Kaius. How are you fine with this?”

“Because I know Louis. Whatever he’s doing with our plan, he’s doing it to save his ass and ours. Our framework has left a lot of holes when it comes to him. My guess is Louis has figured a way to close those holes, leaving himself less open for attack,” he mused.

“Kaius would not approve,” Nichol warned.

“Forgiveness over permission, my good man.”

“You have faith in that rogue?”

“More than in your heartless ass, Nicky,” he grinned. “When Kai finds out Dominic is involved, I’ll keep your name out of the report.”

“You better. Fuckhead.”

****

Dominic glared at the mighty Mississippi River, its navy waves lapping gently at his feet. “There has *got* to be a better way.”

“Fine. Strip down and get in.”

Downstream from the barges, the water’s odor was potent with chemicals. Toeing his sneakers off, he began undressing, mumbling under his breath about the unfairness of it all.

Louis grabbed each item of clothing as it was tossed his way. “Could be worse. Sewage plants provide the same scent coverage.”

“You could at least turn around, you old pervert,” he groused as he stepped into the dank water. Louis’s deep chuckle was muffled as he dove in, immersing himself in the foul stench before bursting back onto the bank.

“If you go for a quick run, you’ll dry off,” Louis suggested, exaggerating his efforts to keep his back to the naked male.

“Just pass me my fucking clothes.”

He ran his tongue over his clipped fangs and listened carefully as Louis outlined their game plan for the night. His role involved shutting up and taking advantage of any opportunity to plant the lipstick tube in Molly’s room. Louis would continue to saddle up to Dovidas and maintain the guise of a mercenary hoping for a well-compensated job.

Dovidas met the males at the gate, his dark hair and jacket obscuring him from human eyes. “Moen. Banks. I’ll be heading out immediately. You can expect me back shortly. I assume there will be no need for you to venture into the house?”

He kept his head down, sliding his eyes in Louis’s direction.

“No reason I foresee, sir,” Louis responded. “We’ll patrol the perimeter and report anything questionable. I can text you at the number you provided Sunday?”

“Of course. See you shortly.”

He watched Dovidas’s silhouette disappeared down the street. “That’s it?”

Louis crooked his head toward the house. “You have two minutes to get that thing in her room before he returns. Dovidas will be watching us, likely from…” Louis glanced around as he passed a thin blade to him, “that tree across the street. Perfect view of the entire estate. Third window on the eastern side of the house. Go.”

He tore across the yard, stretching his senses and noting Louis’s casual gait on the grass and Dovidas’s retreating footsteps.

Third window.

Bingo.

Using Louis's blade, he wedged the window open gently, extending it just far enough for his fingers and the tube to fit through. A faint scent of honeysuckle wafted out. He rapped on the glass lightly, hoping against hope it would be Molly's ears, and not those of Dovidas, that picked up the sound.

"Molly," he hissed. "You there?"

Pale fingers reached through the small opening. "Dominic?"

He exhaled, the sound of her voice soothing his core. Fighting the urge to touch her, he pushed the lipstick into the room. "Hey," he whispered, a grin spreading across his face at the sight of the wiggling fingers. "I only have a minute. The lipstick is a two-way communicator. Use it solely during daylight hours, and only when you're certain you're alone."

"But during the day…" Molly's voice began, hushed and tired.

"I'll answer. I swear it," he murmured. "If you're in trouble, I'll know."

"How?" Molly whispered, her hand worming further out the small opening.

Risking the subtle scent of honeysuckle transferring to his skin, he caressed Molly's fingers quickly and nudged her hand back. "Because I screwed up big time," he hushed. "Once you're back with us, I'll explain it all. I better run. Stay safe. Please." He eased his hand from the window and looked at it. "And wash your hands. He'll scent me on you if you don't."

He closed the window tight.

Mission accomplished.

He rejoined Louis and the two males spent the next hour skulking through the yard. With the knowledge that Dovidas was watching their every move, they made a show out of separating, investigating different nooks, and reconvening to discuss their findings.

Louis found a rat nest.

He found a large branch and spent most of his patrol sword fighting imaginary foes.

Less than two hours had passed when Dovidas made his official appearance. "I trust it went well, Moen?"

"Nothing to report, sir."

Kaspars' gray eyes scanned him. "Anything to report?"

"No, sir."

They stood in silence.

Dominic, anticipating the worst.

Louis, holding Dovidas's unblinking gaze.

Dovidas, sizing the mercenaries up.

With a flash of his fangs, Dovidas broke the stillness. "Next week I will be leaving the area on business. I have guests arriving during my absence. However, there will be two, possibly three nights where my house will be unguarded. As per your recommendation, I will have an increased surveillance system in place prior to my departure, but your presence would be an added deterrent should anyone see my home as a target. Are you interested?"

Louis bowed his head in acknowledgement. "Of course, sir. What are you willing to pay for our loyalty?"

Dovidas barked a laugh. "Two thousand per night.

With the opportunity to match any other offers you may receive, mercenary."

"More than fair, sir," Louis responded with a fake salute. "Text me the night before you go and we take our pay in cash."

"Naturally."

****

Louis was feeling much better after stopping for a quick snack on the way home. Dominic had waited patiently in the shadows while he fed off a middle-aged woman before hypnotizing himself out of her memory and continuing on his way. As the males entered his shack, Mickey met them at the door.

"My prodigal sons!" he exclaimed in a comical falsetto. "Nichol! I told you they would return to us. Such good boys. Such good, good boys."

Rhys grabbed Dominic and pushed him toward the bathroom. "Naughty boys playing in the filth. Mickey, dear, you really must be stricter with them."

Jagg observed the over-acting with a small smile.

Nichol pulled his chair in closer to the computer screen.

"So how'd it go?" Mick asked him as the shower fired up.

"The communication device has been deposited, Dominic found a stick to play with, and Dovidas is leaving town next week. Business. If the timing is right, that falls right at the sixteen-night mark. As in Sixteen Candles. Dom's connected is brighter than you gave her credit for."

Rhys's eyes rolled back.

"Anyways," he continued, "James Banks and Shaun Moen will be working security until Dovidas's guests arrive a few nights later."

Rhys frowned. "Who the fuck is James Banks?"

"That would be Dominic."

"Ah. Gotcha. Any idea who the guests are?"

He shook his head. "No idea. Have to be vampires, though, if security detail ends when they arrive. Trusted by Dovidas since they will be there in his absence. Could be our possible accomplices."

Mickey pulled up a rickety chair. "Does this change anything?"

"Only if you want Kaius to eat Louis," Nichol called over. "I'm game for that."

"Doesn't change anything," he responded while flipping Nichol off. Behind his back. Definitely out of view. "What it does do is tighten our time line. If we hold off until Dovidas leaves to identify his guests, he could disappear for good. Tomorrow morning the repair techs will be here for the explosives. With the communicator deposited, the chance of miscommunication is significantly reduced."

"Miscommunication?" Rhys asked.

"Minute possibility with multiple instructions. Wires get crossed. Human brains often struggle with compartmentalizing various tasks," he replied.

Mickey stared at him. "So there was a possibility that the lipstick would be planted outside and the bombs placed in Molly's room?"

"Minute. Very."

Mickey shook his head quickly. "Okay. But with that done, the techs will lay the bombs and you'll connect them when?"

"Tomorrow night. I'll do up a map for the techs now. I suggest we make this a go three nights from now," he said as he stretched his neck. "That will give Nichol time to adjust any issues, the woman will hopefully contact Dominic, and I can fucking rest."

Chapter Twenty-One

Mick was drowning.

Nichol's obsessive compulsion had been morphing the surly male into a raging vampire with a hair-trigger temper. He ranted. Snarled. Paced. The extended time at Louis's shack, away from his meticulously organized control room in the Kaius haunt, was wearing on him.

Combining that with the close quarters and lack of solitude Nichol desperately needed, the male was quickly reaching his boiling point. Despite his attempts to pull in some of the old vampire's anxiety, Nichol skulked the tiny house like a caged lion, his hazel eyes and elongated fangs flashing in the dim light.

Jagg, who often served as a stoic beacon for him during contentious times, had been retreating further into his own core and out of his reach. The ice-eyed male escaped the rising tension in the house by closing his eyes and hiding within his own thoughts as the others ignored the quiet vampire perched in the corner.

He was unable to follow his humming brother into that muted space and was instead left outside with nothing but Jagg's constant echoed regret.

Hour fifty.

Dominic had held his impatience and worry close to his chest in the passing hours. Molly had yet to activate the communicator and the young vampire had not spoken outside of hourly updates since the previous night. He kept a constant stream open, allowing Dom's fear and frustration to trickle out steadily. With each hourly update, he poked softly at Dominic's core to ensure it remained encased in control.

The box was thin.

He quietly rationalized to Dominic that Molly's silence in both the communicator and in Dom's mind was a good thing. Once the hauntmates established that Molly was active in his head during times of extreme emotion, it was easier to assuage Dominic's concerns regarding the female's safety.

At least, it was easier for Dom to pretend to the others.

But he knew his younger brother had done little more than push the worry off his face and toward his core.

The silence from Kaius was unsurprising. The hauntmates were accustomed to the frequent and extended absences of their creator, and his disappearance had little impact on the mission at hand. They'd grown used to not knowing, to not asking, and to not fighting about it. Kaius did whatever it was he needed to do, and he made it very clear it was none of his haunt's business.

Mickey, however, was battling feelings of resentment as he was left to absorb the increasing negativity of his brethren without the support of the intuitive Kai. With no one to take the reins, he had no break from the emotional onslaught swarming the tiny space night and day.

Rhys's good humor was beginning to flounder amidst the rising tension in the house. With the others withdrawing into themselves or reacting with extreme agitation, Rhys's comments had become less jovial and more biting. Despite his attempts to pull as much negativity into himself as he could handle, Rhys was frustrated with waiting and anxious to return to the luxury of his quarters.

Decades spent imprisoned over the past seven centuries had made Rhys wary of small spaces and agitated by sparseness. Louis's shack was, for Rhys, akin to a cell. The secrecy of their mission meant the hauntmates were sequestered in the house and that removal of freedom sliced at Rhys's psyche.

Though he would never voice it, he feared the day Rhys succumbed to his past.

The solitary rogue vampire provided the smallest relief for him when he was present. Without the restrictions on his movements that the others faced, Louis had spent the past two nights prowling the streets and sidling up to Dovidas. The phone repair techs had done an excellent job of reestablishing telephone connection at the Dovidas home. They had also planted every explosive provided. Louis left at sundown tonight with the goal of connecting the detonator lines to the hidden devices despite Kaspars' presence in the house.

It was a risky move, but Dovidas had made no movement outside the grounds in two nights and the tightened timeline had caused the hauntmates to agree to the calculated gamble. Without a blood connection, he was unable to track his friend and his unease over the delicate assignment compounded the irritability he was absorbing at a rapid rate.

He was drowning.

It had been decades since the hauntmates had worked in cohesion on a mission with such widespread implications. The expedited timeline meant they were going in with less intel than any of the males were comfortable with. There were too many unknowns, too many suppositions, too many repercussions, and too few guarantees.

The likelihood of Dovidas working alone was low due to the expense and consequences of marketing Deepfryers in North America. Kaspars Dovidas was old enough to be an intimidating front man, but young enough to be expendable to a much older vampire. Who that older vampire would be was, however, a mystery.

The rationale behind supplying your own species' death traps was a question in itself. In the long lives of vampires, financial gain was rarely a motive for making such a dangerous move against the fanged population. Without knowing who was backing Dovidas, the hauntmates were left with little more than baseless theories.

He parked himself in front of a small window overlooking the dirt road and watched for Louis. His friend's unexpected attachment to Dominic had been a welcomed turn of events for him. His young brother needed a male around that didn't coddle him, didn't shelter him from precarious undertakings.

Dominic had been exposed to few risky situations in his short life as none of the elder hauntmates could bring themselves to put their youngest member into harm's way. The haunt's overprotectiveness of their "baby brother" had left Dominic vulnerable should he ever be on his own, and Louis was quietly pushing those first necessary steps of independence and responsibility onto Dom.

He was grateful, because his own haunt was unable to see Dom as anything other than that dirty, destroyed boy Kaius had brought solemnly into the haunt three decades earlier.

The tortured, helpless turquoise eyes obscured by blood-soaked hair had been burned into the memories of the hauntmates and was not easily forgotten when faced with the opportunity to push Mini into the real world of vampirism.

"Fifty-one," Dominic muttered into the silent room.

He glanced over at his brethren. Jagg remained motionless in the corner, his soul-piercing eyes closed. Nichol was hunched over his computer, his hands flexing and fisting rhythmically. Rhys was glaring at a glass of cold blood, willing it to taste better than the previous night's had. Dominic was tracing his jawline absently, his dark mood flickering with a serene numbness.

****

It was four hours before dawn. Rhys had passed restless and moved into antsy. Cramped quarters were difficult for vampires in general due to their lack of escape routes, but his personal experiences with small spaces made his perception of the confinement more pronounced.

Staring out the tiny window with Mick helped alleviate some of the pressure, but he was well aware it was Mickey's empathic draw that was keeping his emotions in check and not the dirtied glimpse of the outdoors visible through the glass.

Dominic sat on the threadbare sofa, his head periodically lolling forward before it snapped back up. He motioned to Mick.

"How's Mini registering?" he asked, watching

Dom's eyes drift close.

Mickey paused, then crouched at Dominic's knee. "Hey. Mini. You tired or something?" When the younger male didn't respond, Mick called over to Nichol. "You should come check this out," he said slowly. "He's totally calm. Like, sleeping kind of calm."

Nichol pushed past Rhys and booted Dom's ankle. "Get up."

Dominic's eyes cracked open and he struggled to his feet briefly before falling back onto the couch.

He frowned and knelt by his brother. "What the hell's wrong with him?"

Nichol pulled out his phone. "What the hell's wrong with Molly might be the question." He tossed his phone to him and began checking Dominic over thoroughly. "I've texted Louis. Let me know when he responds."

The males stood around the sofa, prodding at Dom intermittently and watching the silent phone. Rhys returned to his position at the window.

A lone figure appeared at the end of the road, moving at an impressive speed.

"He's back," Mick called, standing up to open the door as Dom burst to his feet.

"She's fucking gone!" Dominic roared, his formerly lethargic body primed for a fight as Nichol went on the defensive. Rhys moved in front of Dominic, preparing to take the male down if needed. "Nothing! I can't feel a single fucking thing! She's fucking dead!"

Louis appeared instantly in the doorway, his fangs elongated and tinged red. His crimson hair was slick with mud that ran in rivulets down his face. A quick, possessive growl bit through the air. “Down, Dominic,” Louis barked. “Rhys, pass him that communicator and be fucking ready.”

He flipped the small device open and tossed it to Dom as Louis slammed the door behind him. “We need to move. Tonight.”

“What the fuck?” Nichol bellowed. “What did you do?”

“Don’t start it, old man,” Louis hissed before turning to him and Mickey. “Most of the explosives are linked. But the woman…*fuck.* Someone get me a goddamn blood. I’m fucking drained.”

He vaulted to the fridge while Mick placed a steadying hand on his friend. Without bothering to prep it, he handed the bag to Louis and watched as the pale vampire downed the entire thing before signaling for another.

Louis had lost a lot of blood.

The minutes ticked by as Louis emptied two more bags before he stood and walked over to Dominic, who had remained frozen in place with the communicator tight in his grip. “You need to hear this. Got it? The woman’s alive, but… fuck.”

He watched Mini’s eyes lock onto Louis’s fangs before nodding slowly.

“It was all good. I got on the property with no problems. The cameras Dovidas brought in are on site, but not active yet, so it was pretty simple to move around the house without detection. I had to avoid the area directly in front of the great room, though, so that area is dead. Will they still detonate with a gap, Nichol?” Louis asked.

"You bypassed that area completely? Then yes. Should be fine."

Louis began pacing the tattered floor. "Good. Not good. Fuck. Okay. I figured while Dovidas was occupied at the other end of the house, I'd try to make contact with the woman." His eyes snapped to Dominic. "I jimmied the window. Figured I'd poke my head in, introduce myself. That was it. All I was going to do, Dom."

He moved swiftly, placing himself in arm's reach of Dominic. Dom was stalking slowly toward Louis, his nostrils flaring as he picked up a faint scent.

"She wasn't moving, Dom. Barely breathing. Who knows how long she's been like that, but you know that scent of death?" Louis locked his gaze with Dom's. "It was there, Dominic. Clinging to everything. Only thing I could do was feed her. It took a lot before she started responding, but she did. Got it? You understand your connected is alive, right?"

Dominic stopped his advance. "Her blood," he growled hoarsely. "It's on your fangs."

Louis stepped back, dropping his arms to his sides. "I've never given my blood before, Dom. I… I wasn't prepared for the pull to bite."

Dominic launched himself at Louis, who stood his ground. Rhys moved to jump in as Jagg pulled him back. "Louis can defend himself."

The hauntmates scattered to the room's perimeter as Louis and Dominic fought, fangs and fists hitting their marks.

"You linked," Dominic snarled between strikes, "to Molly. I'm going to fucking kill you!"

He watched as Louis matched his strength to the

young vampire's. "It was a fucking accident!" When Dominic's fangs sunk into Louis's biceps, the elder male reared up and flung Dom across the room. The sound of tearing flesh made him wince as Louis finally pulled rank and flattened Dominic to the floor.

"Now listen, Dom. Your Molly should be waking at any minute. The lipstick com is in her hand. You need to talk her through tonight, because we need to move now. My scent is all over that room and inside the veins of Dovidas's Tender." Louis paused to check in with Mick.

"When he gets a whiff of her or that room, she's fucking dead and this whole thing is over. We. Need. To. Move."

Mick began pulling his boots on. He and Jagg followed suit.

"I'm letting you up," Louis said calmly to Dominic. "You can take a round out of me another night, but right now is *not* the time."

Dom struggled against the older vampire's hold before submitting with a nod. As he stood, Louis retrieved the communicator and pushed it into Dom's hand. "You're staying back with Nichol. Rhys will bring the woman here."

"I'm coming."

"Not with me, you aren't," Louis snapped. "I'm already compromised with my scent in the woman, and frankly, Dominic, I have a big enough target on my back on that property. I sure as fuck don't want to be worrying about your connected ass ambushing me, too."

Dominic bared his fangs briefly before taking a deep breath. "Rhys," he snarled over his shoulder, "I'm riding with you." Dom looked Louis dead in the eye. "I will hunt you down every night of my post-life if you let her die."

"I would deserve it."

Chapter Twenty-Two

Louis relaxed back into the passenger seat as Mick tore away from the shack and onto the freeway. The taste of the Tender's blood was fading in his mouth and the precarious hold on his bloodlust was finally strengthening its grip.

"Weird feeling, isn't it?" Mick mused.

"The weirdest. Like every drop she took was actually invigorating me, not draining me. You ever exchange?" he asked, his curiosity peaked.

"Only donated to my brothers," Mick replied, his eyes locked on the dark streets. "And your pathetic ass that once, but that was for, like, a second. It's a similar feeling, I think. But less intense since we all share the same line. And I've never had the urge to bite them back."

"Wonder if that's normal. The biting thing. Mick, it was so fucking intense. I didn't even know I was doing it until I'd pulled a good four or five mouthfuls in," he moaned. "Dominic is going to stake me in my sleep."

"Nah," Mick laughed. "You'll send his woman back to him, he'll forget we all exist, and everyone will live happily ever after."

He chuckled and called Rhys's cell phone. "That you and Dominic behind us?" he asked, glancing in the rear-view mirror.

"Yup. What's the plan, guys?" Rhys's voice asked. A feral snarl from Dominic tore through the speakers.

"Dom'll wait for the woman after I release her and get the hell outta the area. You'll take one vehicle and trail Kaspars if he escapes. Speaking of which, how important is it to not kill him tonight?" he inquired.

"Very," Rhys responded. "Unless it comes down to you or him. We'll take you."

Mick glanced at his own phone. "Fuck. Kai's beeping in. Link me?"

Kaius's deep voice echoed in the car. "Explain."

Rhys and Dom's line went dead silent. Louis looked out his window. Mick sighed. "Mission's changed. Circumstances have led us on the road there now."

"Changed. Louis?"

He fought back a wince. "Long story short, sir, the bombs are set and I formed a blood link to Dominic's connected female."

Kaius went quiet.

"Full report before dawn," Kai finally said, a hint of exasperation in his voice.

The line went dead. He looked over at Mick as Rhys chirped in. "Nice summary, you asshat. Now what about Mick? What's his assignment tonight?"

"Spotter, then driver," Louis stated. "I need eyes on the site. There's a tree a few houses over that overlooks the entire yard. Dovidas used it the night Dominic and I played mercenary for him. Once the female is out, Mick will drive her and Dom and I'll run home."

Mick turned down Dovidas's street, dimming his lights and pulling to a stop alongside the curb. The males unfolded themselves from the vehicle and walked over to Rhys and Dominic.

Dom was silent, his eyes boring holes into him as

Mick and Rhys touched base

"If Molly can't move, get me," Rhys stated, looking between him and Dominic. "No fucking around."

Louis and Mick crept along the shadows of the street, staying far from the lamps lining the broken pavement. He pointed to the tree, its branches heavy with greenery. Mick nodded and moved swiftly toward it before turning back.

"We appreciate this, Louis," he whispered. "I've got your back. Know that."

He nodded before slinking toward the northern side of Kaspars's property where shrubbery concealed a perfect infiltration weakness in the brick wall. He scented the air, focusing all his energy on one sense at a time.

Dovidas was still in the great room, his voice a whispered hint among the din of the city noises. The weakness of his scent on his own property was indicative of how cloistered Kaspars had been inside his house over the past few days.

He moved closer to the building, his boots sinking into the perpetually damp moss of the gardens. He rounded the corner, inching stealthily toward the Tender's window. It was still slightly ajar, a fresh scent overtaking the underlying odor of death and decay.

He reached up, hoisting himself easily through the opening before vaulting silently onto the woman's empty bed. Glancing around, he noticed the lid of the lipstick tube lying on the floor. As he picked it up, slow shadows danced under the bathroom door.

Click.

"Dominic?" the woman whispered, her voice

throaty.

A faint crackle.

"Molly!" Dominic's voice echoed quietly in the tiled bathroom.

He moved closer, keeping one ear tuned into the quiet one-sided conversation Dovidas was holding in the great room.

Dom wasted no time. He was impressed. "You're getting out tonight, Moll. Louis's going in, I'm out here. Do what he says. Okay?"

The woman's voice shook. "I'll be home tonight?"

Dovidas's call ended.

Movement.

He flung the bathroom door open and grabbed the woman from behind, one large hand covering her mouth and dragging her toward the open window while the other hand pocketed the lipstick communicator. Her eyes widened in fright as she instinctively began to fight against the unknown force, going limp the moment recognition of him kicked in. Dovidas's footsteps halted in their progress down the hallway toward the kitchen. They closed in on the window, the Tender almost yanked from his grip.

The chains.

An angry red welt was quickly forming on the woman's neck. He ran his hands across the links, his sensitive skin picking up the weakest soldered link. He tightened his hold and tugged, cursing when the chain remained unbroken in his hands. He paused, listening for Dovidas.

Boots on tile.

"Even if you broke it, it wouldn't do any good," Molly whispered, her hands stilling the quiet clank of her leash.

His mind flashed. Never go to rest with one, never give them access to your resting place, and never underestimate the worth of a perimeter collar.

Fuck.

He assessed the house, picking up the approaching maid by the sound of her chain clinking along the metal track. Dovidas was still topside.

Taking them on in full view of the Kaius haunt would be wiser than waiting in Molly's bedroom, trapped like rats. "I'll clear the path. You get to the great room and get as close to the windows as you can," he hissed, tracking the maid and Dovidas. "If you hear anything fizzle or crack, back the hell up and turn away from the glass."

Keeping her in his peripheral, he led her out the door.

The maid froze as she caught sight of them exiting the room, her mouth gaping open before she turned, calling for her master while she raced along her track. Dovidas appeared at the end of the hallway, his silvered fangs flashing and eyes narrowed into slits as he took in the scene.

"Mercenary," Kaspars spat. "My whore is worth your head?"

"Her price is," he countered, moving forward to create a small opening for Molly to escape to the great room. He palmed the uncapped lipstick tube in his pocket, feeling through the denim fabric for the call button. Pressing it slowly, he spoke over his shoulder while keeping his eyes on the advancing Dovidas. "Woman, now. Gentlemen, in thirty."

The Tender shot past him as Dovidas lunged for

her, her path perfectly aligned with the tracks on the ceiling. Louis intercepted the vampire, noting his speed was a good hundred years behind expectation. Providing the vitamin K affected his strength as well, he had a fighting chance of escaping alive. The males fell to the floor with a crash, the feral snarling reverberating throughout the halls as Dovidas growled orders at his maid.

The maid doubled back after Molly, her own movements through the maze uncoordinated, her progress halted by the stoppers scattered on the tracks. He kept one eye on Molly while he fought Dovidas off, mentally counting down the timing of the explosives while the woman lunged toward a small end table, her collar cutting off her air supply.

She yanked a drawer open, booting the maid across the knees and sending her to the floor, the sound of the maid's neck snapping as her chain went taut. Between blocking Dovidas's fangs, he caught glimpses of Molly while she moved enough to take in another breath before diving back to the drawer, her arm extended as far as it would go until she found what she wanted.

A key.

She looked over at the maid's lifeless body, her dark eyes hardening as she began working the key into the chain that connected her to the track.

Twenty-six.

He was losing ground in the fight, Dovidas finally pinning him. "Jump!" he barked as Dovidas's fangs sunk into his throat, ripping across his voice box.

Twenty-seven.

The woman hesitated, gripping her collar before flinging the glass doors open and launching herself forward. His mind registered the crack of electricity as he fought back against Dovidas. He knew he needed to gain the upper hand before blood loss eliminated any advantage the vitamin K had provided.

Twenty-nine. Thirty.

The explosives detonated in bursts, shaking the house's foundation and catching Kaspars off guard. He took advantage of Dovidas's momentary confusion to buck the male off of him, leaping to his feet in preparation for attack. As understanding overcame Dovidas's features, his stance changed from fight to flight. Louis turned toward the hallway and launched himself toward a large painting on the wall, tearing it from the wall and smashing the frame.

Improvised stake.

Tackling Dovidas to the ground, he fought to still the older male long enough to get the wooden weapon embedded in his chest. Dovidas snarled, his fangs snapping and ripping across his arms until he paused his defense.

A faint howling emerged from the kitchen, growing louder and shriller.

Dovidas grinned, bloodied fangs on full display.

****

From Dominic's vantage point, he could make out Louis's movements as he prowled along the exterior and crawled carefully into Molly's window. At his angle, however, he was unable to make out anything inside. Pulling his phone out, he fired off a text to Rhys and Mick.

Dominic: Anything? I'm blind
Rhys: Nada
Mick: Nothing

He resumed scouring the neighborhood from the ground, flicking his attention back to Dovidas's house every few seconds. As the minutes ticked by, he became increasingly nervous.

Louis should have had her out by now.

A flicker of movement on the north side of the house.

He focused in on the source. A tall male, perhaps six-four or six-five was sidling up to the front door. With one eye on the intruder and another on his phone, Mick fired off another message.

Dominic: Big guy incoming front door. Any visual?

Rhys: Don't have sight

Mick: See him. Inside now.

Louis's voice crackled over the communicator, breaking the quiet of the neighborhood. "Molly, now. Gentlemen, in thirty."

He fired off a text to Nichol to detonate, counting the seconds down and jumping as a crackle of electricity burst from the French doors of the great room. Molly cried out and toppled over the ledge of the balcony to the grass below and he ran across the yard, launching himself over a decorative hedge and sliding across the damp grass until he reached her body. Hoisting the unconscious woman up over his shoulder, he tore toward Rhys.

"Where's Mick?" he demanded as he grasped Molly's limp wrist and searched frantically for her pulse.

****

The detonations began, with Nichol's precisely timed explosives knocking out structural supports methodically. Through the dead zone of the great room, Mick entered the house, his vision clouded by smoke and debris and his hearing assaulted by the creaks and groans of the collapsing house.

And howling.

He moved into the hallway, his eyes locking instantly on the bloodied mess that was Louis. Dovidas was nowhere to be seen. With a quick assessment, he scooped up his friend and began backtracking as the howling intensified.

“What the fuck is that, man?” he mumbled to the motionless Louis.

Sirens wailed in the distance as he leapt from the balcony and raced toward the SUV. Rhys tore past them, the car barreling down the narrow road. The second round of explosions began, bringing the weakened foundation down section by section. With Louis prone in the back seat, he turned to check on him and to watch the final collapse of the house.

“No fucking way,” he breathed, staring into what was left of Dovidas’s yard.

He jumped out the door before the car had stopped and jogged down the street, hiding among the shadows of the trees as he closed in on what remained of the Dovidas property. Seven figures moved around the fire-encased house, their movements halting and uncoordinated. An eighth came into view, his face illuminated by the flames.

Dovidas had survived.

Another male, his gait smooth and face covered by a balaclava, joined Dovidas.

The unexpected intruder.

As the sirens drew closer, the masked vampire

pulled a long blade from his back and proceeded to decapitate the seven stumbling males one by one. As each withered to ash, he hightailed it back to the SUV.

Chapter Twenty-Three

Rhys remained motionless in the corner of the shack, the skin of his hands tightening under Molly's drying blood. He, Jagger, and Nichol stood guard in silence, hovering in the periphery of the tiny house to provide as wide a berth as possible for their youngest brother.

The intensity of the territorial growl had reduced instantly once Molly had been deposited back into Dominic's arms, and as long as none of them moved into his range, Dom appeared content to focus on nursing the broken woman. Although he knew Dominic was monitoring the woman's vitals, he found himself listening for improvements in Molly's feeble pulse in case he needed to intervene.

Between the time Dominic had gently laid Molly out in the back seat of the SUV and they had arrived back at Louis's shack, he had rehearsed how he would break the news to Dominic that his connected was dying.

Molly's heart rate had stuttered and bucked throughout the drive back to the house, leaving him little hope that she would survive the travel. Dominic had crouched on the cramped back floor of the car, his gaze moving between Molly and his wrist.

And he had no idea how to help his youngest brother.

Healing a human was a delicate balancing act. Too

much, too little, too fast, too slow. Each misstep came with its own disastrous outcomes. The risk of creating a vampire increased with the amount given and stopping just shy of vampirism ended in a monster driven solely by the hunt for food.

Neither was an ideal outcome in their current situation.

So he drove through the darkened streets of Memphis, formulating his inadequate explanation to Dominic in his mind as Molly rasped beside him. The weight of her imminent death lay heavily as he pulled on to the uneven road leading to Louis's house. It wasn't until Jagger arrived to help jostle the fading woman into Dominic's arms that the burden of responsibility eased.

Jagg's offer of assistance was met with a snarl, and the elder male backed off instantly.

"I won't allow his stubbornness to kill her," Jagger whispered quietly. "If I must step in, I will."

With Mickey and Louis still unaccounted for, Nichol, Jagger, and Rhys stood guard over Dominic as he hunched protectively over Molly. The elder males were wise enough to stay back, wise enough to realize that encroaching on a connected male with his injured partner was dangerous for all involved. So side by side, the vampires watched the deserted dirt road and silent phones for signs of the others.

****

Dominic was in control.

At least, he was in control of his core.

Mostly.

He sliced his wrist and allowed a few more droplets to run down Molly's throat.

Too much? Too little?

As her heart and lungs began to stabilize, his senses became acutely aware of Molly's blood mingled with Rhys's scent. The combination agitated him irrationally. Not trusting himself to speak to Rhys, he attempted to communicate with his brother through narrowed glares and bared fangs.

It wasn't working.

Although he was unable to articulate it, he appreciated the semblance of seclusion Nichol, Jagger, and Rhys were providing. It allowed him time to collect himself, to regain his footing after he'd watched Molly's head loll when Jagger helped to hoist her out of the vehicle, bony arms dangling awkwardly. He'd frozen, his feet refusing to move as his mind processed the smell of impending death.

He was too young, too weak.

The damage to Molly's body was more than the blood of a young vampire could heal.

She would die outside a dilapidated shack.

Die because he chose her.

"Stop your fucking growling and *fix her*," Rhys had roared, snapping him out of his head.

Now, the worst of her internal damage stabilized, he began assessing the blackened skin under her collar. Working a finger under the metal restraint, he growled low as he realized he would be unable to remove the device without causing further injury.

"We will get bolt cutters," Nichol said quietly. "Once the others return, we will get that off."

He nodded, tearing open his wrist again to drip more blood down Molly's throat.

Drip.

Molly had yet to swallow under her own power, and the initial relief he'd felt upon hearing a rhythmic heartbeat was waning as her progress stalled. He was desperate for guidance from Kaius, Jagger, or Louis. Someone who could tell him what he was doing wrong. Neither Nichol nor Rhys had any experience with healing humans, and their obvious discomfort with the situation was making him hesitant.

Too little and Molly's body may give up, too much and he could have a female vampire on his hands.

Drip.

Unable to articulate what he wanted, he kept one eye on Jagger, who stood silently in the corner.

Jagg wouldn't let him fuck up too bad.

He could do this.

Out of the corner of his eye, he spied Rhys motioning toward the kitchen before sidling up to the fridge and pulling a bag of blood out. Rhys held the bag with both hands, walking slowly toward him.

"You need this, Mini," Rhys instructed. "You'll do her no good if you drain yourself."

Drip.

Logic dictated that yes, he required a feeding to regain what he'd lost. Emotion, however, took over as Rhys's blood-covered hands moved into his space. With a fanged snarl, his eyes locked on the offending appendages. Rhys glanced down.

"Fuck. Right. I'm leaving the bag right here and going to grab a shower. Don't do anything stupid, okay?"

He huffed, turning his head from Rhys.

Drip.

Provided Molly was stable, stupid was the last

move he wanted to make. But if she took a turn for the worse, stupid would definitely win.

****

"I'm going to turn here and double back down the alley," Mick called over his shoulder as the SUV tore through an abandoned neighborhood. Bringing the vehicle to a stop behind a lone man, he jumped out of the car, grabbed the male, and dragged him into the backseat where Louis lay prone. Using his own fangs to open the screaming man's throat, he angled the trail of blood through the hole in Louis's neck.

Louis was weakening quickly, his open wounds losing the blood he needed to heal himself. The AB-positive blood poured smoothly as he restrained the resistant man and watched Louis's neck for signs of improvement. When the human stopped struggling, he made the call to allow Louis to drain the man.

Now was not the time to release a potential witness who could provide a facial composite of any haunt member.

As the man's heart sent its final surge of blood into Louis's throat, he tossed the lifeless body back into the alley. "We'll grab another."

It took less than ten minutes before he was confining another human. This one was a heavily made-up older woman who had made the fatal mistake of cutting through a back alley on her journey home. Louis's condition finally made progress with her A-positive blood, his damaged larynx knitting itself together as the surface wounds began closing up. The final pump of the woman's heart found her thrown to the pavement as the SUV tore through the night toward Louis's shack.

From the city alley, he reached the rundown house in record time. As he pulled to an abrupt stop, he helped the disoriented Louis toward the front door and was met with the hard, navy eyes of Rhys.

"About fucking time," he grunted, leading the trio inside. "Stay to the perimeter. Nichol and I are trying to herd Dominic into the bedroom."

He eased Louis to the floor and watched Rhys approach their young brother as one might an injured lion. Nichol moved toward the bedroom door and opened the path as Rhys motioned to the empty room. Dominic was recalcitrant, his posture closing further around the woman in his arms.

"She's hit a wall," Rhys warned Dom, his voice low. "Jagger's going to help you out now. Got it?"

Dominic's growling amplified for a moment.

Jagger traded places with Rhys and led the reluctant Dominic into the back room. Nichol closed the door behind them and took his place in front of the computer as Rhys brought two cold blood bags over to him and Louis. Although he maintained his silence, Louis's eyes were regaining their alertness as he closed his own to process the night's events.

He could feel the anticipation radiating off Nichol and Rhys, the doubt rolling from Dominic, and a whisper of melancholy from Jagger. Without guilt, he found the emptiness of Louis and wrapped himself inside it as he reviewed what he'd seen.

Chapter Twenty-Four

Dominic arranged Molly on the uneven mattress, appreciating Jagger's efforts to maintain as much distance from the pair as he could in the modest room. Although he knew in his rational mind that Jagger was there to help, his core was fighting against any uninvited interference between himself and his injured female. Jagg stood in the corner, biding his time until he finally muttered softly.

"Help."

After a vampire had successfully healed a human a few times, he was capable of maneuvering through the process with more certainty. The situation grew more precarious as the human grew closer to death, but he was confident in Jagg's ability to read the signs of an accidental conversion. Molly was stable, her heart rate steady and breathing regulated. Although her external damage lingered, he hoped it wasn't indicative of her chances of survival.

"Five drops. Then assess," Jagg instructed quietly, staying tight to the wall to avoid stressing him out. As he completed the first round, he looked to Jagger for further instruction.

"Five more and assess."

"You'll help, right?" he murmured as his fangs reopened his wrist.

Jagger nodded, his eyes on Dominic's mouth. "I've been tuned in to her vitals since you arrived. We won't risk an accident."

Jagg stood stoically for two hours, intermittently nodding with encouragement as he nursed the woman. When he moved to open his wrist for what felt like the hundredth time, Jagger's hand reached to stop him.

"Mini. Enough."

He paused.

"Her heart has slowed. The internal damage is repaired and the external is beginning to heal. Examine Molly's neck," Jagg counseled. "It's safe to stop. I'll leave you until tomorrow evening. Are you okay with that?"

He nodded, grateful as Jagger slipped out of the room and resumed humming.

If she would only come back online in his head, it would be okay.

****

"You better be abso-fucking-lutely sure about this, Mick," Nichol growled, phone in hand. "I'm not reporting some half-assed fairytale theory to Kai."

"Fucking positive," Mick insisted as he paced the small room, desperately fighting to keep his brothers' emotions at bay. "Seven of them. No way anyone has seven accidents."

"I heard them," Louis rasped, testing his healing vocal cords. "That freaky howl. Under the house."

"Jagg," he called, motioning for his hauntmates attention. "Conversion takes effort, right? I mean, it's a pretty specific process, right?"

Jagg nodded. "There are fine lines between healing, killing, converting, and deviating."

Nichol typed furiously on his phone. "What are the chances there were more than seven?" he demanded.

He shrugged. "Fuck if I know. The fire would have taken care of the rest, I guess. The unknown intruder decapitated those bastards without hesitation, so I'd wager there's more where that came from."

Nichol sent off his message to Kai, checking his phone intermittently for a response, his brow knotting the longer the silence stretched out.

While Deviants were a risk of the turning process, they were relatively rare occurrences for vampires past the first successful conversion. Standard practice among haunts was to put down Deviants immediately, as they were mindless, exceptionally aggressive, and prone to violent pack behavior.

They freaked him out.

Suspended between humanity and vampirism, unchecked Deviants were a virulent scourge. Prior to the public outing, vampires exterminated Deviants to ensure their continued shrouded existence. In an age of instant global news, haunts worldwide had become even more vigilant in their dealings with Deviants to avoid further persecution from an already wary humanity.

The idea that Dovidas or his accomplices might be purposely creating Deviants seemed absurd. The mental tie between a vampire and his creator was strongest during the first century, and it was during that time that many sires took it upon themselves to exterminate young males who were unable to gain control over their core impulses.

Deviants were nothing more than core impulses.

The mental fortitude required for a creator to separate himself from the id-driven core of one Deviant would be formidable. But seven? Over the years, he had heard stories of vampires who attempted to rehabilitate a Deviant through a delusional sense of responsibility. Every tale of warning had ended the same: the vampire eventually succumbed to the same unobstructed impulses that drove the Deviant and both were hunted and slaughtered.

He watched as Nichol repeatedly glanced at his phone. Without Kaius's guidance, Nichol was the next in line on the power totem of the haunt and the weight of it sat heavy on his shoulders.

"We leave at dusk tomorrow," Nichol finally stated with certainty. "We'll caravan it back home and regroup from there."

He frowned. "There's some serious shit happening around here, Nic. We need to find out who Dovidas is working with."

"If he's creating Deviants, someone has to stay on top of that," Rhys chimed in. "And I don't know of any power haunts in this state that could take that on."

Jagg ceased humming. "Moving Dominic and the woman into an enclosed space like a vehicle could be difficult. For them and us."

"And Louis can't be on his own until he recuperates completely," he added. "Maybe we should hold off for a few weeks."

Although he rarely pulled rank amongst his hauntmates, Nichol's word was law in Kai's absence. "Dusk tomorrow. We're sitting ducks out here. No armor, limited weapons, and no allies. Best case scenario is Mickey's mistaken. Worst case is us getting overtaken by Deviants. During daylight. With no escape network."

He couldn't argue with the eldest brother's

assessment.

The hauntmates silenced.

"Start packing up this place," Nichol added. "Louis, you will come with us."

****

Louis moved slowly and methodically as he assisted Mickey in packing the final electronic components into Nichol's SUV. Though he had healed significantly throughout his daylight rest, his voice maintained a graveled quality since his newly regenerated vocal cords were tight. Thankfully, Mickey filled the tense silence enough for the both of them.

"You ever seen Deviants up close, man? I mean, I wasn't close. But close enough. There's no mistaking those movements, all jittery and spastic." Mick shook his head quickly. "I've never been face to face with one, but Nichol and Jagg have. Rhys, too." Pausing to assess the remaining boxes, Mickey motioned toward the shrinking pile of supplies. "I can shove those in the back of the SUV. You and I are riding with Rhys. I'll sit with the boxes. Your mangled ass can sit in front."

He took a half-hearted swing at Mickey and climbed into the front of the car. Rhys was leaning against the hood, perusing a map. He tossed it in the window at Louis. "I'm not spending tomorrow in a fucking barn. Find something tolerable around the halfway."

Flipping through his mental catalogue of associates, he compared their locations to various stop points along the way. Pulling out his phone, he fired off a quick text and sat back to watch Jagger guide Dom into the SUV. The woman lay limp in Dominic's arms.

Although her eyes had opened briefly at midday,

the Tender had remained unresponsive as her body healed her injuries. Jagger had assured the males it was a natural condition for human recovery, but they worried on behalf of Dom regardless.

Dominic was currently baring his fangs and growling a low warning at Jagger, who took it in stride, calmly holding the back door open for the pair.

From what he knew, the stoic Jagger had experience with connection. He was to ride with Nichol and act as an advisor for Dominic should the woman require more intervention. His patience was remarkable.

He would have eaten the snarling young vampire hours ago.

As the SUV's passengers settled, Rhys and Mickey jumped into the other car. The hauntmates argued momentarily over music before Rhys took a nip off Mick's finger and effectively ended the fight.

"You fucker!" Mick yelled as they sped onto the highway.

"Your plaid-wearing crooners have no place 'round here," Rhys called into the back seat. "Am I right, Louis?"

He grinned and stretched his vocal cords. "Sorry, Mick. Metal is road music."

Mick flung himself back against his seat. "Yeah, well you suck. Do we have any hits on a resting place?"

Scanning his phone, he opened a message. "Contact in Kansas City. Says he has an underground bolt house by an amusement park. Yes?"

Rhys nodded. "I'll let the others know. So, Mick? What are you thinking about this Deviant thing? Would Dovidas have a bunch of vampires creating them or what? No way he'd be so normal with that many lunatics in his head."

"Gotta be," Mick mused. "But even then, don't the creators go insane, too? Wouldn't that just be more hassle than it's worth?"

He cleared the tightness from his throat. "Subduer."

"Fuck me," Rhys barked. "You're right. Get Nichol on the phone. I want his input on that."

Nichol answered quickly. "What."

Mickey shifted himself, leaning his long body forward into the front of the SUV. "Nichol. Louis's suggesting those Deviants could be Dovidas's. He's a Subduer, right? Wouldn't that mean he could mute his own blood connections?"

"Damn. Yeah, that would… Dominic, shut the hell up! No one wants your woman… yeah, that would work, wouldn't it? I have a few contacts I can touch base with to find out more about Subduers. Let's put that on the forefront of our working theories… Jagg. Hey. Jagg. Can't you kill him or something…"

Rhys ended the call and looked over at him with a fanged smile. "I hope Jagg gets some video of this. Nichol hates us all at the best of times. He's going to fucking lose it by dawn."

****

MollyMollyMollyFeedFixMollyMolly.

The hum of the highway under Dominic's feet had lulled him into a serene trance, his eyes staring unseeing out the window. The hours had passed slowly as he adhered rigidly to Jagger's feed and assess schedule, and Molly had yet to respond. She had remained stable but static in her recovery for the past twenty-four hours. Thankfully, Jagger appeared untroubled by Molly's progress and it was his confidence that he clung to every time his wrist healed without change.

Nichol was less patient.

The uncontrollable growling had caused immeasurable tension in the vehicle, with Nichol's snarls of frustration and annoyance intermittently cutting through the white noise of the car and his territorial din. Though he had full control of his thoughts, he didn't trust himself to speak with any measure of civility. His core was focused solely on his connected, and he worried that any verbal interaction with the increasingly aggressive Nichol would turn into a brawl should his core feel Molly was threatened.

And Nichol was one scary bastard.

He resumed his blank stare out the window.

"There we go," Jagger suddenly muttered, his voice barely audible amongst the road noise and growls.

He felt Molly move a millisecond before he heard her screams.

"Holy shit!" Nichol cursed, the SUV swerving as Molly's piercing shriek penetrated his highly tuned ear drums. Molly launched herself across the back seat, slamming her weight against the driver's seat and clawing at the metal collar still fastened around her neck. The vehicle yanked to the left before Nichol regained his lane. "Get her the fuck under control!" he hissed at him.

He held his hands up in surrender. "Molly. It's me. You're safe. I need you to stop screaming, okay? Just… just stop. Please," he begged shamelessly, not giving a rat's ass what his brothers thought.

With her onyx eyes frantically scanning her surroundings, Molly finally settled her attention on him. Her screams died down as understanding sank in.

"I'm out. I got out."

"You did."

She glanced over at Jagger and met his icy glare. "And Dove? He's dead?"

Jagger shook his head. "Dovidas lives. But we're moving farther from him with every passing moment."

With a slow nod, Molly continued to scan the occupants, her gaze settling on Nichol before she recoiled toward him. Nichol's harsh hazel eyes met hers in the rear-view mirror. "You would do well to maintain a silent tongue after that outburst," he grunted. He bared his fangs. "Put those away, Mini. I'm calling ahead to Rhys. We'll pull over so the woman can freshen up."

After much ado and excitement for him from Mickey and Rhys, the hauntmates pulled off the interstate and into the quiet parking lot of a 24-hour gas station. Nichol circled the lot slowly as Rhys drove a counter loop before parking tight to the pumps. Rhys and Nichol exited first and scented their surroundings. He followed, extending his hand for Molly and watching her warily as she stood on unsteady legs. With a small smile, Molly released his hand and teetered over to Rhys.

"I need some things," she said flatly, her voice completely devoid of emotion. "Can I have some money?"

Rhys pulled a wad of bills out of his pocket and passed it over without thought, his navy eyes scanning the empty fields for movement. A flash of jealousy washed over him, long enough for Mickey to wander his way and place a reassuring hand on his shoulder. With a deep, stabilizing breath, he followed Molly into the store and watched her wavering hands pull various items off the shelf. Fighting the urge to carry the unsteady woman through the aisles, he remained close, his senses open to possible threats. Molly made her purchases and disappeared into a bathroom at the back of the store.

As the vehicles slowly hit their fuel fill, he waited patiently. Rhys entered the store, flashing a fangy smile at the anxious cashier before returning to the SUV to chat with Louis.

"You shouldn't be traveling with vamps," the clerk called back to him. "You and your lady friend can hold out here if you need."

"We're good," he mumbled, keeping his fangs and eyes hidden from view.

"Against state law for vamps to pick up hitchhikers. You'd be better off waiting for a trucker."

"We're fine, thanks."

"Your funeral, man."

He pretended to be enthralled with the selection of cold drink cans in the coolers, staying close to the hallway Molly had disappeared down. He was pulling a bright blue drink from the shelf when Molly's sobs caught his attention.

The drink hit the floor as he sped to the washroom and began banging on the door. "Molly!" he yelled, trying the locked knob. "Open up."

He leaned into the door, scenting the air for her blood as her gulping cries continued.

"Come on, Moll," he pled, waving off the well-meaning clerk as he approached. "Just open up. Whatever it is, I can fix it. I can try. Just… open the door, Molly."

The seconds dragged out as he continued to rap on the door in desperation.

Without the link, he had no idea where she hurt. And in that moment, he realized he'd take a thousand lashings to have that link back.

As the sobs lessened, the lock on the knob clicked. He pushed the door to the tiny washroom open. Molly stood at the sink, staring into the mirror with empty, onyx eyes.

"Moll?" he ventured, glancing around the room. The bloodied clothes she'd been wearing since Dovidas's lay in a heap on the floor and were replaced with an oversized truck logo shirt and a pair of ill-fitting shorts. Her hair was wet and tangled, hanging in her face and dampening the back of her shirt. "When we get back to the haunt—"

"Yeah," Molly interrupted, blinking and carefully collecting her things, "when we get back to the haunt."

She looked up at him and gave him a brief smile before walking slowly past him. As he followed her down the hall, Rhys's voice cut through the air.

"Stay in and get outta sight!"

Chapter Twenty-Five

The foul stench of manure had put Rhys and the others at ease, their vigilant gazes returning to the barren highway after assessing the incoming truck and horse trailer for signs of threats. The hooded driver pulled up to the pumps, his face veiled in shadows amid the offensive fluorescent lighting of the gas station. Neither he nor Nichol had paid much heed to the tall male as he exited the truck and wandered back to examine the contents of his trailer. The fetid horse odor wafted off the man, causing the surveilling hauntmates to exchange exasperated looks.

Human men could be nasty creatures.

At his age, he was highly sensitive to assaults on his senses. Bright lights, excessive noise, and offensive aromas were often augmented as his finely tuned survival instincts clashed with his desire to curtail the discomfort that accompanied the full stretch of his senses.

And humans encompassed everything unpleasant.

He had been negligent, not recognizing the danger in front of him until it was stumbling en masse in his direction, pouring from the back of the horse trailer. He called out to the most vulnerable of his hauntmates as the Deviants descended, alerting the others in the process.

Pulling a small knife from his combat pants, he launched into the mob with his blade and fangs exposed. The knife, whetted by the meticulous Jagger, sliced keenly through the first Deviant he encountered. Malformed teeth sunk deep into his shoulder and he sliced back, injuring another Deviant and roaring in fury as a large chunk of his own flesh fell back with his assailant.

"Intel!" he yelled above the howling Deviants.

"With you!" Nichol shouted back, his bladed hands slicing fiercely through the crowd.

"Twenty," Louis's graveled voice called out. "Jagg's holding them back at the door."

He spared a quick glance in the direction of Louis's voice to find him crouched on the roof of the vehicle, fangs dripping and a small serrated knife working through the spine of a particularly large Deviant.

He continued to cut through the mob, decapitating the mutants as quickly as they descended on him. Mangled teeth bit into his legs, arms, and shoulders. The amplified strength of Deviants was no match for a fully turned vampire, but the sheer number and blood loss were wearing at his stamina. Tossing one particularly aggressive Deviant to the ground, he removed the head before pulling a lingering malformed fang from his biceps.

"Status?" he barked, bucking another mutated goon off his back.

"Ten!" Louis called out, jumping off the car and into the fray. He closed in on the truck as the hooded driver turned the engine. With a pop, the truck backfired and tore away onto the highway, smoke billowing across the battle zone.

"Fucking *fuck!*" he snarled, turning into the hazy bloodbath. Nichol and Louis stood back to back, finishing off the last of the Deviants as Jagger took care of a straggler. The putrid smell of decay and manure hung in the air. "Did anyone get a good look at that guy?"

Nichol wiped his blades off on his pants and shook his head. "No. I got some blood in my mouth. Fucking rancid."

Mickey and Louis assessed the damage. "We better start scooping what's left of these things and drop them into the fuel storage," Mick grumbled, shoving his bloodied knife back into his pocket. "I'll hunt down a hose to wash the lot down. And someone needs to deal with the human inside."

Nichol ran a hand through his blood-soaked hair. "Any major injuries?"

A chorus of negatives and he watched Nichol saunter into the store to eliminate the witness.

****

Molly watched in fascination and horror as the surly, freckled vampire restrained the cashier and proceeded to drain the man of every drop of blood he had. The sight was inordinately more gruesome given the chunks of someone else's body speckling the vampire's face and clothing. As he finished, his hazel eyes caught hers and he grinned, droplets of blood falling from his fangs onto his leg.

Ew.

Dominic continued to keep her view of the outside obscured, his hulking form blocking the glass door and the commotion on the other side of it. She could identify Rhys's authoritative voice easily amidst the sounds of rushing water. Its familiarity soothed her frazzled nerves. Between Rhys's clipped commands and Dominic's cocooning arms, she was feeling safe for the first time in months.

At Rhys's shouted warning from outside, Dominic had responded instantaneously. She hadn't felt her feet leave the ground when she suddenly found herself balled on floor, an imposing beast wrapped around her securely. The howls she had heard at Dove's house reverberated throughout the narrow hallway, punctuated with inhuman shrieks of pain and furious hollers.

Ten, maybe fifteen minutes had passed before Dominic had allowed her back to her unsteady feet. She had refused his assistance earlier, but now clung to his arm as she rose from the floor. The humming vampire with the ice-blue eyes entered the store and murmured something only Dominic's ears could hear. As the pair moved toward the door, the auburn-haired male had strode in and announced that they would be on their way after clean-up.

She knew instinctively she did not want to see the mess.

Now she stood quietly observing the scary male as he flipped the cashier's body over, gripped one leg, and stormed out the door.

"We're hauling ass in two," he called over his shoulder.

Dominic grabbed her purchases and escorted her to the car, his hand guiding her swiftly across the wet cement and past the snarky, hazel-eyed vampire who was being hosed down by Louis. The parking lot looked no different than it had when she had entered the store.

Except everything was dripping with water.

As she and Dominic took their places in the back seat, Rhys stuck his head into the SUV. "We need to beat it to Kansas City if we hope to make it before dawn. Princess, limit what you drink because we don't have time to stop. Clear?"

"Crystal."

"Good girl. Dom…keep that growling shit under control. Nichol's had a hard night and there's a fifty-fifty chance he'll kill you if you keep it up. Got it?"

Dominic nodded sheepishly, glancing at her.

"He's still doing that?" she asked Rhys, her voice tinted with amusement for the first time in months.

"Like a fucking chainsaw, angel."

Dominic reached up and pushed Rhys's head out of the car as the other males climbed in. The vehicles ripped out of the parking lot and blasted down the blackened highway. She leaned in to Dominic. "What's his name again?" she asked, pointing to the humming vampire in the passenger seat.

"Jagger. He's…" Dominic paused, "he helped me heal you. Without converting you."

"And him?"

"That's Nichol. He's a bitch."

Nichol flashed his fangs in the rear-view mirror and pinched his fingers together. "I'm right there, Dom. Right. Fucking. There."

As she shrank back in her seat, Dominic leaned in and feigned a conspiratorial whisper.

"What we are witnessing here is a classic example of PMS. Post Massacre Syndrome. Sufferers exhibit poor conversation skills, the inability to laugh, and are prone to uttering open-ended threats because they know they can't eat me because Daddy Dearest would *chain him up for a century*."

****

“We’ll make it,” Rhys assured the others as he kept one eye on the eastern horizon. “Hey Louis. This place is at the base of that amusement park, right?”

Louis nodded, pulling up the address his contact had supplied him. “We’re about twenty minutes out.”

“That’s about three minutes past sunrise,” Mick pointed out. “Maybe we should have kept one Deviant alive to drive us in.”

He frowned. “Damn. Maybe we should have. Let me pull up Nichol on speaker.”

Nichol answered immediately. “What.”

“Nineteen to go, sixteen until sunrise. What do we do, great leader?”

“We pull over at the next turnoff and stash the car until tomorrow. The woman will drive us in,” Nichol huffed as he disconnected the call.

He followed the SUV off the highway, dipping down a gravel path to camouflage the car amongst the trees. As the males began transferring the contents of the SUV into the vehicle, Nichol became increasingly agitated.

“Over thirty thousand in gear being left in a rental with no security.”

He motioned for the others to start loading themselves into the SUV with Molly at the wheel. “It’ll be fine.”

“It’ll take me months to replace some of that shit. We don’t have months.”

“Get in, Nicky.”

While he could understand Nichol’s hesitation at leaving the customized surveillance and computer components behind, the time was tight and the danger of the sun was inching closer. Nichol moved toward the

SUV before doubling back to the vehicle. “Gimme two minutes.”

The sun would rise in seven minutes, leaving potentially twelve minutes of sun exposure. Jagger and Mickey had blacked out the SUV’s windows and created a light-tight divider between the front and back seats using bags, clothes, and most of Nichol’s stash of duct tape, but the risks were still more than he was comfortable with. However, two minutes might provide Nichol with some peace of mind which would translate into peace for everyone.

“Two minutes,” he confirmed as he crawled over Louis to talk with Molly. “The GPS is programmed. Follow it exactly and do not speed. Last thing we need is to get pulled over. Questions, sweetheart?”

Molly shook her head. “Got it.”

He waited a moment before reattaching the light-tight divider and finding a seat in the cramped vehicle. Molly had been through hell and was still physically weak, but he had hope that she would quickly regain some of her impetuousness. This docile, subservient female was ideal Tender material and definitely not a woman Dominic would be content with.

But it was nice not to be told to go fuck himself.

The passenger door swung open and Nichol propelled in. “If anything happens to me, the code to turn off the detonator is eight, six, seven, five, three, zero, nine.”

A snort from the front seat.

He contorted his legs in an attempt to make room for the sixth large vampire in a space meant for four. “You armed it?”

Nichol grinned. “If I can’t have it, no one can. Just

an extra assurance that all that intel and mods don't fall into the wrong hands. The detonator is under the ass end. Disengage it before opening any doors or you're fucking toast."

And that, he thought, was what made Nichol a genius. Forget tweaking computers and cameras and contraptions. Forget codes and hacks and backdoor access. Nichol covered their tracks like no one's business and was likely the sole reason their haunt's location had never been compromised.

Nine minutes to go. Two until sunrise.

"I can see a roller coaster," Molly called to them.

The males were tense. Sun exposure hurt like a bitch and took longer to heal than simple flesh wounds. A shiver ran up his back as his body acknowledged the sun's early morning rays.

"I hate this," Mick grumbled. "This must be what it's like in a Deepfryer."

Louis smacked the back of Mickey's head. "Thanks for the visual, dickhead. We've got, like, six minutes to go."

"Deepfryers typically take ten to fifteen minutes to completely bake a vamp," Nichol informed the group. "Direct sunlight takes around half that."

"You're a socially stunted ass, Nicky," he shot back.

"Merely pointing out that anything under the five-minute mark is survivable for all of us."

The males fell silent, feeling every turn of the SUV as it drew closer to their safe haven. When the vehicle slowed to a stop and reversed, he turned to Louis. "Is this place unlocked?"

Silence.

"Princess," he called, "are we here?"

"I think so," came a muffled voice. "What should I do, Rhys?"

He ignored the jealous growl and threatening glare from Dominic. "All right, angel. Get out and check the door. I need to know how many steps from the back of the car to the door and we need a clear entry inside."

The males waited anxiously as Molly investigated their situation. Relying solely on a human for survival went against everything the vampires knew, and skepticism in Molly's ability to assess the circumstances was thick.

"It's fourteen steps to the door, but the door's locked," Molly called through the back window.

"Code or deadbolt?" he questioned.

"Deadbolt."

"Wood or metal?"

"Metal."

"Push or pull?"

"Push."

He turned to the others. "One of us will need to be the battering ram, and the others will have to follow."

Mickey was quick to volunteer. "I'm the biggest. If Nichol is behind me, he can be the backup."

Nichol nodded his consent. "Louis behind me, then Dominic. Jagger, you stay hot on Dom's heels and Rhys, you'll bring up the rear."

"And Molly?" Dominic asked.

He called to the woman. "Okay, darling. You have a few jobs. One, grab whatever you'll need today from the front seat. Two, on my count, you'll open the hatch. Three, stand back and wait until we're all in before you follow. Yes?"

"On it," she said as her faint shadow moved to toward the front of the SUV. The males adjusted their positions accordingly in the cramped space, preparing themselves for a dash through the sunlight. After a rustling of plastic, the front door slammed and Molly moved toward the rear.

"Everyone ready?" he asked, crouching in place.

As the murmured affirmations echoed, he called out to Molly. "On three. Yes?"

"Ready."

Mickey and Nichol's muscles tensed in anticipation.

"One. Two. *Three*."

The hatch opened, filling the SUV with sunlight. Mickey launched out of the back, his smoldering shoulder aimed at the large steel door. His eyes tracked his hauntmate in the seconds it took for Mick to slam into the entrance, knocking it off its top hinges and sending Mickey up and over the metal barrier. Nichol, smoke rising from his back as the rays penetrated his shirt, adjusted his angle and took out the lower hinges of the door. Louis's speed out of the SUV was impressive but slowed instantly as the direct sunlight beat onto him. His blistering arms disappeared through the doorway.

Dominic hesitated before following.

Young vampires were more susceptible to the destructive effects of sunlight. He watched Dominic veer off course, his vision marred. Jagger corrected his own path, tossing the youngest hauntmate over his shoulder before the smoking duo vanished into the dark entrance.

His arms were already showing damage from the

rays reflected off the pavement. His face felt tight, a sure sign it was beginning to char. As he sprang from the SUV, he felt the instantaneous searing of the sunlight on his exposed skin.

One.

Time slowed as he fought through the pain of the burns and the instinct to turn back toward the shadows of the vehicle.

Two.

His feet propelled forward as his vision became obscured. He was vaguely aware of Molly's presence at his right as she gave the males wide berth.

Good girl.

Three.

With his head bent, the rays blistered the back of his neck, the smoke from his own body further clouding his impaired sight.

Four.

He crossed the threshold and catapulted himself down the unlit stairwell, crashing into a cement wall. Dust from the fractured concrete settled on him as he took a moment to compose himself and listen for the arrival of the final member of their group. Molly's hesitant footsteps echoed in the darkness, her breathing labored.

"Rhys?" she called out quietly.

"Down here, sweetheart," he grumbled, attempting to hide the searing pain from his voice.

"What do I do about the door?" she inquired, her voice growing closer.

He strained to see her silhouette in the stairwell and was met with blackness. Fucking sun blind, he thought in frustration. "We'll deal with it after we join the others. I'm on the landing. Don't trip over me."

Molly approached him with calculated steps. Hoping at least one of the others had their eyesight, he called out. "Marco!"

"Polo," Mickey responded gruffly, his voice echoing in the darkness. "Go eighteen steps forward and turn right."

He rose to his feet. "Lead the way, princess."

He was met with silence as small bursts of air passed over his face.

"You *are* blind!" Molly exclaimed as the fanning ceased.

"It'll heal. Now stop making those faces at me and let's rejoin the others."

"So creepy," Molly whispered as she began feeling her way down the hallway with him tight to her back.

Chapter Twenty-Six

Nichol despised being without his electronic arsenal but being without his impeccable eyesight was infinitely worse. The shadows in the dimly lit bolt hole danced and flickered as Rhys and the woman made their way into the dank cement room. While his hauntmates and Louis were suffering complete sun blindness, his age had fought off the damaging rays enough for him to distinguish contrasting hues.

It wasn't enough to allow him to aid the others.

"Woman," he snapped, "how are your eyes?"

"Fully functioning now," she replied softly from across the room. "What do you need?"

Need?

He needed a lot of things right now, and none of them were available or possible.

He needed fresh blood for himself and his brethren. He needed his surveillance equipment and monitors.

He needed to be back in his control room with his gadgets and computers. He needed Kaius to guide their next steps.

"Is there a fridge or freezer anywhere in here?" he demanded harshly. "Anything that might contain blood bags."

"Nothing."

The males needed blood. With their eyesight damaged and their surface burns extensive, their bodies would take longer to heal than they could afford to wait. He could hear Dominic deeply inhaling Molly's scent. The others, himself included, were more subtly scenting the air.

Confined quarters.

One walking meal.

Six injured, hungry vampires.

"How compelling are your feminine wiles?" Nichol queried.

Dominic snarled low in his throat as Rhys responded. "About as effective as yours."

"Both of you, shut it," Molly retorted. "Why?"

The territorial growl ceased and Rhys chuckled. Nichol spoke carefully, selecting his words with precision. "It's unwise for you to remain down here with us. We're injured, we're hungry, and you're the only nutritional option." He paused as Louis and Mick swore under their breath. "While I'm fairly certain none of us would lose control, we are also facing disadvantages which threaten your safety." Dominic's boots scraped on the cement as he rose. "We're weakened. Sun blind. Sitting ducks in an unfamiliar tomb."

The woman's shadow moved toward Dominic's.

"Dominic will give you his phone, we'll compile whatever cash we have on hand," he continued, "and you'll go topside. What you choose to do from there is entirely up to you."

****

Intoxicated was far too civilized a term for Molly's current state.

Inebriated.

Sloshed.

Plastered.

She was plastered.

Her wad of cash was rapidly decreasing as she indulged in greasy chicken wings and shots of bourbon with her new compadres. She leaned her elbows on the sticky table for support as she twirled her damp hair. Her retinue was crowded into the small booth of the bar, their raucous laughter and jostling for her attention keeping her muddled brain from analyzing precisely what she was doing.

The four men were around her age, all in their late twenties. She had chosen their group carefully, listening in from the adjoining table as they scouted the room for their evening conquests. When their hushed discussion had turned to the pills the tallest man had brought for the night's hunt, she made her move.

She was just an out-of-towner looking for a fun night.

In town for the music festival.

Staying on a friend's couch for the weekend.

The lies rolled off her tongue with ease, her fingers ghosting over her metal collar to anchor her when her resolve wavered.

Molly smiled absently at the men, her thoughts flickering through the past few hours.

With a pocket full of cash and the freedom of the sun, she used Dominic's phone to call a taxi.

Escape.

As the driver wound through the streets toward the bus depot, she contemplated her life after captivity. The months surviving under Dove's leash had been spent plotting and dreaming of liberation. What she had never thought about was where she would go and what she would do once she broke free.

She had no home.

No family.

No friends.

No job.

No clothes.

Her fingers caressed the bills in her pocket as her eyes took in the ill-fitting shorts and baggy souvenir gas station shirt she was wearing. The flip-flops on her feet were too small. Her hair felt greasy.

"I changed my mind," she blurted to the driver. "A mall. I need to get to a mall, please."

The driver nodded and altered his path.

As she entered the heavy glass doors of the shopping center, she was momentarily overwhelmed by the chaos of it all. Her former self had reveled in the anonymity and confusion of the assaulting sights, sounds, and people, but after months of virtual solitude, she found herself intimidated by the crowds and noise. She walked close to the walls, kept her head down, and blocked the music, the laughter, the chatting, and the beeps of scanners. Slipping into a deserted department store, she breathed a sigh of relief and marched quickly to the women's clothing.

"May I help you find anything?"

Her hands in a reactive death grip on a hanger, she assessed the speaker before her brain recognized the woman was not a threat. Shaking her head, she turned her attention to the racks of clothing, pulling a variety of sizes as she attempted to compensate visually for her drastic weight loss under Dove's thumb.

Once her arms were laden with garments, she sought out the elderly saleswoman, murmuring her thanks as she took shelter in the sanctity of the private change room. Tapping the wad of bills in her pocket in reassurance, she began to undress.

Ribs.

Hip bones.

Knobby knees.

Gaunt cheeks.

The barking guffaw of the blond man at her table pulled her back into the present. He was conversing loudly with his taller friend as he watched for her feminine approval. She rolled her eyes slightly, gave a lopsided grin, and tightened her grip on her drink. Content, the man returned his full attention back to his friend.

With a new backpack filled to the brim with her purchases, she hopped in another taxi, destined for a truck stop with shower facilities. The idea of wearing her new clothes over her spot-cleaned body was unacceptable. She needed to wash her hair. Shave her legs. Douse herself in scented lotion.

The truck stop was quiet midday. Although her inner poor girl screamed as she dished out excessively for shampoo, razors, soap, and shower privileges at the gas station counter, she rationalized that starting fresh meant she had to smell fresh.

And as the water poured over her face and down her back, she accepted that her only plan after escape had been to sleep safely in her bed in the Tender training rooms and finally explain to Dominic precisely why no music created after 1977 was true punk music.

Allowing her eyes to roam over the men surrounding her, she worked up her determination. Although the alcohol consumption of the group had been great, only the tall, lanky man was showing signs of being drunk.

And herself. But that didn't count.

What she wasn't was drugged. And neither was any other unsuspecting woman in the bar as long as she could maintain the group's interest. However, the more she drank, the more careless she became.

Her situation was precarious enough.

She checked Dominic's phone nonchalantly.

"Are you guys up to moving this back to your place? Maybe swing by my friend's work first so I can grab a few things?" she offered as she pursed her lips flirtatiously. A shiver of disgust ran through her as the men passed pleased looks amongst themselves before standing.

Tossing a few more bills on the table, she stood with them. "My treat, gentlemen. You can grab the beer on the way there."

****

Nichol sat with his back to the damp wall, his clouded eyesight watching over the shadows of Louis and his resting hauntmates. The sun had set hours ago, yet none of the other had stirred. He had deliberated going topside to find an unwilling meal, but the risk of running into another vampire while visually impaired was too great. So he sat, waited, and cursed Kaius for leaving the haunt's survival in his hands.

Rhys's navy eyes flashed open. "Fuck."

"No better?" he inquired.

"Nope," Rhys huffed as he stood. "Surface burns are healed though."

He hummed in acknowledgement. His own skin had healed throughout the day, but the deep tissue and organ damage had shown no improvement.

Rhys joined his hauntmate along the wall. "I take it by the fact I'm fucking starving that Molly took off for good?"

"I believe so."

"I'm holding out hope on her," Rhys mused. "We'll give her another two hours. If she doesn't return, Mini's going to be crushed."

"He's better for it," he stated. "Fickle bitch."

Another hour passed. Jagger was next to wake, with Mickey and Louis rousing slowly. Each male assessed their situation silently before joining the others against the cold cement. Periodically, humans would pass the broken door and their voices would waft down into the cell. The vampires would listen with interest briefly before disregarding the sounds.

"Dahlia! I'm here!"

Rhys leapt to his feet and grinned in his direction. "Fickle bitch, my ass. That's a Rhys-trained Tender, fucknut."

The rest of the males rose to their feet swiftly, positioning themselves around the cell doorway as heavy uneven footsteps echoed in the darkness. He placed himself in the lead attack position, the weakness of the others at the forefront of his mind.

"Frickin' dark down there," a male voice called over the sound of clinking glass. "Slow it down a bit. I don't wanna drop the beer."

"Follow my voice," Molly answered, her steps reaching the base of the stairwell as she broke into an off-key rendition of *Good Golly Miss Molly*.

"She's drunk!" Dominic whispered from the back of the cell.

"Stay there and shut it," he muttered back.

"Morning, sunshine," Mickey responded quietly while they tracked their approaching meals.

As Molly's horrendous singing grew closer, he cursed the sun for taking his eyes instead of his ears. The woman's throaty voice was straining unnaturally to hit the higher notes, piercing his hearing.

"Through here, guys," she sang loudly, her slurred words betraying her intoxication.

****

The body of the tall, lanky man hit the cement wall before the case of beer he had been holding shattered on the floor. Louis's crimson head descended on the unconscious male as Molly's eyes were ripped toward the blond man's shout of surprise.

Jagger's arms shot past her to grab the blond guy while Nichol and Rhys bolted from the room after the last two retreating men.

Their screams echoed in the dim chamber as the sound of snapping bones reverberated in her mind. She closed her eyes to the carnage for a moment before steeling herself to watch the result of her decision.

Jagger dragged the blond man toward Dominic, shredding the man's jugular before pushing Dom's head against the blood flow. As Dominic latched on, the faint silver hue of Jagger's fangs sunk into an exposed wrist. Louis was joined by Mickey, the ovaled slits of their eyes barely visible as they indulged in the blood of the dying man.

Rhys entered the room, dragging one of the unconscious men behind him. He glanced in her direction, but his inability to meet her eyes told her he, as well as the others, remained blinded from the previous morning's sun exposure.

Only Nichol, his hazel irises eclipsing his pupils, met her stare. His victim was awake, howls muffled and movements restrained by Nichol's hands. She watched as the confusion and agony in the man's blue eyes turned to comprehension while he strained his eyes around the cell and Nichol's hand tightened around his throat.

She blinked away.

As horrendous as the last victim's strangled screams were, the amplified sounds of slurping that followed his muting were acutely worse. She took in every cadaveric spasm, every final gurgled exhale as Nichol stood silently beside her, his victim maintained on the cusp of death.

"You aren't feeding," she whispered.

Nichol remained still, his eyes flicking across the others. "They may require more."

"Do they," she choked on her own words. "Do they have to die?"

He adjusted his hold on the man, casually shifting his arms. "Despite what the Species Purifiers claim, we can't erase memories. Even those with hypnosis abilities have their limits." He looked down at his meal. "Events tied to strong emotions are impenetrable. I believe this would be one of those events."

She focused on Dominic, his dark hair swooping forward across his brow before his hand moved to brush it away. The commonality of the gesture as his fangs remained buried in a dying man's neck caught her off guard. She felt a hysteric giggle rising in her throat. Clasping her metal collar, she let loose a low chuckle.

Another.

Louder.

The insanity and ruthlessness of what she'd just done washed over her as she sank to her knees in a fit of laughter.

Molly Wagner couldn't hold a job.

Couldn't remember to pay her rent.

Was incapable of holding onto a cell phone for longer than a month.

But she could plan and execute the luring of four men to certain death at the fangs of a ravenous band of vampires. Of all the life skills she had attempted to master only to fail miserably, accomplice to murder was her forte. An accomplice to vampires.

Her crazed giggles halted and she looked up into Dominic's worried turquoise eyes. "What did I do?"

Chapter Twenty-Seven

Dawn came and went with little more than a shiver down Dominic's spine. Molly lay sleeping on a small nest of shirts the males had donated awkwardly as she sobbed and whimpered into the early morning hours. Even Nichol now sat half-naked, his head lolled to the side while he finally rested. A backpack of women's clothing was tucked under her face, angling her away from the blood-stained cement.

As Molly had fallen into the enormity of her actions, Nichol had snapped the neck of the final human in a failed attempt to reduce the damage of the night's events on the woman. Molly's howls as the bones crackled punctuated Nichol's error and left the frazzled male with a hasty, unsatisfactory meal that he lamented over once Molly finally fell asleep.

Rhys had been the first to try and console her after passing his unfinished meal over to him and Jagger. He had listened while Rhys cajoled Molly with promises of safety and his flippant terms of endearment. Mickey was next to venture in, echoing Rhys's guarantees of safety and looking to Louis for help when Molly's wails turned to gulping sobs. Louis merely shook his head quickly and began dragging his finished meal out of the room.

MollyMollyMollyFixMolly.

Although his core had screamed to go to her, he held back. He had no idea what to do, how to help her.

Jagger had looked at him pointedly, his icy eyes rejuvenating from the fresh blood. He glanced away until Jagg forcibly brought him to his feet and moved him next to Molly.

Once he sat beside her, instinct had taken over. He had stayed beside her, his arm wrapped tight around her as she sobbed into his shirt. Despite knowing he would be teased mercilessly once the hauntmates resettled back home, he sang quietly to his connected female, inordinately proud when his off-tune verses lessened the heart-wrenching cries. The others took the opportunity to clear the rest of the bodies into the hallway before returning to confer quietly amongst themselves.

"It is too close to dawn to leave," Nichol had stated. "We'll leave at sundown and rest in shifts in the off chance we're found during the day. I'm on first shift."

"No, you aren't," Rhys argued. "You've barely rested since we got here. Dominic and I will take the first shift, Mick and Louis the second, and I'll be up with Jagg for third."

He listened for Nichol to counter and had been surprised when the eldest male merely nodded his agreement. Rhys moved into Jagg's line of sight and repeated the plan softly, cognizant of Molly's presence. Dominic lowered his head toward Molly's ear. "We're going to make you a bed over there. You heard Rhys? We'll be guarding you in shifts until we leave here and go home."

As he murmured the word "home," he had watched as Molly's jaw tensed in determination and she stood. He led her to the far back wall as he pulled off his shirt and laid it out on the floor. Jagger sat forward and followed suit, motioning for Mickey to bring Molly's backpack over. Rhys's shirt flew across the room as Mick came over with the bag. He handed it over, hesitated a moment, then added his shirt to the pile as Louis joined in. With her eyes fixated on the barren wall, he had eased Molly to the ground, arranging her bag under her head.

The emptiness in her eyes worried him immensely and he placed a hand on her shoulder as she continued to stare without seeing.

The tears were almost preferable to the sullen silence.

A small scuffle erupted across the room, with Rhys and Nichol smacking at each other before Nichol huffed over and tossed his large shirt over Molly's frail body.

He lowered his head to hide his grin.

The males had spent the final hour before dawn sitting uncomfortably around the cell and ignoring the sniffling and hiccups coming from the despondent woman. When she finally fell into a restless sleep, Rhys ran his hand through his hair and dropped his head back.

"You guys always see the end result, my perfectly cultivated Tenders. This… this is what I deal with for weeks, months, before I release my works of art upon the world."

"You're a saint," Mick chuckled quietly. "All this time, I figured your entire job was fucking them until they were too tired to argue. I'll never be jealous of you again."

"I fail to see what the issue was," Nichol grumbled. "The woman had no part in their immediate deaths."

“That’s because you’re an insensitive Neanderthal completely out of touch with today’s modern woman,” Rhys jabbed. “Some of us have evolved, adapted to the emotional needs…”

“Shut the fuck up,” Nichol snorted. “Women are as big a headache now as they were in my youth.”

Mick and Louis hummed in agreement.

“Though I admit she chose well,” he said, reaching into his cargo pocket and holding out a handful of white pills. “My unpleasant meal had these on him.”

Dominic could feel his irises ovaling. “She shouldn’t have risked it,” he snarled, glancing down at the sleeping woman. He nudged her softly, pleased when she frowned and shifted positions.

“I want that shit buried before we hit home,” Rhys growled. “No way are my girls stumbling on that.”

With a nod, Nichol placed the pills in his pocket. “I’ll bury them when we pick up the car,” he agreed. “And I think,” Nichol continued, “that Dominic and the woman should ride with Rhys tomorrow night. She will be covered in all our scents from those shirts, and I will kill both of them if I have to spend the drive listening to crying and growling the entire time. Agreed?”

Rhys barked with laughter. “Fair enough, man. Hear that, Dom? No snarly-snarly-roar-roar-grrrrr. Clear?”

He rolled his eyes. “Crystal.”

Rhys positioned himself in front of the cell door in preparation for dawn. As each male fell into their rest, Dominic ran a hand across his connected female’s brow while he listened to the sounds of morning filtering down the stairwell.

“You realize when we get back to the haunt, Molly

won't be bunking with you, right?" Rhys put forth quietly.

He frowned. He hadn't considered that she would be returning to the Tender area. In all his musings about their return, he had mentally placed Molly in his bunker while he took up residence on his sofa.

"I can fix a lot of shit," Rhys said. "But Tenders who've been in the haunts of vamps like Dovidas require a lot more help than I can usually provide. Boy and I usually end up putting them down."

"So how… what can…" He struggled with his thoughts as he absently stroked Molly's hair. "So can you fix her?"

Rhys contemplated the idea in silence as he mulled over his guilty conscience. If he had turned a blind eye when she ran from him that first night, dropped her off at a gas station and driven away when he first felt the pull toward her, acted on his desires to be with her before she was sold, spoken up when Nichol gave her the choice to stay or go…but he had hesitated, and she was paying the price for it.

"Don't start that shit," Rhys demanded. "You getting all mopey and kicking your own ass will do nothing positive for Molly. No offense, brother, but the only way you can make this connection a two-way street is if you grow the fuck up."

His eyebrows shot up.

"A big part of that is our fault," Rhys continued. "Well, mostly Kai. But you were created during a time where we could afford to be lax with your responsibilities and training. Hell, you were, what, a decade in when the exposure occurred? The rest of us had been hiding for centuries. Over a millennium for

Nichol and Kai. Probably Boy, too. You were able to walk into a fucking store ten years into your post-life and buy DVDs. With the political stagnation here, you haven't seen vampire warfare. You haven't been tossed out of the haunt to find your footing. You've been sheltered, Mini, and with the tides of human acceptance turning against us, being a pussy isn't an option anymore. Even less so if you want to have a woman by your side."

He snarled at Rhys's assessment. "I'm more than fucking capable of being on my own if you guys would ease the hell up on me once in a while. I never asked any of you to go easy on me and I sure as fuck never asked to be…this!"

"Oh please, Mini," Rhys scoffed angrily. "Where would you be if Kai hadn't found you? Dead on the side of a road? Or maybe you would have survived and spent the past three decades wallowing in self-pity while your body died around you. You'd be in your sixties now, right? Wasting away in a one-bedroom apartment, drinking your self-deprecating ass into oblivion. You're a fucking spoiled brat."

Molly's rhythmic breathing combined with the sweet scent of honeysuckle was the only thing keeping his temper reigned in as Rhys unloaded on him. He flashed his fangs but had no comeback to the harsh truth his older brother was spewing.

"Yeah, yeah," Rhys grumbled as his anger dissipated. "Snap away. You're going to do whatever you will with what I've said. But when we get back to the haunt, Molly returns to my primary care until I feel she's stabilized and only then will I decide if you've matured enough to court her."

He glared at Rhys through his mop of hair. “Court her?”

“It’s the twenty-first century, Mini. Connected vampires no longer have the luxury of stalking, kidnapping, and chaining up their connected interests for decades until the woman finally concedes. You’re probably rusty, but I’m sure it’ll come back to you. Get some rest. I’ll get Mick and Louis on patrol.”

Chapter Twenty-Eight

The knock on the Tender training room door came like clockwork. Rhys sauntered over to the door to find Amy holding yet another elaborate bouquet of flowers. "Thanks, sweetheart," he chuckled as he accepted the offering, scanning between the foliage for whatever junk food Dominic was "smuggling" into the training rooms for Molly.

Sour gummies. Gross.

"Will Molly be joining us for dinner this evening?" Amy asked anxiously, her worry for her fellow Tender evident in her voice.

"Perhaps."

He closed the door and secured the lock before setting the extravagant display on the table. The shower continued to run, steam pouring from under Molly's bedroom door. With their second week back at the haunt winding down, she was beginning to take back control of her most basic decisions.

Until yesterday, she had showered only on his command. Had woken with considerable prodding. Had eaten under the strictest of orders. Conversation had been limited to a one-sided stream of thought from him as he monitored her behaviors and moods within the safety of their secured rooms.

Dominic had been physically absent from the Tender halls but had sent Amy to the training room every evening with flowers, his chicken scratch writing quoting song lyrics on the attached notes.

He found it sappy.

But they always drew a small smile from Molly, so he didn't discourage it.

He also pretended not to notice the candy. Or the crinkling of the wrappers.

Amy, Dahlia, and Justine had been painstakingly attentive to his instructions, providing opulent meals, laundering clothing, and running messages between him and the other males. The Tenders were given sparse information regarding Molly's time with Dovidas, but the women were wise enough to recognize his prolonged seclusion with her was a necessity. Amy had been especially worried, her nightly requests for Molly to join the others for meals often accompanied with personal messages of comfort and support for the absent woman.

He reclined on the sofa and placed his bare feet on the table. For two weeks, he had ensured his actions and words were slow, nonthreatening, and unobtrusive. Tonight he intended to push Molly a little, to poke at the core being hidden behind the guilt and fear of her ordeal. The shower ended and he bided his time playing Solitaire until Molly emerged from her room.

"Morning, princess," he called, subtly wiggling his toes.

Silence.

"Amy and the girls would like you to join them for dinner this evening. Shall we give it a go?"

With a slow head shake, Molly climbed onto the sofa beside him. It had become their routine for the past few days, starting their nights off sitting quietly on the couch until he pushed her to eat. Pointing at the bolt cutters leaning across the room, he drew Molly's attention.

"Remember what I said last night? The collar comes off tonight. In one hour."

The collar had been an enigma to him. On their first night back, he had sent Boy to bring bolt cutters up from the bloodslave compound only to have Molly lock herself in the bathroom and refuse to come out until he had left her room. He had tried again on the second night only to be met with the same reaction.

Last night, he had prepared her for its removal. While her fingers often traced the cold steel, the collar was a constant reminder to Rhys of his failure to properly vet a Master for one of his girls. His brash decision had cost the woman dearly and removing the last physical token of her time under Dovidas's roof was imperative for her sake. His, too.

Even if she didn't agree.

Molly's hand skipped across her covered throat without thought. "No."

He opened his mouth to point out it was not her decision again, before changing his tactic. "Why not?"

Silence.

"Not good enough," he said in response as he rose and walked toward the bolt cutters. He anticipated a breakaway, an escape back into her bathroom, but Molly remained balled on the sofa.

"When you take it off…"

He froze in place and waited.

"When it comes off, I'll be sold again."

Oh. OH.

He tossed the bolt cutters over his shoulder and rejoined Molly on the couch. "You won't be retrained and sold."

"Then I'll be on the street."

"No, for now you'll be here until we feel you're ready."

"Who's 'we'?"

"You and I."

"Ready for what?"

Fuck.

What was he supposed to say? Molly was never going to be released from the compound as a free woman. Her freedom would be a security risk and a danger to the haunt. She couldn't be sold to another Master without Dominic losing his mind. Ideally, she would choose Dom and they would live happily ever after in his bunker, but nothing with Molly had been easy or ideal.

Keeping her on as a Tender within the haunt has been a fleeting thought, but he had squashed it quickly upon realizing Dominic would likely end up being beaten nightly by his elder brothers. She truly belonged nowhere and somewhere simultaneously. "Ready to decide where you best fit."

He watched Molly's reaction carefully. She knotted her brows, her fingers linking into the collar and tugging softly. Her long legs unfolded from beneath her and she rose up, tilting her head with her arms lax at her side. He joined her, exaggerating his movements so as not to spook her out of her compliance. He brought his hand to the offensive steel, gauging its slack before lifting the bolt cutters. "Do you want someone else to do it? Dominic, maybe?"

She shook her head. "I don't want him to see me like this," she muttered, refusing to meet his eyes. "I want to be…me… when he sees me again."

"I won't push it," he replied, aligning the snips. "But I will say Dom won't be scared off by whatever you think will spook him. He wants your good, your bad, and your questionably unattractive clothing selections."

As the cold metal slipped around the collar, it sent a shiver through Molly before she steadied herself. With a quick snap, the first cut was made. He realigned the cropper and with the press of his hands, the metal clanked to the floor.

"So?" he asked quietly.

Molly reached up to her neck, feeling her skin for the first time in months. "I can stay?"

"You can stay."

"And I won't be resold?"

"You won't."

"Will you pass me to Dominic?"

"Only if you choose him."

Molly contemplated his words a moment. "That choice is mine," she stated without question.

He watched as Molly bent, retrieving the broken collar from the floor. She turned it in her hands slowly, tracing the sharply sliced breaks before marching purposefully into her room. Minutes ticked by until Molly returned and took her place on the luxurious sofa. He held his position, observing in stillness.

"I'm never leaving here, am I? Even if I wanted to."

"If," he began slowly, "we came to the agreement that you should no longer be housed in this haunt, we would look into other haunt employment."

"Nichol let me go."

"Nichol took a calculated risk in an unforgiving situation."

Molly mulled his statement over, leaning forward to examine the plate of fruit sitting on the coffee table. "He knew I'd come back."

"He, we, banked on that possibility," he said, hiding his pleasure as she selected an apple and bit into it.

"Did *you* think I'd come back?"

"Yes."

"Did Dominic?"

He hesitated. "I think Dom hoped you'd do whatever you felt you needed to do, and the risk was worth it for him."

"Will I see the red-haired guy again? Shaun or Louis or whoever he is?"

"Of course you will. Bastard lives here right now. So could you at least pretend to make an effort not to talk with your mouth full? The smacking of your lips is driving home my failure to make you anything remotely resembling a lady," he snarked in response.

"Maybe if you cover those nasty feet, you fucking Neanderthal."

****

Dominic sat at the conference table, his hands linked behind his head and booted feet on the polished surface. His posture belied his anticipation of Amy's return. The Tender had taken another carefully selected bouquet into the training quarters with instructions to return to him immediately afterwards. His ears were tuned to her soft shuffle through the halls as he reached for his phone and began scrolling for tomorrow's arrangement.

A muted *knock*.

"Dominic?" Amy called into the control room quietly.

"C'mon in," he muttered, his large fingers fumbling with the order button on his phone.

Amy approached quickly, smiling. "Delivered them to Rhys. I didn't see Molly, but I heard the shower going. Same time tomorrow?"

He stretched his senses. "Yup. Thanks."

Amy flashed a flirtatious smile toward Mick before she strode out.

"You are a sick, sick puppy," Mickey muttered, shaking his head.

Lolling his head back, he closed his eyes to revel for a moment before responding. "Sick? No. Perverted? Possibly. Pathetic? Yup."

Nichol looked up from his monitor. "I vote pathetic."

Louis grinned. "Pathetic, but resourceful."

He kept his eyes closed, staying his senses.

MollyMollyMollyMolly.

The moment the group had returned to the haunt, Rhys had sequestered himself in the Tender training area with her. Forced to acknowledge that Rhys's revelations about his weaknesses held much truth, he hadn't attempted to push himself into Molly's recovery. With the exception of an inordinately large bacon order passed through Nichol.

Throwing himself into every aspect of the haunt that he could, he managed to compartmentalize his yearning for Molly as he honed his sword skills with Jagger, worked alongside Mick and Louis while they tracked Dovidas's travel from Memphis to Beijing, and assisted Nichol in scanning thousands of pages of internet chatter.

He'd even made time to assist Boy in the bloodslave quarters, carefully running IV lines and refilling water canisters.

What he didn't do was venture down the Tender hall. Every morning as dawn broke, he would select a floral bouquet online for Amy to pick up and carefully choose a song he hoped sent the right message. Or was at least catchy enough to loop in Molly's mind subconsciously. He would pore over his growing collection of gas station junk food, carefully matching the packaging to the bouquet for better concealment. And every evening he would summon Amy to bring the arrangement to Molly's room and report back with any changes.

It was sweet.

Unobtrusive.

Courting.

And every night, Amy returned to him like clockwork, the scent of honeysuckle clinging to her clothing and skin.

He was a resourceful bastard.

That faint, lingering smell was enough to keep his core content, to keep himself from charging down the halls and confronting Rhys about his connected's well-being. Her scent had been barely noticeable the first few nights, but its strength had grown exponentially over the past few evenings and he clung to it greedily.

"You just going to sit there with that stupid-ass look on your face or are you in on this meeting?" Mickey called out as he tossed a pen at his chest.

Dropping his feet to the floor, he sat up. "Yeah,

yeah. I'm in."

"Good," Louis drawled, pulling his chair in. "I'd hate to interrupt whatever scent kink you have going on there."

Try as he had, he was unable to maintain a grudge against the affable Louis. While visions of Molly's blood on Louis's fangs periodically flashed across his mind, he was quick to separate his emotion from the facts once they had set foot within the familiar walls of the Kaius haunt.

Louis had given him a wide berth initially, allowing him time to come to terms with knowing his connected's blood had mixed with that of another vampire, a vampire who now had an intimate link to Molly's emotions.

A vampire now living down the hall from him. A vampire who slipped seamlessly into the haunt's operations.

A vampire he respected.

It still stung.

Nichol angled his computer monitor toward the males as Jagger entered the conference room, humming softly. With a nod, Nichol began. "Thanks to Molly's intel, we've narrowed Dovidas's location to the northern outskirts of Beijing. Whatever he's doing there, we can assume he has taken residence with or close to the Chen haunt."

"Fuuuuuck," Jagger breathed.

"Fuck is right," Nichol agreed. "Four thousand years of Chen vampires have resided there. No one knows how many of the old guard have survived, but we are working on a worst-case scenario basis."

"Meaning?" Louis inquired, his brow knotting.

"Meaning at one creation every century or two, we're looking at twenty to forty vamps ranging in age from four thousand down to one hundred. Plus however many those have sired. It's unlikely all would have survived given the history of that area, but we should assume Dovidas is backed by some serious power," Nichol explained. "We'll monitor the situation but concentrate our efforts Stateside. No point shitting in someone else's backyard when we haven't even dug our own latrine."

"We don't shit," Mick pointed out.

Nichol tossed a withering glance his way. "Figure of speech."

"In what universe?"

Nichol, ignoring Mick, pulled up the documents he and Dominic had perused over the past two weeks. "Senator Green has been keeping his nose clean. No communication with Dovidas, no mention of Deepfryers. He is, however, signing off the registration bill. All vampires have until the first of next month to receive their mandatory facial mercury tattoo before they're considered enemies of the state."

Louis flopped back in his seat. "No fucking way. They can't seriously expect that vamps are going to voluntarily line up for this."

Jagger stopped his humming. "They're hoping we won't."

Nichol nodded and looked pointedly at Dominic. "The young ones may go willingly. Perhaps a few who still hold on to the hope of integration into human society. But the rest of us…this bill lays the legal groundwork for the Deepfryer implementation. By making us enemies of the state…"

"Execution for treason," he huffed in disbelief. "Independent vampire hunters gunning for us I understand, but can the government actually do this? Make our existence illegal?"

"They can and will," Nic confirmed. "This bill means no more hoops to jump through. A catch-22. No tattoo, no rights. Get the tattoo, place a bullseye between your eyes. Despite the propaganda, up until now we have been considered "persons" in the eyes of the law. It's our feeding methods that have been outlawed recently, not our right to exist peacefully…"

"Tried to fucking starve us out of existence," Mick muttered.

"Pretty much," Nichol concurred. "The difference with this new law is that unmarked vampires will be considered traitors through nonaction. Meaning not getting the tattoo is the only crime required for prosecution."

The table fell silent as the males digested the information.

"Anyone heard from Kai?" Mick asked quietly.

The others shook their heads.

Nichol sat back in his chair. "I think we can assume Kaius has been called back to his creator."

"On what basis?" Mick demanded, his frustration with Kai's disappearances echoed in the expressions of the others. "Does anyone even have proof Khthonios is still around?"

"On the basis of my belief he wouldn't willingly abandon his own haunt when we're being legislated out of existence," Nichol replied tersely. "And until Kaius confirms the final death of his creator himself, we need no proof. Anything else?"

Looking around the table at his older brothers, he ran a hand through his hair. “So what do we do?”

Chapter Twenty-Nine

Free from her metal collar, Molly turned a corner quickly. She was no longer silent, her onyx eyes glazed and empty. She became agitated, angry, fearful, and teary. Night after night, Molly unleashed on Rhys, her rants begging for comprehension of the events she had endured.

Despite his best efforts, his attempts to help Molly reconcile her experiences had fallen flat.

"That's cute," Molly mused, pulling his attention back to the computer screen and the shapeless grey sweater she was admiring.

"'Bag Lady' is not a style, even if you add 'chic' to the title," he grumbled.

"I'm adding it." Molly tapped the touch screen.

He leaned back. "Fine. But you have no shoes to match."

Molly's hand froze, her back stiffening. "I don't want my shoes to match."

Exasperated with the shopping, he put his hands behind his head. "Shoes to match, or you go naked."

The computer shattered on the hardwood as Molly tore back to the sanctity of her room.

He dropped his head and ran a hand through his hair before following her, knocking softly on her door.

"I'm coming in, angel," he warned as he opened the door.

Molly sat on her bed, her fingers tracing her throat

as she drew in deep breaths. He moved slowly to her side, unwilling to startle the skittish woman.

He knew his limits.

He sat down next to her and leaned back on his elbows. “I can’t fix this, Molly,” he said quietly.

Her shoulders tensed. “You never call me that.”

“Relax, princess,” he chuckled, “I’m not going to put you down. I’m going to give you two choices.”

Molly looked back at him. “Door number one?”

“Dominic,” he replied, holding up a finger when she opened her mouth. “Hold that tongue for a minute while I explain.” He waited until Molly’s lips tightened, ignoring the protest already forming on her face.

“Subconsciously, you associate me with Dovidas. As you rightfully should. Everything that happened in that house stems directly from my failure to properly verify him.”

Molly’s eyes dropped to her hands, her brows knotting.

“Despite Dominic’s role of driving you here on that first night, I think the two of you fit. Under different circumstances, in a different time, your meeting would have led to marriage, kids, and the white picket fence. But that’s not the reality you, or Dom, was dealt. And no amount of wishful thinking is going to change that.”

He watched as a tear rolled down Molly’s cheek.

“Dominic’s entire existence is centered on you,” he pressed on. “And I’m thinking he may be better suited than I am to help you through th—”

“I don’t want him to see me like this,” Molly muttered.

“He’s seen you looking worse.”

When Molly rolled her eyes, he grinned at the small glimpse of her former self.

She leaned back and looked over at him. “I don’t want to have to see him,” she said. “And I don’t want him to be obligated, either. I want…a cleaner slate, I guess. What’s door number two?”

He grunted and tossed a tattooed arm over his eyes. “Fuck if I know, kitten. I’ll get back to you on that.”

****

Boy was wary, his vacant blue eyes assessing Rhys’s every movement.

“I just need to ask the bloodslaves a few questions,” he assured the mute male. “Then I’m out of your hair.”

Boy turned his back and resumed slopping a chunky, foul-smelling soup into large metal bowls. He began winding through the halls of the cells, scanning the contents. He paused at the first cell that held females and rattled his knuckles against the bars.

“Ladies,” he drawled, “I’m looking for someone with training in psychology. Human mental disorders. A quack, perhaps. Anyone in here fall into that category?”

The women cowered against the back wall of the cell, their legs pulled tight against their chests. Their dull eyes averted his gaze as whimpers echoed within the cement chamber.

“No? How about here?” he inquired as he moved to the adjoining unit. “Psychologist. Anyone with therapy experience?”

Cell after cell, the humans ignored his request, crawling frantically over each other to escape his reach. Hesitant to move into the male population, he crossed his arms and stared intently at the floor.

"Why?"

He zeroed in on the strong, demanding voice. "I have a human that requires assistance."

The woman moved toward the bars of the dungeon. "I have a degree from Berkeley. What are you offering?"

He cocked a brow. "Offering?"

"What goods are you offering for my services?" the woman asked, her back straight and proud despite the filth of her appearance.

Flashing in front of her, he bared his fangs at her insolence. "I'll let you live."

The woman smiled sweetly, her cat-like brown eyes sparkling. "He lets me live," she retorted, motioning toward Boy. "You'll have to do better than that."

He noted the woman's cellmates covering their eyes, unwilling to witness the impending massacre of the smart-mouthed female. "How do I know you're trained?"

"If I'm lying, you can kill me or return me. You lose nothing."

Jaw clenched, he narrowed his eyes. "If you are found to be acceptable, you'll have a room, food, clothing, and a limited range of movement."

"And a shower."

"Of course."

A long, thin arm reached through the bars. "Audra Verdi."

As Boy escorted Audra out of her cell, he took a good look at the woman. Her long black hair was snarled into knots and clumps from neglect. She was of average height with an ample bosom, despite her thinness from months of underfeeding. Her light brown eyes were large and slightly turned up in the corners, giving them a feline quality. Her arms were goose-bumped as the tattered remains of the clothing she had arrived in did little to warm her in the damp space.

Audra walked briskly at his heels, her bare feet brushing softly along the floor. As they exited the bloodslave compound, he paused. If he returned to the Tender training area with the woman this disheveled and filthy, Molly may buck at her assistance. Resolutely, he led Audra toward his abandoned bunk in the main haunt.

The haunt was outfitted with a multitude of hot water tanks, and Audra appeared to be making it her mission to empty them all in one shower. He sat on his sofa, shifting restlessly as the woman showered in his bathroom. His work quarters adjoined to the Tender training area was his primary residence, its opulent decor and sensual fabrics making it his preferred place to feed and fuck while between trainees.

This bunker was located amongst his brethren and was, in his mind, his hideaway. Spending one or two nights a year in the barren room served as a good respite when he needed time to simply rest without being on call at the whims of his females.

Audra was the first woman to step foot in the bunker room, and she had already taken over the place.

He glared at the notebook and pen lying on his coffee table. Upon realizing she would be clothed and tended, Audra had requested the items so she could make a list of "necessities."

Requested.

She had damn well demanded.

He contemplated draining her.

The shower finally turned off, steam seeping from under the bathroom door. Moments later, a very clean and very pink Audra emerged dressed in his spare weapons-training clothes and strode to the table. She flashed a smile at him before sitting beside him and collecting the book and pen.

"How quickly can I expect these things?" she asked, her eyes narrowing. "I'll make two lists, one for immediate purchases and one of things I will need in the near future. The quicker you get on this, the quicker I can meet whoever it is that requires help. I assume I'll be staying here for now? I don't sleep well on couches, so I'll be needing the bed. I also don't fuck random men. Or vampires."

Her cat eyes bore into him. "I…I don't want." He grimaced as he stumbled over his tongue. "I very don't want."

Holy fuck.

This was a mistake.

Audra snorted. "Here's the lists. If there's nothing else, I need some sleep. You can wake me when these arrive."

Justine and Amy arrived shortly after sunset, their arms loaded with the supplies Audra had insisted she required. Audra greeted the women pleasantly, her eyes holding no judgement at their positions within the vampire haunt. He puttered around the room for a few minutes, nonchalantly monitoring the interactions of the three women.

"I'm sure you have some place you need to be," Audra called from the bathroom, her voice less inquiring and more authoritative.

He glared at the door before skulking out of his own bunk in search of Dahlia for a quick meal prior to his evening with Molly.

As sunrise peaked, he returned to his bunk to find a very different Audra. Her tangled black hair had been brushed sleek with dyed chunks of cobalt blue flaming up her locks. Manicured brows framed her cat-like eyes, a light dusting of shimmering eyeshadow and charcoal eyeliner accenting the hardness of her gaze. Long gone was Rhys's ill-fitting shirt and in its place was a fitted black suit jacket and pencil skirt. Audra was reclined on the sofa, pen and notebook in hand.

"I'll meet with the woman tomorrow," she said without glancing up. "The Tenders… Justine and Amy? They gave me a little background information on this Molly." She sat up, serious eyes narrowed. "You really should have sought me out weeks ago."

He frowned. "I'll bring you to her tomorrow, honey."

"Audra. Or Ms. Verdi. I am definitely not a honey."

Not a honey was right. Lord help any male that thought so.

****

Molly pulled her Wednesday panties over her hips, smirking to herself as she consciously noted it was Monday on the puppy calendar Rhys had hung in her bedroom. Her wardrobe had been switched out again, with the smaller items of her malnourished size boxed in the corner and her regular sizes hanging neatly in the closet.

Rhys had struck again.

Pulling a gray sweatshirt over her head, she listened for Audra. Despite having been sheltered within the haunt for over two months, Molly was still finely tuned to her surroundings, her ears constantly tracking the whereabouts of her bunkmates. She smiled as she heard Audra's authoritative voice conversing with Rhys and she happily joined the pair in the living area.

"About time your lazy ass appeared," Rhys quipped, the slight upturn of his lips giving away his satisfaction at seeing her filling out her clothes. Audra raised a perfectly shaped brow in his direction.

"I smelled bacon," she hinted, glancing at the plate sitting in front of the male.

"Of course you did," Rhys retorted with an eye roll as he passed her a plate. "We have something to discuss, so get comfortable."

She lolled her head back against the sofa. "I hate when you say that."

"And I give a total of zero fucks about that." He leaned forward and rested his elbows on his knees, his gaze darting to Audra. "We need to talk about you and Dominic."

With the rolling of her eyes, she swallowed the bacon in her mouth. "What about us?"

Audra's legs crossed, her notepad appearing on her lap. "We've noticed an increase in communication between the two of you over the last month, and I have some concerns about details that were previously held from me." She fixed Rhys with a harsh stare and his lips drew into a thin line. "Namely, the blood taking and sharing."

Rhys huffed and flopped back against the sofa. "I

explained all this when she was tied to Boy. Which, I'd like to point out here, resulted in me getting kicked in the balls." When Audra responded with nothing more than the lift of her brow, he returned his attention to her. "You know Louis's taken over the tie, right?"

She licked her lips and nodded. "You mentioned it a while back when I asked to meet him."

Rhys rapped his fingers on the back of the sofa. "We're keeping you and Louis separate to avoid mixing your scents. Nothing good would come out of Louis walking around Dominic smelling like you."

"Does it bother you?" Audra interjected, pen poised.

She shrugged. "I don't really think about it."

The psychologist adjusted her skirt, and Molly knew she meant business. "It's something you definitely need to be considering," Audra stated, ignoring Rhys's mutterings. "There's a vampire in this, what is the term you use, Rhys? Haunt? A vampire in this haunt that's capable of monitoring your emotions and possibly reporting them to Dominic."

"He's not reporting to Dom," Rhys barked, running his hands through his hair. "Fuck, Audra. It's not a big deal."

"It is if Molly isn't fully experiencing her feelings for fear of having them reported," Audra replied calmly. "And I have concerns about the level of potentially coerced affection she's experiencing for a vampire that's capable of creating the 'super-link' you and Dominic spoke of yesterday."

Rhys rose to his feet and began pacing the room, wholly focused on Audra. "Louis's overridden whatever Dom started, so just back the fucking train up on that thought," he snarled. "The only thing going on between Molly and Dominic is stupid texts about stupid shit." He snatched her phone from the table, completely ignoring her as he waved it in Audra's face. "Wasn't that your edict? I'm required to monitor communications? Take a fucking look for yourself."

Inching the plate of bacon and pancakes closer, she watched as Audra plucked the phone from Rhys's hand and placed it on her lap as she drew in a deep breath. "I also expressed concern that Molly's communication is limited to those within this building, but I see we haven't managed to extend her list of approved contacts. I suspect there are residue connections between her and Dominic that stem from his attempts to turn her and limiting her ability to interact with the outside world is only hindering her."

Rhys's eyes were completely ovaled, his gait becoming predatory. "I'm gonna drain you."

"You're changing the topic."

Molly's eyes widened and she bit her lip as her psychologist and her trainer squared off.

Audra set her notepad on the coffee table. "Does she know he was able to feel her experiences? That he was capable of seeing through her eyes? I spoke with Dominic at length about it, but I have some reservations about his insistence that there's nothing outside of his one-sided connection remaining."

"Dom isn't lying to you," Rhys groaned, scratching at his arms. "Fuck, Audra. The kid's been fighting some seriously primal internal shit just to keep himself away until you give him the go-ahead to see Molly. He's the one that wanted us to have this whole discussion with her in the first place."

"And that permission won't come if I–"

"What do you mean, Dominic felt it?" she interrupted, sitting up straighter as Audra and Rhys spun to face her. "He… knew?"

Audra's mouth opened, Rhys stepping in front of her. "He was having weird visions here, but didn't tell anyone, so we had no idea there was a direct line between you and Dovidas and the shit going down on this end."

"Because Dominic feared he'd be put down like a rabid animal," Audra stated, earning a glare from Rhys.

The trainer rolled his shoulders out. "Because a link that strong has rarely been documented and has never been known to occur in younger vamps." He crossed his arms and sneered at Audra. "When we hit Memphis, he started getting physical echoes of what was happening at Dovidas's. It was how we were able to monitor your condition until we could get you out. How we knew when we had to get you out."

She stared at the coffee table for a moment. "What do you mean by 'echoes'?"

Rhys shoved his hands in his pockets and glanced at Audra, speaking only when she gave a quick nod. "The lashings, for one. Not a mark on him, but he felt the entire thing. He woke up choking once, which freaked us out since we don't breathe."

"Cleaning the floor," she mumbled, inhaling deep to remind herself she could. "Is it weird that I actually feel better knowing I wasn't totally alone in there?"

Audra knelt at her knees. "Not in the least."

"If he was going through the same things…was it too much? Did he ask Louis to take over the link?"

Audra's brows lifted at the question and Rhys

snorted. “Bastard tried to take Louis out for it. It’s still grating him.” He looked at her for a moment. “He would’ve raced through the sunlight to get to you if we’d let him, angel. So no, it wasn’t too much.”

She nodded, her eyes moving to her phone. “He never texts me first.”

“He isn’t allowed to initiate contact with you, princess. My orders,” Rhys said as he stepped closer to her and held out his own cell. “But he’s been messaging me every ten minutes since he got up.”

She scanned the screen, trying not to laugh at the barrage of texts Dominic had sent Rhys, a forced casualness in every ‘hey, how’s it going down there’ that had popped up every ten minutes exactly. “What about the connection thing?”

Rhys pulled his phone back and began tapping away on it. “He’s exited the feral phase and seems to be handling the separation well,” he muttered, glaring at the cell for a moment.

“Sweetheart, that kid adores you with or without the connection. If you doubt it or have any questions, text him. I guarantee he’ll answer, and he’ll answer honestly.” He walked over to the door. “I need to head topside for the evening, ladies. Any other useless discussions we need to have before I go?”

Audra’s lips pursed and she took her seat again.

Rhys doubled back and nudged her foot with his. “If you need anything, send Amy to Nichol. He’ll track me down. Good?”

She nodded, stealing another piece of cold bacon before he could snatch the plate away.

“We’ll be fine,” Audra replied. “You and I can talk when you return.”

Rhys sauntered out of the room, muttering about bossy humans and his superiority over them.

Audra turned her attention to her, pen in hand. “Let’s move on. What’s the goal tonight?”

****

Rhys listened at the door for a few moments as Molly giggled and explained the lyrics on Dominic’s latest flower arrangement to Audra. Once he was satisfied Molly’s mood was good for the evening, he strode slowly through the halls of the haunt toward Nichol’s control room, rapping on the door before entering. “Keys?”

Nic tossed the keys to his SUV, his eyes remaining glued to the computer screen.

He angled his head to see the monitor. “If anyone comes looking for me under Audra’s orders, you can reach me through that new GPS system, right?”

Nichol grunted.

Content with Nic’s answer, he moved swiftly topside into the haunt’s garage. Dominic’s custom sports car was backed tight against the far wall, ensuring neither Nichol’s SUV nor Mickey’s horrendous 1970s compact would accidentally scratch the impeccable paint. Pulling a small clot of dried mud off a tire, he spread the dust across the sports car’s hood before climbing into the SUV and pulling out into the night.

The highway was virtually deserted, with searing headlights of the odd determined truck driver the only break in the darkness. He was en route to meet a new contact, a vampire from California shutting down his haunt and had enough bloodslave stock to replenish the Kaius haunt’s dwindling numbers.

The meeting was merely a formality, a gesture of good will on behalf of both haunts. He had already transferred funds to the vampire, and a load of fifty humans was expected to arrive within the week. Boy was highly skilled in keeping the bloodslave stock alive, but the events of the past months had resulted in the urgent need for a large restocking.

He hadn't bothered sending Dominic out. Dom was needed in the haunt. And he needed a break.

He pulled the SUV smoothly into a quiet subdivision grocery store on the outskirts of town, running his tongue along his clipped fangs and blinked a few times to ensure his colored contacts were in place. His associate, one Jonathan Minks, was due to arrive any moment. He exited the car and scented the air as he listened for the sound of friend or foe. Turning toward the sound of an approaching motorbike, he raised his brows. Vampires were not fond of open-air transportation.

The bike slowed as it turned into the parking lot and halted in front of him.

"Rhys Kaius, I presume," Minks said as he removed his helmet.

With a nod, he responded. "Jonathan Minks. Nice to put a name to a bank account."

Minks chuckled. "That bank account is funding my wanderlust right now. The bloodslave issue was the last thorn in my side. I appreciate your work in that realm."

He assessed the motorcycle. "It doesn't bother you, being so exposed?"

"Not a mite," Minks replied with a high British accent. "I'm heading through to the Canadian tundra. Not a lot of enemies residing in those parts."

"Then I appreciate this quick meeting even more so. Should you find yourself overrun with humans again in the future, I hope you'll give our haunt first run at a price," he offered.

"I will," Minks assured him. "Doubtful I'll tie myself down to anything like that again, though. I admit I was surprised to get a response from you. I assumed the Kaius haunt would be shutting down their rescue work in this climate."

"We're adjusting our priorities right now," he said, his voice indicating there would be no further information on which priorities had taken precedence.

Jonathan Minks pulled his helmet back on. "Pleasure doing business with you then, Rhys Kaius. Keep my number and should your…priorities… require assistance, the Minks haunt will be at your service."

He watched as Minks drove off into the darkness before he climbed into the driver's seat and made his way out of the winding neighborhood.

Chapter Thirty

Dominic looked around the common room one last time, second-guessing every meticulously planned detail.

The candles were probably going overboard.

Maybe the roses, too.

Fuck.

He flopped onto the sofa and checked the time on his phone.

Ten minutes.

The shit Jagger had told him to put in his hair wasn't holding, the stray strands flopping back into his eyes defiantly.

This was a fucking mistake.

He flicked open the last text he'd received from Molly.

Can't wait!

Grinning stupidly into the empty room, he scanned back through their hundreds of messages over the past two months before he stood up and headed down to the Tender quarters.

Being late on their first official date wouldn't set a good tone for the evening.

As he approached the bright hallway leading to the training rooms, Rhys intercepted him with a smirk.

"Nice hair, pretty boy," Rhys snarked, joining him on his trek. "You sure you want to arrive empty-handed?"

He froze in place. "Oh shit," he groaned. "I left everything in the common room. Is Mickey back yet? I don't want the food to get cold." He took in an unneeded breath. "I'm so fucking not good at this."

Rhys gripped his shoulders, looking him dead in the eye. "If I was a better male, this would be pep-talk time," he stated seriously. "However, since I've never had to put this much effort into wooing a woman, my only advice is to chill the hell out. It's just Molly."

Just Molly.

Just their first date.

No pressure.

"Ah, and Mini?" Rhys muttered sheepishly. "I couldn't negotiate Audra's complete absence, so she'll be hanging around outside the common room until curfew."

He snorted.

At least he wasn't the only one intimidated by Audra.

With a quick rap on the training room door, he waited to see his connected female for the first time in two months.

****

"Right. The music."

Molly tugged at the hem of her dress as Dominic jumped up from the candlelit table and knelt beside an expensive-looking stereo. When the awkward silence of the room was broken by an R&B song she couldn't quite put her finger on, Dom returned with a tight smile.

At least she wasn't the only one overcome by nerves.

The longer she and Dominic sat in silence at the table, the worse she felt. The amount of effort he had so obviously put into the evening was evident in the numerous flower arrangements and pillar candles lining every surface. Her meal was so gourmet, she couldn't fully identify half the dishes spread before her on the red silk tablecloth.

It was so polished, so fancy, so formal.

And so, so awkward.

As she prodded a suspicious-looking meat slathered in a red sauce, a new song caught her attention. She set her fork down under Dominic's watchful eye and subtly pulled her phone from her purse to fire off a text.

His phone buzzed in his pocket and she looked at him pointedly. After a brief flash of confusion in those incredible turquoise eyes, he took his phone out and scanned the message.

"Marvin Gaye. 1973. Tamla Records. Twelfth album," he said confidently, crossing his arms and leaning back in his seat.

"Ooooooooh," she breathed, shaking her head. "So close. Thirteenth."

****

Dominic owed Mick big time.

The elaborate meal sat cold on the table, long forgotten as he and Molly lounged on the floor in front of the record player, a pizza box, and a collection of open candy bars ready for more sampling.

"I'd forgotten how much I love pepperoni," Molly moaned as she bit into her third piece. "Any chance Mick brought back an extra for tomorrow?"

"If he didn't, I can run out at first dark and pick up a few," he offered, the compulsion to ensure his connected female was fed and happy surging to the forefront.

It was the same urge that had stocked the Tender freezers with an epic stockpile of bacon.

She nodded emphatically, flipping through his massive record collection.

Wrapped in a large blanket with a hot slice of pizza in one hand and a collector's edition album in the other, she looked exactly how he had imagined her over the past months. Their first tentative texts, supervised tightly by Audra and Rhys, had been a godsend for him, and the initial impersonal exchanges had morphed quickly as Molly began reaching out more frequently.

It had taken him every ounce of restraint he had to allow her to set the pace.

Had he had his way, they would have been tethered to their phones from the moment her first tentative message had come through.

Her brows furrowed as she carefully removed an orange record from its casing. "I would sell my soul for this album," she gasped, gingerly lifting the record into the light.

He added the rare vinyl to his mental catalogue of albums that would be making their way into Molly's room the next evening. Nichol wouldn't notice this one missing.

"Toss it on," he suggested, laying back on the rug and admiring the view when she scrambled to her feet and began fiddling with the record player. When the first song crackled to life, she flashed him a devastatingly happy smile and wrapped herself back up in her blanket.

She dropped to the floor, hesitating a moment before curling up against him.

"Hey," he whispered, reaching into his pocket awkwardly to tug his phone out. "I have video footage of Wyatt's punishment, if you still want to see it."

He'd been holding on to the footage since Nichol had emailed it to him weeks ago, not wanting to forward it to her without being there. It wasn't particularly gruesome, but the time stamps on the spliced video indicated Wyatt's disciplinary action had been meticulously carried out over months.

Molly held her hand open, her fingers wrapping around the phone as she brought it closer to her face. "How do I delete this?"

Reaching around her, he pointed to the trash icon. "There."

She swiped it without pause. "Did you watch it?"

"I did."

"Was it suitable?"

He flashed through the images in his head.

Nothing would be suitable in his eyes.

But by vampire standards, it was adequate.

"Yeah. Yeah, I'd say so," he muttered, pushing the visuals from his head before his anger rose and soured their evening.

"Then it's done," she stated. "Pass me the pretzels, please?"

Her honeysuckle scent drifted languidly through his mind as they lay on the floor, its formerly ravenous affects now tempered into a calm sense of wholeness. The strong, reassuring beat of her heart against his ribs and he drew his arm down to pull Molly a fraction closer.

"Five minutes, kids."

Molly giggled into his shoulder and threw a leg

over his hips. As she rose up to straddle him, he craned his neck back toward the doors, noting the shadow of Audra's heels.

"We're gonna get grounded by the warden if she catches us like this," he warned, folding his arms behind his head in case Audra actually did walk in on them.

No way in hell was he going to risk Audra's wrath.

She smirked and lowered her lips toward his, her black hair draping down and creating a cocoon around them. "Totally worth it," she smiled before her lips descended softly onto his.

A word about the author...

Katja Desjarlais is a music teacher by day and a paranormal romance writer by moonlight. She is an unapologetic music addict and has an obsession for bad Bach puns despite her irrational aversion to Baroque. Her favorite words include "plethora" and "dapper," and she is physically repulsed by the word "moist." Katja's interest in the paranormal can be traced to her early childhood film choices and to the revolving book collection on her phone.

Desjarlais lives in northern Canada with her husband, three children, and polydactyl cat. Her ideal summer vacation is spent traipsing through the United States with her family and attending heavy metal concerts.

Thank you for purchasing
this publication of The Wild Rose Press, Inc.

For questions or more information
contact us at
info@thewildrosepress.com.

The Wild Rose Press, Inc.
www.thewildrosepress.com

To visit with authors of
The Wild Rose Press, Inc.
join our yahoo loop at
http://groups.yahoo.com/group/thewildrosepress/

www.ingramcontent.com/pod-product-compliance
Lightning Source LLC
Chambersburg PA
CBHW050027030726
47506CB00001B/149

* 9 7 8 1 5 0 9 2 2 1 4 4 8 *